Praise for Levon

Gentile surprises all in his debut novel. He seamlessly combines poetry and prose in this heartbreaking novel.

Thomas J. Esquire -- The New York Underground

Gentile combines multiple story lines, footnotes and a complex weaving of characters to highlight how a simple romance can tear anyone apart. His writing is going to attract a special group of readers that will be sure to cling to whatever he writes next.

Sybil Vane -- The Waltham Inquirer

I didn't know whether to cry, laugh, or take a shot of bourbon after finishing this debut novel. It pulls on all the right strings in all the right ways.

James Hunter -- Hamilton News

There is a rhythm to his writing. Its soulful, honest, yet spontaneous. It bursts off the page like a 1920's jazz band then slows to a Nashville blues.

Olivia Lange – The Boston Harbor

His words seem to come from an old soul, not a 24-year-old.

Frederique Alpina – Maycomb Gazette

On face value this book could be a simple love story, but deep underneath its layers of footnotes and pop culture references it is a study of an entire generation.

Malcolm Oris – Breitling News

You will fall in love with Levon, as he is a part of all of us, and we are all a part of him.

Adelaide Bronte – The Bremont Sun

Gentile eases you into his scattered mind with an unconscious organization you will only understand when you try and explain the novel to someone and find yourself saying, "It's about everything. You know, life."

Ulysses Panerai – The Stowe Seamaster

Gentile is real. And he explains the world as only an honest cynic can.

Emily Allende — Le Pain Quarterly

No ten-dollar words, but a love story that will keep you reeling after you end the last word.

Kilgore Proust — The Tudor Prince

Gentile keeps it simple enough for the novice romance novelist, but complicated and intricate enough that one could teach an entire class on his novel.

John Heuer — The Portofino Times

A riveting novel that reminds us what it is like to be a human.
A courageous novel that you will want to give to everyone you know.

Pierre Le Coulture — Merci Strand

Audaciously original, and an unsettling narrative of what can drive us, as well as destroys us.

Jaeger Fox — The Vacheron Daily

LEVON

~First Edition~

BY G.R. GENTILE

~ 55th and 3rd Publishing ~ New York ~

ISBN: 978-1-7343612-0-9

Library of Congress Control Number:

Front cover image by G.R. Gentile
Book design by G.R. Gentile

Printed by KDP Amazon Inc., in the United States of America.

First printing edition 2019.

This book is dedicated to you.

"I do not know a truer phrase than *fell madly in love*. To fall madly. To fall madly in love. It has been overused and corrupted by a world that destroys good phrases with overuse and commerce. A lazy, stupid, regressive world that beats the meaning from words, beats them to death, until they are only noise, only filler. And I know I sound like a crank, I know. Still, I'm saying take a second and consider the phrase is all. Nowhere have I read a better description of what happened to me. I fell madly in. Pronoun, verb, adverb, preposition. Flawless. A mad falling."

~*Alexander Maksik, Shelter in Place*

CHAPTER ONE

"Maturing is necessary but growing up is optional."
                                                    -- Jake Roberts

I hated moving. Change gave me anxiety. The closer we came to our final destination the more my palms sweat. My heart raced. I couldn't tell if it was because of my SVT, (supraventricular tachycardia) or if it was my normal anxious self. I could say there were many thoughts going through my head, but that would be no different than today, as I try to sit down and write this story. My mind is always racing. It is why I don't sleep. I am not sure how the insomnia began. It has been with me for so long I do not believe I will ever find out how it started. It may have been when the nightmares manifested, or when the bags under my eyes began to bulge, or even when my heart started to harden.

I have tried to tell the story of Levon since I met him as a teenager, when my family moved to Branford, Connecticut.

When I met the old man, I recently moved into the small New England beach town with my mother and father. My three older sisters were in college and my parents wanted to downsize, as well as prepare for retirement. I was 16 years old, and a functioning ball of delinquency like most adolescents. I had a constant feeling that nowhere around you is someone close enough to yourself to ever understand you.[1] It was comforting knowing others felt just as alone.

Moving into the oversized home made me feel like the new kid in the Sandlot. I became a shell of myself, quiet, reserved, and a bit of a loner. The world felt drab and empty after I left my New York City. I was a city boy at heart and was ripped from my roots like a bad carrot. The way I left didn't leave a good taste in my mouth. I remember my knees shook when I closed the door to the house that helped shelter and raise me. Sometimes things don't feel right, or at least that is the way I interpreted the ache I felt but couldn't describe. This didn't feel right.

I hated the way we left, leaving my friends, and my life behind me. However, the alternative of boarding school, rehab or jail were not any more appealing. So, I followed orders and moved.

My house in Branford stood on a rock. It was set back from marshland with a trail that led to some of the best clamming around. Just over the marsh to the East was the marina. Ships came and went in an orchestrated carousel of shapes, sizes and colors. Some boats were crewed by hardworking fishermen with salt laced beards and whiskey on their breath, other boats were filled with cadres of loud youth looking to escape into the ocean and toss a few Budweiser's back. The house came with a good size yard where our dog Broadway could play and not run away. Broadway was found tied to a pole on Broadway as a puppy, hence the name. The house was modern in its design but country in decoration. The outside was painted in a cold grey and was littered with hard angles and triangle shaped windows. But the inside's pine floors, wood shelves and warm hearth gave a completely different vibe. I always said the house had an identity crisis it could never figure out. The house was vacant for many years. I never met anyone who could tell me exactly how long, mostly because it had been abandoned long before most moved into the town. Despite its loneliness, the house was very well maintained and had all of the modern amenities one would expect today. A family owned it for 50 years but was unable to solidify a buyer, until my family decided to take a flyer on the house.

---

[1] Irving, John. The World According to Garp

My father said, "It was a deal that even a deaf, dumb and blind man couldn't pass up." I was never sure what that meant. My father liked to sound intelligent and boastful, but most of his intelligence came from a few regurgitated lines from *Ben Hur* and *La Vita e Bella*. Anyway, I digress. I never liked seeing vacant houses. It reminded me of the Joyce Kilmer poem my grandmother used to recite to me during bedtime. She tried to pass it off as her own, but I knew better.[2]

No one ever gave us an explanation as to why the house wouldn't sell. However, I later found out.

When we first pulled down Lotus Lane, he sat in a large brown rocking chair on the front porch. The chair was extremely ornate to be

---

[2] Whenever I walk to Suffern along the Erie track
I go by a poor old farmhouse with its shingles broken and black.
I suppose I've passed it a hundred times, but I always stop for a minute
And look at the house, the tragic house, the house with nobody in it.

I never have seen a haunted house, but I hear there are such things;
That they hold the talk of spirits, their mirth and sorrowings.
I know this house isn't haunted, and I wish it were, I do;
For it wouldn't be so lonely if it had a ghost or two.

This house on the road to Suffern needs a dozen panes of glass,
And somebody ought to weed the walk and take a scythe to the grass.
It needs new paint and shingles, and the vines should be trimmed and tied;
But what it needs the most of all is some people living inside.

If I had a lot of money and all my debts were paid
I'd put a gang of men to work with brush and saw and spade.
I'd buy that place and fix it up the way it used to be
And I'd find some people who wanted a home and give it to them free.

Now, a new house standing empty, with staring window and door,
Looks idle, perhaps, and foolish, like a hat on its block in the store.
But there's nothing mournful about it; it cannot be sad and lone
For the lack of something within it that it has never known.

But a house that has done what a house should do, a house that has sheltered life,
That has put its loving wooden arms around a man and his wife,
A house that has echoed a baby's laugh and held up his stumbling feet,
Is the saddest sight, when it's left alone, that ever your eyes could meet.

So whenever I go to Suffern along the Erie track
I never go by the empty house without stopping and looking back,
Yet it hurts me to look at the crumbling roof and the shutters fallen apart,
For I can't help thinking the poor old house is a house with a broken heart.

outside. The gloss shimmered from afar, making me wonder how it kept such a shine after years of being pelted by harsh New England weather. The chair was out of place on the simplistic Colonial porch. The porch had a white railing attached to a dark weathered wood floor that wrapped around the entire house. He rocked incessantly, at a pace that was far too fast for anyone in a rocking chair to reach... and he waved at us. That was it. He never came over and never spoke.

Most people who will be important in your life usually don't make it known until after their first impression has already been cemented in your mind. This is god's little way of reminding us, we are all inherently shallow.

At first, I couldn't tell much about the old man other than he was old and alone. His house was an ancient white farmhouse. For a house that looked to be built pre-war, it was in incredibly good condition. Not a single shutter hung astray, not a single shingle gone rogue. The porch was swept, and the paint looked fresh. There was another deck on the second level that faced East and the ocean behind us, however, I never saw him out on that balcony. This struck me as odd during the first two weeks I lived at 16 Lotus Lane because it was a beautiful two weeks of weather and not a single person stayed indoors. The entire town was out enjoying the summer weather. The old man was a constant presence on his front porch ignoring his million-dollar view from just on the other side of the house. Why would he stare at the street and forest of pines instead of a Country-Living-magazine-worthy view of the ocean? The house was accented by dark red shutters and a white picket fence that lined the well-groomed yard. I wanted to describe the old man as Boo Radley, but he was too well kept, and the house too well maintained to ever be the fateful grumpy old man at the end of Main Street in Maycomb, Alabama. He had two dogs that always sat near him; a large black Newfoundland who he called Kurt and a brindle colored English Bulldog named Ernest. His mailbox said Levon. He was house 28.

By day seventeen (Yes, I counted) of living in the new house, my mother saw the old man sitting on his porch alone and decided it would be a nice neighborly gesture to say hello. My mother believed that kindness and compassion could change the world. I believed the world just changed. Who gave a shit how it went about the changes? "Not eye, said the blind man."

I knew I had no choice but to go along with my mother as she bopped her way, in a neighborly strut across the yard to the well-manicured garden. I never saw the old man in his garden, but it always looked as if a team of illegal immigrants spent hours a day fumbling over the hedges, forget-me-nots, sunflowers and an array of lilies that would make a funeral home owner blush.

The two dogs were polar opposite in genetic makeup and size. They stayed loyally by their owner as we walked up the wooden steps to the porch. Up close, the porch and house looked much bigger, the rocking chair even larger, but the man was much smaller. Short in stature, with a stocky build, he stayed slightly hidden in the shaded region of the porch, concealing his most detailed features. He did not say anything as we approached. He did not move. I couldn't tell if he was dead or alive.

My mother, never one to notice the awkwardness in situations, decided to just go for it. Her blissful ignorance at 60 years of life always made me smile and cringe that someone this inept at social norms was so successful in their professional life.

"Hey! We are the new neighbors from down the road. Number..."

She was cut off. "16, I know. I saw when you moved in. The move go well?" The old man said with an earnestness in his voice that was eerily familiar, terrifying and also intoxicating.

"Yes, all is well. I want to introduce my son Jake. We just moved here from New York. I am Ruth and my husband is Angelo."

"Nice to meet you guys." he said.

Then we reached the awkward part in all conversations. This is when all conversations are decided. Immediately after any introduction, there is always a slight pause where the conversation can go one way or the other. You have to be quick, and decisive, and for god's sake do not mention the fucking weather. Nothing makes me sicker than forced politeness and forced interaction.

This is when the old man should have introduced himself, but he didn't. It was an odd gesture for a man who appeared to be docile and well spoken. My mother, not picking up on the social cues continued," And may I ask your name?"

"It's Levon."

"Isn't that your last…" I shot in but was cut off…

"Sport, It's Levon. It's what they call me."

Sport? Who did this guy think he was… Gatsby? It felt slightly demeaning and in any other situation my undeveloped brain would have a petty immature response such as, "at least I can play a sport." Or even more couth, "Don't call me Sport, you old fuck."

However, my filter clicked in and I said… "Okay."

Levon and my mother continued to speak about his garden and mutual affinity for lilies. We walked away, and despite two entirely different interactions, had a similar impression of Levon. He was lonely.

The first few weeks were weird in the new house. I was used to the loud horns and commotion of the city lights, not the New England country. The crickets were louder than the sirens that echoed off the alleys of a New York City night.

Every day, as I drove back and forth to my new school, I saw Levon sitting on his front porch with Kurt and Ernest. He would wave and sit there. Almost a year went by before we had an actual conversation. It happened as I snuck out my back window to smoke a blunt by the water. It was routine for me, like my glass of wine at night. As the blanket of night engulfed the small beach town I ran to solitude. The nights were troubling for me, so I self-medicated the best way I knew how.

The ocean had a calming effect on me, like Vicks Vapor Rub for the soul. One night, while down by the water I sensed in my stoned-paranoia someone was near. Although, when I turned around and peered through the nighttime mist, I saw no one. I smelt pot. I thought it was my own but then I saw the orange glow coming from the jetty, about 100 yards away. I froze in the dark chill of the night unable to make a decision between approaching or minding my own business. So, I minded my own business and pretended as if no one else existed in this world but me. I tried to not look in the direction of the fellow stoner, but just like when you tell kids not to snoop for Christmas presents, and they do regardless, I turned and stared down the glow. To my surprise, the person was coming closer. The image slowly became clear as the distance between us disappeared.

Like a scene from a movie, the stranger approached through the descending fog onto the beach where the moon shown down on the glossed sand. It wasn't that dramatic, but wouldn't you know it... Levon appeared, hobbling closer. He wore a tattered University of Rhode Island hoodie, which lost all of its elastic from years of wear, a pair of dark blue Levi's and boat shoes. He was dressed like a frat boy but was easily in his 60's. His joint was tightly rolled, the obvious skill of a man who has been rolling joints near the ocean for a while. Anyone who smokes pot knows that joints in windy situations are about as compatible as an emotional woman with an insensitive man. He moved slowly down the beach. It was a walk that seemed so familiar to him... he knew every iota of sand that was strewn throughout the beach... he knew where to step, and how hard or soft to step. It always helps if you know where to step next.

When you see someone doing something that is out of character, despite the fact I didn't know the crotchety old man or his character, it always takes you back. Seeing an easily 60 plus year-old man smoking a joint at midnight on the beach was something that was out of character. It is like seeing a teacher in the grocery store and you say, "What are you doing here?" Failing to realize they do in fact, eat food, just like you.

I turned toward him as smoke billowed from his joint creating a cloud in the already hazy night. I didn't know what to say. I wanted to be like, "shit I am busted," but really... so was he. Either way, what did this lonely old man care? I felt social, so I sat down with the man on the rock wall behind us. We did this without speaking, as if we just knew it was time to sit.

"Who are you?" He said as if in the middle of a conversation.

"Jacob, I mean Jake, Ruth's son, your new..." I was cut off...

"That's not what I asked, Sport."

"How many nicknames are you going to have for me Fitzgerald?" His bushy eyebrows raised but he didn't turn.

"My first question," he blurted, now in a lower and raspier voice that was new to me.

"Sorry Levon, I don't get what you are asking."

"Yes, you do."

"You struggle with hearing? Or just..." He cut me off again...

"I see it Sport. I see it. I hear it too. Who are you?"

"What is that? A fucking Haiku?"

"No, you little brat Haiku's are 5,7,5. And you knew that too, you pretentious little…" I cut him off…

"Okay then, who do you think I am if you know, if you see it too?"

"There he is."

"I am too high for this right now." I mumbled to myself.

"I just want to know who you are. You are obviously Jake Roberts who lives at 16 Lotus Lane, but I want to know WHO you are. What do you see? What do you hear? You observe, don't you? Your observations are what make you who you are. How you convey them creates how you are perceived. So, when I ask, "who are you?" I want to know what you see and hear in this world. Your eyes are old kid, but your heart is still young... Tell me."

It didn't make any sense. I didn't know how to respond. No one ever asked me this before. But what caught me in my one-track mind was his allusion to my heart and mind. It was as though he was so hurt by age; the innocence of youthful eyes, ears and heart were like medicine. Some expect the old to be grumpy, some wise, and some jaded. But what I find is they are all of the above, they just wear their pain on wrinkled hands and heavy eyes. The heart can only take so much pain after all the years of living. However, it can only know the pain of life, if it has enjoyed the blessings life provides as well. A well-worn body shows a well-lived person.

For some reason, I burned the candle at both ends slowly holding onto the idea I didn't have a drug or alcohol problem mixed with the unconscious desire to wear myself out…to become a wretched old man. I wanted to look exhausted, burnt out and down trodden. I didn't know why. The tired old man with eyes sagging low and hands worked to the bone, was attractive to me. I see them, and I see a life well lived. I see a man who has seen things. I see a man who has loved. I see someone who has survived the worst the world can throw at him and come out on the other end flipping everyone else off.

The pause lasted much longer in my head than reality.

Up close his face was made of granite, however, his hands were smooth. The usual protruding spider veins and calluses were absent. His nails were well manicured. He spoke slow but harsh, his words drawn out by an airy tone. He was so wound up when he thought, but when he spoke;

it was tranquil, like with each passing syllable he was able to breathe a little easier.

I attempted a stuttering answer of immaturity.

"I don't know; I am who I am. I see people for who they are...yeah I know cliché... and I am allergic to incompetence."

"Allergic to incompetence," He repeated.

"Yeah you know what I mean. I don't care if you are stupid that's not your fault it's god fucking you in the ass, but incompetence drives me crazy. There is no excuse for incompetence."

"I understand Sport."

"But I also think everyone is too damn serious all the time. I get maturing is necessary but why isn't growing up optional? I don't know... 'I am just far more certain about what I am against than what I am for.'"[3]

"Mandela...Good, good."

Didn't think he would catch my plagiarism.

He continued, "It's okay to feel that way, 'Something is odd if a person is not liberal when he is young and conservative when he is old.'"[4]

"Mandela, I suppose?"

"You catch on quick kid."

What the hell was this crazy old man talking about? My skepticism about his overall sanity rose but I did not run... I should have run.

He gently put out his joint, gingerly stood up and gracefully disappeared back into the night. As he slowly faded away, I yelled, "Isn't smoking at your age bad for you!?"

"I ain't in it for my health kid,"[5] he said.

When I woke up, I wanted to convince myself it didn't happen. But the next day when Levon winked at me I knew it was definitely real.

This was our first chat on the beach that turned into many. Eventually, I brought whiskey down for us to drink. Levon would bring his tumblers. Each night the sun gradually set as a soft moon left a shadowy glow across the skipping waves. It was our happy place, like two kids who snuck out of the house at night to giggle and play games without the

---

[3] Mandela, Nelson. A Long Walk to Freedom
[4] Mandela, Nelson. A Long Walk to Freedom
[5] Helms, Levon. The Band

burdensome eyes of their parents. But what started as a coincidence became something more.

During the day, Levon would come up with a way to signal that night we were meeting. Some days it was a wink, some days it was letting Kurt shit in our lawn, some days I found a lily petal on the porch. I think he enjoyed the game. There were days when he didn't contact. I never asked about it. I never pried into his life. I think he appreciated this part of our relationship. People should not have to speak about what they do not wish to mention voluntarily. He was a good listener and pushed me in my thinking. The way he talked was reminiscent of Lord Henry from *The Picture of Dorian Grey*. He had words of wisdom with an underlying cynicism that made sense if impressionable and damning if weak.

Our ability to listen without speaking was imperative to our relationship.

The relationship was slow building. Levon would ask me to tell him about my day. At first, I gave the generic, "It was good," response I usually yelled at my mother, as I slammed the door behind me trying to get upstairs as fast as possible. It wasn't because I didn't have a good relationship with my mother, it was because I was young and immature and didn't realize her hearing about my day was all she waited for at 4:05 each evening.

The last thing I remember from that night was the smile Levon gave as he walked away. It was a sincere lie. We all wear masks. Some intentional and some not, but the deliberate veil of happiness[6] is the most seductive of all masks. I was okay with his honest lie. Society has lost the value of a white lie, however be wary, you can never trust an honest man.

---

[6] Keats, John. Ode on Melancholy

CHAPTER TWO

"A million hungers and not one of them appeasable."
-- Albert Halper

The nightmares started when we moved into 16 Lotus Lane. My parents didn't notice my lack of sleep. Life is always easier in the commotion of the daytime, but at night, silence becomes loud in my desolate room. To keep my mind occupied, instead of imploding on itself, I would read as much as I could and numbed my brain with shots of whiskey topped with a bowl or two. Self-medication is self-deprivation at its finest.

Intelligent, I suppose I was, but "happiness in intelligent people is the rarest thing I know."[7] I was an underachiever, not a moron. Plus, I would do anything to calm my troubled mind.

I was haunted. It only happened at night. He was always there… watching me… Broadway would sit at the end of my bed and bark into the blank spaces of the room. The nightmares became so real my veins shuddered as I woke. My room felt like a vacant cave and my mind the narrow passages connecting all its haunted places. I didn't see it coming. I was a happy child, an outgoing kid… I always did well in school. Why did my brain turn on me? Mental illness was not in my family, but I knew something was off-kilter in my quirky brain. A lack of sleep most definitely did not help my severed sanity. My parents assumed it was a traumatic reaction to Johnny. I didn't think so, but he tormented my every move.

---

[7] Hemingway, Ernest

Each night I heard his voice, the words he last spoke to me. "It's like a locomotive in my chest...a restless hurricane driving me into unbearable sleeplessness. I am just tired, and I am too young to be this tired."

At the time, I was waking up to the world around me. It happens to all of us as we grow up. Everything I once perceived true was now a lie. Maybe Johnny's death is what brought me to this realization that nothing was what it seemed. The subtle shifts in the sands of time under my feet shook my soul. It didn't take long for me to begin destroying every assurance of reality and normalcy in my life. Restaurants became overwhelming and crowds became terrifying. Trains made me claustrophobic and classrooms were daunting. I sat alone at lunch too afraid of even the chairs that weren't attached to the lunch tables. Everything gave me anxiety, from school lunches, to stop signs; the world overwhelmed me. I fought the good fight when I was younger. I fought as hard as I could to remain intact but unhinged and broken was my destiny. So, I gave in. I caved. I went into hermit mode. I hid from the world. I read furiously, wrote fast and tried to drown my mind in more intoxicants than a Russian whorehouse.

Johnny taught me how to do this. He taught me the game...The drug game...The numbing game.

The only thing in my life that gave me comfort was words. There are 26 letters in the English alphabet and a handful of grammatical rules you must follow. This limited ability in the English language was much more comforting than the infinite mass of bullshit we call math. Where does it end!? No one knows.

When I moved to 16 Lotus Lane time began to skip. It wasn't retrograde amnesia,[8] which is like PTSD for the drunken soul. I couldn't remember my last sober night. My actions weren't mine. Life was good despite my internal reservations. I don't think anybody saw a difference. I felt like a scratched cd. I was supposed to be the calm and steady one...

I could no longer recall moments and memories.

We tell ourselves we are just living our lives, living it to the fullest, but when living your life to the fullest, leaves you brain dead and alone... was it truly worth it? We get fucked up to make memories, but it is the very thing that makes the moments so enthusiastic that causes you to forget. The

---

[8] Smith, Daniel B. Monkey Mind

problem of trying to recall past nights of incessant mixing of alcohol and marijuana is that they counteract each other. The alcohol hits your circulatory system and time rips by. It speeds up to the point where your brain shuts off because it is going by too fast. When you smoke weed, life slows down. So, when you combine the two substances, life around you skips like a Mexican jumping bean. You don't know whether you are coming or going. You forget what room you are sitting in. Your brain functions about as well as a Jenna Jameson in a convent. But the plethora of upper and downers and tobacco products didn't help either.

Once you hit the play button in life, there is no rewind or pause, just stop and eject.

One night it became too much... All of it was overwhelming and I was never taught how to cope with the feeling of guilt and loneliness that constantly rested on my mind. Johnny's face was too clear in my nightmare. I felt his presence everywhere I went. I didn't know why I couldn't shake this demon of a best friend. I remember seeing him hanging there above the stairs. His eyes still open, neck broken, but his features calm and placid. He seemed at peace. That is what I like to tell myself knowing how tormented he was. The torture of the needle and gun[9] was gone from his battered mind. Such a waste at 16... such a waste at any time. I was angry with him. I was sad. I was scared I had the same future. Johnny walked where I walked and spoke when I spoke. I still hear his voice with every 'flick of my bic' and every slurp of Maker's Mark.

My parents thought moving away from the scene where I found my best friend hanging in my house would help me. They believed a new place equaled a new chapter. Plus, my parents couldn't handle the fact they were living in a home where a young boy killed himself. They wanted to hide, but never admitted it. My mother was ashamed. My father shunned by the community and I, once popular, became the outcast of society...the dunce in the front of the classroom. My mother never looked at me the same. I felt she blamed me for his death. I don't think my mother believed anything in this world happened naturally.[10] I was angry at the world for everything. It was a futile emotion because being, "angry is like drinking poison and expecting the other person to die."

---

[9] Young, Neil
[10] Irving, John. The World According to Garp

It was a Tuesday when I tried to kill myself. All tragedies happen on a Tuesday. It was about a year after we moved to Branford. I woke up from a night of Bulleit Bourbon and an 8ball of cocaine up my nose. I was on my floor. I don't remember what I did before this as I lost track of what chemicals I was ingesting, snorting and smoking. He was in my room again. Johnny was there again. I saw him. I couldn't take it anymore. The clock struck 4:00 am... at least I thought it was 4am. My Nana's old clock chime rung throughout the house and an emptiness filled my body as I couldn't tell if I caught the chime on the first second or third ring. My phone gone and my clock still packed away in the closet; the vulnerability of being lost in time took its toll. I wrote no note. I said nothing to anyone except Johnny. I said, "I can't do this alone anymore."

I went to my desk drawer. The same desk I had since childhood. The same desk I learned to read, write and even lost my virginity on. Despite having suicidal thoughts, I was still a teenage boy who saw sex everywhere he went. I smiled briefly while I grabbed a slew of Xanax, OxyContin, morphine patches, Tylenol pm, mellow yellow's, Vicodin, Percocet, Lortabs and a bottle of Robitussin. I figured if I was going to go, no better way than fucked up near the ocean. I grabbed my favorite books, God Bless You Mr. Rosewater, House of Leaves, A Moveable Feast and the Giver. Grabbed a bottle of water, rolled a blunt and snuck past my unsuspecting parents without an iota of thought as to the decision I was making, other than I was tired of not being able to sleep. Like Johnny, I was too young to be this tired.

Like I had done a half dozen times over the past couple of weeks to meet up with Levon, I hopped out the second story hallway window onto the roof, flung my feet through the lattice work, a couple of steps down I reached the garbage cans and hopped down onto the patio. It was only a jump over a fence and three-minute walk that meandered through the marsh until I reached the rock ledge and jetty that met the ocean head on. It was the exact spot where I first met Levon. I emptied everything I took from my desk onto the weathered limestone rock. The array of colors made me smile. I lit the blunt and began... one by one. There was no rhyme or reason to the order. Just one at a time. I began feeling the morphine patch before I was even done taking all of the pills.

Finally, I finished. Leaned back. Took another pull from the blunt, looked at god's thumbnail in the sky and thought about all of the stars I have seen in my life. Then I started to warm up. The warmth turned into a burn. The world became blurry. My throat dry, my palms sweaty, my heart slowing, my toes cold in the wet sand... Then the calm left and only panic stayed. I ripped my clothes off, unable to scream, due to the plethora of mellow yellow muscle relaxers. So many downers I couldn't even conjure a gag reflex. I tried to stand up and sprint into the ocean. I fell. Crawling, stretching every muscle and summoning every piece of strength not taken away from the "medicine." It felt like crawling through the sands of Normandy, but this was not going to win me any medals of honor. Then it went blank. There were no thoughts of Johnny, no images of my first love, my mother and father were not there, no memories from my life, no images of learning to ride a bike or my first Lego tower. There was no bright light, no angels singing on high. It all faded to black. I may have died. No one knows. The last memory I had was sucking down sand as my body melted.

_____
_____Black_____Blank_____
_____Thoughtless_____Selfish_____
_____Cowardice_____
_____Scared_____It
all went empty into nothingness _____No more
pain, no more pleasure_____Everything was beautiful and nothing hurt.[11]

Like Schrödinger's Cat, I was neither alive nor dead.
Then...Then...I was throwing up. Levon held me like Mary holding Jesus in *La Pieta*. I was still naked; we were soaking wet. I was cold. My bones shivered as I continuously threw up over the side of my face. Levon's sturdy grip on my shoulders and waist, my head pounding like a kettledrum at a Reggae concert, I could barely see the outline of the old granite man above me. Once I regained some feeling, I latched on like a newborn baby. Unable to throw up anymore and having some muscle movement, Levon

---

[11] Vonnegut Jr., Kurt. Slaughterhouse Five (aka A Children's Crusade)

lifted me to my stumbling feet. He spoke no words. I still didn't have the ability to talk, and I didn't feel like it.

He walked me back to his house. It took a long time for the man with his creaking bones and arthritis to assist my abused and wretched body to the white house at the end of Lotus Lane. The memories are fuzzy as he dressed me in old grey sweats and gave me water. Then I fell back asleep, exhausted.

My eyes slowly opened through crusted eye boogers. At first, I had no idea where I was. Despite my blurred vision, I scanned the room. I was lying on a worn black leather couch. The coffered ceiling loomed above me and mahogany bookshelves lined the walls. Not a vacant spot on any shelf. The array of books was terrifyingly magical. Nothing was in any particular order. The room looked more like the mind of a madman or a hall of fame episode of Hoarders. A stack of books or an empty whiskey bottle occupied every free spot in the room. The musk in the room was unmistakable. The odor was a mix of college library, nursing home and campfire, an intriguing mix to my virgin nose. Where did I wake up? I was struggling to put together the brief pieces of the past couple hours.

I sat up slowly. My head felt like someone put a balloon in it and filled it to max capacity. Not remembering much other than sitting on the beach and throwing up in Levon's arms, I tried to get my bearings. I walked around the cathedral of a room looking at the extensive collection of novels, biographies, memoirs, short stories, textbooks, anthologies and everything else in between. Not a single binding unbroken, showing someone who truly reads, not just a pretentious douche who buys books to show off a facade of intelligence. I stood in front of the fire and noticed on the mantle a few pictures of what seemed to be a family. Next to the scattered frames were the books I brought to the beach.

"Feeling better Sport?"

I jumped, not expecting another presence in the room. Levon was there the entire time while I went on a book safari in his library.

"Uh..uh…" I was at a loss of words for the first time in my life.

"You are a lucky bastard Jake."

"Umm."

"You are also a dumb fucking kid. If you didn't almost just die, I would consider killing you myself."

"Not really what I need to hear right now."

"I don't give a shit, I am not one for sympathy and especially not empathy in this case."

"Levon…"

"Listen carefully kid, just listen for a second because I never took you as a coward."

"Coward?"

"Suicide is the ultimate form of cowardice. What is so bad you felt you needed to kill yourself?"

"Hell of a collection of books."

"Don't change the subject Sport."

"I don't want to talk about it…"

"That's fine… then write about it."

"What?"

"We have a lifetime to talk about this… but you have only a short time to write about it. The best way to forget is to write."

"I am not in the mood Levon, my head is killing me, just please…"

He put a laptop in front of me already open to a blank word document.

"Write." He demanded.

"I really have nothing to say."

"Hit the keys. We all have a voice and you aren't using yours. Don't be a fucking coward like you were last night."

This had to be a joke. He was belittling a kid who just tried to kill himself. I tried to figure out what the hell I just attempted, and here was this crazy man yelling at me to write…he didn't even tell me what about. Levon obviously never took a psychology class.

"Are you going to tell anyone?"

"WRITE!"

"Fine! For god's sake, stop yelling, I told you my head." I turned towards the computer and mumbled, "fucking nut."

"What was that?"

"Nothing."

"Whatever you say boss."

I stared at the keys, the blank screen, and I didn't know where to begin, what to say... I just wanted to be done and back in my bed.

So, I began typing...

It was the nightmares...I didn't mean to...I thought I could save him. I couldn't take the guilt. I am tired of someone's soul resting on my heart. I only had enough heart for one. I thought I was a good person. How could such pain be given to me? What did I do to deserve this life? I have never felt so broken. Like a broken clock in a clock store I feel locked in this world watching everyone run by me while I remain stuck. I am a stagnant mess of fluttering emotions. I don't want to see the sunrise, or the moon set anymore. The lust of life has become a burden.

I paused.

Levon was standing over my shoulder. I could feel him nodding. He slowly moved to the couch next to me and spun the computer around. He rested his fingers slowly on the keyboard, closed his eyes, and took a deep breath as if he was entering a trance worthy of Edgar Cayce. Then all of a sudden in a flurry, in a frenzy, his fingers pounded the keys with a ferocity of a dog digging up an old bone. His bushy eyebrows twinkled as he caressed the keys in a blind daze. In a few short moments that lasted a lifetime, while I rubbed my temples trying to ease the pain, he spun the computer around and said nothing. He looked away.

But the sun still rises tomorrow. Tender will become your nights. Tender is the crisp fall air. Tender is soft lips. Tender is smooth moving hips. Tender is a broken heart. Tender is a heart in love. Tender is a moment passed. Tender is a memory had. And in these tender moments we remember why tomorrow will always come. And in these tender moments is why we strive to better ourselves. Remember kid, it is okay to be afraid. It is okay to fear the unknown. This is why people are afraid of the dark, because of what it hides, not because of a lack of light. So, remember kid, tender is the night. [12]

I got the references to the literary greats. I read it over and over. He still said nothing, but the silence was comforting. His words were silk as they flowed through an array of grammatical atrocities, but it still worked.

"Who brings books to kill themself?" Levon asked in a whisper.

"You don't understand."

---

[12] Fitzgerald, F. Scott. Tender is the Night

"Oh, but I do. I do more than you know. What's more interesting is your book choice."

"You aren't going to tell my mo…" he cut me off as usual.

"Don't worry. I won't on one condition."

"Which is?"

"2000 words a day and spend some time with me."

"What?"

"Do you want me to say something to Madre and Padre kid?"

"Are you blackmailing me with my own suicide? You are blackmailing me into a friendship…you know how insane this is right?"

"I have never claimed to be moral, fair, sane, compassionate or empathetic, so why assume I was such a person?"

"Was that a poem?"

"You always have a response."

"Should I apologize for that?"

"What's your decision?"

"Your face, my thane, is as a book where men
May read strange matters. To beguile the time…" I mumbled under my breath…

"Look like the time; bear welcome in your eye,
Your hand, your tongue: look like the innocent flower,
But be the serpent under't." [13] He finished the line before I had a chance.

I didn't expect him to finish my line. He was a fool, but I always had an affinity for fools. I place a lot of faith in them. Better a witty fool than a foolish wit.[14]

"So, I take that as a reluctant yes?" He asked.

I answered with a glaring stare and no words.

Levon had a way of saying a lot without saying much at all. He spoke as if we were lifelong friends and I knew every detail of his past.

"I am gonna be honest with you Sport." He said breaking the silence. "I am pissed. I watched you the whole time, luckily, I still had some Ipecac in the cabinet otherwise you would be dead. Life is only precious because it doesn't last. You may think what you did was noble, but

---

[13] Shakespeare, William. Macbeth
[14] Shakespeare, William. Twelfth Night

whenever a man makes a stupid decision it usually comes from a noble motive.[15] I am going to do something for you no one did for me."

"And that is forcing me to write 2000 words a day?..."

"Jacob." I knew when he used my formal name, he meant business. "Come back tomorrow at noon. I want to show you something."

I passively agreed, knowing this man now held my biggest secret and saved my life. I had to oblige Levon's crazy request. If he told my mother, they may actually send me away. And I felt a comfort in his presence I never felt before.

"Got it boss," I said.

Without another word I left the immense library and walked into the white and black tiled foyer. The rest of the house had hardwood floors, so the tile stuck out immediately. Across the hall was another room with stacks of worn books piled into mini towers. As I opened the front door, I looked back into the house and noticed a third room with the floor covered in printer paper, blue pen marks all over the blurred words. The stairs on my left went up to the second floor. All the doors were open with a similar scene of tattered books lining the pine floors and covering the maroon walls. The house was in such disarray on the inside, but abnormally well put together on the exterior. I thought, his house had an identity crisis just like mine, and smiled to myself. Before I closed the door, I looked into the library where Levon sat hunched over his knees still staring at the screen. Just like before, he closed his eyes, tilted his head back and gracefully pounded away at the keyboard in a symphony of clicks. "He created in a beautiful frenzy."

"Noon?" I said.

There was no response.

Then it caught my eye. It stood out in the open layout of the old white colonial. The one door, which remained closed. I said no more and left.

_____

[15] Wilde, Oscar. The Picture of Dorian Gray. ("Whenever a man does a thoroughly stupid thing, it is always from the noblest motives.")

CHAPTER THREE

"...All sorrows can be borne if you put them into a story or tell a story about them."

--Isak Dinesen

Twelve noon on the dot I stood atop the imposing front porch. Levon seemed like a man you didn't want to disappoint. I was at the awkward point in any friendship (I guess that's what we were...friends), when you don't know if you should knock or just go in. Sometimes you get to the coveted "allowed to enter through the side door or garage" status and that is pretty much the equivalent of being family. And if you are going through the side door, sneaking in the garage, and don't fall under this category, you are either a hooker entering a brothel or 12-year-old sneaking into a girlfriend's house. Anyway, I digress.

It was a typical fall day, when the air was a little cleaner than the day before and the leaves still had a luminescent shimmer from the nighttime frost.

There was music playing inside the house. I couldn't exactly tell who it was. Levon always had music playing but I rarely knew the artists. He had a Victrola record player from 1922. It was a piece of furniture that doubled as a record player. The wooden monstrosity was polished daily. It was one of the only things in the Levon's household that was consistently cleaned. The record player belonged to his father, a musician who studied Jazz composition at Berklee College of Music in Boston. Levon had a real pension for nostalgia; none of the music he played was recorded later than 2000. He believed every age prior to his was the "golden age." He never liked to accept the reality of the world around him.

Sam Cooke was playing. Odd combination considering the household... stuffy old white man and one of the smoothest black guys in history. Sam Cooke could sing the feathers off a chicken. (I have no idea what that actually means, but it sounded good). Either way, I hesitantly entered the house, not out of fear but a feeling of uncertainty.

What was going to happen? He makes me write a couple short stories about some king and queen in a castle surrounded by a river of lava and a bridge guarded by a fire-breathing dragon? Maybe he will make me write some weird Asian poem, most likely because a hippie friend of his told Levon it gave his soul peace. I had no idea about all the above.

The door creaked open, very cliché, but it actually did (I am trying to include every detail and there was a creak that day). Levon was tending the fire in the library with his back turned towards me. I say library despite the fact every room in his house looked like a library. He wore the usual old dark blue Levi's, a navy-blue hoodie, but this time from a summer camp in upstate New York and a pair of Nike Roshe Runs.

"If you are early you are on time, if you are on time you are late, if you are late don't even bother showing up." He said with his back still turned.

"Levon, with all due respect and everything...I know you saved my life but really? Come on, this isn't boot camp. I am here so you won't tell my mom the shit I pulled the other night, so let's get this over with. I will be here at noon, so quit being a dick about it." (As I now think about my words, it scares me how quickly I let the failed suicide attempt run from my mind. Even today it falls in the wayside of traumatic events in my life. I think I block it out just to protect myself).

"I said what I meant, and I meant what I said, said the elephant,"[16] he continued, "I hear you, but this is the way I operate, don't worry we will figure it out."

"You really do struggle with communicating huh?"

---

[16] Dr. Seuss, Horton Hatches the Egg

He ignored my last comment and sat on the same leather couch I woke up on a few days earlier. At this point, I put on a good, "fuck it" attitude and decided to go along with the crazy old man. It beat sitting at home on this Saturday listening to my dad attempt, and fail, to put up a new ceiling fan in the man cave downstairs. My father had a real stubbornness against directions. I never understood why. Even when he read them, he became frustrated, sweaty and moody. What my father never realized is that directions don't account for human error. My mother would be nearby in the kitchen bitching about how easy it is to rip holes in piecrust. Piecrust was my mom's one and only nemesis. So it goes...[17]

He didn't ask me to sit down but I did anyway. I was tired of standing. I sat across from Levon on the overstuffed armchair of the same color leather as the couch.

"Why do you think I want you to write?" he began before my ass hit the leather.

"I honestly have no clue. I can see you obviously enjoy books. You ever publish anything?"

"Some stuff." He quickly said, "But this isn't about me."

He caught my usual tactic of turning the conversation away from myself and onto the person I was speaking with; it was a true conversation saver. Everyone likes to talk about him or herself. It works every time. Especially with women, women always love to talk about themselves.

"Alright...Well my answer still stands, I have no clue why you want me to come over here and write. It sounds honestly like the actions of a nut bag," I said.

"Do you talk to everyone like this or just the people you like?"

"You assume I like you?"

"Do you need me to list the plethora of reasons you should like me? Let's start with saving your life."

"This is getting kind of ridiculous."

"You mean stupid?"

"No, Ridiculous is exactly what I mean...I am leaving.

"Pussy," Levon said.

---

[17] Vonnegut Jr., Kurt

"Ummmm. Did you just call me a pussy? Are you a bully or an old man?"

"Can't I be both? Grab that computer…" He motioned to the desk in the corner of the room.

I reacted without question. Our quick-witted banter brought me into a trance. I knew he was joking but Levon was quick and I had to be quicker. This man was like a grandpa. And you can't lose to a grandpa.

As I picked up the silver MacBook Pro, which sat next to three other different versions of Macs, I said, "Are you ever going to tell me why I am here?"

"If you haven't figured it out, then I don't want to tell you."

"Why do you have to act like that? You talk in parables, hyperbole's, incomplete thoughts and metaphors no one uses today. It is like I am in a conversation with a nobleman from middle ages."

"There is a better way of transferring the same idea and meaning. Why say hot when you can say scorching? You ever watch Dead Poets Society?"

"No."

"In the movie Robin Williams said, 'words are meant to woo women and nothing else,' something along those lines. He also said to never use the word 'very,' that it is a word for lazy people. I have a few rules picked up along the way. Never use a semicolon; they are the hermaphrodites of writing,[18] write one true sentence,[19] and stay out of the passive voice. Let's just start with those."

"You do realize I have no idea what you are talking about? And just to mention this is real life not a fucking movie."

"Have you ever scribbled a poem, an angry note to an ex… anything?"

"Yes"

"Okay well that's a start."

I am not sure why I was so hesitant to tell Levon that I enjoyed writing and always kept a journal. I never really wrote anything substantial, no actual attempts at a story or a news piece. But my essays were always

---

[18] Vonnegut Jr., Kurt
[19] Hemingway, Ernest

spot on. I used to charge kids in high school to write their essays. School was never difficult. I never understood how kids struggled. They give you the answer. Just say it back. (As you can tell my critical thinking skills were yet to develop but I could regurgitate states and dates better than anyone). I think my fear of letting Levon in was because I wanted to keep expectations low. I liked having a secret. Secrecy is okay. It makes life special. "It seems to be the one thing that can make modern life mysterious or marvelous."[20]

"Hmmm…" He hummed some tune to himself on a completely different beat than the Sam Cooke album, which still spun in the background. He groped his nonexistent beard and said, "Okay."

Profound I know…

"Okay what?"

"Go grab a book off the shelf over there." Levon pointed to one wall. It looked no different than the others. Completely out of order, dirty, with titles that were unrecognizable. The room was not as big as I remembered. "Take any," he said.

I looked back, rolled my eyes, "Come on Levon what the hell?"

"First of all, roll them back, second of all just trust me, I saved your life for Christ's sake. Why not just take a chance and maybe you will have a new experience and learn something instead of being the questioning and condensing piece of shit you have been until this point, in what you believe to be a worthless life."

"Ruthless man. You do know that is no way to motivate anyone, right?"

"Will you choose a book, or would you rather clean my windows?"

"Got it boss."

I looked back towards the infinitesimal number of books at my choosing. Quickly scanned. Some, I recognized, some, I didn't. I had read none. So, I grabbed the first familiar title. I chose <u>The Picture of Dorian Grey</u> by Oscar Wilde. As I brought the book back to the couches in front of the now blazing fire Levon asked what I chose. Without saying a word, I flashed the cover and the old man shot a cynical, conniving smile I have never seen before or since. It was a look that said, "Got you good fucker."

---

[20] Wilde, Oscar. The Picture of Dorian Gray

I sat with the book in front of the computer now open with a new word document up. Again, this was by far, the weirdest thing ever for a 17-year-old suicidal kid. I accepted the situation at the time because in hindsight there is no way any sane person could consider this situation normal. You can never rationalize the irrational. It was Levon that made it not weird. He spoke with such passion, even when discussing what chair to sit in that you couldn't help but follow. Throughout the later years with Levon I never encountered a single soul who was not comforted by his presence despite his lack of social decorum, or at least lack of social knowledge.

"Open it, to any page, read it and choose a line, any line, and I want you to type it exactly. However, include the sentence above and the sentence below but underline the one line you chose so you can separate it."

Like a soldier in the army I unquestionably followed the directions. I closed my eyes thumbed the book like a man thumbing his cash after a big win in Vegas, and then stopped. I rested my right index finger on the page and opened my eyes to page 89. I read the line to myself and then began typing.

She is very lovely, and if she knows as little about life as she does about acting, she will be a delightful experience. <u>There are only two kinds of people who are really fascinating -- people who know absolutely everything, and people who know absolutely nothing.</u> Good heavens, my dear boy, don't look so tragic!

"Read it to me now," Levon said seemingly knowing I was done just as I pushed the last exclamation point. I read the three sentences.

"Good, now write them in your own words."

"Why?"

"I will tell you after, just try it. Read it to yourself. Think about what the words are saying as a whole. Ask yourself, what is Oscar trying to tell me? Use the lines before and after to help connect it to your life."

"Levon, I don't…" He cut me off.

"Try Jake, no hurt in trying. Don't worry about grammar, political correctness, nothing… Just straight stream of conscience. Read and react. It is okay to react emotionally from time to time."

"That's how I got into that situation the other night. I don't know…"

Levon ignored my last comment.

The world is filled with all sorts of people. Fat, happy, skinny, sad, tall, short, depressed, anxious, angry and everything else in between. With all the characters of life at our disposal one would think we find them all equally intriguing.

I paused…and heard… "Don't you dare stop kid…keep writing!…"

However, there are only two types of people, which capture our imagination the same way a child's imagination is captivated by magic. The ones who know everything and the ones who know nothing. This is because the ones who know everything are lying pretentious ass holes and those who know nothing are an absolute waste of a god given brain and body.

"Don't you dare fucking stop…I can hear you Sport," Levon screamed for absolutely no reason…

We gravitate towards the extremes. We fall in love with the extremes and dream the unobtainable. We humans are wretched things built for extremes, whether it is disappointment or pure ecstasy. We struggle to find a middle ground and when we do it is considered mediocrity.

I stopped. Levon looked directly into my eyes. He had light brown eyes I considered more honey colored than brown. He was a man you learned details about the more you hung out with him. He gave very little away at any one point. His eyelashes were longer than any man's eyelashes should ever be. Not that I ever noticed eyelashes before, but something about being around Levon gave you a heightened sense of observation due to the fear he would question you on some detail, which seemed so obvious when asked.

Levon grabbed the computer without asking. He took his honeysuckle eyes and scanned the words on the screen. I didn't know what to expect.

"I was right," He said, talking to himself. This made me feel pretty awkward. What was he right about?

"Quick, who are you?"

"Just a kid."

"No Jake, you will never be anything if you always believe you are a child. WHO ARE YOU!?"

"I just want to be me! Jesus, why do you have to make everything an argument, or just super dramatic? I just want to be me, okay? Is that all right with you? Or is it not enough? What do you want me to say? That I will be the next Hemingway? Or I will be an incredible athlete like Jordan? I don't know what you want me to say. So, who do you want me to be Levon because I have no idea and don't particularly care anymore? Stop fucking with me, pretending to have some 'Good Will Hunting' or 'Finding Forrester' moment. Those are movies, this is real life and sitting here isn't helping me do anything productive towards it. I am depressed, I am angry, and I don't want to do this."

"Use that anger, use that hate, and use those emotions kid. You don't think this matters? You don't think you matter, do you?"

"To matter is bullshit Levon. I used to say I was anxious to matter.[21] It's all a lie. It is all bull shit. The truth is we don't matter. It is a lie powerful people want you to believe. They want you to think you are special and have some purpose. They say our biggest fear is that we are inadequate,[22] in hopes to motivate us. Levon I may only be 17 but I know more than most about this thing called life. Most of us are just stuck in the bull shit of life destined to live mediocre middle class lives, in their mediocre middle class house, with their mediocre middle class kids, going to work from 9-5, taking vacations to Disney and dying on their black leather mediocre middle class couch, in some overpriced, over taxed suburb, their children can come back to and visit, and live out their years thinking they have the "all American life" we strive so desperately to obtain. So, I don't need your pestering old man babble about who I am, or my purpose, because it is all shit, just heaping loads of smelly horse shit."

"What happened to you? How can you talk so bad about a life and world you have yet to encounter? You are wrong. I will tell you that first. Accept it. People who live those middle-class mediocre lives, such as your parents, worked their ass off for it. They chose that life because they chose you. Many of them find great enjoyment in life despite not being famous, or wealthy, or all knowing. This is when you need to make a decision about

---

[21] Affleck, Ben. Pearl Harbor
[22] Williamson, Marianne.

who you are. And you need to like it, because if you want my honest opinion, I think you are afraid. I think you are afraid to go after your dreams, to do anything worthwhile. You are afraid to fail. If you aim low, you will never disappoint yourself. You decide to sit back, observe, and throw in a plethora of backhanded comments for brief moments of comic relief. This is a cop out. This is when you realize you are much more insane than you ever imagined. You are a joke. Everything you are doing is a joke because if you can't wake up every day and say I am going to take the world by its scrotum and fuck shit up then you might as well not wake up."

He could be open in a charismatic way that drew out other people's secrets, but he held onto his own.[23]

"I want you to let go Jake." Levon continued. "Just try. I know it sounds like a load of shit. But try to trust me. What can it hurt? Just let go."

"Let go of what?"

"If I told you to start a story, what would you say?"

"I'm not starting a story."

"Jake, get out of this shell already...why do you think someone is going to take away your 'cool card' if you care about something, or are intelligent?"

"I...I don't." I stumbled over my words.

"Do you remember the feeling you had when you put Oscar Wilde's line into your own words?"

"I just did it, there was no feeling."

"Wrong kid. You won't admit it, but 10 years from now when you read what you wrote, you will see the meaning and relevance. It may not win you a Pulitzer, but it will still mean something, at some point. Always save your words, they are all you have."

"Why do I always have to be wrong?" I asked.

"And you say I am the one with the communication problem?"

Flustered and angry I followed direction out of some innate reaction unknown to myself before this moment.

"But I don't know what to write about. What do I know? I am only 17 Levon! So, my best friend killed himself in my house. But who doesn't

---

[23]Johnson, Joyce. The Voice is All

know someone who committed suicide? I "loved" one girl, but I don't even know if it was real or true love. Nothing makes my life, my story worth reading by anyone. I did get laid a few times, that was fun." I quipped trying to lighten the growing tension.

"There is such thing as true love, but to say you will only have one love is an ignorant statement of a lackluster cynic."

"I have absolutely no idea what that means Levon. Anyway, I don't want to just write anything. I want it to mean something. Like if you are going to make me sit here and waste my time typing every day for god knows what reason, it better be at least worthwhile. I want it to change the way I think, or you think."

"You can't change the world if all you do is try and blend in and be just like it. You can only make a difference if you piss off the world, stand out from the crap and simply say what you feel. No one says what he or she feels anymore. And don't worry because in the end of the day 'all art is quite useless,' anyway."[24]

"It's not that easy."

"Yes, it is."

"Do you enjoy belittling me?"

"Wait until you see what it actually means to be belittled you little shit."

"Harsh."

"Fear is the ultimate restraint. Don't be afraid to piss people off. Don't be afraid to get angry. Don't be afraid to set the world on fire. Too cliché again?"

"Why do you speak like you are trying to incite riots and preach to the masses? It's just me here. Calm down Stalin."

"Shut up and listen to someone other than yourself. I swear you kids today think the more you know, the smarter you are. You miss the point Jake. 'The more you know, the more you know you don't know shit' about this too big world.[25] Start something... Start anything...You almost killed yourself. I know you have something you want to yell at the

---

[24] Wilde, Oscar. The Picture of Dorian Gray
[25] Combination of lines from Ben Folds "The Bastard," and Kerouac's line "Too big world."

world...start that story. Tell us...there is only one way to free it...just do it...only action...WRITE!"

My face was flushed; I was angry...he was pissing me off. Everything was pissing me off. His words made my blood burn. I was like Jack Nicholson in The Shining breaking through the door. I wanted to scream. So, I screamed. No one heard. I couldn't put the anger into words yet. It needed to be filtered.

I thought about all the pain, the uncertainty, anxiety.... and I hit the keys harder than ever before. I began sweating and was suddenly lost, like a runner who catches a running high. The thoughts moved smoothly, and the fingers gracefully skipped across their surface never missing a beat almost as if I never thought the words. They just went straight from synapse to reflex...I blacked out and I have never experienced anything like it since. It must be what heroin addict feels the first time they shoot up. I have been chasing that dragon ever since. It was word vomit. But like throwing up, I felt much better after this came out...

God hath not promised shit. We were born into this[26] world with nothing but our dick in our hands and our eyes wide open. If my mother read that opening line, she would kill me. Let me try again.

As the sun lay gently over the velvet grass of northern France and the dew seeped onto the musty hills, my eyes wandered from the soulless black of the night to the blue in her eyes, as I could remember nothing before, and remember nothing since. "Romance Sport, is a young man's game." We race and fight for the beautiful, the smart and strong. We look for the perfect bodies and the most compatible souls; however, the problem with romance is that no one looks where they should be looking. No one looks at themselves. They are too concerned with everyone else, they forget how to make themselves happy. That doesn't come until one is old.

Nope that's not how I can start it. It's not my voice...

I can still see the smoke rising up in the room. I can feel the slow burn down my throat as my diaphragm spasm'd telling me no more, but like a victim of emphysema I sucked and pulled until my eyes rolled. I put the blunt down. Then I put the joint down. Then I put the bowl and the bong down and stopped eating the brownie. I took two

---

[26] Bukowski, Charles.

Xanax and left for work. I came home took an Adderall, kept working then smoked a
bowl, then a joint then went to bed.

Nope that is definitely not it...Too crackhead-ish.

You ever meet someone and afterwards say to yourself, "what the fuck?"...
Can't start with a question...

Nope...Think...Think...Type...Write... Ugh fuck this shit. Crazy ass old
man yelling at me, looking over my shoulder probably smirking while I intend to insult
him...

I can feel the breeze. I have felt that breeze before. But not here. Not like this.
I felt that breeze when I was running once as a boy. I felt that breeze on the Indian
Ocean, no wait, maybe it was the Mediterranean. I felt it as I stuck my head out the
train car whipping past townships in Argentina, and I felt it while standing on the Black
Hills of the Dakotas. I am 24. I should be 19. No, I am 20. When I wrote my first
book, I was 19. When I wrote my second, I was 22. When I hit 30, like everyone else in
my life I had a quarter life crisis, terrified the adventures were over. No more 4 a.m.
dance parties in the living room. No more hard drugs. No more fucking girls in elevators
on cruise ships. No more drinking until your eyes begin to spin around like a dreidel in
Israel. Perpetually underachieving, I have become the poster board for mediocrity. No
doubt I will get stuck in my job, never to travel, never to caress a stranger's figure while
knowing we are only in it for one night of reactionary passion, they make porn after. No
longer can I sleep until 4, get up, smoke a joint, eat some Chipotle and fart for 6 straight
hours without shitting my pants.

It's that breeze. It cools me down, warms me up and slaps the back of my neck
with a five star bigger than a Converse billboard.

...Where was this coming from?...I kept going...It felt really good.

We all get those feelings, the unrelenting desire to run... to get up and run.
Maybe for self-discovery, which is usually a stoner's way of saying no more responsibility.
Maybe it is to learn...maybe that desire comes from a gypsy soul engrained in a few
whose nomadic heart can't hold them in a society, which glorifies stupidity and mocks
intelligence. Or maybe it's just a breeze and we tend to over analyze shit.

There is no starting point for this tale. There is no lesson. It is not
entertainment. It is not a memoir, it is fiction. But like all fiction it is based on fact. Fact
cannot be ignored, and it is only facts that we can rely on. The fact is that I live in the
worst, period. Generation, period. That has ever been privileged to grace this planet and I
am fucking proud of it.

Levon smiled. "I knew it."

I hated when he said, "I knew it." Cocky son-of-a-bitch.

Levon closed the computer and said we were done. He didn't say goodbye or ask me to leave. He just walked away, went upstairs and left me alone in the library with a closed computer.

Only about an hour passed since I arrived at Levon's, but I figured he was done, so I left without a word. Levon never said goodbye.

CHAPTER FOUR

"For he had learned some of the things that every man must find out for himself, and he had found out about them as one has to find out-- through error and through trial, through fantasy and illusion, through falsehood and his own damn foolishness, through being mistaken and wrong and an idiot and egotistical and aspiring and hopeful and believing and confused."
                                                    -- Thomas Wolfe

The next day came like they all do. The sun rose. School was such a formality, which I dreaded. It had nothing to do with the actual school, or the teachers, or the work. I hated school because of the other students. They were all phony.[27] There is nothing more fake in this world then a kid in high school. They have yet to discover any true identity and find themselves skipping from trend to trend hoping to discover a persona that sticks. Their stubbornness to admit their ambiguous personalities was the biggest problem of them all. Not much in the world scares me more than a teenager on the path to discovery, they are such lost souls, but it is a necessary trail we all travel down at some point.

I could never understand the open disrespect towards teachers and apathy towards failing. To me, failing was horrible, to the majority of my classmates, failing was the least deterrent of all. There is only so much motivation a teacher can instill on a student. They can provide all the

---

[27] Salinger, J.D. The Catcher in the Rye

extrinsic material necessary to get a kid to get up and go...but the intrinsic motivation comes from that student and that student alone. When that motivation is not there, usually due to uneducated parents or siblings who claimed education wasn't important because they didn't get one, or a job, but the government will still pay for their lazy ass to have a child, there is not much left for a teacher to do. I ignored the ignorance and just did my own thing. This is not to say all students in my high school fell under such a stigma, but I have traveled so much over the years, observing other education systems and schools, I still find it flabbergasting that in a country as rich in resources, knowledge, and ability, we still have one of the worst education systems of the western world. Anyway...I digress.

Instead of participating in the rabble-rousing, and immature debauchery (I was way past spit balls) I kept to myself. For some reason my English teacher found it necessary to tell my parents my social abilities were lacking. My parents did not like this report after parent teacher conferences. Mrs. Dellina was concerned my "social health" wasn't developing properly. It was an interesting assessment coming from a woman who wore purple cocktail dresses to school. My parents failed to mention Johnny. They tried to bury all that was our past, when your past is all that makes you, you. We are all comprised of our past demons and angels, whether we like it or not. I never understood why she singled me out? I may have been quiet but at least I wasn't any of the other peasant children who attended that god forsaken brown building on the corner of Fair St. and Route 311. The students ignored the teachers, spoke back to them and belittled the privilege of a free public education. God forbid the adults in this world wanted to bestow the gift and ability to think. Yet, I get the negative report because I was quiet. Fuck her.

But why is education in such shambles? In every generation they blame the "times." I have no idea what that means. First, it comes down to the value education has within the culture. American culture lost the value in education because of the welfare state perpetuating incompetence and complacency with doing donkey shit and getting paid for it. While this is going on we have an Enlightenment model of a free public education being forced into an Industrialist ideal. We treat students like cars on an assembly line, slowly giving them one piece at a time as they flash by in 180 days, declaring they have now moved a grade up. However, kids are not cars on an assembly line, and this isn't the Enlightenment and Industrialization has passed. Sometimes kids move to the next station on the assembly line missing parts from the previous station. Remember, no child left behind, leaves all children behind.

We are a consuming people who do very little to produce, whether that be goods or knowledge. If no one here is producing the knowledge, then we are conceding to other countries. You may ask, then how do we fix this if you are so omnipotent about education? You didn't ask this, I asked it for you. It can only change if our views about education change. It should no longer be a right to an education, but a privilege. Take away free public education and see how quickly people will begin to fight for it again. Then, we will see who values what in this country. (Not a real suggestion).

I received a great education growing up, but it was because of the work I did. I worked for it. I went and found the books, I read them, I wrote about them. School had very little to do with my education and development as a man. All school did for me was teach me reasons to hate society and its glorification of stupidity. The fact the popular kids had an IQ of 73, made me sick to my stomach. Intelligence should never be mocked. It is important to surround and uplift intelligence and when all of our resources are being pooled to help the learning disabled, we forget there is an entire population of gifted students either not being enriched or falling to the wayside.

The reason I am bringing this up is because outside of myself, I attribute my education to Levon. Going to his house was my education and I am forever indebted to the man. Levon was a tough cat to read. The more I grew to understand Levon, the more I understood I would never understand the old man. His emotions were erratic with the smallest of events setting him off into tantrums fit for a 3-year-old whose lollipop was just taken away. I learned to laugh at his outbursts because of how juvenile they were for a man passed his prime. Well, they were juvenile for anyone who graduated elementary school.

I began to show up at Levon's after school, whether I was invited or not I would stop in at 16 Lotus Lane. It was always better than going home. Levon's library was more of a home for my gypsy heart than my own house. Some days we would write, others, Levon never showed his face and I sat in the library thumbing through his collection. Levon was always home, which I found odd for a man with pictures strewn throughout his home that showed him in one magical place after another. He had traveled to Jordan, Turkey, South Africa, Iceland, Peru, Argentina, Senegal, Thailand, Maldives, Nepal just to name a few of the places I could identify in his pictures. He was a certified scuba diver; I knew this because I found his certification being used as a bookmark in *Slaughterhouse Five*. He apparently knew how to surf, hiked Machu Picchu, K2 and backcountry skied. His exploits were evident, his stories nowhere to be found. For a man who wrote constantly and had a love affair with words, he shared very little. One would think after a year of afternoon visits, I would know all about the old man. All I knew about Levon's personal life came from his annotations in his books, and the pictures he left on the walls. Anytime I pressed about his past during the first year we lived in Connecticut, he would change the subject, or become unreasonably angry and make me leave. I never took his fits personally. He reminded me of *Esteban Trueba* in how his irrational anger caused him to always apologize with his tail between his legs. Levon knew he was irrational with his reactions, but it felt as if he truly had no control. So, I never faulted him and would return the next day. Forgiveness is a skill, not a trait.

It was a friendship that required no discussion of being friends. The friendly banter was all that was needed. He never explained why I was writing, he never explained anything other than I had a gift and it needed to be shared. Now, by this point I should have thrown it back into his face that he never shared anything with me. But his loneliness was hard to bear. I felt, why rock the boat if I am a source of companionship for this old man? He had his outbursts, but something about Levon was calming. Some days, when I would be off writing in the library, I'd look up from the glowing screen to catch Levon staring off into nothingness. I asked him one time what he was thinking about. His response was, "Can't a man think about nothing?"

"Yes, a man has that right, but you are a horrible liar. No man with a gaze like a lost child in a theme park is thinking about nothing, but I will let it go Levon."

"Good." He silently smirked as I looked back down at the screen.

My parents were oddly okay with my relationship with the old man. They were so focused on their lives, even if they disagreed with my daily ventures, they knew I wouldn't stop if they requested. I was free to my own devices, to discover my own world, form my own opinions, make my own mistakes. This of course was only okay if I didn't screw up their life.

In the summer I helped with landscaping and he would pay me. Levon never said it, but I think he enjoyed my company. I also didn't mind being his landscape prostitute. Despite his ever-changing emotions and sporadic temper, we got along well. He appreciated my brash sarcastic and pessimistic view of the world, and I enjoyed the fact he wasn't a complete babbling moron. Also, I felt, regardless of whether Levon would admit it, we were both alone, our companionship was comforting. Humans are communal by nature. We are not meant to travel this world alone. And for my first 17 years of life, I was alone. I found it hard to believe Levon had been alone his entire life, but he wore no ring and there were no pictures of kids anywhere in his home.

I found peace in his home. I found comfort in Levon's loneliness and I found my voice in the imposing library.

It was after school on a Thursday when Levon gave me a real lesson on writing that wasn't him nodding behind me as I wrote nonsense. Though I still wrote daily, it served no purpose but to get my thoughts and emotions on paper, so I didn't officially go bat shit crazy.

It was snowing and I picked up pizza for the two of us. Thursday was always my pizza day, not Friday. When I was growing up, Thursday was when my mother had graduate school, so my father ordered pizza. I was a creature of habit and kept this tradition my whole life.

When I walked into the old white colonial, Levon wasn't anywhere to be seen and didn't answer my usual bellows from downstairs. This was normal, so I thought nothing about it. While I scarfed down my second slice of buffalo chicken pizza, Levon appeared in the doorway that led into the kitchen. He looked exhausted. He always looked tired, but his eyes were lower than usual and his movements slower. It was the 21st of August.

"You are ready," he said, starting in the middle of a conversation as usual. A simple "Hi, how are you, how was your day?" was not in his vernacular.

"Ready for what?" I asked.

He walked over to the wall of books, rubbed his non-existent beard, ran his fingers along the bindings humming to himself. He picked up a book and with an adolescent yell of "think quick" tossed it in my direction over his back shoulder. Not thinking quickly, the book flew over my head and crashed into his globe. The globe popped open to reveal a bar inside, with all empty whiskey bottles. I got up from the laptop and picked up the book. *On Writing* by Stephen King.

"Stephen King? Really? I am not a big fan of horror or mysteries Levon, how is this going to help?"

"Trust me, he knows more about writing in general than I could ever teach you. I want you to go through the book and copy my annotations and underlines into your journal."

"Why?"

"Trust me Sport. Do you like writing?"

"I do, but it is just for fun."

"It can still be fun. Just read some of my underlines and try to soak some of it in."

"Okay Levon," and I rolled my eyes.

"Roll them back."

"Got it boss."

I thumbed the book like I have done innumerable times before to other books. This one was worn more than other books that lined his shelves. Its cover had a tear from right to left right across the image of Mr. King writing at his desk. The copyright page was missing. Little post-its and neon colored tab stickers stuck out the side. The inside had his usual blue pen graffiti the rest of his books contained. I wrote down as much as I could. It would have taken a man 10 years to try and decipher every one of Levon's scribbles.

We began a snappy dialogue that garnished its own rhythm. I read a line he underlined out loud, Levon would elaborate first, putting his own baroque style into it, then I quickly rebutted in some fashion before moving onto the next line. Even if we had complete opposite reviews/opinions, we moved on with no further discussion.

No one ever asks about the language.

"Most people think since they know how to speak, they know how to write. If there is any single biggest mistake a writer can make, it is writing how they speak."

"Or they could just be original. Dialect and dialogue are important regardless of grammatical correctness." I responded.

To write is human, to edit is divine.

"I hate editors. No one enjoys divinity when it is not them. All editors do is muddy up the waters and confuse a writer from his path."

"Or her path…" I corrected him. "Their job is to make your writing better; I don't get how you can hate someone whose one job is to improve your craft."

I realized that almost every writer of fiction and poetry who has ever published a line has been accused by someone of wasting his or her God-given talent. If you write (or paint or dance or sing I suppose), someone will try to make you feel lousy about it.

"Everyone who hates on the arts has never experienced the thrill that comes with creation. They are one celled paramecium brains[28] with no imagination. They get off on being critics of those who supply a lifeline to the world. They make a living by criticizing, how much lower can you get? Bunch of scum."

"Isn't there an old saying that says a man without a critic is a man who has never accomplished anything?…"

In my character, a kind of wildness and a deep conservatism are wound together like hair in a braid.

"Ah, this is a good one. So many authors have written about the duality of man and life. You know the usual lesson of you can't have light without the dark statement. Regardless of the corniness and pure obnoxious repetition of that line, it has much truth to it. I agree with Mr. King here. My body is made up with the struggle between what is proper and okay to say and what is outlandish or wild. I don't give a shit what you think about my statements. I have always written in a somewhat

---

[28] Williams, Robin. Hook

unorthodox way. This form of "wild" writing combats my desire for a pure prose and grammatically spotless writing. In the middle is where you find the world falling apart. We desire moderation, gravitate towards extremes and struggle with reality. That is the human way. However, when it comes to writing, you must find your desire to shock and be original, but always know one day your mother might read it. Know all writers have different voices, some are their own, others have been comprised from all they surround themselves with and a few come from the reader's own imagination."

"My whole life I have warred within myself with stuff like this."

"Stuff like this? Why don't you be a little more specific."

"Let me finish… I mean it applies to everything. My father always tells me to be humble, but then you are told to have confidence. You are told to try hard but not be an overachiever… I don't know, I just know I don't have a balance between my wildness and conservatism. When one is in full bloom the other is quivering deep within me."

When you write a story, you're telling yourself the story.

"You should always write what you would read. This is why the number one job of a writer is to read, not write. Why write something you aren't entertained by?"

"I have never written a story."

"You have written more stories than you know."

"That makes no sense Levon."

Write with the door closed, rewrite with the door open.

"Does he need to say anymore? Writing should be done in solitude, so you can only hear one voice."

"My door will stay closed even if I am on draft 47. Those are my words," I responded.

"You should share."

"This coming from you?"

"Next line," He commanded.

Having someone believe in you makes a lot of difference…Just believing is usually enough.

"It is always important to know that someone out there has your back and believes that what you are saying is important. If you don't have this person, writing is a long dark lonely road, only to become harder when the uncertainties of what lies ahead smacks you in the face."

"Someone is a bit needy…why can't you just believe in yourself?"

"You will never believe in yourself as much as someone who truly loves you, believes in you."

For me writing has always best when it's intimate.

"Don't let anyone kid you, everything is best when intimate. Large groups are overrated."

"I don't even know how to be intimate."

"You will learn."

"Apparently I have a lot to learn."

"If only you knew."

Sometimes you are doing good work when it feels like all you're managing is to shovel shit from a sitting position.

"What do you think this is saying?"

"That sometimes you need to shovel shit."

"Keep going…"

"I don't know Levon."

"Sometimes when you feel like you are doing shitty work it is actually much better than you imagine. Even if work isn't going well it is important to keep chugging along. It is important to flex the muscles even if it is painful to get the words from your heart to your brain down to your arms and through your fingers. There is a lot of places for your words to go rogue. So, shovel that shit, because even shit helps the flowers grow."

I am convinced fear is at the root of most bad writing.

"Fear is the basis of all poor decisions. Fear about tomorrow, the past, and even fear of right now is the root of evil. You can't be afraid to say what you feel or want. It may offend some and inspire others at the same time. Fear will lead you to a timid life and don't stray down such a path to meekness, because kid, the Bible lies, all the meek will inherit is loneliness."

"Fear is a natural human reaction Levon, don't be so dramatic. Sometimes shit is scary. Like clowns. I hate clowns. There is no rationale behind my fear of clowns, but they scare me."

"You are on the surface."

"Huh?"

"I'll put it this way, don't be afraid to say what you feel. That is why the world falters day in and out. We thrive on our connections to each other and if you lose the ability to speak free and openly, you lose honest communication and there is the center of the crumbling foundation of humanity."

"Bit dramatic but noted."

Good writing is often about letting go of fear and affection.

"If you become too wrapped up into your own world what you write you will never be truthful."

"Is this why you always tell me to let go?"

"You have to. You hold onto too much."

"I think I hold onto what is necessary."

"Then you will never write truthfully."

If you intend to write as truthfully as you can, your days as a member of polite society are numbered, anyway.

"Polite society is overrated anyways."

"Why do you assume the truth will always be negative or offend someone?"

"Because the truth is not fair, and fair does not mean equal."

"Huh?"

"Because the world is too damn sensitive. That clear?"

For me, good description usually consists of a few well-chosen details that will stand for everything else.

"Be simple and move on. Don't linger on unnecessary details. Write what you see and hear then get on with the story. You hate when your mom gives 3 hours of back story for such a simple thought. Do the exact opposite."

"Are we done yet? This is a bit much now Levon. I got it...read the book and I can learn how to write."

"No."

"Got it boss," I said reluctantly, not to piss off the volatile man.

Sometimes the book gives you answers, but not always, and I didn't want to leave the readers who had followed me through hundreds of pages with nothing but some empty platitude I didn't believe myself.

"Never, I repeat never, write to find an answer. No book will give you an answer; nothing you can devise in that brain can either. If you are writing in order to find an answer you will be left very disappointed. Be careful about expressing your soul, because you will lose it.

"Yes boss."

"Not sure if that was condescending or not but I don't particularly care."

"One more Jake, I am tired now."

All novels are really letters aimed at one person.

"You always have an audience in mind. Sometimes the audience is just one."

With this last line Levon looked away. It was more of a shudder than a twitch. As if those words pierced some deep-down place he hasn't visited in a long time. Every bone in my body felt the uneasiness that spread through Levon's veins. It sent us into a silence that lasted one tick too long for it to be called accidental.

CHAPTER FIVE

"You can lose your way groping among the shadows of the past."

-- Louis-Ferdinand Céline

Day after day, the routine remained the same. School from 7:30-2, football practice from 2-5, Levon's from 5:30-7, sometimes 8, then home for a late dinner, off to bed to do it all again the next day. Weekends brought an overwhelming depression that caused me to never leave my room. Some weekends I drank with the few friends I was able to collect over the year. The other option was going to Levon's. Sometimes I thought it was because I enjoyed his company, sometimes it was because it felt like I was helping the old man, sometimes I felt bad about his loneliness, sometimes I was thinking about my loneliness. Either way, in the end, regardless of why it happened, we hung out quite a bit on the weekends. Levon was a different man on the weekends. The sensitive, moody, drill sergeant was gone, and a Jimmy Buffet clone was suddenly before me. It was crazy the difference between Monday Levon and Saturday evening Levon.

No writing happened on the weekends. Levon always said, "You must never work when you can play." However, he considered every minute of the 5-day work week time when you should be working. He killed himself slaving over whatever it is he slaved over. There was never a single time I went over Levon's on the weekend when he wasn't already out on the porch, with drink in hand. There were Saturday mornings I showed up at 7 or 6 am and that son-of-a-bitch was out there, whiskey in hand. I eventually gave up trying to beat him. He lived for the weekend. There is a saying that you shouldn't just live for Friday. If you ever told Levon this he would drink a bottle of whiskey without moving the bottle from his lips, only taking it away it to promptly smash the bottle over your head. Not that I ever saw him do this, I just assumed he would. I couldn't imagine a statement getting him more irritated.

There was one Saturday during that first year when it was so putridly hot there was no way anyone was going to stay out in the cauldron of an earth. It was like standing in the devil's ball sack. There was no way anyone could survive in that heat. It was a heat that melted ice cubes before you could bring them to your mouth. Levon sweat in the winter so this was stroke worthy weather for him. But sure enough, that day I showed up and Levon had his feet in two pots of ice water, with an umbrella hat equipped with a fan and water mister. He looked like a mix of Bill Murray in Caddy Shack with Bill Murray from Space Jam. He had on a bright red bathing suit that was easily 30 years old, now faded to burnt orange and 3 sizes too small. Gazing through his faded Wayfarer's he said, "Soon you will be bitching that it's too cold outside. Go grab a bucket."

And like so many times before I obeyed without question.

On my way out the door I grabbed Thomas Wolfe's, *Look Homeward Angel*. The two of us sat on the porch overlooking the corner of the marsh. Off in the distance you could see the lobster boats coming in and out of the harbor as the sun rose in the East. We didn't say much to each other having over time become comfortable in each other's presence. The book was, as usual, littered with Levon's blue pen marks, underlines and annotations. Levon was reading *Journey to The End of the Night* by Louis-Ferdinand Celine. Whenever I was with Levon, things happened for a reason. It was as if serendipitous moments followed the man everywhere, he went. I was convinced I chose this book for a reason today, I met him for a reason and the marks in his books were for my eyes and no one else's. It happened so often that I began to expect moments of revelation and inspiration whenever sitting with Levon. I wonder if anyone else felt that way around him?

I read in the blistering heat, soon forgetting the temperature and becoming lost in Wolfe's mind.

She was buried in his flesh. She throbbed in the beat of his pulses. She was wine in his blood, music in his heart.

This was underlined, with an arrow that pointed to, *"I'm sorry Phia, I still feel you, though, I lost the sound of music."*

Who was Phia? What type of name was Phia? Was it short for something? It was the first time I ever read or saw the name.

This was one of those moments when you unconsciously decide to solve a problem. If you didn't solve the problem it followed you for the rest of your life like the comment you heard online at Walmart that sunk into your brain, never letting go of its grip on your sanity. When you heard the statement, you turned around to find the old lady who said, "My stockings are the reason I had 3 children." Just when it sinks into your brain and you process the idiocracy of the statement and you go to ask what the hell she meant, she vanished, vanquished. You wonder was it even real? No one could say such a stupid thing. But you will never know for sure and all you can do for the next 72 hours of your life is ponder and think to yourself, what the fuck did that mean? Anyway, I digress...

I had never seen another reference to a Phia in any other annotations. Levon's annotations were usually underlines of descriptions, circling of 10-dollar words, usually so he remembered to never use such ostentatious terms. Levon believed using such words was a disservice to all readers. Books should be accessible to everyone. He agreed, some books are meant for people with higher intelligence; however, he once said "large, 10-dollar words, such as the ones Faulkner litters in his writing turn people off." Rarely did he actually write words in his annotations. He later told me this was out of respect, because he was already breaking literature decorum by marking books and dog-earing pages.

But now my curiosity was perked. Behind every great man is a tragedy. Was Phia his tragedy? This could be a death, or the losing of a loved one, an accident, anything... But no man leaves life unscathed. Some scars are visible, some are hidden. The fact I knew so little about this man after a year, I needed to find out the story of Phia even if it was just an old high school love. I was determined to break down the walls of Levon. To this point I didn't even know Levon's first name.

I looked up at Levon sitting above me like a king in a thrown, humming to himself. I was nervous he would remember what he wrote in the book. Despite my good-hearted intentions and innocently stumbling on the annotation, I knew Levon would be pissed I saw a piece of his past.

I quickly took out my phone and snapped a picture of the page with the quote, to use as a possible reference. My mind was swimming with possible love stories, scenarios about Phia and Levon. I was getting that spine-tingling feeling that I needed to write. The creative juices were bubbling at my very core. I had an epic love story of Levon traveling in Italy and falling in love with a Phia, only to be forced apart by an angry dad who loathed the thought that his perfect daughter would fall for a ruffian, aspiring author who never showed anyone his work. Boom...there was my Pulitzer and I wasn't even 18 yet. The images of grandeur flooded my brain, the parade, the praises, the underwear that would be thrown at me. All of the sapiosexuals unloading their every fantasy and desire onto me.

As I took the picture, a blue Dodge Caravan pulled down the driveway. Never having seen the car before, I tapped Levon's elbow to alert him of the possible intruder. He did not look up. The van stopped, but no one got out for about 5-minutes. Then an elderly woman climbed out of the driver seat, maneuvering her way to the side door where she unloaded spades, shovels, loppers, lavender, hydrangeas, lilies, and mulch. She did not look familiar. (One universal truth about women...they all take forever to get out of a car. Why? No one will ever know). She was not a neighbor and had a hint of Spanish that led me to believe she was not related to Levon. Was it Phia? Did she show up now as I just read that line? The universe could not be so serendipitous.

The sweat was pouring down my face like I was standing in a shower, but a hot, salty shower. Despite my pit stains reaching my waistline, my only focus was on the first person I ever saw visit Levon. She was a tall woman, wearing stained khaki clam diggers, royal blue crocs, a green floral blouse unbuttoned a tad low for an older lady. From first glance she appeared to be roughly Levon's age, maybe older. She walked gracefully from the driveway to the garden, not even acknowledging the two males on the porch, and Levon did not budge, still entrenched in his book, which he already read multiple times.

Finally, I received an answer to some of my many questions about Levon. How the hell did his garden and yard stay so meticulous? The woman went straight to work. It was a garden worthy of Versailles. She had the skill of a surgeon. She was a botanical surgeon. I wondered how I never saw her before today. She quickly went ever to the hostas and began digging out the roots. I knew this plant because my mother always referred to them as the "devil plant." Our yard had a row of hostas when we moved in. My mother and I spent an entire weekend trying to dig them up, but the root system was so deep it was like digging up a casket.

Levon still did not move, so I decided to take my feet out of the water buckets and go over to the woman and see if she needed help. Despite being an ass hole self-righteous teenager, I still believed in chivalry. When I saw her embarking on this task, I knew she would need help.

I put the book down and strolled off the porch back into the heat. Before my right foot stepped off the pathway, the woman turned and saw me.

"Don't you come over here empty-handed Jake." she said, startling me. She had a thick Spanish accent.

"How do you know my…" She cut me off in Levon fashion.

"I know all about you Jake. Bring that shovel over here."

"I hope you heard all good things."

"That depends on your definition of good."

Is she the Spanish female version of Levon?

I skipped over the blazing walkway to the car and grabbed an extra shovel. It had a short handle. It was a shovel you used to dig up small plants. I knew it was going to be insufficient.

Without any direction I jogged over to the old lady standing next to the hostas and went to work. She quickly realized I knew what she was doing and instead of dictating to me, she started working herself. At first there was no dialogue as the sun hammered the back of our necks and sweat showered off our brows. Neither of us put suntan lotion on, classic mistake. (The only other spot you always forget is the back of your knees and the tops of your feet).

We moved in synchrony around the large leafy bushes. She began yapping, without prompt. Most people above the age of 50 always have something to say. You would think they are talked out by that advanced age, but anyone who has been caught on the phone with grandma around a holiday, knows I speak the truth. She told me her name was Evelyn Lopez, mother of 5 children. She had twin boys 30 years old, two daughters 32 and 33 and another son 27 years old. She openly claimed he was a mistake. Evelyn said, "we didn't have birth control, we had rhythm." Obviously, that rhythm was not as effective as birth control. Evelyn moved to the States from Columbia when she was 17, learning English through random odd jobs she was able to pick up. Her story was like many you see on Dateline specials and Oprah. She was the American dream working her way up, supporting her family through her natural ability and skills passed down to her from generations to generation. Evelyn, who went by Evie, said she was about 10 years older than Levon and has been doing his yard and garden for 36 years, since he moved into the area. However, she'd known Levon much longer. She did not tell her story chronologically, instead skipping around giving bits and pieces from childhood to present day. Her mind was quick despite her body being old. It became tiresome attempting to follow the skipping allegories while battling the heat and the devil plant at the same time. If I didn't chime in soon, I knew I was going to drop right into the cedar mulch.

"Evie, slow down a little. First off, how the heck do you know so much about me and what do you know?"

"Levon of course." she said forgetting to mention what she knows. Or at least neglecting to mention… a way out of lying…solid tactic…

"But I have never seen you here."

"Just because you have never seen me doesn't mean I was never here."

"True, but that doesn't answer when you come to work on the garden. I have been here many other Saturdays and you weren't here."

"You didn't ask."

"When do you come to garden?"

"When the yard needs work."

"This yard is always spotless."

"See, I come at the right times."

She was quick for a woman speaking in a second language.

"So, what has Levon told you?"

"A lot."

"Couldn't be more descriptive?"

"He said you remind him of him."

"I hope not."

"Don't you dare say that child."

"I am not a child."

"Don't be so sensitive... Levon would have reacted the same way," she mumbled under her breath.

"If you have known Levon for over 30 years you must know all about him."

"I know more than you know."

"I am sure, I know nothing."

"I know you know nothing...that is how Levon works."

"Evelyn..."

"Don't use my formal name."

"Come on Evie, tell me something, I am dying here. You know all about me and I know about you now, how come Levon gets a pass?"

"It's not my place."

"Can you at least tell me how you met him?"

"We knew each other in graduate school, in the city."

"What city? Wait you have a masters?"

"You can't learn everything about a person in a lifetime, what makes you think in 15 minutes of gardening with someone you would know all about me?"

"I can see why you two get along."

"We hated each other."

"Past tense?...though you still do his gardening."

"Look at the man...how can I not come over? A garden is good for your soul. It's the least I can do for him. His soul needs all the help it can get, to keep it at rest."

"You are a better person than me."

"You still have many years to learn the person you are."

"Why here?" I shot in changing the subject.

"Excuse me?"

"How did you both end up here in Branford?"

"It's a long story."

"Do you know how long it is going to take to transplant these devil bushes?"

"Devil bushes?"

"It is what my mother calls them."

"Mother?....that's pretty formal."

"Formality is a way of life in my house of facades."

"Levon was right."

"About?...What did he tell you!?"

"Do you want to help or not?"

It was obvious I was not getting anything out of her, but she intrigued me the same way Levon intrigued me. They both had this dialogue, like an Aaron Sorkin film, it was fast, faster than fast, your brain needed all of its capacity to fire back at them. I had so many other questions, but they remained unanswered. I wanted to ask, but the defenses these two people shared were like the walls of Troy and I needed to find my Trojan horse. (I apologize for the cliché).

We continued to work into the late hours of the day. Levon never got up from his chair other than to pee and make nachos...a personal favorite of his. He only used Santitas tortilla chips with Sargento shredded sharp cheddar cheese and splash of Frank's Hot Sauce. Place on high in the microwave for 30 seconds. It was a "28 Lotus Lane Special" as Levon referred to it. The simple snack was like his whiskey, a home base for the lonely man.

The old man never came over to visit us for most of the day. Just as the sun was disappearing over the pine trees across the street giving the blue backdrop of the ocean a violet glow, Levon appeared behind Evelyn and I with two glasses of whiskey. Most would expect lemonade, water, maybe some pigs in a blanket or bruschetta. No, Levon had one thing and one thing only to serve...whiskey. We each picked up our glass and tipped towards the center of our triumvirate, and without hesitation Levon said,

"To the crazy for they make the rest sane. To the liquid sunshine,[29] may it burn on the way down."

I watched Levon and Evelyn ferociously shoot their drinks back not letting the brown liquid grace their mouths, going straight down their throats. I was surprised by Evie taking the drink for a lack of better terms, "like a man," despite the fact the best drinkers I know are women. At the time, I never saw a woman drink like Evelyn. Levon walked away with a little more pep in his strut. Evie and I went back to work, trying to transplant the devil hostas. The sun was still molten lava hot but was slowly starting to set. About 30 minutes later, Levon came with another shot. I tried to take it like the two vets but failed, pouring a good portion of the liquid gold down my face. Taking a shot is an acquired skill and I was an underage rookie. After a third shot I could tell Evie was starting to loosen up. Her accent was thicker as she lost focus on her speech. I gave up trying to pry more into Levon's past. I figured I would have my time and place for such inquiries. However, she began to tell me all she knew about the plants in the yard, and even a little bit about what Levon told her of me. She said, Levon told her a couple months ago he had been teaching a kid who moved into 16 Lotus Lane about writing. She said, I was the first person in 15 years, other than her, to go in the house. I said very little. A lot of subtle chuckles and well timed, "you don't say," "That's so interesting," "How do you feel about that?" I came to learn it doesn't matter who you are talking to, or what about, but there are a few little tricks in all conversations that can be lifesavers.

By the time the last hosta was moved from the cedar mulch and transplanted across the road into the woods, the sun was gone over the pine trees across the driveway. Evelyn and I were soaked from our toes to our nose in sweat. We were also about seven or eight shots in, I lost track after 5, between the gardening and Evelyn's consistent stories. Levon was still sipping his drink on the porch completely unfazed. In hindsight it's extremely odd for a 17-year-old boy to be drinking with an old man and his elderly Colombian gardener, but at the time, it was what it was.

---

[29] Shaw, George Bernard

"So, I see you guys hit it off," Levon yelled from the porch, even though it was only 30 feet away.

"You should be nicer to him," Evelyn shouted back. Again, I still didn't understand why they were shouting. I would come to find out this was how they communicated. They constantly yelled like middle school children on the playground.

"I am always nice, what the hell did you tell her Jake?"

"I didn't say anything… Evelyn…"

"Calm down Jake, I am joking," she said to me, walking towards the house. "You never mentioned he is as sensitive as a chick!"

"Don't compare people to your insensitive self, Hitler, Stalin and Columbus had more sensitivity in their fingernails than you have in your entire body Evie," Levon shot back.

"Don't be a dick."

"I was born an ass hole Evie, I haven't been working at it."

I stood in amazement and watched the exchange of banter. It felt like I was watching Animal Planet exploring some newly discovered species. My only experience with the elderly was visiting my two grandmothers in their nursing homes. Both of my grandfathers were dead by the time I was born. Both died from heart problems. My mother's father had a massive heart attack at 73 and my dad's father, Papa, passed away during a valve transplant. Apparently, the pig heart didn't agree with his body. I just think they got tired of living and left the rest up to us. But Evie and Levon bickered like brother and sister, if she wasn't Columbian, I would have bet money they were brother and sister.

Were they lovers? Inappropriate again…I was missing a plethora of puzzle pieces in order to complete the jigsaw. Between the note to Phia, and a chance meeting with the self-proclaimed master of the garden, my mind spun in circles as to what the missing pieces could possibly be. So far, I knew they met at grad school in the city. Levon moved to Branford 36 years ago. Evie has 5 kids, all of whom were older than 27, one of which was a mistake, nothing about her babies' padre. I knew nothing of why Evie gardened for Levon, why he is in Branford, why she is in Branford, nothing about Levon's family, or where he used to live, if he had kids or not, nothing about Phia… It was like watching a TV show that never tied up the loose ends and only leaves you with more questions, but the show is so well done and entertaining you come back each week to watch a new episode, only leaving you with more questions as you curse at the television yelling, "What the fuck is going on?"

When I was about to tell Levon that I was heading home for dinner, he looked at me like a red headed step child, and said, "Come on man, how are you going to leave Evie like that, I just ordered some food to thank you guys for your work."

"You ordered food? You never order food Levon."

"I gotta pay the bitch somehow."

"That's how you lose the last piece of chicken you ass," Evie shot back at Levon.

"I don't have a choice in the matter, do I?" I asked.

"Nope." He ushered towards the door.

The three of us went in and Levon opened a bottle of wine. It was the first time I saw him drink anything other than whiskey, water and coffee. We all walked into the library, unconsciously knowing there was no other room to go into, no other room we were allowed to venture. I never saw Levon in the dining room or the family room. It was either kitchen or library.

His personality shifted with Evie there. The Gestapo, Trunchbull, and crotchety old man I have grown accustomed to shed his hard exterior. He was cracking jokes, smiling and leaning back in his chair. Levon was usually so wound up he sat up straight clutching his body at all times. It made him look smaller than his 5,5" stature already did. One of the many masks I would learn Levon wore, shed away in the cool Saturday evening air. I forgot about all my questions and loose ends. The moment was overwhelmingly enjoyable. It was my first family dinner. Levon was getting much drunker than the rest of us because he hadn't put a drink down since the sun rose. He began these epic rants. They were personal soliloquies, external monologues, or manifestos. Alcohol amplified Levon's personality. He usually preached when he spoke, but when he was drunk, he transformed into a literary, life philosophizing, Das Fuhrer. He wasn't speaking with us, just at us. He wasn't being rude, but he was not looking for a response. Evie and I sat there and soaked it in. If you are too sensitive it could definitely rub you the wrong way, but to me, it was intoxicating. He demanded attention and you couldn't look away, hanging on every word. I am sure Evie has dealt with this more than I. Later in life I learned that much of his long rants was him combining original thought with that of his favorite authors. He never shared his verbal plagiarism, but as my own book collection grew and the more I read, many obscure lines from the most random books sounded familiar.

   "You have to love alcohol; it makes the world more beautiful, like seeing it through rose colored glasses.[30]It yanks you out of your body and your mind and throws you against the wall. I have the feeling that drinking is a form of suicide where you're allowed to return to life and begin all over the next day. It's like killing yourself, and then you're reborn. I guess I've lived about ten or fifteen thousand lives now."[31] Levon said, sounding like a proud alcoholic.

   He talked about topics ranging from cuisines, existentialism, Buddhism, politics, sex, the education system, other cultures, utilitarianism, the missteps of our forefathers, and of course, literature. He would mention his travels, but that was all we heard about his past while we chowed down our well deserve Chinese food. But it was never what we wanted to hear. I guess those rants were his way of telling beautiful lies about the world he left behind when he moved into his old white home.

   Kurt and Ernest were sleeping by Levon's feet when the alcohol finally took full control and Levon passed out. By that time, it was just Evie and I discussing my time in New York. She knew the city well having lived there from her mid 20's to early 30's after she had her children. We both visited the same restaurants and bars. If Evie were my age, we would have been very good friends. She made me feel comfortable without making me feel young. Something that always drove me crazy about the older generation is when they made me feel young. I hated when people made me feel young, or like I couldn't understand, it was a complex of mine. I guess that's why I forced myself to always grow up faster than I needed to.

   I mentioned my ex-girlfriend to Evie when I slipped. I usually don't talk about relationships with anyone, but Evie had me on a roll and my

---

[30] Fitzgerald, F. Scott
[31] Bukowski, Charles.

alcohol induce filter no longer existed. The masks were gone and all that was left was Jake Roberts, a drunken boy, who thought he knew the world, but will wake up the next day and be just as scared as the day before. I digress… I was explaining how Rose, my ex, and I didn't last because of my insecurities and impatience, but how strongly I believed if we met during another time, we were perfect for each other. Then I said, "I bet it was the same with Phia…" I don't know why I said it, it just happened.

Her reaction was unmistakable, it was anger, fear, and the wrath of Hades mixed up with unstableness of the Hulk. She shifted like a therapist who just heard a mob boss confess to a murder during a session. Her weathered hands clenched as her whole body stiffened. Dark clouds crowded over the coffered ceiling, thunder roared as if the very mentioning of the name unleashed the dogs of hell.

"Did you say…?" Evie questioned…leaving it open ended, making sure she did not put words in my mouth.

"I…I…"

"Did you say Phia?" She said impatiently, but calmly, with slight hesitation to make sure she heard the correct name, as if saying it out loud helped her double check what I said.

I owned up to it, "Yes."

"Before I say anything else… Please tell me how you know about her and what you know? I need the truth Jake. This is serious. Because I know it was not from Levon."

I never heard that tone in Evie's voice. It felt like being questioned in an episode of Law and Order. The dim lit room was searing hot and the lights shone down on my face, my cheeks were flushed, palms damp with sweat. Hell, waterboarding had to be more pleasurable than the inquisition about to come down on me.

"I saw it in one of his annotations, in one of his books, I really don't know anything…"

"Whatever it said, forget it. Just erase it from your mind like a bad memory. Take it and lock it away, for your own good, for my own good and especially for Levon."

"What's the big deal? I don't get why so much of Levon's past has to be locked away as if it were the Sorcerer's Stone. Who is she?" I was now frustrated and becoming defensive.

"Do you like spending time here? I know Levon enjoys your company, you challenge him kid, you remind him of his childhood and have been a blessing to him, but don't ever mention that name again."

"So, that's it...?"

"Yes."

"I won't accept that." I was determined to learn something.

"You have to."

"Why do I have to?" I questioned in a very typical adolescent way.

"Because, you can lose your way groping among the shadows of the past.[32] Phia was extremely important to Levon. In due time Levon will let you know more about his story, but Phia is his, that's his story, sometimes it's okay to keep things to yourself."

"Did you know her?"

"Yes, we all did."

"Was Phia her real name?"

"If I tell you her real name, will you promise me you will never mention we had this conversation, or her name, to Levon, ever? You must promise me."

"I promise." It was a promise I knew I would break.

"Her name was Ophelia."

"I will leave it alone now."

"Please do Jake."

The moment was somber. The name Ophelia rang in my head. Originally from the Greek *Ophelos* meaning to help, Ophelia was first used as a name in Shakespeare's Hamlet. She was Hamlet's lover. Ophelia struggled with her duality in life, she wanted to please all around, but didn't know how. She went insane by Hamlet's irrational behavior. But she was a lover of all that was beautiful and had a strong desire to express herself in anyway necessary. Not to ruin Hamlet for anyone who hasn't read the story,

---

[32] Céline, Louis-Ferdinand

but Ophelia eventually drowned herself because of the madness she was driven too by Hamlet.

I gracefully changed the subject to travel and the night continued.

Levon peacefully slept off the booze on the couch, dogs by his feet, fire still crackling in the corner. Levon's slumber gave the room a subdued feeling, causing us to relax as the cool air of the night crept in. We were like a small family from the start. The fire gave a tranquil glow throughout the wood lined house. Our hearts comfortable and my mind for the first time ever, at ease.

Evie spoke to me like my mother never could, like my mother never tried to do. She was interested and concerned about my life and emotions. I wasn't sure if this was because of what Levon told her, or if she was someone who would always be a mother. Some women are maternal at their core, and Evie was one of those people. The hours ticked away without us ever acknowledging the time. Once we both yawned at the same time realizing it was 1 am, Evie and I began to shuffle out of the house, turning off the lights and putting the glasses in the sink.

"I hope to see you again Jake," she said.

"Why wouldn't you?"

"No reason, I just enjoyed myself. It has been a while since I have spoken to anyone under the age of 60. It has been refreshing. You have a good heart; it is pleasant to be around."

What about her kids?

"Thanks Evie, I enjoyed it too. You are much less moody than Levon."

"Leave the sleeping man alone. He has a good heart; it is just tired."

"Goodnight Jake, get home safe." She said ushering me to the door.

"Goodnight Evie."

As I left, she said, "Remember, Dream of the Angels."

While leaving I saw Evie lean in to Levon and whisper something in his ear. They weren't words for me, and I didn't ask or try to guess. She took a beige afghan and draped it over the silent, resting man.

That night, alone in my room, I pulled out my older sister's version of Hamlet. The name Ophelia still buzzed in my head, unable to escape, like a fly trapped inside a jar. The name trapped in the bell jar of my brain. The book was still stuffed in the bottom of a box in the attic crawl space. My sisters never visited our home in Branford. I wasn't reading looking for an answer to anything, but more because I found the name serendipitous. It meant something to me as well.

> *"Doubt thou the stars are fire;*
> *Doubt that the sun doth move;*
> *Doubt truth to be a liar;*
> *Never doubt I love."*[33]

---

[33] Shakespeare, William. Act 2, Scene 2; Hamlet.

CHAPTER SIX

"Unlike most of us he was the sort of person who insisted on living out his own beliefs."

-- Jon Kraukner

I never saw Evelyn before that fateful Saturday, but after that day I saw her every weekend and some weekdays. She never explained why she started showing up more often. I like to think it was because of me. Maybe, I reminded her of her sons? She was as secretively open as Levon. Evelyn told you enough to make you think you knew everything, but when you walked away the questions flooded. I didn't care either way because these two adults became the only steady thing I had in my life. My parents were still lost in their own lives, ignoring the troubled youth under their roof. I think they just didn't know what to do with me, it wasn't their fault. I was an orphan in my own family. Deep down my mother believed I was better off spending time with Levon and Evie. When she saw us interact, she wore a sad smile as if to tell me she was happy I found a family that accepted me, but sad it couldn't be her.

Levon and Evie bickered like a married couple, spoke like brother and sister, and cared for each other on a maternal and paternal level. They filled a void within each other, soothing the cold sting of a lonely day. During the daylight, Evie and I gardened, knit, discussed philosophy and helped keep the old white colonial clean by washing windows and fixing shudders, or anything else that may have deteriorated over time in the salt drenched air. By night, I was lectured, tutored, and learned about writing, reading and becoming a man. As these events happened in my life, I did not understand the gravity, however, in hindsight I see the way this odd hodgepodge, pseudo family, helped mold me into the person I am today. From the day I moved into 16 Lotus Lane to the day I left for college 2 years later, I spent time learning and soaking in all I could. Then came the week before I was to leave for school. I was headed to Brown University in Providence. Levon helped me with the essay; of course, it was kick ass.

Levon was quiet that week. He had weeks, where he didn't say much but grunted in my direction and motioned to different books, lines, quotes, lyrics, poems etc. I called it his "Tim the Tool-man Taylor speech." I ignored the moodiness by this point because of how frequently it changed.

The night before I left, Evelyn planned a family dinner for the three of us. She was making her homemade empanadas and fajitas. She told me it was a special family recipe. It was always a special family recipe. God forbid the Old ever Googled how to do something. Evelyn told me to set the dining room table. I couldn't believe it. I don't even think I ever walked into the dining room before. Come to think about it, I was not even sure which room the dining room was, because of the excessive piling of books in every crevice of the house. Evelyn hummed throughout the house as she bopped from job to job, chopping, cleaning, preheating, slicing, defrosting, and cleaning some more. Her presence made the house feel like a womb, nurturing and comfortable. Not that I ever was in a womb that I remember, but she made it warmer, much warmer than when it was just Levon and I. She made 28 Lotus Lane a home, something only a woman could do.

I cleared the table, one empty whiskey bottle and book at a time. There were unused ashtrays, blue Pilot G2-07 pens, all drained of every last drop of ink, used napkins, ripped pieces of paper, and stacked pictures in frames of far away, exotic places Levon may or may not have visited. There were lists everywhere. He constantly made lists but never completed them. It was a subtle understated compulsion of his. It was like going through a storage unit of a manic hoarder.

I could smell the sizzling onions and peppers from the kitchen. Levon didn't know what was going on. He knew I was leaving the next day, but his melancholy state infected his whole being. He stayed huddled in the library by the fire like it was winter and there was no heat. He was wrapped up in the same afghan I saw Evie drape over him almost a year ago. He kept fumbling over Sylvia Plath's, The Bell Jar, mumbling to himself as he reread his annotations. Evelyn and I knew when he got into these modes of desperation and temporary insanity to leave him alone.

As I rummaged through the sea of artifacts, that in some way, some order, outlined a part of Levon's life, or many parts, who knows, a ripped piece of moleskin paper fell on the floor. I learned not to read these scraps of paper that littered his house. Whatever was written on these notes was not meant for my eyes. But as the ripped, dirty, long forgotten paper fluttered to the ground ink stain up, almost yelling at me to take, to read, I couldn't look away. It was marked in Levon's usual royal blue ink of but there were two types of handwriting on this note. I quickly jammed the piece of paper into my pocket before anyone saw me.

I ran to the bathroom to analyze my discovery. I felt like a treasure hunter who just found Cortez's gold, the lost city of Atlantis and the Holy Grail, all at once. My elevated heart rate took me by surprise. I didn't understand why I desired to know so desperately about Levon. I think it

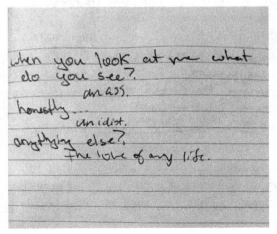

was because it was such a mystery and whenever you are told you can't do something or know something, it is human nature to fight your ass off to do it or find out. In the two years I have rummaged through Levon's books and scraps, not once did I find someone else's handwriting. There was no date on the paper. Not that a date would matter, I didn't even know when Levon was born. He never celebrated a birthday, although I am positive he had one. My gut told me this was Ophelia, my heart wanted it to be Ophelia. I read it over and over again while pretending to take a shit. I knew without asking, I would never know. I knew I could never ask. I folded the paper like a school note from mom and went back into the dining room and finished clearing the table.

Dinner went on as planned. It took a little to get Levon from the floor to the table, but he eventually made it after a few enticements of whiskey. Evelyn cooked the crispiest, freshest, spiciest empanadas on this side of the Mississippi. The outside was crispy and flakey, the inside soft and moist, tantalizing every taste bud on the way through. Her fajitas made me smile from ear to ear like a kid who successfully planted evidence on their sibling. Levon remained silent staring into his plate, eating at a pace better suited for Gandhi than any real human trying to sustain life. Evelyn was upset I was leaving the two of them.

"I know Levon won't say it, but you will be missed Jake. It has been fun having some young blood around again."

Levon grunted in agreement.

"Don't forget about us," she continued.

Evie was just doing what all older people do when they say goodbye. It is a way of hedging their bets in case they die. They say goodbye in a way, that allows for another meeting, but is still complimentary and appreciative in case they don't wake up the next day. The hopeful morbidity never fully made sense to me, especially at the time.

"Oooo stop Evie," I said, lightening the mood. "It's not like I am flying across the country. You guys are like family, and we always take care of family."

I got up from the table to clean up. My mother was texting me about getting home to finish the packing I never started. A pain shot up my left arm as I walked away. I quickly glanced down at my wrist, Levon was squeezing my wrist with crazy-mother-trying-to-lift-a-car-off-her-baby like grip. I jerked away without budging but didn't say anything to him; I didn't know what to say. Levon looked up at me through the tops of his eyelids, only exposing the white of his eyes underneath. His burning Lucifer-gaze shook me to the core. Evie tensed and slid her chair back quickly.

"Levon…" She said softly at first.

"Go Evie…Right now," He said calmly in return.

"Levon, what has gotten into you? Let the boy go…We were having such a good night."

"We still are…" He responded in a devilish tone.

"Levon, that actually really hurts now, can you let go…Are you okay?" I hopefully interjected.

"Shut up! You don't get to speak!"

I jumped back at the sudden elevation in volume. Evie shot up from her seat. "Levon this is enough. What the hell are you doing?" The tension in the room was rising like when the Jaws music begins to play.

"Give it to me," Levon said without looking at either of us.

"What do you want?"

"Before I do something I regret, give me it."

I didn't know what he was talking about. Over the 2 hours of prepping dinner and then eating I completely forgot about the note in my pocket. But I realized what Levon was talking about when he didn't take his eyes off my front right pocket. Angry silence crept into the room, the tension at the surface of everyone's skin, boiling, leaving us blistered in jadedness. The pause lingered like a long sigh. I pulled my arm with all my might in a swift sudden movement but to no avail.

"I will not ask again son," He said without looking me in the eye. Levon always looked you in the eye.

"Levon I really don't…" Just before I lied for the billionth time in my life I stopped. Without a word I reached into my pocket with my free hand. My fingers rubbed the paper as I contemplated what to do. I rubbed it like a wishing stone, hoping it could give me the answers. I didn't consciously make the decision, but eventually, before I knew what I was doing, pulled the note from my pocket with my head down. I felt like a scolded puppy that was caught eating a shoe. I didn't want to look at him while I unveiled my thievery.

I held out the rogue sheet of moleskin paper.

"Jake, please leave. I am going to try and be rational. So, I am asking you to not question this and just go out that door right now."

This was far from rational…

"Levon…" Evelyn said trying to gain his attention.

"Evie stay the fuck out of this!" He snapped back.

"For Christ's sake Levon! He doesn't even know what he is holding, or why you are so upset. How is he supposed to know? He is still a kid. Let's enjoy our dinner before Jake leaves for college tomorrow."

With the stubborn tenderness of Atticus Finch, he said, "My decision has been made. Jake I would like you to leave the paper on the table and leave."

So, I left. I didn't look back inside the home. Part of me felt I might never see Evie or Levon again. Part of me ashamed I couldn't resist the temptation of unknown, unrequited love. My heart angered by my own betrayal and confusion over the drama that warred within Levon. I wished he could just say and release all that hurt him. But it was not my battle to fight for the man. He constantly fought battles, telling me, "There is always a battle worth fighting for. Sometimes the battles have guns, sometimes they are internal, but you will always be fighting."

The morning came quick, as all my mornings. The sun always arriving two ticks earlier than the day before, driving my insomnia to monolithic proportions. I shuffled out of bed and began packing the car before my parents woke up. I needed to occupy my mind. The red Jeep Cherokee was covered in the beads of night dew. The pearled sky made way for the lilac darkness covering the seaside. I could see my breath, but the air was neither cold nor hot, yet still made its presence known on the tips of my nose and ears.

I jumped, startled by the lights in my house, which unexpectedly illuminated the windows, one by one. My parents were obviously awake. Once the driveway floodlight turned on, I knew my father was awake. He had a routine and turning the floodlight was step five, after shit, shave, shower and coffee. I don't remember what day of the week it was. My anxiety grew, as I knew the parting hour climbed closer. I sat on my stoop, put my head in my hands and tried to talk myself down off the ledge of emotions. Everything ran at Usain-Bolt-speed through my head. What about Levon? What about Evelyn? What about Ophelia? What about my parents? Am I going to be okay? Did I make the right decision? Did I forget to pack something? Do I have my nail clippers? What about my toothbrush? When do I get my books? What's my schedule going to be like? Do you think my roommate will be cool? What does cool even mean today? I am going to miss Broadway. I am going to miss Levon. I wish he wasn't so mad at me. I didn't mean to...

The thoughts continued, but I will spare you the insanity that is my mind...

"You will be alright Sport."

I looked up through my shaggy hair and fingertips to see the granite face with pearl shaped honeysuckle eyes staring back at me.

"Glad I caught you before you left," Levon continued. "I wanted to tell you something."

I said nothing, just looked back at him.

"After you left, Evie yelled at me. A man always needs a woman to tell them when they are being a moron and you and I both know she doesn't hesitate to tell us when we are wrong."

"Levon, it's okay..."

"Let me finish Sport. That note you had. It wasn't for your eyes. You have done a good job respecting my privacy, but I felt violated. That was from a special woman in my life and right now, that is all you need to know."

"Will you ever..."

"Let me finish."

"Okay."

"You are ready for this world kid. You have a good head on your shoulders and a mouth to match. Always remember to use that god given brain and not waste it. If you need me, I am here. Sorry, I am not good at this sentimental bull shit."

He stopped looking me in the eye and was staring at his shuffling feet like an elementary school kid talking to the principal. There was an awkward pause in his speech. It was a mix of apology and badly worded life advice.

"As I fell asleep last night, I decided I needed to give you something, just in case.

"In case of what?"

"I have something for you...I want you to have something."

He held out a worn, brown leather folder. It was McGraw-Hill-textbook-thick. The age of the leather did not match the age on his hands as he stretched through the pollen-ridden air, handing me the gift.

"I think it's time for you to learn a little about me. I think you are ready for this. It is my first manuscript."

"I thought you never published a book before?"

"This has never been published. It has never been finished. I started it my sophomore year in college."

"Levon, you have no idea what this…"

"Just take it Sport, maybe it will give you inspiration, maybe it will help you when you are in a hard spot like it helped me. I don't want to tell you too much about it, some is fact, some is fiction, which is which, is for you to decide."

"Levon this is too much…"

"Just take it before I change my mind."

I flipped back the velvet leather covering the title page. _Yellow is Underrated Color_ by J.H. Levon. I opened the car door and placed the manuscript in my backpack in between Hamlet and my moleskin journal.

Without another word Levon slipped back into the dawn. My parents appeared on the front steps.

"Did you pack the whole car already?" My dad asked.

"Couldn't sleep Padre."

"Hey, less work for us. You sure you got everything?"

"I think so." I looked back into the car and saw the backpack sitting on the seat, containing Levon's unpublished, unfinished manuscript with some fact and some fiction. "Yeah, yeah...I have everything." I walked closer to the backpack, pulled out the book, began reading and never turned back.

"Great! I'll cook breakfast and then we can shove off," my mother shouted.

~Authors Note~

The aim of this novel is to give light to my friend Levon's life and work. After much deliberation with friends, family and editors, I decided to include just a few excerpts from Yellow is an Underrated Color. I attempted to choose carefully to highlight the growth, range and depth of Levon's ability, even beginning with some of his grammatically atrocious early works. No offense Levon. Levon saved everything from the time he was 14. He wrote on coasters, napkins, notebooks, phone notes, Google docs, Word, and Apple pages.

Reading all of Levon's letters, books and notes drove me into a small spiral of insanity. His neurosis was clear and scattered brain more evident than ever. His work was a scatter plot of a man who lived in the extremes of life...

Levon started writing Yellow when he was 19 years old. From what I have gathered he gave up around the age of 22. I say "gave up" because it begins to pitter off toward the end and the story eventually disappears. I will continue to make references to Yellow, while I tell the story of Levon, but reading the novel is not necessary.

However, a brief synopsis of the novel does help. The structure of the unfinished novel fluctuates between two story lines. The novel begins with Drew traveling to South Africa when he finds a journal under his seat in the waiting room. The Journal was that of Timothy Oliver, who is hopelessly in love with Sutton at the University of Rhode Island. When I first read Yellow, I tried desperately to figure out whether Levon was Timothy or Drew. Levon went to the University of Rhode Island and also spent time in South Africa. Perhaps we will never have this answer. Perhaps he is neither.

Consider this section the "quote highlights" of Levon's first attempt at a novel. Each quote/passage rotates between regular and **bolded font.**

J.A. Roberts

P.S. This section is only to give added depth to the story of Levon, however if you wish to continue, skip to page 92. Goosebumps style.

This book is for my generation. "We are a lost generation."[34] We have no great war, no great depression. We are not the Baby Boomer's and we are not the "trophy kid generation." We were born during a time when we weren't learning how to survive. Survival is easy for us. But it is a time when we are learning how to live. Now, learning how to live is much harder.

Do not read this and be critical of me…if you are offended, you weren't meant to be. If you can't figure out the sarcasm… learn, and in the words of Vonnegut, "god dammit you've got to be kind." There will be no "ten-dollar words." I do not write in the fantastic prose of a Hemingway or Faulkner. I am not a poet like Robert Frost or Poe. But like them I am true. I am true to me. I am true to my abilities. I am true to those around me.

This book is about you. It is not for you. I hope she never reads this. I hope she does. I hope this helps me become sane again. But "hope is a dangerous thing. Hope can drive a man insane."[35]

Some memories will always be engrained in my mind. I will remember what I saw, the feelings I had, the smell of the terminal, and the feel of the carpet. I remember that feeling in the pit of my stomach when I lost view of my parents and went through security. It was that feeling you get when you drive over a frost heave, but it wasn't a feeling of surprise and glee but one of anxiousness and fear. I didn't know how to handle these feelings; I didn't know I had these simple human emotions.

Eyes can tell you a lot about someone. If you look the right way, you can know everything you ever wanted to know about someone just by looking into his or her eyes. The same way Forrest Gump said you can tell a lot about a person "by them shoes," you can tell a lot about a person by his or her eyes. Next time you accidentally lock eyes with someone in a room just keep staring at them. People get scared when someone pays attention to them.

---

[34] Palahniuk, Chuck
[35] Shawshank Redemption

As the music from my IPod played in my ears and I kept the eye fuck game going with the girl, who I would soon know as Leah. Simultaneously, the flamboyant flight attendant went about his spiel pointing out exits and emergency procedures, like it even fucking mattered. Not that I know from experience, but if I'm on a plane that's about to crash, no way in hell am I about to tuck into my legs and grab my seat cushion. I would be pushing grandmas out the way like George from Seinfeld.

Turbulence... I can see the old lady in front of me grab her husband's arm. You can tell there was so much trust and love in the way she touched him and relied on his presence...

I had an uncanny gift/curse, which allowed me to have people hear what they want to hear. I am doing it right now. For some reason I can judge what someone wants to hear, and I say it. I make them see the person they want to see. It's good in that I can manipulate people easily, but it is bad because it is not right to do it, especially if you don't mean to, which was my issue.

By the time I was a senior in high school, I had worn so many masks I forgot which one was real. I was the smart ass, the jock, the nerd, the stoner, the rebel, and the best friend... I was, and did it all... but who I was, no one knows.

I am not a religious person, but I am faithful. I believe in coincidences. Some call it serendipity...but I don't care to put a singular word on it. All I know is that there are signs out there and either you take the time to notice them, or you pass on by, divinely unaware of the missed opportunities.

I lucked out with an end seat on the middle isle. There was no one in the two middle seats but then there was Kayleigh on the other end. I judged her immediately as a spoiled little brat. I came to this conclusion due to the queen-sized pink fleece blanket. I mean, what the fuck? The second thing she said to me after she found out we were going to the same place was, "and I hear they don't wear deodorant down there." What a little ignorant stupid girl. Someone, who no doubt will give the rest of us Americans a bad name, one of those ditsy, sad specimens of a human being whose life revolved around ballet classes and mommy's Tupperware parties. And we took off...

On the plane...to South Africa on an adventure. Will I see happiness or sadness? Will I survive this adventure?

So many interesting people on this earth. So different. Who is right? Does anyone need to be right?

Will I find inspiration? My path? My career out of this?

As the plane bounces up and down on the invisible hands of the divine, I think about my life, the choices I have made, the women I have kissed, the words I have said. If I had died today, would my life be as fulfilling? Do I have enough faith? There are so many questions I have no answers to. I want the answers. Look at what men have created, is it grand or sad?

Up, up, down, down
Who wears the crown?
No control
Was it full?
Do I go along for the ride?
Do I quiver and hide?
Should I be facetious or gracious?

To see half a face is to see half a sunrise or sunset, you don't know
what they are doing, coming or going
But momma would you be happy
To know that your son will rise
Or will it be better
To know that your son is set
It's the questions between striving for the best or being content with
the rest

"Behind every exquisite thing that existed, there was something tragic."
— Oscar Wilde, The Picture of Dorian Gray

This is not a love story. This is not a happy story. This is not a sad story. This is a real story. This is a story of a boy and a girl. This is the story of two lives colliding like the stars in the night sky bursting into a thousand beautiful pieces to be sprinkled on the world. But the two stars did not make it. They did not survive, but the world was a better place for their life's to have met in that one microscopic moment. [36] Henry Miller once said the best way to get over a girl is to turn her into literature,[37] to immortalize her in the words on a page. So, I am going to try and turn Sutton into literature. Just to make my mind shut the fuck up. Cause, "my head won't leave my head alone."[38]

First class was Philosophy 101 *(seriously)*. I lucked out with the most stereotypical college professor ever conceived. He was balding but had a dominant grey beard. His teeth were far from white or straight, but he wore them with pride as he sucked down his 3rd cup of coffee, which he continuously filled up from the thermos he kept in his "Indiana Jones" satchel. In reality it was a man purse, nothing more, nothing less. He was tall. It looked like he was taller than he was supposed to be, as he stood slightly hunched over his toes, his chin always pointing down. He wore a jacket that professor Robert Langdon would have worn in a Dan Brown novel and he donned Merrell climbing shoes that resembled clogs. He was always covered in chalk, despite only using a whiteboard, something I never figured out.

You can tell a lot about people, particularly my generation at this time. First thing you will be able to pick out is who are freshman and who are upperclassmen. The upperclassmen were never dressed up, usually rocking normal sneakers, sweats and a North Face jacket. The freshman, especially the girls, look like they just walked out of Bloomingdales wearing everything they just bought. The room slowly filled with eager young minds to soak up a topic that has no bearing on real life situations.

In college there is rarely assigned seating but in reality, there is unofficial assigned seating. It is a type of unspoken social law. Choosing where to sit on the first day was crucial to the rest of the semester, because the seat you chose was forever your seat. You could go a couple different directions in this regard. I try and sit near an attractive girl, but not too close so you don't look like a creep, but still close enough to chime in on

[36] Levon later told me this line was inspired from the famous "Roman Candle" line from Kerouac in On the Road.
[37] Not confirmed if Henry Miller actually said this. It was said in 500 Days of Summer. It was Levon's third favorite 'chick-flick' after Just Like Heaven and Sleepless in Seattle.
[38] Matthews, Dave. Rhyme and Reason.

random conversations. Then it gives you an "in" if the person between you was absent. You can't be too close to the professor for obvious reasons but not too far, because you want them to know you are paying attention. There is a strategy to everything.

After Obama was elected to office that November, she turned to me the next morning and said, "You may not know this now, or are able to see it, but this is a huge day for me, for us. This is something I will tell my kids about. He doesn't need to be successful, but the fact he has made it to the presidency shows that we all can do it. The world can't hold us down anymore."

"But Cassie, 'you guys' have been able to do it for years, I don't believe you can make excuses anymore about the world being racist. Look around you; you are sitting in a class with 10 other ethnic students. You don't know any slaves. Your parents don't either. No one is holding you back. Listen, if you want the cops to stop targeting black neighborhoods, profiling minorities, then tell them to stop committing crimes. If cop came up empty every time they profiled someone based off race, then believe me they would stop searching you. It is all excuses by now. Its 2008, if you want something, stop making excuses and go get it."

"I know you aren't racist; you just don't get it. These aren't excuses, this is reality. It is built into the system. You don't see racism because you don't choose to, and don't say that I am looking for it because I am not, I have just lived with it my whole life. It is still there though, I see it," She finished.

I mention this because this is the way I view love and relationships. Love is always there; sometimes you just need to see it and just because it may have not happened to you, doesn't mean its not real.

Her blue eyes are what caught me. Without being too corny or cliché, I will just say they were beautiful. Simply beautiful, and there is not much more too it.

During all of my classes I usually wrote poetry. I am not sure if it is considered poetry, literature or lyrics, but it beat writing in complete sentences. I tried to write at least one a day to keep my creative juices flowing. I probably wrote so furiously from the combination of two Dunkin' Donuts coffees and an Adderall diet that would kill a small horse.

Though, I am not sure why a horse would ever be given Adderall, anyway...I digress.

She stands with a slight lean
Her white hair shimmers and gleams
With her hands in her pockets and chalk on her back
She preaches to a choir that doesn't sing back
Instead they sit in front of her
Some sleep, some slouch, some yawn
Others look out the window at the break of dawn
Drink your coffee, take your Adderall
Just sitting there, stoned, staring at the wall

She turned around and walked towards the blackboard
Her words made no sense twisting like the veins that protruded from her hands
Why does she still try?
The kids are not like they used to be she would say...
But why?

Her voice cracks as she talks over the heaters drone
A girl continues to text on her phone
Yet, she goes on teaching
With just that little hope
That there is a student somewhere out there listening

Absence always leaves us jaded.

She pondered questions like, "Why is yellow an underrated color?" She saw the world differently and I couldn't figure it out. I couldn't see what she saw. If only I could view the world through her beautiful blue eyes, I would be able to understand what made her tick for it still is a complete mystery to me.

Her life seemed to be driven by the unrelenting need to find happiness that lacked somewhere else in her life. She was so beautiful and could have any man she wanted. She was smart and talented in all ways of life. Her family, from an outside perspective seemed normal, well, as normal as any family could be.

Everybody says his or her family is crazy. And usually they are correct, but that is just because you know your family the best. We are all crazy. You just need to get to know someone to find his or her crazy. I like the crazies. I like the chaos. It is the crazy, chaotic, mad people, which make this world go around, not the meek and passive.

Musicians are the only honest people I know. They aren't put through the filters of authors and newscasters etc… well that is if you listen to the right music…Everything they put into their music, whether you agree with it or not, is honest and we expect this honesty and appreciate it. I feel the artists who reach people the are the artists who are the most honest. She was someone who truly listened to music and appreciated it. You could see it when she listened, she closed her eyes and swayed. She was a girl who you could take home to mom, cook a dinner with, go out to a club or a bar, who could get along with and be friends with everyone she met, play video games with the boys and talk girl crap with the girls. She was someone who would climb a mountain and camp but also able to go to an art gallery that night. She never answered to anyone and was the freest spirited person I have ever known.

When a guy meets the girl's friends it is do or die. They either like you and you are "in" or they don't, and you are "out." Good thing she was meeting my friends at this moment and she got along with them well. We talked all night as she drank gin and tonics and I crushed[39] Bud Lights. That night she only met my close friends Rebekah and Jamie.

There was something addicting about her. It was something magical to behold. I always thought she was beautiful, gorgeous and every other adjective of the sort, but I never really watched her in this atmosphere. This girl, this woman, who stood 5 foot 2 on a good day, had a certain look. She was skinny, but not too skinny. She was fit. Sutton had dark brown hair, with blue eyes that held you still when she looked at you. Her face was defined with definitive cheekbones and slightly pointed nose. Her lips looked soft and honest. With the facial structure of an eastern European model and the dark hair of an Italian, with a quiet confidence, she was louder than hell.

---

[39] Levon would cringe if he read this again. He hated terms like "crushed." Levon said they were words for people who didn't know how to use better words."

I tried to help her confusion and make her feel better.
Sometimes the only gift we have for people is our confusion.

It is in those moments of silence we really learn who each other
are.

Then she just said it
Scorned by the world and feeling alone
I could tell she missed home
Gripping her phone as she confessed
But it wasn't her confession to make for she was betrayed
For it was another man who strayed
Too far he went, the unforgivable act
But in those few moments, in her eyes I saw pure bliss
For the more she says it, the more alive she becomes
Trying to figure out something to run from
Neither of us moved, no more need to run
I am here now

So full of life, I didn't see it coming
But I saw a hole in her story
There was something behind the mask she created
So confident and alive, how could a man try and take this from her?
Why did she have to be affected so?
Why was I supposed to know?

If you are lonely, please tell me[40]
If you are scared, please tell me
For I am hooked, I am intrigued
There is nothing you can say to change my mind
Just let me know what you need
Is it time?

The moment stood suspended
Unable to react, not able to be comprehended
I no longer saw a victim, but a person
No longer a setting moon, but a rising sun

---

[40] Tell Me by Good Old War

Today is a new day, so she will put on her headphones and forget the
conversation
Hide in the words of the artists who give her release
Cause in those brief moments, that pain will cease

She was running with the wind in her hair
Regardless of where she was going, she did not care
For she was running from what was, what could have been, what is
She was running because life was not fair
The more she ran the harder it got
Her body said no, it strained, it fought
Stained by the memory of past
Chained by what will not last

There is no use is asking what she is running from
There is no use in asking who we will be when our time is done
But I will always remember the girl who ran
The girl who captivated my attention so greatly if at least for only one
night
The girl who taught me more about myself and the meaning of self-
wealth
The girl who, no matter how hard she tried, I would not go
Just hoping to see one last smile, one last glimpse
For I will never know when she may just pick up and go

     The sky was red; like nothing I have ever seen before. A rusty mist
lay over the land where so much blood had been spilled. If one has ever
seen the movie *Blood Diamond,* you would know this statement for they say,
the land in Africa is red because of all the blood that has been spilt fighting
over it. A fight, I learned was still going on.
     The drive to Stellenbosch was eerie as the rust in the sky bled
black, and the humidity made me sweat from my armpits to my waist. I
tried to look out the window to find anything that looked like home. I
looked out the window at the ruins of Apartheid hidden in the black night.
It was a drive that in the daytime was lined with beautiful vineyards but
seemed barren and run down through the darkness.
     The first night was the worst. The shower burned because I didn't
understand how to use the knobs. You never question your intelligence
until you try to use someone else's shower.

But the next morning when I woke up to a whole new world, the loneliness of the night before was a fleeting memory for I knew I was in the right place to gain this wisdom. I was finally ready to live.

I remembered a quote I once heard that morning when I stepped into the searing sun. Bukowski said once, "I wanted the whole world...or nothing." And I added, "I wanted every last bit of it."

She was one of those girls that made you feel like you were holding the whole world in the palm of your hand. She made complicated things simple and simple things complicated. She made you uneasy and comfortable. She had a desire to live each day like one has a desire to breathe...She wasn't real. She was driven to find something. She was always looking for the next adventure reaching on to ideas and lofty dreams unable to grab them. She didn't want the world to stop spinning in nights of drunken shenanigans. When the world came knocking, she kept the door closed but when she wanted the world, she expected open arms. It was impossible to hate her but impossible to love her as well. The problem was that it wasn't her fault. The problem was that even though she put you through so much pain, she didn't know she was. She had no idea the torment she put on people. She lived in a perpetual state of bliss. Some call it selfishness, I say it was just someone being more in tune with who they truly are.

When I said goodbye after the game...She saluted me. What the fuck?! I didn't even get a hug goodbye. A salute is just as bad as thumbs up with a wink and a gun and maybe a hip check thrown in for good measure. Can you believe that, a fucking salute? I am contemplating just laying it all out on the table and saying how I feel. But how do I react if this back fires? I can't take any more of this. My life slows to a halt when she is around. I can't shake her. I could just be fucking with myself and playing head games with a head case.[41]

After reading about Timothy and Sutton I felt this urge to document what was going on around me. I wanted to feel what it felt like to bleed on paper, well in this case on a keyboard. I wanted to

---

[41] It was around this point in reading the tattered manuscript that I realized how deep the war within Levon went. He was a constantly conflicted man. His writing reminded me of someone having a conversation with themselves.

strip myself down bare and see who was underneath the plethora of masks I wore. I wondered if the story was real at all? I wondered if the way it ended was truly the way it ended or if the saga of the two doomed never-been lovers continued? As I sat on my ledge overlooking beautiful vineyards in this exotic land my mind raced with questions, but something was different. I wasn't concerned about the answers. I thought, in due time they will come. It will all work out. But I knew if they didn't, these questions would brand who I am. They would create more masks; they would build me up and tear me down without any warning. So, I did not care about these answers, but I cared so deeply it scared me.

By this day my liver was having convulsions and sleep was as rare as a good Nickleback album.[42]

I quickly turned around and asked the first person I saw. It was a weathered 40 something or old mother of two young boys whom she dragged along with her by loud nippy and backhanded comments in Afrikaans. The kids did everything but walk. They jumped, skipped, bounded, barked, sang, hummed, spun, twirled, swirled, stumbled and kicked the air like they were in a 1980's Jackie Chan film. I am sure in their mind they were coordinated, quick and agile. In their minds they were part of the "elite" human being class. To Stefan and me, it seemed like a bunch of drunken kids. I saw drooling, stumbling, mumbling and blabbering children. Yet, they continued to spin, hop, skip, side step around in an invisible land of ninjas and epic battles.

We were high on the spirit of the new. New things get everybody stoned if at least for a little bit of time. We were stoned on a new place and this was going to be a long-ass high.

We were destined to be damned but knew how beautiful we could be. Beautifully damned and well aware was the way I liked to live life. That was the way I felt when I was with her. I thought, maybe this could be more. But I was really fucking drunk, so needless to say control over inhibitions meant nothing and decision-making skills lacked.

---

[42] Levon always had a serious hatred of Nickleback.

When a crowd of people walks down a sidewalk together positioning is key to how enjoyable that walk will be. I lucked out in my positioning, walking arm and arm with Leah. As we walked behind the crowd of loud Americans we watched as they swayed in and out of formation in sync with the conversations and their duration. You saw the girls making friendships, which are the toughest friendships. When a guy meets another guy, they are usually friends until that guy does something fucking weird. An example would generate this reaction, "did you see what that guy did, and that was fucking weird. I am never talking to his grimy ass again." When a girl meets a girl, they hate each other and view new acquaintance with the grave suspicion of a house cat that just broke into the always-locked guest room. They only become friends when they find a topic to connect on. Popular examples of common points are, having a boyfriend of the same name, nail polish color, having a previous boyfriend of the same name, Saved by the Bell, who had the bigger collection of TY beanie babies, thoughts on Cory and Topanga's tumultuous relationship and a personal favorite, which comes up more often than one would think, is common hatred of Nickleback.

There were puffs of smoke which billowed over the crowd because most of the Afrikaans were chronic chain smokers. The majority of them could have rivaled the most notorious cigarette smokers of all time such as, Humphrey Bogart, Lucille Ball and Don Draper. We all grouped together and tried to maneuver our way closer to the front of the crowd. There are a lot of methods to do this. You can scream out a random name and point like you see them. I personally like to use "Larry" as the name I scream, because it is a fucking fun word to yell when extremely inebriated.[43]

There are a lot of variables involved to why I am struggling so much right now. My first thought is because she is not around me anymore. My second thought is that I need Adderall. My third thought is that I need to be in the college atmosphere again. My fourth thought was that my problems were due to the subject matter and that what I was writing about happened so long ago. Maybe it was all of these reasons. But when I thought about how long-ago Africa truly was, I should be able to remember more. It was two years ago, and I remember details about high school better than Africa. Was I too fucked up the whole time? Do I actually have a

---

[43] A famous prank from the television show Impractical Jokers.

problem? Naw, it couldn't be that. I know I had a great time and that I learned so much about the world and myself. I know I felt every feeling known to have ever existed. But I couldn't remember in what order or exactly when. I couldn't figure out who was involved. I couldn't remember conversations. Was I really that stoned? Is it really that bad?

I keep worrying about what people close to me will think or how I am going to be viewed. Will they think of me any different? Am I too sensitive? Do I do too many drugs? What will they think is true? What will they think is false? Better yet, what did I want them to think was true or false? What did I want them to think of me?

Jack Kerouac had 30 Essential Beliefs & Techniques for the Modern Prose. A few have always and will always stick out as I go about my everyday life.
Number 4: Be in love with your life.
Number 6: Be crazy dumbsaint of the mind.
Number 17: Write in recollection and amazement for yourself.
Number 19: Accept loss forever.
Number 25: Write for the world to read and see your exact pictures
of it.
Number 29: You're a genius all the time.

I was struggling to live up to these expectations. I once had them. When I was in love with waking up every day to see her. I was crazy about her and I wrote every day because it just came pouring from me like a broken faucet. I didn't know what else to do with what I was going through. But I always accepted that I would lose her. I knew we were doomed without ever having lived. Yet, I was not prepared for what that feeling actually felt like.

I will say this; I think I am a genius. That will never change. No matter what test score I get, I think I am the smartest man that ever lived. The reality is that I am definitely not the smartest man in the world. I am borderline on the spectrum, but it can't hurt to think you are the smartest man in the world sometimes.

Just when you think you are about to change the world, the world spits on you. We walked and talked with an unintentional elitist tone. We thought we were coming to see and conquer. We wanted to

change the world around us, and if we could get fucked up in the process, that was cool too. But we walked around on those first few nights like we knew the world, like we knew of pain, of sadness, of happiness, of joy, of anger, of hate. We were angry that we were being told to think a certain way, live a certain way. We were angry nobody was listening, but they were. We only heard what we wanted to hear.

What if the sidewalks, and buildings and trees could speak? Would they tell us about the racism, the hatred, and the violence, which left this land ragged and hostile for centuries? Would they choose sides?

I know I danced, as I got dressed. I suggest everybody does it and pretend to be like Omar Epps in the beginning of Juice. You can never be in a bad mood when you dance while getting dressed.

Alice was awkwardly hot. She was someone who I would describe as a .08. This means I would definitely hook up with her if I was drunk. This comes from the ancient scale of woman hotness created by a group of adolescent boys from Boston in 1787. They decided to create this scale after stealing some of their pops gin and stumbled around town gawking at the local woman. They discovered at this moment that women needed to be broken up into three categories. The scale had three levels, 0, .08, and 1. The true underlying motivation behind this was to have a basis for how much shit one needed to receive from their friends after hooking up with a female. The boys decided that if a girl was considered a 0, then she is ugly, and you would never fuck. So, if you hooked up with a 0 you were due for a good ribbing. If a girl were a .08 it means that you would fuck her if intoxicated. If she is a 1, then she is good looking enough to fuck sober.[44]

This form of classification has been passed down from generation to generation.

Alice fell in the .08 range. She had a great body but didn't show it well. She had some sex-appeal, but that could have been due to the tongue ring and knowing she had a little freak in her. All women want a bad man who will be good just for them, and all men want is a good girl who will be bad just for them.

---

[44] You can really tell how young Levon was when he wrote this. It is insane to see the maturity in his later writing, compared to this.

Leah and I stayed close most of the night. We finished whatever alcohol we had, because wasteful we were not. We stepped out into the night. Like butterflies emerging from a cocoon, we stepped into the new world that is the night. Nighttime is a special time. When the sun falls out of the sky and just the moon stares over you, the mood of the world changes. The rules change. You find a decisive line in the day because what was so simple by the moonlight is never as simple once the sun rises and morning breaks.

Around 1 a.m., just before the bars closed, I locked eyes with Leah. We knew what each other were thinking. Sometimes you can connect with someone so quickly and you don't know why. Despite 20 feet and 30 people in-between us, in that moment, when our eyes connected, we accepted the challenge. It was the challenge of taking on that person. Taking on who they were, the good and the bad. In that look we said to each other, "I hope you are ready."

She said, "let's go."

I ignored the fact that any decision made, or words uttered, when intoxicated are the farthest thing from natural. Did anything happen naturally?

We crept closer together.

"You don't want to do this," she whispered.

"Yes, I do."

"Why do you want this? I told myself, I wouldn't do this with anyone down here."

"So then why are you?"

"I don't know."

"Should I go?"

"No, don't..."

We were now embracing each other in the middle of the room. We swayed to our own pace as we warned each other we shouldn't be getting involved. We made us being together wrong in our minds. Yet, with every warning we got closer.

On cue, with a stiff wind that ripped through my windows she mumbled, "Please be nice..." And we kissed. So it began.

Then she looked up and took a deep breath. It was as if she was trying to swallow the moment. She would swallow it and savor it.

As Leah talked, she scrunched her shoulders and crinkled her nose whenever she said something, she thought was funny or cute. I laughed, more because of the innocent gesture. Sometimes I would get lost in our conversations because they became so hypothetical and massively metaphorical.

The moment in the room slowly died as "Drunk Again" came on the shuffle. The usual crowd filed out when I felt a tug on my shirt. It was Leah, nudging me to stop and stay. I was unable to pick up any signal and motioned for us to continue so we didn't fall behind the rest of the group. Then she grabbed my arm with an airy sigh.

"You are a fucking idiot you know that," Leah said as she tossed me into my room and slammed the door close behind her. She dropped her fire-engine red sundress from her shoulders exposing herself in all her glory. Proud, to stand there in her natural beauty. She slowly walked towards me leaning on her toes and shoved me onto the bed. She leapt with a ferociousness of a pouncing jaguar, straddling me and clenching down with her naked thighs.

It was a playground love. It was a foolish yet fun bout of excitement and lust. It was a short-lived burst of flavor meant to shake up our worlds and spice up the sky. It meant something and it meant nothing. There was no winner or loser but a whole slew of fun. It was a playground love. It was just beginning.

CHAPTER SEVEN

"How we need another soul to cling to."
— *Sylvia Plath*

<u>Yellow</u> was roughly 180 pages of scattered run on sentences, however it gave a glimpse into the mysterious mind of Levon and his shadowy past.

    I never came home my first year while enrolled in Brown. When I left, it felt like I had no home anymore. My house on Lotus Lane was a shell of a home, just a place where I kept all of my shit. My old home in New York was such a distant memory only its smell lingered in my brain. Levon's old white colonial was still not my home, but it felt more comfortable than my own abode. College was simply a place where I slept in between eating, fucking, reading and writing. So, when I arrived at Brown, I found odd jobs, got an apartment and began my own life, free from the belittling glare of my parents. There was no way I would move home permanently again; Chinese water torture was a more appealing option. I went home for Thanksgiving and Christmas, but never stayed longer than a couple days. It was usually to re-up on supplies, toiletries, Ramen, Andy Capp Hot Fries and some type of cheese, usually a sharp provolone or a manchego. I get pregnant women's cravings for cheese.

    The year was full of new experiences. The typical college bull shit of general education classes, kegs, cocaine benders, copious amounts of

MDMA, interesting sexual encounters, and grain alcohol. By years end I still had a 3.8 GPA and only two trips to the hospital. I decided to call it a win.

I devoured Levon's unfinished, unpublished manuscript in the first week at school. Despite Yellow's lack of cohesion, plot, excessive use of conditionals, minimal character development and abundance of cliché's, I was still entertained, mostly due to the personal connection and the cornucopia of questions it raised while slowly answering a few as well. I constantly went back to it, reviewed and annotated the scattered messages from his brain. I never asked Levon anymore about his words, what was true, what was false, or even if Sutton or Leah were actually Ophelia? It was just nice to know a little bit more about the man, how he grew up and his struggling writing. It gave me a little hope with what I compiled over the past eight months in Providence. If that was Levon's writing at 19 I should be okay, because I felt I surpassed his ability at the same age. I was excited to return and show Levon, maybe even Evie about what I had written. I felt more compelled to show them than my own parents.

The drive back to the Connecticut shore brewed with unrelenting anticipation. Before I ever made it home, I pulled into 28 Lotus Lane. Not to my surprise, Levon was there on his porch, drink in hand, as if he knew I was coming at that very moment. There was no way he could, he did not own a phone, he never looked at a calendar, watched the weather or even had a clock in his house. He only wore a broken Frederique Constant watch with a brown alligator strap. He wore it every day. It was the one object Levon was never without. When he became nervous, uncomfortable, excited, or cheerful, he rubbed the sapphire crystal with his thumb, never actually looking at the timepiece. The watch always stood out to me because of the ratty old red string he always kept tied to the same left wrist. It was not until later in life I realized the timepiece never worked. Stuck at 5:13 on the 21st. Time was forever at a standstill for the old man.

"Hey Sport, you survived," Levon yelled before I even opened my car door.

"Technically speaking."

"Ah, you look like shit, so it must have been good." In a tone that was a question and statement mixed into one.

"Nice to see you too, you only aged 20 years."

"You would be lucky to have my looks at this age," He said standing up lowering both hands simultaneously from his head to his waist "Vana White-ing" his own body.

"I would be lucky to have three naked women drenched around me and a swimming pool of marijuana, a steak on an island, while watching Sports Center, but we all aren't so lucky."

"Glad you came home. Evie misses the shit out of you. She should be here soon, why don't you head home, say hi to your rents and come back here. Evie will want to cook dinner for you and hear all sorts of stories. You know how she is."

"Sounds like a plan."

I drove up the road and saw my parents waiting for me. They were standing on two different steps. They knew I was coming home. However, they did not wear faces of cheerful reunion, but of sadness and confusion. My mother didn't look up as I pulled into the driveway. She stared off into the lavender bush next to the porch. My father rubbed the bannister, in some compulsion like he wanted to scrape the paint off. My gut sank. My heart sped up, my SVT in full swing...I almost fainted getting out of the car. Good shit happens to bad people and bad shit happens to good people. Karma is crap.

"We need to talk," My father began. No good conversation begins with this statement. The sun was now setting over the pine trees across Lotus Lane, darkness and a chill crept over the shore. The waves became pronounced and loud, causing the floor to shake underneath our feet as I waited the impending news, which was sure to be crippling. I didn't even turn my car off before my father said, "Your mother and I are getting a divorce." And the thunder struck, the lightning flashed, and simple comprehension disappeared.

I understand, until this point, I have not painted my parents in a favorable light, however, they are still my parents and unconditional love is unconditional love.

"It is a lot to get into now, but your mother is going to live with your sister Nancy. I am moving back into the City. Listen Jake, we will still see each other, but this is what is right for us."

I didn't answer or respond immediately. Still digesting the words and the reality that I have become another statistic in the era of divorce. Somewhere along the timeline of humans we forgot that when something is broken you are supposed to fix it. I didn't yell. I turned around, got back in my car, called for Broadway who jumped in my passenger seat, and drove away. I never said goodbye, never asked what their plan was for me, why they wanted a divorce. I didn't care to know. They gave up. That is the only way I saw it. They gave up on love, on each other, on commitment. It didn't matter which one of them asked for the divorce. They had four children, almost 30 years of marriage and they threw it all away. For what? Now they will be alone, old and miserable, rather than together and miserable. Well, "fuck them," I thought. At least I had real parents down the road.

My stunned moment soon turned into confusion, fear, frustration and eventually anger. I was angry with them. I was angry with anyone who ever got a divorce. I was angry with Henry VIII for starting the trend. Sometimes you become angry and it is okay.

My phone vibrated incessantly with calls from my sisters and parents. I turned it off. I told myself never again. No longer did I want to be the orphan in my family. I now could choose my family. I chose Levon and Evie.

I pulled back down Levon's driveway and saw Evelyn's car parked in its usual spot near the side garden, in front of the forget-me-nots. My smile from earlier now gone, it was replaced by dejected anger. Still in shock, Levon knew without a word. Put his arm around my right shoulder and looked me in the eye. It wasn't like any time before. He looked at me like a father.

"You got the room to the top right of the stairs. I'll help unload your stuff…"

Before he uttered another sound, I latched onto the man. Finally feeling the old man embraced in my arms I realized how small he truly was. Levon didn't grab back at first but when my tear hit his shoulder through the Tommy Bahama shirt, he hesitantly raised his hands and embraced me back. And for the first time in my life I felt like someone truly cared about me. I felt a connection with another man, I felt like a son. His embrace was solid and warm. I felt the strain under his weathered muscles and his slow heartbeat. My heart mimicked his, eventually slowing down. I became a waterfall. It was the first time I cried since I broke my arm falling off my bike when I was 5. It didn't feel good nor bad. It was an emotion I couldn't control. For what seemed like an eternity in his arms, I eventually stepped back and screamed. I needed to scream so I yelled, I howled like a wolf, I jumped around like the wild things.

"I am fucking angry! This isn't fair. Why now? Why to me? Why is love so difficult for people to understand? Why must I always be the one left? I am tired of being alone in this too big world Levon! When is it my turn for something good to happen to me? I feel like this dark cloud of the devil follows my every move. Was I a fucking Nazi in my past life? What. The. Fuck!"

"Son…" Levon said, slowing my rant. "Remember, it takes more than love for a relationship to work."

"But what do I do now?"

"Whatever you want Sport."

"That doesn't help Levon." I looked away from Levon, leaning over the porch afraid to look up in fear I may see 16 Lotus Lane on the horizon, knowing I can never go back. Not to that house. It was vacant again. It failed another family. Fuck that house.

"Jake, you aren't alone. You will never be alone."

"But I am. My sisters are gone, my parents are gone, my friends are fake and too busy trying to become imbeciles…it is just me here. It isn't fair! The only place you should never have to worry is when you are home and I have no home."

"You have me…you have Evie."

"But you guys will go eventually…nothing stays forever."

"That is why this world is beautiful…Jake, if everything lasted forever, how could we cherish it? We couldn't. Listen, you still have so much living to do. I won't lie and say life doesn't suck, life sucks, life is hard but that is why we drive the rocky roads. The view is always better at the end of the unpaved roads. You need to keep driving and soon the sun will rise on the horizon, your dark cloud will subside and the anger you feel now will make way for hope. Hope is dangerous, but also the greatest of things we have. Always hope for a better day, a better moment, a better kiss, a better sunset…"

"Levon…"

"Go inside Jake."

I went inside. I walked in looking at my feet, only maneuvering my way through the house by memory, the way a blind man feels his way in the dark.

Evie was inside making paella. The aroma spilled throughout the house. With my eyes still swollen and fists still clenched I hugged Evie, who heard everything. She maternally kissed my forehead. Her warmth was apparent in touch and soft words.

"Go take a nap Jake. Dinner will be ready soon."

As I walked away, she said, "Jake…"

"Yeah Evie?"

"You are loved. Remember that. I love you dearly and I know Levon does even though he won't say it."

I smiled a smile that one reserves for kind words, even when they don't believe them, and went into the library to lay down on the very couch that cradled me after my failed suicide attempt two years prior.

Just before I fell asleep, I heard Levon say to Evie, "I feel bad for him, he is too young to learn the truth. Youth dies when you learn the truth about this world."

When I woke up all of my stuff was moved into the room at the top of the stairs. The books, which prevented anyone from sleeping on the bed, were piled in another bedroom. The sheets were fresh, and the desk cleared with a laptop already open and on. The all-dark wood furniture matched the rest of the house. Orange lilies sat on the windowsill that overlooked the southeast corner of the beach. When I stuck my head out the window, I saw the forever-locked room to the left, the porch spotless and as always, empty. As I walked out of the room following the scent of Latin spices to the kitchen, I gently glided my hand over the doorknob. As I expected… Locked.

It wasn't until my third day living at Levon's that I noticed something, which didn't make much sense until many years later.

I was always attracted by Levon's book collection. The catalog of books must have been worth a fortune just due to sheer volume. He wasn't a book collector in the sense he loved first editions and shit like that. He was a collector of art in his mind. Despite his belief that "all art is worthless," something he attributed to his love of Wilde as many of his quirks. The names of authors, editors, titles, colors, sizes were enchanting. How they all settled on each other in precarious situations looking like a poorly engineered bridge in many places. A toddler would have a field day playing "the floor is lava" in Levon's house.

I liked to run my fingers over the bindings, feeling the different surfaces from cloth to leather to paper, until I would feel like stopping and pull one out. The titles were endless... *Fahrenheit 451, Cosmos, Closing of the American Mind, Outliers, The Voice is All, Outlaw Journalist, House of Leaves, The House of the Spirits, Rabbit Run, Big Sur, Into the Wild, Slapstick, Cat's Cradle, Catch 22, Long Walk to Freedom, A People's History of the United States, The Divine Comedy, This Boy's Life, For Whom the Bell Tolls, The Sun Also Rises, This Side of Paradise, Journey to the End of the Night, You Can't Go Home Again, Look Homeward Angel, The Stranger, The Portrait of a Young Man as an Artist, The Bell Jar, The Complete Tales and Poems of Edgar Allan Poe, Complete Work and Poems of John Keats, The World According to Garp, Things Fall Apart, The End of Faith, A History of the Modern Middle East, Where the Sidewalk Ends...* The list could go on and on. I pulled one out and thumbed through it looking for Levon's annotations. They were my favorite. It was impossible for me to choose a book voluntarily, so I left it to Levon's annotations to decide for me. He either belittled the author directly on the page or kindly underlined in his blue pen. I am convinced Levon owned stock in Pilot pens. He carried the same Pilot G-2 07 blue pen. Levon twirled the pen in his fingers, spun it around his thumb, had it tucked behind his right ear or clipped inside his front right jean pocket. I never understood how the pen didn't break in his pocket. I digress...

By at least the 10th or 12th book I pulled off the old dusty, and musty shelves that day, I noticed there was something similar between all of them. Somewhere in the last 100 pages, there would be a page dog-eared. At first, I thought maybe he is marking something to come back to. However, I noticed he had another system with his blue pen for such needs. Somewhere along the line I paused and went back to the books I previously opened, and sure enough there was a dog-ear somewhere near the end of every book. It clicked that he never finished any of these. There were 800-page clunkers, he must have died trying to get through and he dropped them with 10 pages left.

Much began to make sense. No wonder he never finished anything. No wonder he never finished Yellow. I couldn't tell if this was intentional or not. But it had to be. Was it a commitment issue? I had no idea. It didn't make sense for someone as intelligent and well-read to have never finished a book.

The days continued to pass as the summer heat swelled.

One day while he was asleep upstairs, I was on a poetry kick and began to pull all the books about poetry from Poe to Keats to Yeats and as I was almost finished, I picked up one more book and then I found it. I came across a letter. It was handwritten on a sheet of Moleskin paper that had been ripped from the black leather-bound journal. The piece of scrap paper was jammed on page 89 of *The Complete Tales and Poems of Edgar Allen Poe.* It was not in Levon's blue ink or handwriting. This time it was dated. It was from Valentine's Day. I couldn't tell if it was the beginning, middle or end of a chain of letters or how it fit into Levon's life other

2/14/14

My dearest

It's an old Chinese myth that at birth, the gods decide your soulmate. They tie a red string to both people, and no matter how many times the thread twists and tangles, those two people will inevitably find each other. Ironically enough, my whole life I have worn a red string tied around my left wrist. It's an old Jewish myth (Kabbalah) that it will protect you from the evil eye. Our string may have been stretched thin, there may be many knots on it as well, but the world spun us together at a time when we needed each other most. I have never known a love so true, so unconditional, as our love for one another. You are always on my mind, and forever in my heart.

I love you,
your sweetheart,

than the date. Where the woman signed was cut off, so I didn't know if this was Ophelia, Sutton, Leah or maybe someone I didn't know. One thing was obvious…it was a love letter. I gushed at the possibility of learning a little more about the old man who took me in.

I saw Levon come into the library. I knew he would not be happy about my nosiness. Without a thought I turned around with the letter in my hand and immediately Levon lost all color in his face as if he saw Elvis rise from the dead.

"What the hell do you think you are doing!?" he bellowed. I shuttered slamming the book with letter inside.

"Levon, come on man, I wasn't trying to be nosey, it was just there."

"It doesn't…Just forget whatever you just read." He walked over to the fireplace to throw another log on. "We have been through this before. I thought my manuscript would have satisfied."

"Levon…"

"What Jake?"

"Why can't you ever talk about your past? I have known you for almost 3 years and I barely know anything about you."

"Good."

"You always tell me to let go, why don't you? It is obvious something fucked you up royally."

"When did you become Freud? It's just none of your business … Leave it."

"Levon, I live with you now, you know almost everything about my life. I let you read my writing. Share something with me, something that means as much to you as she did. Behind every man there is always one. I get it she broke your heart, but I have never met someone who keeps so much of his soul to himself."

"Stop. Jake."

"Levon, what can it hurt to let someone in, just a little?… I am not asking for much, but let's be real, you have no kids, you have no wife, who is going to know your story when you die?"

"I won't."

"I have no idea what "I won't" means, but I do know that it isn't good to keep stuff in. That shit boils until you pop. No offense you are way too fucking old to survive a good emotional blast."

I stopped pushing. His face was flushed, and his hands were clenched as he now sat at the end of the recliner. I opened the Poe book and took the letter back out. I rested it on Levon's lap and walked out. Just before I reached the door jam, he started talking. Not directly to me, but out loud. I paused and turned around. He spoke without ever turning back towards me. I wasn't sure if the words were for me or not, but I stayed to find out.

"Ophelia..." He said out of nowhere, conceding.

"Was this letter from her?"

"Yes." The short answers were unlike the robust speech-giver I have grown accustomed to.

"What happened? Like tell me what actually happened. This letter makes it seem like she truly loved you."

"Past tense...Will you just leave it alone Jake?"

"You already know the answer to that," I said, now gaining momentum.

"Listen Sport, it's complicated and too long of a story for you to understand."

"Try me." The seconds seemed like hours, time froze.

"I chose her, but it was too late." He started in the middle of a story as always. "She was exquisite, brilliant, sensual, sexual, hyper-intelligent, intriguing, funny and the most addicting substance I ever came across. She made me shake with love and passion. When I was with her it was pure bliss. I loved her with the wild passion of youth and rage mixed together. Unfortunately, I was ignorant on how to do love. Remember, love is a verb, not a noun. You have to have action for love to work. The stress of our passion became overwhelming to hold onto. Love became difficult for a myriad of reasons, but it was mostly me. My mind was straying... I tried to not focus on our stressors, but it was futile. Every day, when we were together, I chose her a little less. I forgot all the blessings she brought into my life. I focused on all the negatives; her insecurities, anxiety and past grinded away at my subconscious. In turn I began showing her my negativity. We spiraled... Her fear I would leave, led to her anxiety. Her anxiety frustrated me, pushing us further apart. It was a fool's errand. Only a fool presses on when the world tells you it is not meant to be. Only a fool believes in destiny or fate. However, I am a fool, a silly damn fool[45] and I was too proud to admit otherwise. Simply, I abandoned the one love of my life. Regrets are shadows of the past that make the sea turbulent to sail and the fog too dense to see through...Regrets prevent progress. Don't be me. Have patience with those you love, hold onto them otherwise you will end up like this."

He finished with a tone in his voice that said more than his words. His voice cracked and became stern towards the end. It gave the feeling he made an irrevocable decision. A decision he wished to take back but knew was impossible. I knew this was all I would get for now. It was okay with me. I simply responded with, "Thank you."

I didn't need more. I didn't truly understand everything he said. It was the first time he showed any true emotion outside of anger and frustration, and the brief paternal sympathy when I sobbed on his shoulder. He believed showing affection and emotion was somehow the characteristics of an inferior being.

The summer continued as Evelyn and I worked outside in the day and I came in to write with Levon at night. Living with Levon was like living with a crazy college professor who doesn't know up from down. He dropped everything he touched but knew exactly where he placed it. Levon left a trail everywhere he went in the old colonial. Nights were filled with laughter by fires or quiet sighs under the stars. Days were no longer tiresome burdens, but peaceful dreams. I felt comfortable, I finally felt home.

One night out drinking by the fire, I blacked out on Makers Mark. Evelyn opened up about her husband Emilio. Emilio and Levon were good friends. Emilio was a chef in NYC and one of the most promising young chefs in the country. One night when returning home to his beautiful bride and their children, Emilio saw a man harassing a woman at the Bleecker stop in Manhattan. He yelled at the man to stop but suddenly the homeless

---

[45] Fitzgerald, F. Scott, The Great Gatsby. "All a girl can be in this world is a silly fool."

man lunged at Emilio. In pure reaction and without thought Emilio stepped aside and punched the man square in the teeth knocking him unconscious. He hit the man with such force one of his teeth was left stuck in Emilio's knuckles, the man's blood all over Emilio's hand. A week later the wound was infected. The homeless man he punched had HIV. Emilio contracted it and within 3 years he died. Evelyn always spoke about Emilio in the present, as if he was still alive.

I spoke of my first love again. How I fell so hopelessly in love that the emotions doomed us from the start. It was juvenile in hindsight, but we all must live through juvenile love in order to reach one worthier. I was drunk enough and feeling emotional enough to ask about Ophelia again. At this point I saw a letter from Ophelia, a note between the two of them, Levon even opened up briefly a few weeks prior but the whole story still remained a mystery. With each piece I gained, the more it strained me to find out the whole story. It was like staring at a portrait and everything was there, the background, the legs, hands, torso, beautiful necklace, but the face was missing. She knew the story… she had to tell me.

"Evelyn, I need to know about Ophelia." I demanded through drunken slurps of bourbon.

"Don't say that name child. I told you to never bring it up again. No reason to bring up pain from the past. We have talked about this. The more you dig the more you will become lost in the shadows of your past. It is better to keep moving forward."

"What do you know?" I asked, ignoring her previous warning. "Earlier this summer I found one of their letters. But Levon just told me he ruined it. You said you knew her or know her, you said "we" knew her…Why won't anyone talk about her? Is she dead? Did she cheat on Levon? What the fuck Evie…I feel like we are a family, but this isn't fair anymore. I deserve to know something about you, about him, about Ophelia."

She heard my frustration. She heard my anger growing.

"To be honest Jake, I don't know why you care so much."

"It is like a festering wound Evie. The more I am told to forget about it, the more I need to know."

"You know what Jake…Fuck it. You deserve to know something. Maybe you can learn from it. I have known Levon longer than anyone else left in his life. I remember when he was just an ambitious, cocky boy, who woo'd women with his words. He was smooth, he knew exactly what to say, but Levon never understood the impact of his words. He threw them out with zero responsibility. When he met Ophelia, everything changed. She was engaged to an older man when they met at graduate school in New York. We were all in the same education program. Despite the ring, they fell in love. They fell fast and hard. It was a ferociously passionate love and they couldn't comprehend its magnitude or impact at first. Overnight they were inseparable. Ophelia was an amazing woman and Levon became so blinded by her unconditional love. Then it happened. There was a tragedy… Anyway, this tragedy weighed on them and they held on as tight as possible."

"Tragedy?" I shot in.

"They knew the engine on the train was broken but still hopped on in hopes they could help direct it to safety," She continued ignoring my inquiry. "Some rides aren't meant to get on despite how fun they seem in the beginning. It was Levon's first love and he struggled with what to do as the relationship grew tense and Ophelia began to hide from the world she once embraced. Whether or not they chose to admit it, the tragedy casted a shadow over the relationship. Levon stopped coming out with us, he stopped answering calls, texts, and he disappeared. When we did see him, he was constantly talking with Ophelia. At first, it was pure honeymooning status. They were high on the new. After a while all of Levon's friends became nervous they were losing him. Levon didn't know how to balance the two. Ophelia became insecure out of fear Levon would leave and clung on more and more. She became trapped by her anxiety, which only became worse when Levon came around. She felt him moving away. He only was moving away because of the anxiety. The harder he fought for her to not be anxious, the more anxious she became. It spiraled. I wish it were as simple as he fell out of love, or he cheated on her... It was never an idea of falling out of love, he just chose her less and she felt it. Levon became exhausted trying to hold on and eventually did exactly what Ophelia feared and left. He thought he was doing the right thing for her. He thought he did all he could to help and be there for her, but he gave up. He believed she would only be happy if he stepped away from the picture and allowed Ophelia to move past the tragedy. She would have been happy with him. All she wanted was Levon. In the end she hated him so much for abandoning her, there was no repairing that wound, not even time can heal a shattered heart…"

"Tragedy?" I asked again and slurped the ice trying to get every last morsel of whiskey left in the glass.

"That is all you need to know Jake. I know more, but what is important is to understand Levon never recovered. He buried himself in reading, writing and traveling. He lost connection with his family. He moved from his apartment and abandoned his friends. His heart was never the same, his anger grew day after day. There was life before Ophelia and there was life after. She will always remain at the center of his story. Listen child, Levon is no monster. He is one of the sweetest men I have ever known. But what happened to him also happens to many others."

"So, you are telling me the gist of the story is that Ophelia and Levon fell in love and one day he said he must leave because it was what was best for her, but he never actually fell out of love? Why the hell is he so fucked up by this if he was the one who left her? I don't get it."

"It's not your tragedy to understand."

Most of my days in that first summer were spent with Evie. The older Levon got the more recluse he became as well.

The following evening, I was helping Evelyn in the family room reorganize the china cabinet, which had become overrun with dishes from five different sets of china. Some were littered with multicolored floral patterns, some had simple silver accents, others chipped and dusty. It looked like an estate sale threw up. As I shifted the tea cups, dessert plates, serving platters I kept throwing the old yellow paper that separated them onto the floor and replacing them with newspaper. The paper was crumpling and felt older than the house. I turned to gather the remains when I noticed some writing. Every time I didn't want to find something in Levon's house, something would appear. Coincidence? Fate? Who the fuck knows, but I realized that instead of using cloth to protect the china, Levon used old letters to someone named Sophia. Ophelia was mentioned but according to the dates and content they were written after Levon and Ophelia broke up. They weren't love letters; they were letters of depression and despair. They were letters of hope. If the dates were accurate, which I assume they were, it led me to believe many letters were missing. I quickly jammed them in my backpack. I knew Levon would never read them or miss them. Levon couldn't find sand on a beach.

That night I sat up under the glow of my desk lamp and mercilessly read each and every word between Sophia and Levon. At the time much did not make sense.

~Author's Note~

I included these letters here in chronological order for you to read them as I read them, not yet knowing the full story. Though these give many clues to Levon's life, much is confusing without context. However, I found them to be so beautifully written they had to be included in this book. What I found most interesting about these letters is that after years of reading Levon's words, letters and notes, never have I found another reference to Sophia. We may never know who she is. Some were handwritten and others typed. I did my best to include what was salvageable in its entirety. Levon's letters are written in regular Garamond and Sophia's are in *Italics*.

September 2, 2015

Air is thick on the fourth floor. It has a musty feel. Smells all the same, looks pretty much the same minus the waxed floors. The hallways are bare, and I am still sitting here sweating like the day before. I have a concert tonight. A little music to cheer my soul. Though, I don't feel melancholy, I still strive for uplifting sounds. There is smog that sits over the city today. Makes you angry. Well, it makes me angry. I had a dream last night. It felt so real. Like I was there again, like I could feel it all again. But morning came and the soft gentle touch of her skin left. I am kind of use to it at this point. I think eventually you never really get over someone you just get use to thinking about them on a daily basis.

She asked me to write (you asked me to write). She asked me to write about something we could write together. We spoke honestly. We spoke openly. So why her? Why you? Why was I to share this with her? With you? Why was she to share this with me? Why must I repeat the beginning of sentences? Well, it doesn't matter that much so, I digress. Her voice always made me a little nervous. Your voice. She spoke with such gusto about life it was truly intimidating. She had a lust for adventure, whatever that meant to her, it was infectious yet daunting to keep up.

But she asked me to write. Sophia's head was swirling with words, thoughts, emotions, ideas, similes, metaphors, adjectives and music that could fill a stadium and then some. It was intoxicating how she was able to be honest yet keep so much of her heart a secret. She was eccentric, but most good things in this too big world are always first considered eccentric.

She knew what she wanted to write about. It was about a street. I said I would look it up. I didn't.

Huddled masses of souls yearning to breathe free.[46] The new colossus we search for, the beacon to take us home in a world wrought with pain.[47]

I guess we all search for the green light across the bay.[48] I don't think it is bad to search for something more than this. Whatever this is. I

---

[46] Lazarus, Emma. The New Colossus.
[47] This was scribbled into the typed page. I am not sure why but included it regardless.

have never been good at living, but I am good at living. Do you know what I mean by that? I mean I have always been good at waking up and filling my days with adventures, new experiences, happy faces, thought provoking conversations and a myriad of ways to expand my brain. However, I always struggled at the generic idea of "living." The idea that you wake up, go to your 9-5, make your money come home, kiss your wife, tuck your kids in, wake up and do it until the weekend. You may even have guy's night that consists of dick jokes, whiskey and football. Then you rinse and repeat. I am very well aware the latter option of living is most likely what will happen to me. But it scares me because of how bad I am at living it. The routine keeps me in check but also drives me into a spiral of inner insanity.

But then tomorrow comes and all is well again.

Sincerely,

Your Levon

September 4, 2015

I'm running to catch my train today; my heart is racing, lungs expanding, and that recognizable panting noise is rippling across the air as I struggle to wipe my brow clean. It's a hot sunny day in Toronto, but the people wouldn't dare complain. We appreciate the warm summer days and hold onto them like children do when clinging onto their favorite, worn out teddy bears. Winter's arrival and departure is a cruel one in this country, as it starves us of our natural light and good spirits. I don't mind the snow that much; it's more so the cold that bothers me. It reminds me of a past life, one not too long ago actually, in which our grandparents lived in. The wars, the starvation, the loneliness. It's almost as if that life still echoes loudly during the long winter months. All around us we can see people dragging their boots in the snow, their heads held low with their backs slumped over. It's depressing really, but there is something so electrifying when you breathe in that cool, frigid air... feeling nothing but the burning of your nostril hairs, cheeks and extremities. Maybe that's why I can appreciate winter...because it makes you feel tremendously alive...as if all your senses are intensified and your eyes can't help but widen and tear up. I speak of winter not because it's coming up, but because it reminds me of one of my passions. No, not the good old game this country is known for...the other

---

[48] Reference to The Great Gatsby.

passion. Nursing. The snow reminds me of the tracks I leave behind as I head to work with a simple goal in my mind. To have a good day, to brighten someone's day, to make a difference in someone's experience… whatever that may be. It reminds me I can still make an imprint in this world, while others less fortunate cannot. It reminds me of something beautiful my father once told me when I was stricken with grief after ending a relationship. I can vividly recall him stomping his foot into the snow on one of our nature hikes saying, "see honey, I made this imprint in the snow. I cannot erase what I have done. I can either try very hard to eliminate what I have created or come to terms with it and continue walking. If I don't walk, I will remain in the snow not having advanced very far. However, if I continue to walk, I make great progress and eventually I will get somewhere. So, tell me, what are you going to choose to do?" The melancholy of winter seemed to lift for me that day, carrying one of the many life lessons my father has shared with me. He is a beautiful man, a family man, a gentle soul, a wounded soul. Yet he lives this life with nothing but strength and optimism… and always love of nature and her children, his children. That is why I love winter. Because even though my father hates it, ironically it reminds me of him, and how he has survived for me. How he continuously encouraged, supported and relished in my passion, the same passion of my mother, the one that saved his very soul…a passion in nursing.

Your Friend,
Sophia

September 6, 2015

It has been a bit since I have been able to sit down and write. I am alone in my apartment. There is still a brief sting of marijuana in the air from the bowl earlier. Whiskey still lingers on my breath after the 4-day bender that has crossed six state lines and put a dent in my wallet that may take until spring to recover from. I try and think about how to respond to such intimate words. I try and think about all the events since last week that can be the focus of this letter. For some reason we chose each other to share all the thoughts and feelings we can't with the rest of the world but for some unexplainable reason feel comfortable with each other. Despite having only shared two weeks out of our lives with the other, we still feel this insatiable desire to remain close in any way possible.

The whiskey gets easier to drink as the sun falls on the city. The nights are cooler, and fall is on the horizon. One of my favorite quotes of all time is from one of the most recognizable authors of all time. F. Scott Fitzgerald, as mainstream as he may be, he will always be a favorite writer of mine. Whenever I read, to me the story is not what the author writes, but the author's life as he wrote the story. I like to know about why the author is writing what he is writing. Does that make any sense? Well anyway, he said, "Life starts all over again when it gets crisp in the fall."

It is interesting your thoughts about your father. I find my relationship with my dad has grown extremely strong recently. I find myself talking to my students like my father with the same stern yet caring voice that demands a reaction. I find myself imitating my mother in my teaching strategies and how I make up student names, jump on desks, cold call, run around the room and pretty much put on a show worthy of a Broadway ticket. But the other side comes through. I take on the very things about my parents I considered negative. I remember my father telling me a story about his father, my Papa. My father would become frustrated at his dad's quick temper and reaction to certain situations. My dad went on to say how he realized he reacts very similar and it kills him.

I now become frustrated over my inability to write again. It is painful to hit the keys and I can't figure out why. It is as if the thoughts in my head are still too convoluted for even me to decipher. Anyway, I digress.

My aunt died. It was the weirdest funeral I had ever been to. It seemed as if the formality of burying someone was the focus. There was no mourning for a woman who was murdered. I don't care if she was crazy. As my Papa always said, "family is family, no matter what." She was family.

Everyone around me dies.

Take care,
Your friend

September 7, 2015

I know I only wrote you yesterday, but I couldn't wait for a response.

I didn't sleep well last night. Too much on my mind. Too much solitude again. Lost in my whiskey and marijuana, I would do anything to stop from thinking, yet my only sanity is thoughts that refrain my mind from wondering.

I just got off the phone with my parents. I asked them about my future. I find I have these grand ideas all the time but never the wherewithal to execute. My whole life I have flown by the seat of my pants never looking past the immediate decision. Now, I am in a position (fuck adulthood) where I can no longer do that. I realized when talking to my parents this is the first decision in my 25 years on this planet, I am actually doing just for me. When it was choosing college, or grad school or to break up with Ophelia I always was able to say I made this decision for other people.[49] But what about me? Is it okay to finally be selfish, flip everyone else off and do what I want? Well, I have no idea what the fuck I want. I can teach abroad and put myself in a financial hole, with no professional certification, but think of the adventure and the juice it could put back into my convoluted, schism preferred brain. I could move to New England, teach and travel in the summers… But how alone could I end up? Would I regret never teaching abroad? But if I get back from being abroad, I will be 28, alone, and poor with parents who live 10 states away. I hate this.

I spent time with Sutton this weekend. She is crazy.

I talked to Ophelia…She was with her new boyfriend and told me to not contact her.

Patrick is with his friends in Montauk. Rick is at the Shore. Kevin is at Notre Dame.[50] I am alone, staring at the same computer, writing the same thoughts, confused about the same future. Why do I feel like the older I get the less I know for sure?

My editor wants more. I can't write about Ophelia anymore. It doesn't help get her out of my mind. I can't write about Sutton anymore. I can't write about myself anymore. I struggle to become creative with fiction

---

[49] This line helped me put these letters on Levon's timeline. It helped me decipher these came after Ophelia and him broke up.

[50] References to Levon's old roommates when he was in graduate school at Columbia.

and I am lost with a passion and no subject that makes me get up in the morning.

Then you look around and go what in the fuck am I complaining about? I have seen the dregs of society. I have felt the sting of poverty; the pain of violence and it makes you wonder how can such a cruel world look so beautiful in the morning? It becomes exhausting to smile when nothing feels right. I want to write happy, but it gets harder and harder with each day.

It makes me think about my Nana. One of the strongest women I have ever known use to look at the world with her diamond colored lenses. Now her eyes only see a grey mass of confusion, her will broken. Is this all our fates? I hope not, but it makes you hope there is more to this thing we call life that I haven't tasted, because Mondays don't seem a brighter shade and the weekends are only filled with hedonistic debauchery that could make the Five Points seem like a convent.

Too many questions and not enough answers. So, I will go on hoping in good Karma, trying to be a good man and hopefully it all comes around. I will always remember what Janet said to me my last day at the Memorial[51] when I asked her about Karma when explaining the black cloud that seems to follow me around. She said, "I don't believe in Karma...What I believe in is life. You don't choose a future you are given it, just do your best to make it beautiful. "

Your Friend,
J.H.

September 8, 2015.

I didn't sleep very much last night, maybe four hours tops. I spent the entire night lying beside my Nonna giving her the company she needs right now. It was incredibly hot and humid in her house, as we lay there motionless, trying to conserve

---

51 There was a period in Levon's life when he worked odd jobs all around NYC. One of those gigs was at the 9/11 Museum and Memorial. Other jobs included Ellis Island, the Statue of Liberty and the Cooper Hewitt Museum.

energy and moisture from our seeping pores. The anterior part of my body was faced the open window, trying to cool down from what felt like Middle Eastern weather in the western part of our hemisphere. "I wish we had fricken air conditioning in this 100-year-old house." My Nonna tossed and turned and sighed with a great relief of discomfort, sadness and annoyance. "Nonna, try and get some rest," I said. Nothing. Throughout the twilight hours, I awoke to Nonna staring blankly at the ceiling, her eyes fixated, as she was lost in deep thought as evidence by her furrowed brow. Her lips parted, a clear sign of dehydration. She doesn't want to drink though, and my mind ruminates over all the things I have learned about with regards to the human body. She isn't well. She isn't well at all. She turned to her side and I turned with her, placing my warm hand on the top of her back. I stare at her petite body, recognizing the old remnant of a scar located on her neck, a reminder of the big surgery she had three years ago. I paused, looking for something to say. "Nonna, you are going to be okay". Nothing. I even wondered if I believed in what I was telling her, she seems so far gone right now. The morning came and I rolled over to see my Nonna staring at the ceiling once again. "What the fuck is wrong with her," I thought. Snap out of it. But then I quickly realized this is how major depression works. It paralyzes you, numbs you, dissociates you from the world, your friends your family...you. My aunt came into the room and they began speaking in Italian. I'm not fluent in Italian but I can understand a lot. "I am not well. I won't be well again. I don't want you getting sick from taking care of me. This is la vita from now on. I want to go to Homewood" said my Nonna (Homewood is a well-known psychiatric facility in Ontario, located in Guelph). My aunt and I both looked at each other with the same stare. What are we supposed to do or say? Finally, my aunt said, "okay ma, let's get up and start the day. Put on new clothes and get dressed and I will make some breakfast. Let's enjoy the day, it's nice out". My Nonna continued to sit on the bed with no affect or eye contact, as my aunt made her way downstairs. I watched her for a bit, saying and staring at nothing "Common Nonna, let's get up". Nothing. I got up and she decided to lie back down. "FUCK" I thought. I wish I was more experienced in nursing...this is where therapeutic communication skills really come into hand. I stared at her and finally said "Nonna, imagine how Nonno would feel if he saw you like this. He wouldn't be very happy". I almost choked on my own words, holding back tears; ashamed I had even mentioned his name like that. I never had the opportunity of knowing my grandfather, as he passed away from bone cancer when I was six months old. However, the effect of mentioning his name in this very moment caused me to react with great emotion. I imagined the love they shared, the bond they had, the struggles they went *through before and after they immigrated to Canada, the beautiful memories they made. And boom just like that my Nonna was made a widow. I don't blame her for feeling this way. She has gone through so much in life, it's understandable she has reached her breaking point. Her two sisters have just passed away one year apart from one another in January. Her husband has passed away. Her friends are starting to. She no longer feels that her body can function and do the things she loves to do, the things that keep her going. What a sad reality. I don't understand life sometimes. She stares blankly, and I am out of words. I picked up the rosary I gave her yesterday, one of my favorites, and I held it in my hand. Please God, help me to help her. Please help my Nonna. For the first time she actually looked at me with those innocent, gentle eyes of hers. The stare was indescribable, as if she was waiting for me to start praying or say something holy. She didn't say anything, but I knew what she wanted. I just stared back at her in awe of what I had just experienced. I was in shock. Her eyes spoke to me. And just like that she got up and started to move like her normal self again.*

Pray,
Sophia

September 10, 2015

It comes and goes in waves. Sometimes I think I am so good, I am over it and other times I feel as though I have needles sticking me from the inside of my stomach while simultaneously being sea sick and standing on hot coals. The body shudders, lips quake, throat becomes dry, thoughts become so scattered all you do is tense up so much you are sore the next day. But no, no, I do not have a problem. I do not need to speak to a therapist even though I have even come so close I actually looked them up. Do I think I need Xanax, no. But do I feel my body is completely out of whack right now, yes. I haven't felt right since I was in HS. I think I have been so fucked up for so long I am starting to lose control on things. I have chemically imbalanced my body to a point that sobriety doesn't know what is up or down. Maybe it is because I am a rational thinker that I can understand when my body is making me feel and act ways that I know are irrational, that I can catch this chemical imbalance and true junkies don't have this type of metacognition? When I really try and think about it, I haven't gone a single week without getting fucked up on something since I was about 15 years old. I am 25 now. That is 10 years of abuse. I went from weed and opiates to booze, back to weed and booze, mix in Adderall, cocaine, ecstasy, molly, more weed, whiskey, more weed, packing lips, Xanax, Klonopin, and some more weed and whiskey on a rotation, all at different times, all in different quantities for 10 years, or 120 months, or 720 weeks, or 3,650 days of fucking with the chemistry in my brain. I may have finally reached the tipping point. Maybe it is because I am high right now.

All I know that in the words of the great Hank Moody, when asked to see a therapist, he responded, "I am a writer Karen, I don't give this shit away for free." That is how I feel. Even though not a single word of this has been published. I only have truth in what I put on paper. I may stray and lie to myself, but it is as honest as I can be to anything or anyone. How I feel are the words I type, not the words I speak and the first person that realizes that I am forever in their gratitude.

I had a friend named Leah.[52] I studied with her in Africa. She used to say, that all great art comes from a place of pain. (I know this is not her original thought and she definitely paraphrased it from somewhere, but I will attribute it to her). She said that if you are truly happy you couldn't create art. Do you think that is why I could never write when I was with Ophelia? But since I have slowly come back to life pounding away at the keyboard night after night hoping something just begins to flow and I begin to write as furiously as I used to... I do not know but it feels as though Leah may have been right. However, this scares me. I don't want her to be right. That would mean if I followed my passion of writing and really push to get this stuff out there than I will have to suffer and be sad the rest of my life. Who the fuck wants that? I should just write the one book, get the girl back and be done with it. Move to the New England coast and post up. Get a couple dogs and chill with my beautiful wife. Viva la underachievers!

How do you know if you are going crazy? How do you know if you are becoming a little unhinged, a little stir-crazy, the master Looney at the

---

[52] First confirmation Leah was a real person in <u>Yellow.</u>

Looney bin? When do you know you have officially 'Brittany Spears' snapped?

But then today happened. Last night happened. My mind in a constant bind between what is in your control, what is out of your control, what you should control, what is worth your worry, what can wait until later, the woulda coulda, shoulda, maybe's, probably's, what your vision of yourself is, why things don't work out, karma, are you doing the right thing, is it okay to be selfish, should I give more, when is it my turn, where is my sunshine, but I am blessed, so many blessings, but I don't want these blessings, am I insensitive, do I not care enough... It goes on and on and on and on until you think and go what the fuck is even going through my head. I have always dealt with the reality of moments and worried about what I could control but I feel like those few moments of Dharma are so long past all I am left with is enough insanity and undiagnosed anxiety that the world spins and nightmares become mountains to climb.

How could I have become so unhinged?

I had a dream last night about Ophelia. Bradley was in it.[53] Bradley laughed at me. Ophelia smiled. She seemed so happy in my dream. I kept shaking. I don't remember where it was taking place but the three of us were in a bed. Bradley said, "Karma is real." Ophelia lifted her hands and touched mine. Then I felt a rush of anxiety, a shake up my spine and a coldness that seemed more real than I want to recall. "I feel so much better," Ophelia said. "It is yours now," Bradley said glaring at me, "You take her anxiety now, her fears...it is my last gift to her." Bradley looked at her and they kissed. She said thank you and they walked away. The bed turned into a cave. I was there. Alone. Shaking...

Has she really been able to give me all this pain? Does he now haunt me? Is this why I can't sleep at night and the thought of being alone is scarier than Jared from Subway at a 5th graders birthday party?

I truly believe I have her burdens. I have taken them all from her like I said I would. And now the king masochist must live with his cloud, for I don't remember when I last saw the sun. The winter lasted through

---

[53] First reference in any of Levon's writing to someone named Bradley.

summer and I smiled. They were hidden tremors of fear, like an old lady's nervous laugh.

Terrified,
J.

September 12, 2015

I'm on the go train as per usual, this time I'm heading westbound towards home. As we approach the big city my stomach drops. That old, familiar feeling of not being able to breathe properly slowly surfaces yet again. Anxiety. I always wondered where my anxiety stemmed from. I have some speculations as to why but for now I will keep those to myself. I haven't been able to decipher the feelings or why it is getting worse. Crowds, lots of stimuli, feeling trapped in a particular situation, unwell relationships...the unknown. These are a few examples of what seems to trigger the suffocating emotion of anxiety, but why now? Why as I approach the city does my throat began to swell invisibly, making me feel like I am having a severe anaphylactic reaction. The train ride screams claustrophobia, and my senses highlight the fact that I cannot open a window. I am stuck. Enclosed in a metal cart with stale air.
   I stare out the window.

Breathe, you are fine.
S. Cantare

October 22, 2015

It has been over a month since I last wrote in this. You texted me last night. I didn't respond. I was too tired. Lately, I feel I am always too tired. I figured writing in this could keep one of my best friends updated as to why I have become so distant, so quick with words. It has nothing to do with lack of happiness, I am quite happy, stressed but still cheerful. Getting back into the routine of school has made me much more stable. My health, much more reliable. I have been running every day, eating well, trying to read more. I have been doing everything within my power to keep moving forward.

I found someone as well. It happened the night I saw the picture of her and him[54]...the picture my mother liked, which caused me in a drunken stupor to text my mom and berate her for doing such an idiotic act for a woman with three master's degrees. I put two bottles of whiskey down my throat an 8-ball of cocaine up my nose, blacked out and when I woke up, I had a number in my pocket. I don't remember how it happened. My roommates told me when we went into the bar, I saw this girl and went straight up to her. They said I wouldn't give up until I had her number. We have been seeing each other for six weeks now and I know the conversation is coming. She reminds me a lot of her. She said she is a strong independent woman who doesn't need to know what is going on in my life 24/7. This isn't true. She has already become a stage-5-clinger,[55] texting me she can't sleep at night without me anymore. She texted me, "how am I supposed to make it two weeks without seeing you." Bitch you did it before what the fuck. I like spending time with her, but I have my walls up. I know I do. I am not honest with her like I was with the other. But it is still fun. However, she is just not bringing anything to the table. She doesn't listen to music, she doesn't love awesome food, she does drink beer, which is a plus, she isn't a big traveler, but like all the rest I feel I need to teach them. I once said to the other one, "I am going to bring you on a little life revolution, you need to learn how to live." I feel I will be back in the same rotation with Lisa.[56] They devoured every bit of life I have, because I feel they need it, only leaving me tired cold and alone in the end. But I am happy. Isn't that a cluster fuck of the mind?

This is the first thing I have written in over a month. It doesn't feel great, but it feels better than not writing at all. Just hearing the click of the keys and getting that morning coffee down as I pound away at trying to decipher a convoluted brain of emotion.

---

[54] Reference to when Levon saw a picture of Ophelia's new boyfriend after they broke up. Levon later told me about a guy named Alex. He was a 35-year-old banker who was shorter than him. He said, "She did all she could to find a richer and more marriage ready version of me."
[55] Wedding Crashers
[56] Lisa was Levon's first relationship after Ophelia. He called her his "bridge" girl. Outside of this letter, Levon actually spoke highly of Lisa and how much she helped him during this time in his life.

I told my roommates I am moving out. I disappointed two of my best friends from elementary school. I don't do well with disappointment. In high school I was suspended, kicked of student government and was fucking my quarterback's (I was the starting running back) girlfriend.[57] My mother also worked with both their parents and if that wasn't enough, I was arrested for being involved with a drug deal all in the same year. I thought after that, my idealism toward disappointment vanished with the cold heart that grew from a boy not yet a man, fucking up time and time again. But in reality, I did grow during that time. But I feel I met my quota of disappointing the world. I am not in a position that even the slightest frown can ruin my day. I hate the feeling of letting someone down and in this moment my best friends from elementary school who have seen me in every possible state of mind and condition and still love me regardless look at me like a stranger in their house. But as I try to always tell myself, "worry about what you can control." I always say, "This too shall pass." They are little mantras that keep the everyday ups and downs in check.

But regardless, I had to be selfish and this move will be good for me. Another step, another adventure, another way to learn and grow and be a better person. Because after 25 years, I think that is what it's about. In five minutes, I may change my mind, but I do think life is truly about growing. Why stay stagnant in such a dynamic world, push, pull, tug, stretch who you are, push the boundaries of your comfortability and take risks. I have taken many risks, and some pay off, some don't. But to live is an awfully big adventure[58] and no one remembers the poor schlep who sat on the sideline during the championship game. So, stop watching TV kid, jump ship and howl[59] with the best of them. The night sky is too pretty to burn without a flame and the heart too pure to have no love to give. To live a life where you do at least one thing every day that scares you[60] is how I want to live. To live a life of emotion is not something to hide but be proud of. You should laugh, think, and cry every day[61]. That is a full day.

---

[57] Another confirmation of what is fact in <u>Yellow.</u>
[58] Hook, Capt. James.
[59] Reference to Allen Ginsberg's famous poem HOWL.
[60] Roosevelt, Eleanor.
[61] Valvano, Jimmy. From his famous speech at the ESPY's.

Next stop Toronto, because for the first time in my life, I no longer need to appease anyone but myself. Time to finally live up to the expectation of reality[62] I set. Time to finally finish my books. Time to love without looking over my shoulder. Time to breathe without the worry of bad breath. Time to finally live kid, even if it scares you.

Optimistic,
J.H.

October 30, 2015

I should wait for a response, but I can't anymore.

I didn't tell you the whole truth… about the sleep thing. I know you already know this. My stoic persona prevents me from actually expressing what is going on. I know you could tell I was leaving information out. There is never enough time in a day to think. When I sit down to think it becomes burdensome. It becomes too difficult to even put in place my thoughts and begin to rationalize what is going on. Maybe typing this stuff out is my therapy. Maybe this is where I can just relax and let my brain expand and try to understand what the fuck is going on. But then I think, why is this so dramatic. Life is pretty good. I don't have any "real" issues. My students have real issues. Broken homes, prostitute or crack addicted mothers, fathers with empty promises, shelters, worrying about shootouts, drug busts, how they are going to eat dinner. I guess it is all-relative in its own right. Most of them are in such denial over what they are going through it is easy for them to associate their situation with "normality." And in turn disassociate with life. They live so sheltered, in their own bubble of violence, debauchery and degradation.

The truth is Sophia, I am afraid to sleep. She always comes back in my dreams. I never dreamed a day before last February. She used to always tell me I was in her dreams. Since she is gone, the minute my eyes close she comes back. As real as if she were standing right in front of me, the smell, the touch, the sound of her voice, like she never left. However, I do believe

---

[62] 500 Days of Summer.

I am "over it." I do believe I have healthily moved on. But I am scared because with each passing day it continues and becomes more real, more alive. It as if she passed away and haunts my nights not letting me live with the decision, that although has been miserable to live with, I truly believe deep down it was the right decision. Sleep... sleep is for dreamers[63], I've seen too much in this life to dream. I just don't know how much longer I can keep up this pace while I am haunted.

My father once told me to never live with regrets, that they would haunt you forever. He had a couple regrets. He always said, he wished he paid more attention to us growing up. I feel you truly never regret something until years later, when one day, you are walking to your car after buying a cheese platter and you unlock the door fumbling for your keys because your hand is shaking from the extra coffee and it hits you. That spine-tingling feeling[64]. It creeps up your back and shoots to your head like a bad bong rip. Then you realize as you drop the keys on the floor that something is off. Something doesn't fit. Something is wrong in your life. You may not be able to pinpoint exactly what it is, but that empty feeling like a piece of you left. It is that feeling you get when you walk into the kitchen and forget why you walked in there. Regrets are a scary thing kid. Be careful.

But again, I don't think I regret much of anything in my life that I can pinpoint. Ophelia used to say I would never be satisfied. She called me a gypsy soul, constantly wandering, looking, searching for something more. Maybe she was right? Maybe that is the emptiness I feel, despite carrying a smile and enjoying my life. I keep it buried knowing I will never be fully satisfied. A man with an unquenchable thirst, an insatiable appetite, is a scary man. He will stop at nothing to find his nirvana, never stopping to realize that maybe, just maybe, it is the journey that is quenching his desire. It is the searching that will fill his void. But until then, the walking man walks[65], even with no direction.

J. Levon.

---

[63] Dylan, Bob.
[64] Pearl Harbor.
[65] Taylor, James.

CHAPTER EIGHT

"Don't do what you want. Do what you don't want. Do what you're trained not to want. Do the things that scare you the most."

-Chuck Palahniuk

The more I read from Levon the more questions I had about this man who took me in. The more curious I became about his speculated, and tattered past, one kept so hidden in the doldrums of his mind. He spoke of the past like a war he tried to forget. The most arrogant, emotional, yet gentlest man I ever knew, had a war wage on within himself, one only he could fight. I didn't know if I should give empathy, sympathy or ignore it all together and live on.

Levon's art concealed himself much more than it ever revealed him.[66]

The summer was flying by as most summers do. Like a gust of wind, the summer lifts you up into the crisp morning and drops you just as the heat of the day disperses into the dark of the night. The minute you get used to the freedom of living, is the very second the freedom gets ripped from your hands. The minute you get your summer routine, you don't need it anymore.

---

[66] Reference to V for Vendetta.

Levon grew more and more recluse over the season. As long as I knew Levon he always went into hermit mode at the end of the summer, becoming even moodier. He later told me it was because he feared the winter.[67] Snow brought him sadness and the cold shuddered his bones like a bridge in an earthquake. He said, "everyone dies in the winter, no one dies in the summer Jake. The winter is when the world leaves and it is just me."

It was mid-August when I woke up in the middle of the night to thundering coughs. The room was still pitch black as I fumbled my way to the light switch all the way across the room, stubbing my toe on my boots and tripping over a week's worth of laundry on the floor. They weren't my coughs, and Evie didn't live in our frat castle, but they came from Levon's room. The walls shuttered with every bellow from Levon. I wasn't sure the proper etiquette in this situation. Levon was a very private person. He never liked to show any weakness, but what if he was truly in trouble? Was it my responsibility to help? I am the only other person there who was able to help. Eventually, there was a hacking of lung butter that sounded like Vesuvius just erupted across the hall. I paused at my door and weighed my options. Fuck it. I ran to Levon's door and just before I busted in Kramer style, I paused again, stared at the door and gently knocked. No response. I rapt again on the solid wood door, making sure he heard me.

"Hey Levon," I whispered." Not sure why I whispered.

No response other than another hacking of phlegm sounding like a wet water balloon being deflated. I tapped again... nothing but hacking away.

"Levon if you don't answer I am either coming in or calling Evie," I yelled through the door.

Then there was a crash, a thump. I grabbed the door handle. It was locked. "Levon," I yelled again only to be responded by the sound of smashing glass. What the fuck is going on in there? The house was dark, only shadows directed my way through the maze upstairs as I sprinted

---

[67] Levon said this to me many times over his life. He never explained and I never asked why the winter made him shudder. Evie told me later that everyone close to Levon died or left in the winter months, specifically the last two weeks in January and first two weeks in February. Levon never ventured out of the house during that 4-week period.

across the hall back into my room to grab my cell phone. On the way I screamed, "That's it Levon, whether you are dying or not I am calling Evie. When she gets here you better be dead, or she will kill you for scaring us like this." If that didn't get the old man motivated to answer my pleas than nothing would. It took three calls before Evie answered her phone. She probably had no idea where she put her phone. It was in her maroon Mulberry purse her granddaughter bought her on Seville Rd. in London. It was the most expensive thing she owned, and she cherished the old bag dearly. Her phone was always in there. The old will never learn.

"Evie, I don't know what's going on with Levon! I heard him coughing and I think he fell, there was a smash, sounded like glass, do I call 911? I am not sure. The door is locked, is there a key? I can't break it down. You know I am not that big to break it down. (Trying to throw some humor in an otherwise dire situation). You think he is okay? Does he do this?"

"Slow down, slow down Jake. Open the middle drawer of the table at the top of the stairs, there should be keys in there. One of them is for his room. I am on my way. And yes, call 911! I am going to fucking kill him if he isn't already dead."

That's my Evie.

I ran back down the hall to the table. I must have walked by this table a thousand times and never noticed it. Dawn was breaking through the east facing windows allowing for better visibility as I darted my way around the second floor of the colonial trying to not waste a single precious second as the coughing stopped and I feared the worse. I grabbed the keys pushing away the old letters, batteries, string, tape and old pocketknives that were also in the drawer. There were 4 keys on the red Camp Wilbur lanyard. The moment took forever. A long sigh was quicker than my sudden movements as I sprinted around in only my briefs. I slammed the first key into the door. Nothing. Second key. Nothing.

"Levon! You okay?"

"Sport." He finally responded. He sounded exhausted struggling to get even the one word out.

"I am coming in Levon, just hold on one more second."

Third key. Nothing. Of course, it would be the last key I fucking try. Fourth key. Nothing. What the fuck. "Levon none of these fucking keys work!"

Just as I finished the last syllable of "work," a key flew out from under the door. "Levon why the fuck would you have the key inside the...Never mind..." I swung the door open to find Levon lying prostrate on his stomach with blood all over his chin and shirt. There were blood splatters on his sheets and ground. The bedside lamp was on the ground shattered into a million glass and cedar shards, Levon kept pointing at his legs. Evie's car door slammed outside and before we could react the front door crashed open. Evie's heavy-footed stampede came prancing up the stairs, echoing through the house.

"Levon you better be really fucking hurt or dead otherwise I am going to..." Evie paused her rant as she came around the corner to me holding Levon upright wiping blood off his face. Levon still had aftershock coughs that shook his whole body.

"OOO Jesus, what happened?"

"I have no idea I just got the door open."

Kurt and Ernest made their way up to the second floor to find out what the commotion was about. When they saw Levon on the ground with Evie and I surrounding him they quickly came over and licked his face. In between coughs Levon was able to tell us some of what happened.

"I...I had a cough. Then I looked down. There was blood. I stood up to go to the bathroom, but my legs gave way. On my way down I grabbed the lamp. I couldn't move. I can't...I don't know..."

"Sounds like a stroke, maybe an aneurism?" Evie said.

"I'm fine, seriously," Levon stoically attempted to brush off his near-death experience and catch his breathe.

"Shut up Levon, this isn't normal. You need to go to the hospital."

"They aren't going to tell me anything I don't already know," He said. "I ain't in it for the health."

"Don't be such a mule, you are coughing up blood and your legs are paralyzed... this isn't negotiable you ass."

I watched the two go through these exchanges as I slowly backed out of the room without saying a word. It scared me to see Levon in such a weak and vulnerable state. The man, who was teaching me to be a man was reduced to blood filled coughs and shaking legs. What if he died? I had no one else. The reality of mortality finally hit me as it does all people at some point is his or her life. The moment you realize you can't hold on to everyone, the moment you realize that life is a fleeting blur and every man, woman and child will eventually have the same fate, is the very moment innocence is completely lost. It is in that very moment of realization that people choose their outlook on the rest of life. Either they choose to have everything taste a little sweeter, a little brighter, a little happier, or they choose to have the world become greyer, slower, and bitter. Neither Evie nor Levon saw me back out of the room, shaken to the core at the fragility of life.

"Jake, call 911 again. Tell them he is stable but still doesn't have full motion of his legs. We need an ambulance now," Evie shouted.

"Jake if you call the ambulance, I am kicking you out of my house. I am fine," Levon rebutted.

"Levon if you don't shut up…"

"Yes, yes I know you are always right."

"That's better," Evie said with a victorious smirk.

I called 911, blacking out the conversation entirely and went straight to my room, stunned, at how quickly this man who I have become to know, admire and love was almost ripped from my grasp, leaving me alone, again.

Before I knew it, the EMT's took a bitching Levon out the front door. I did not move from my room. Suddenly it was silent in the house. The air was stifling and the sepia glow on the shadows gave the world a nostalgic feel. You can become lost in the past if one is not careful. It could turn into a lotus flower trance, stuck on repeat.

The house silently creaked under the strain of each step as I crossed the hallway into Levon's room. The blood remained, the glass still scattered on the pine floors. I began cleaning up and collapsed to the floor exhausted in the dawn light. The room looked different. I never paid close attention to the decor and layout of Levon's personal den. His room was not like the rest of the house. It was orderly, bright, and well kept. No books were randomly placed in stacks, his wallet neatly placed next to his

Frederique Constant watch. His closet was packed with the care of a person with some of the most intense OCD I ever saw.

I eventually got the strength to stand up and clean the crime scene, returning the spotless bedroom to its original state of conformity. As I finished cleaning, walking out the room I grabbed the ring of keys on the Camp Wilbur lanyard. I walked back over to the light brown table, opened the drawer and placed the keys back. Then suddenly I stopped. I put down the brown Whole Foods bag filled with shards of the lamp Levon made when he was in 11th grade shop class. Directly in front of me was the room. The room I have never seen. It was the room that was always locked. It was the room with the beautiful porch overlooking the Atlantic. I looked back at the table with the newly discovered keys sitting inside. Why the fuck not try?

First key. Nothing. Second key, third key, the same…Nothing. Then finally the fourth key, it felt perfect. There was no way it wouldn't work. The knob didn't budge. Discouraged, I put the keys back and went downstairs to make some coffee and try to digest what the fuck just happened. I called the hospital and they confirmed he was admitted. Evie called me back and told me it was a stroke and would eventually get full recovery of his paralysis. As I hung up the phone, it hit me. I knew how to open the door. Levon's key. It had to be the master key. I sprinted upstairs skipping a step with each leap. Slid down the hall and stopped at the door. The key was still in the doorknob. I snatched it out, did an about face and ran to the east.

I gently opened the door and was absolutely terrified. I should have been excited, or maybe a little apprehensive but I was terrified. It felt like opening a tomb or mausoleum. The door was heavier than the others in the house. It took all my might to push the door ajar. There is something about opening a locked door. No matter the circumstance, it always comes from fear of the unknown. In reality, it is such a primal instinct. The curiosity to learn, the curiosity to grow, the curiosity to explore places you have never been, seen, smelt, tasted. We were built to answer questions and explore what we do not know. Curiosity may have killed the cat, but that cat lived an awesome fucking life before it died.

The sun crept in bit-by-bit, illuminating a line down the hallway behind me. A golden glow showered the room as the sun peaked over the horizon and beamed through the lace curtains covering the glass French doors, which led out onto the sprawling, pristine porch, jutting out over the ocean.

There was an easel with a white stool set up in front of the doors. All of the paintbrushes and cloths were set up as if someone just was getting ready to paint. There was a sewing station and what seemed to be a knitting station. Resting on top of the knitting station equipped with spools of yarn and every size needle, was a half made navy blue blanket. It looked like someone was making it and dropped it never to return. There was a wall of books, none I ever saw before. After a quick glance I realized the theme. Most of the books were about women during revolutions, an odd subject to find in Levon's house. There were dog bowls labeled Madeline. As far as I knew, Levon never had a dog named Madeline. It was always Kurt Vonnegut Jr., and Ernest Hemingway. Levon did tell me about a dog he named Booker T. Washington and a turtle called Thomas J. Esquire. Anyway...I digress... Around the corner there was a small fireplace with a brown leather love seat. The wood piled and ready to be burnt. A large wooden chest with animals carved into the side, adorned with brass handles, loomed in the far corner of the room at the foot of a queen bed with all white linens. The room was locked in a time capsule. Despite never having seen this room open, nor anyone clean it. There wasn't a speck of dust. It was vacuum-sealed in time. It was frozen in the past. I was terrified to disturb the presence of the ghostly room. It was an abandoned room in a well lived home. It remained frozen, an ageless room forgotten by the outside world.

The air was colder, cleaner and punched you in the gut. I finally fought through the fear to completely open the door. Softly, I stepped into the room crossing the threshold with much hesitation. My second foot crossed the threshold and immediately something in me shuddered and I jumped back. Something was not right. It was that spine tingling feeling you can never explain, like when you know someone is watching you, or when you know exactly what someone is going to say. You don't know why you get those feelings; you only know you do.

Without any help from myself, the door slammed shut in my face. I reached back for the handle and it was locked again. With chills running up and down my body I backed away, put Levon's key back on his dresser and swore I would never tell anyone what occurred.

Sometimes it is best to forget what you can't explain.

CHAPTER NINE

"No man steps in the same river twice, for it is not the same
river and he is not the same man."

--Heraclitus

When Levon returned from the hospital Evelyn decided to move
in to make sure she could keep an eye on the old man when I returned to
college. There were only a few weeks left in summer and she wanted to
acclimate to the new setting, despite spending the majority of her time with
us. She lived alone and her kids were spread throughout the country. I think
she was lonely too. Sometimes two lonely souls can be the best of
company. I had no desire to return to the den of iniquity known as college.
I am sure in the 1920's academia colleges were incredible places to expand
your brain. Now they are liberal vacuum's where drugs are more prevalent
than books. I knew the atmosphere was not the right place for my tortured
mind. There is no greater tyrant than the brain. Having almost lost Levon,
my parents off god knows where, doing god knows what, my sisters with
their husbands, forgetting they even had a brother, their children growing
up without knowing their uncle, my best friend dead, I had nothing left
other than my brain, my hands and my words. And Levon. I had Levon. I
couldn't lose him. I didn't want to leave him either. What if he needed me?
There is no greater service in life than to help. He was all I had. Him and
Evie.

Everyday Evie and I helped Levon out of bed. It was demoralizing
for the old man. He bitched and complained the entire time, but we knew it

was out of love. Besides, if he didn't have us helping him, his lazy ass would have stayed in bed the rest of his life. The temporary paralysis was slowly receding to the abyss from which it appeared. The doctors told Levon he needed to slow down his drinking. So, he followed directions and drank more. The doctors told him to start taking vitamins, so he ate an extra potato with dinner. It wasn't as if Levon wanted to die, he just didn't like to be told what to do regardless of who was telling him, or their intentions. Evie was the only person I ever saw stand up to the arrogant stubbornness of Levon. It was an honest spitefulness that coursed through his veins.

People react differently to near death experiences. Some rebound to feel more driven than ever and others, shell up and hermit. They hide themselves from the world. Others become bitter and angry. Levon was all of these, it just depended on which side of the house the sun rose. Levon definitely had bipolar disorder or borderline personality disorder. In reality, he had PTSD from a broken heart.

To this point in my life, while writing this book, I have had 11 near death experiences.

For some reason, someone still wants me around. It was a random Monday when my friend told me he was about to see a sheep herding competition at a state fair. I mentioned being rammed by a ram when I was four. Then I went down the lineup of near-death experiences.

1. When I was 1, I ate my grandfather's heart medicine. Had to get my stomach pumped.

2. When I was 2, I ate a balloon and choked on it. My Uncle tried the Heimlich and it didn't work. He had to reach down my throat and pull it out.

3. When I was 4, I was getting eggs from the chicken coup at my uncle's farm and a ram, reared its horn-ridden head and launched into me repeatedly until I was knocked out. My mother beat the shit out of that ram and saved my life.

4. When I was 5, I brushed my teeth with Bengay thinking it was Colgate toothpaste at my aunts. I couldn't read and she said it was the white and red bottle on the sink. She had to call poison control.

5. When I was 6, while selling Girl Scout cookies with my sisters I picked up a random bag in the road to move it to the sidewalk and a needle fell out and stabbed me. I had to spend 2 nights in the hospital getting all sorts of tests done.

6. When I was 16, I almost overdosed on my birthday. I took a full 80 mg oxy and put on a 15 mg fentanyl patch, which is for cancer patients. I had to pull over 3 times while driving to throw up. I slept for 48 straight hours.

7. When I was 21 living abroad, I wandered away from the bar thinking I knew the way home. Found myself outside of a township, waved down a random car. It was a janitor. He drove me back to where I lived. Wandered off again blacked out. Got in a car with a bunch of random drunk kids. Got lost again. Finally, the police found me sleeping on the side of the highway and brought me home.

8. While hiking I had an extremely poisonous spider crawl on me that would have for sure killed me because we were a two-day hike from any civilization.

9. When I was 22, I blacked out in NYC and fell asleep in Stuy Town. Enough said.

10. When I was 23, I was roofied and drove my car and totaled it in the woods. Woke up the next morning in my totaled car with no recollection of what happened.

11. When I was 24, I was supposed to get on a train to my girlfriends. I missed it. That train crashed and over 150 people went to the hospital. Dozens died.

However, I digress. This isn't about me. This is about the old man.

I didn't see any benefit in going back to Brown. I spent most of my time in the library, reading the same books Levon had in his house. I studied History and Journalism, all of which you can't be taught. These are studies of self-discipline where the only way to learn is to keep reading and keep writing. Eventually the shit will stick. The idea I had to pay $50,000 a year to have someone direct me to what books to read was nauseating. I could get the same education with a library card.

I couldn't bring myself to tell Levon and Evie I didn't want to go back to school. I knew they wouldn't approve. Every time I thought of going back, I tried to push it to the back of my mind. I knew I needed to tell them eventually. They weren't exactly my parents, so they had no real say in my choices. I did appreciate all of their input, but it was my life and my young adult stubbornness forced me to only do what pleased me in the now, not thinking 10 minutes past any moment. So, I continued my daily routine in the old white colonial. Many of my evenings were spent with Evie as Levon slept off his food coma, or an afternoon bottle of whiskey.

While Levon was sleeping we decided to clean the house. The bookshelves weren't dusted since Nam. It was absolute chaos trying to make sense of every scrap of paper. You never knew what was written on, what was important or what was a napkin that has been used to wipe pizza sauce off Levon's face.

While doing the dishes, all I thought about was the room. Houses always have a way of keeping secrets. But as the nursery rhyme goes, "secrets secrets are no fun they should be shared with everyone." It wasn't that I wanted to go in the room, it was the idea I didn't know. It was the idea the door remained locked. That it locked without me touching it. It was the feeling of coldness I couldn't shake from my bones since I crossed the threshold. I couldn't ask about the room. My gut told me it had to do with Ophelia, but my mind knew to stay away from the topic, regardless of how close the three of us had become. At night I stared out the window of my room onto the empty deck, and the moon shimmered and skipped across the glossed white of the porch. Maybe Evie knew. She was a little more rational. I was like a child playing his parents against each other, knowing their personalities and using them to gain an advantage. This is where it was important to have a strategy because I couldn't bring it up out of the blue.

"Hey Evie, wouldn't it be nice if we cleaned and straightened the whole house for Levon. It will be nice for him since he is still struggling."

"Not a bad idea," she replied. "But you hate cleaning."

"I know, it just seems like the right thing to do. My mother always said there is no greater feeling than giving and giving for the right reasons." I clenched my teeth under my breath knowing I didn't want to do this for the right reasons but only to find an answer to a question that was nagging me and twisting my insides.

"Levon won't notice if we clean the whole house, you do know that, right?"

"Doesn't matter to me."

"Well, you know me Jake, I stress clean and I stress cook."

"If you were 40 years younger, I would marry you."

"If you were 40 years older, I still wouldn't marry you."

"Harsh, Evie."

"I am too old for your flirting."

"You know you love me."

"Ooooo shush child."

We both laughed at our banter.

"You want to clean the bathrooms?" She continued.

"Was that a rhetorical question? You are funny."

"It was your idea to do this good deed. I am not doing the worst job."

"Rock paper scissors?"

"How about bear ninja cowboy?"

Evie was able to be a grandmother, mother, and best friend all at the same time.

We began cleaning at opposite ends of the house. She started in the library carefully navigating around Levon and I went into the dining room. Lysol wipes galore, we sifted through all of the clutter that hadn't been moved in decades. Levon snored away in the library by the crackling fire. We played Leon Bridges Pandora. You have to listen to music when cooking or cleaning. Dust flew in the air with each movement. Dog hair coated the molding on the floor. There was so much Uncle Scrooge from Ducktails could have dived headfirst into it, like he did his money pit. Bag after bag piled up of random shit. Thankfully this time I did not find any notes, or letters by accident. There was just a lot of old receipts, dirty paper plates, napkins, bottles and shoes. I never noticed how many shoes Levon owned. Evie and I met in the middle of the foyer, both exhausted and disheveled.

I looked at Evie as her hair slowly fell out of her tightly woven bun on her head. Her hair flowed around the contours of her face framing her ancient beauty. The brown locks gently held to her face from glistening in the summer heat. (Women glisten, men sweat). For the first time, I noticed her bright green eyes.

"Should we go upstairs?" I asked.

"You want to keep going?" She said, exhausted and obviously done with the idea of cleaning anything. But I needed to push on.

"Well, what else are we going to do? It can't be nearly as bad as the first floor, all he does is sleep and shit upstairs."

"Fine, I am just not doing any bathrooms," she said again.

"No worries, I will, but I am going to start in the room on the right."

Evie snapped her head around and glared. "Which room?"

I pointed to the closed door without saying anything hoping for some reaction or statement to give me an idea as to the origins of the room.

"You ever been in there?" She asked.

"No." I lied. "But it is always closed, so why not explore I am sure Levon won't care. I tried to speak innocently enough to egg her into giving me more information. However, she seemed more curious about the room than I did.

"You think we can even get in there?"

"I have never tried. So, I am not sure." I lied again. Never misplace the value of a white lie.

Evie looked at me with large innocent eyes of a child. Her tense body loosened, and she looked back at Levon in a deep slumber on the couch, looked back at me, back at Levon and before turning her head back said, "Well, let's fucking find out now. I have been trying to get in there for years."

"Wait you have never been in there?" I acted dumb letting her run with this one, making her think it was actually her idea. Inception at its finest.

"No, never."

"Why is it always locked?"

"I have no idea Jake. As long as Levon has lived here it has always been locked."

"So weird."

"All I know is that when Levon bought this house and he told me he bought it for a room. The first time I visited, I asked about the room and he completely ignored the question. I know Levon well enough to know that when he doesn't answer a question it is best to not press. But fuck it. I deserve to know what the big deal is. Let's do this shit."

"Never heard you curse like this before."

"Carpe that fucking diem Jake. Carpe that fucking diem."

I never saw Evie like this, but I loved it. She acted as if she got a shot of youth straight to the veins. Youth is truly wasted on the young. She was more excited than me. Her excitement made me feel like I never saw inside the room or knew where the key hid in the desk upstairs. She made me forget the gut wrenching, spine tingling fear that coursed through me when I first entered the room. Evie moved quicker than ever before. I played along, thriving off her enthusiasm. We ran up the stairs like two kids fleeing school in the middle of the day. She grabbed the handle, "Its locked," she said as if surprised.

"Really Evie? Thank you, captain obvious."

"Watch it Jake, you need to be smart, to be a smart ass."

"Touché, Touché."

"You think there is a key?"

"I have no idea." I lied again.

"Okay, you go into the guest room, I will go into Levon's room."

I played along and went on the key safari. We rummaged through everything. It was more of a ransacking than an actual search. I heard Evie overturn everything; desperate to get into the one part of Levon's life she knew nothing about.

I finally yelled out, "I can't find anything in here. You have anything?"

"No! But it has to be somewhere."

"Is it possible he keeps the key on him Evie?"

"No, Levon only kept his watch, his lucky coin from 1880's town in South Dakota and his red string bracelet, on him."

"You think there even is a key?"

"It is a locked door. There is always a key."

As we pondered for another solution, I opened the table drawer where I last left the key, hoping to surprise Evie with my great discovery. It was gone. My face went white. Levon must have taken it back. How? The guy couldn't even fucking walk...

"We are getting in," she said with determination and frustration on her face. I was scrambling for ideas.

"Should I climb up the deck?"

"Shut it Jake, that is crazy talk..." She paused and then asked, "You would do that?"

"Well how else do you want to get in? We have no key; the door is locked, and we are on the second floor. We can't break the door down."

We stood at the top of the stairs in silence. Evie tried the door again. "You really think it was going to miraculously open?" I said sarcastically, slightly scared it would unlock and swing open, the way it shockingly closed on me. We panned the second floor, scurrying from room to room looking for any possible solution. We were infected by the idea of the unknown and were unable to shake its hold. You can't kill an idea.[68] You can kill a person; you can take over a country or government, but an idea can crawl into your brain and infect your whole being like a

---

[68] V for Vendetta

virus. The way I was infected with the story of Ophelia was the same way
Evie was infected by the idea of the room.

"Any way we can get to the deck from your window?"

"Maybe," I said.

I always looked at the vacant deck from my window. I thought
about making the leap before I found the key, but never had the balls or
desire to venture out of the two-story window. The two of us crossed the
hall to my room. We stuck our heads out the window and saw the deck an
arm's length away.

"You think the sliding doors are locked?"

"Only one way to find out," Evie said. She looked at me with
encouraging eyes.

"Are you promoting this delinquency?"

"Can a woman have fun you fucking stiff?"

"What has gotten into you?"

"Are you going to try or not?"

"Are you peer pressuring me?"

"I am pressuring you. Yes. However, you are not my peer."

I put up a fake fight. I knew I was about to climb through that
window. There was no way to say no to Evie. You don't say no to a woman
who has conviction in her eyes. She was the head of the household. She ran
everything like all women do. Growing up with all women in your family
you learn quickly that control is a complete illusion they want you to
believe. In reality, they have all the control. An easy way to get through life
as a man is being mentally prepared that you will always be wrong. "The
man may be the head of the family, but the woman is the neck and she can
turn the head any way she wants."[69] I stuck my head back out the window
in the night. It was as dark as a thousand midnights, because the moon was
cloaked behind the clouded sky. Evie was behind me with the chair from
my desk. I stood on the chair and stuck one leg out the window straddling
the sill like a horse. My balls now jammed up on the metal window frame
and Evie's smile looking closer to the Grinch than the tired gardener I first
met. It was obvious she was a wild child in her youth and this event

---

[69] Big Fat Greek Wedding

brought her back to the days of pool jumping and running from the cops. Both our heart rates elevated because of the honest mischief. I shimmied closer and reached out with my foot, gingerly touching the railing of the deck. I reached with my right hand holding onto the window with my left and grabbed the gutter, which ran perpendicular to the railing. In one swift movement I swung my weight out the window pulling on the gutter praying it didn't snap off the house. I balanced on the edge of the railing teetering back and forth. Evie screeched in fear, loud enough to startle me. Waving back and forth, hoping to avoid the two-story plunge into the hydrangeas below I regained my balanced and hopped down onto the deck. With a sigh of relief, I looked around. Standing on the deck felt like standing on Mars. One small step for me one giant leap for us. (One more line of corny clichés to make all writing professors cringe. Anything is better than saying "trials and tribulations").

I looked back at Evie poking her head through the window. She had the look of a young girl waiting at the top of the stairs on Christmas morning. I tried the closest sliding door. It silently opened exposing the white curtains on the other side and Evie shrieked from behind and quickly disappeared back into the house. With my heart racing I sprinted into the room hoping to get to the other door as quickly as possible, terrified to be alone in the void. Immediately, as I unlocked the door, Evie swung it open. Her silhouette stood tall over me as the foyer lights illuminated her back, leaving her jubilant facial expressions hidden in shadows. She slowly took each step into the darkness of the room. She walked by me as if in a trance. She had the look of someone walking to the gates of St. Peter, with arms open, and heart clear. I slid back out into the hallway to give her time to herself. Just as I stepped out into the second story landing, crossing the threshold, the door abruptly slammed. I lunged back at the door terrified for Evie.

"Evie! Are you okay!?"
Silence....

"Evelyn! Don't do this to me! Tell me you are okay...Anything." Still no response. I started banging the door. It was locked. Just before my third strike slammed down, ensuring Levon woke up, I heard, "Child..."

"Evie are you okay?"

"It's okay Jake, relax." She said in in a soothing voice a mother uses to calm their child having a panic attack over losing their first love.

"But the door is locked, I don't know how to get you out…"

Again, my pleas were met with silence. I ran to my bedroom window; the sliding door was closed. Terrified, not because of the situation, but because I didn't have an answer. I hate not having the answer.

I sat on my bed, took a deep breath and tried to assess the situation. A sudden tiredness rushed over my body like I never felt before. It was overwhelmingly warm, traveling from my toes to my nose. My body felt weak, my hands felt weak like I just woke up and was unable to grasp anything. I tried to hold on as much as possible, but I couldn't fight it. It was like taking 3 mellow yellow's, 2 Xanax, a Klonopin and 4 Ambien's, not that I know from experience. Then like the best-drunken black out of all time, I fell asleep.

The next morning, I shot out of bed. However, it wasn't morning. I woke up to the smell of fried chicken. I slept through the entire next day until dinnertime. The smell was overwhelming and nauseating. Confused how it was already dark outside I ran downstairs to see Evie in the kitchen and Levon out on the porch, with drink in hand. Evie didn't say a word or turn to me. She continued to slave over her homemade fried chicken. There was something about the making of fried chicken that never made sense to me. It wasn't actually an idea of not making sense, it was the fact that in order to make fried chicken you use an egg wash, and that is like dipping a chicken into the pulp of its own fetus. That is about as fucked up on the food front as it gets. It is worse than feeding pigs leftover pork.

I softly walked up behind Evie at the counter. My body felt different today. I went to put my hand on her shoulder. Before I got close enough, she snapped around. Evie's face looked different. Some wrinkles had disappeared. Her green eyes turned bright, piercing through me. Her posture was relaxed and the limp she never explained, disappeared. Evie looked like she lost 10 years of age. Like the room was her fountain of youth. I was startled by her appearance.

"What happened last…"

"Child…" She said in the same tone that was used the previous night. "Don't worry. I am okay. We don't speak about it."

"But Evie what the hell happened?"

"It is not important, we are here now."

"Evie what time is it?"

"We are all affected differently in life. I hope you feel rested."

"You aren't answering anything."

"Jake, it is okay to not have an answer for everything. Sometimes just accepting the world around you is okay."

"Is that a fucking Haiku?"

"Just know I no longer need to know about that room, and you shouldn't worry either. Today is a new day and yesterday is over. By the way, Levon wanted to talk to you."

I knew the conversation was going nowhere. I cut my losses and figured I could readdress it later. Levon was in his normal position on the porch.

"Hey Levon, Evie said you wanted to…"

"Sit down Jake," Levon said interrupting me as always. It gets old never being able to finish a sentence. Incomplete thoughts are as bad as a twitter rant about a Kardashian. "You go back to school soon."

"Technically…"

"I wanted to know what you are thinking, because a lot happened this summer."

"I don't know what you mean."

"I can see it on your face, you are scared to leave. You haven't talked once about heading back and you leave in a week."

"I don't know Levon…"

"Don't lie to yourself, it is okay to lie to me. But always be honest to yourself."

"It is just not the place for me…"

"You can make it your place. College is like eating ice cream, they are all different flavors, but at the end of the day you are still eating ice cream. It is what you make it."

"You don't understand Levon…"

I couldn't tell Levon exactly why I didn't want to go back. I was surprised how astute he was at picking up my apprehension in returning to college. The truth was I was terrified to leave. Levon and Evie were all I had. We were truly a family now. Levon made me concerned. I was worried about his physical and mental health. I don't know how he survived all these years without Evie and I taking care of him. Perhaps, god sends you unexpected people at unexpected times. Perhaps, things do happen for a reason.

Then Levon got irrationally angry, like he had been holding in this resentment. In hindsight, I think he was trying to be a dad, and didn't know how.

"You are a fucking idiot if you think you are not going back to school Jake."

"No offense Levon, but you aren't my father. You can't tell me what I can and cannot do."

"Even if I was your father you still wouldn't listen."

"I am not going."

"Please, you son of a bitch, tell me some good reason, and convince me. Sell me a pen I already own.[70] Do something to make me think you not going to college will benefit you in life."

"Levon you just wouldn't get it."

"That's a bad sell. You need to discover who you are, you need to expand, laugh, get angry, be happy, cry, and push yourself. Jake you are similar to me and you need to be pushed… college will push you. Life isn't just 28 Lotus Lane."

"Why can't you trust me?"

"This has nothing to do with trust."

"Then why are you being such an ass about this? You have never acted like this. You are acting like my dad. I don't need another dad."

"Jake don't belittle me."

"This isn't belittling. I am being honest. Something you struggle doing."

"You little fuck. I have opened my house, my friendship, and my life to you. Who do you think you are?"

"Yet, I still am faced with secrets with every turn I take in this house. You want to talk about trust, honesty; you have more secrets than

---

[70] Wolf of Wall Street

the KGB. So please stop asking me this! I just want to be left alone already. I am tired of everyone riding me, telling me I am smart, or I can do better, or I have more potential. Maybe I don't believe it, and isn't that what is truly important? What I believe? I don't care what you believe or Evie or anyone. I only care about me, and what I believe. I am average and that is okay with me."

"You don't mean what you are saying."

"Don't tell me what I mean or what I think!"

I hated when people told me what I thought. I hated when people thought they knew how I felt. The next week the battle brewed between us. I spent most of those last days in my room writing away, hiding from Levon and Evie. I knew Evie would side with Levon. I was outnumbered and didn't know what to do. Then the day before I was to leave, I woke up and knew what I needed to do. I needed to come to the solution on my own like most teens. I didn't want to go because I was scared. To tackle one's fears is one of the hardest things to do. It is rarely okay to react emotionally. I spent my life reacting emotionally, ignoring consequences, and it didn't get me very far. After sleeping off the screaming match I decided I needed to apologize to Levon. It killed me how rude I was to the man who cared so deeply for me.

It is never easy to say sorry to someone. There is no exact way to say it. There are no rules. The person always reacts differently. Depending on why you are saying sorry, how you say it, how they heard it, where they heard it, the mood they heard it in, what happened before, what happened after. The variables are endless. The variables can drive your mind mad. When all you want to do is have one person forgive you and take you back, that sorry always becomes a distant island you will never reach. The odds are forever not in your favor. However, you have to play in order to win, so throw back the sleeves and toss your money on the table. This motherfucker is called life. I was going to go back to school, but I needed to apologize to Levon first. I wrote him a letter before I left.

Dear Levon,

This is to say I am sorry. I am sorry for the arguments. I am sorry for the moodiness. I am sorry for the anger I sent your way. I now realize you only wanted the best. Who am I to cast off your concern? I feel so alone in this world. There are 7 billion people on this planet, and I am a lost soul wandering for some form of existence. You and Evie have become my parents and like any parent child relationship, we will not see eye to eye. But please know my reasons for not leaving were out of concern for you. The only time I don't feel alone in this too big world are when I am wrapped up in your words and books, in between Evie's dinners and your philosophical questions. Your stroke reminded me we only have a little bit of time on this earth and I want to spend it with those I care about. I can't lose anyone else I am close to.

However, this brings me to the point I made earlier this week on the porch. Levon, I feel you know so much about me, but the mysteries of your life keep me at a distance. I am afraid to lose you because who will know your story when you are gone? What about Sutton? What about Ophelia? What about the room? You know the room I am talking about. It isn't fair anymore. I want to tell your story. Your tired eyes say much, but your heart hides much more.

I promise to make you and Evie proud. I promise to be the best man I can. Not for me, but for you and Evie. However, to get to this point I know I need to like myself. I do not like who I am right now. I feel so unhinged to the world, going through the motions, trying to find my place. You have always helped me in this regard but now I understand it is my turn to find myself, whatever that means. Please know, I am sorry, and I will make you proud. I just need you to make me a promise. I want you to promise me that life does not end like this. You have too much heart and spirit to sit in the house anymore. If I need to go out and face this too big world, then you need to as well. Take your own advice. Find your happy place again. But promise me after you rediscover the Levon who once had a lust for life, before the world's ugly head reared its pain on you, that you will come home. Every man needs a home. 28 Lotus Lane is my home. Until we meet each other again.

Your Son, Sport, Your dumbass,
Jake

Back to school I went.

CHAPTER TEN

"The best life is a true life. The only stories worth telling are the ones that have already happened. Tell me a story to help me fall asleep... but also keep me up at night."

--J.H. Levon

About a month into the semester I received a frantic phone call from Evie. She was screaming. It wasn't a panicked scream but one of frustration. I couldn't follow everything; she spoke in Spanglish when she was anxious. From what I deciphered, Levon called a cab to bring him to the airport, didn't say anything to Evie and just left wearing an old blue jacket she hadn't seen in 30 years. Levon wouldn't tell her how long he was going to be gone or where he was going. The last thing Evie said before she slammed the phone down was, "Typical fucking Levon, he isn't 25 anymore..." Despite the insult I smiled a little hoping Levon took my advice...his own advice.

About a week later I received a letter from Levon. The postmark said Hostel Lodi, Rome, Italy. He was living.

~Author's Note~
The following are most of our correspondence but not all. I chose a handful of our letters to try and show Levon's adventures and how our lives were growing together despite being miles apart. To include all the letters would be a book in its own right. Levon's letters are in regular Garamond and my letters are in Italics.

Dear Jake,

I can breathe a little better over here. I feel a little younger. When I stepped on the plane, I didn't know what to expect. I haven't traveled in 30 years, but there is something about the feel of new pavement under your feet as you pump further and further away from your home. Something familiar rushed over me. I am still not sure what it is, but I have been walking a tad faster ever since. I decided a good place for this journey to start is Rome. When I was 23 years old, I spent 3 nights at the very same hostel I am staying in now. Not much changes in this city. I suppose not much ever changes here. I don't know where I will be going next, but I know it will be worth it. I cannot waste another moment. Please, tell Evie she is a nasty needy old hag but thank you for everything.

Forward all mail to the address on this letter until you hear from me again. Don't fuck up in school.

L.

Dear Levon,

You sly son of a bitch. Why didn't you say anything? Well, I will skip the formalities. Thank you for being alive. I am happy for you and wondering why the hell you didn't take me? But here we are. I can't wait to hear all about your adventures so please make sure you write as often as possible. Also, so I can inform Evie of your escapades.

The words don't come as easy as they use to. I usually have the words to describe or convey my feelings about this situation, about informing you how school is going and my new girlfriend. But since I have been dating Cecilia my mind goes blank at night when it used to stir. I am not sure what to do about it. Life is good though…I know you would be proud of me. My grades are good and I have become friends with the Journalism Department Chair. He is the voice of cynicism I was looking for since I left Lotus Lane. I enjoy journalism. However, news story writing is frustrating. The confinements of structure limit how I can write. They don't allow you to stray. There is no art, except for the subjects. I love the stories of the people I interview, the topics; you can't make that shit up. But the conventions of journalism force you to write bare bones and it leaves very little room for artistic styles to flourish. Maybe my inability to write has to do with me wasting my entire daily writing debit on school assignments. I always find it hard to balance what I want to do and what I am obligated to do. But maybe it is because of Cecelia. She is great Levon. You would really enjoy her. She is a thin little blonde with bright blue eyes. (See even there I couldn't even write poetic about the woman I am infatuated with… even infatuated is a cliché).

I will tell you more later. I have nothing else to say…I am good. I wish you all the best and remember, "I'm whitch you…I don't mean it like an expression like I know what you mean…I mean, I'm whitch you…"[71]

JR.

P.S.

You would just get up and go and scare the living shit out of Evie. She is going to kick your ass, but I told her that you said you love her and secretly want to marry her. Evie told me to tell you, "Spit, sit and spin on your thumb." And in case you didn't get the directions she wants you to, "shove your thumb up your ass." Direct quote. She made me write it down.

---

[71] My Blue Heaven

~Author's Note~

While at school Levon and I wrote letters back and forth. We did it the old school, snail mail way. We talked about my love interests, my writing projects, and good food recipes. We talked about Evie and the adventures of Lotus Lane as seen from Levon's front porch. There was no legitimate flow to our conversations; we discussed our lives not expecting advice or a response about our problems, but just an open mind and someone to read them. It's important to have someone who is there to just listen.

Jake my boy,

I have made it to Florence. I know not where I am headed, but I know where I have come from. I met a nice young lady on my train from Naples to Florence. Her name was Kelsey from Texas. Don't even ask, not your style. She was fat, but a sweet young lady.

She reminded me of the life I once lived. I once lived a life I don't remember. I once was a boy running from whim to whim on impulse alone. I once had a drive to feel all I could feel in the shortest amount of time. But then it happened. I felt this way before…there was that moment when I realized I couldn't trust anyone who was around me regardless if they loved me. I couldn't trust the ground I walked on anymore and I couldn't trust the sky above me to stay blue or hold the stars. I was locked in a world I no longer knew and had no direction but to keep moving. I had no other desire but to live with a fire, desirous of all I could desire. But that is just me.

Where I stayed, the bed was hard, but the pillows were soft. The red, green and brown colors, which lined the bed, blended together. For some reason I couldn't sleep, with much tossing around in my mind.

When the sun sets and the moon rises, it takes your mind with it. At night people are different beings entirely. We become an alter ego, a side, which is not allowed out during the daytime. When the sun rears its neglected gaze and the world darkens everything you once knew as normal now becomes a bit different.

Tossing around I couldn't get her words out of my head. What was so simple by the daylight was not as simple by nighttime. I have been on my own for five days now. In Rome for two and Florence for three. I never really mind being alone. It reminds me I am still alive. When traveling alone you tend put yourself out there more. We humans are communal people. We live together for a reason. We rely on human contact to survive. Studies have been done that if babies are not held and loved in infancy they will actually die.[72]

Kelsey's words ran through my brain. They sprinted through my head. They must have been tired. As my synapses spun, like a figure skater, with elegance, but difficulty. The friction burned. How did she know? How could she know? Was she real? At first she kind of seemed like an 80's sitcom bully. The person who made fun of you for doing obvious, normal things, such as brushing your teeth, "haha check out that kid brushing his teeth, what a loser…"

It happened two nights prior, after our train arrived in Florence. She couldn't have been a day older than 25 years old.

I hate awkward moments, so I introduced myself. I quickly realized she was not a normal Texan. Kelsey had an overwhelming, boisterous personality with a voice that echoed off the white stonewalls. There was no southern accent and no racist remarks but some allusions to her meth addicted friends. She asked where she could find a good salad. I knew of a spot around the corner where I recently ate a Caesar salad. She asked if I wanted to go because it was nice to talk to someone who spoke English, though she did most of the talking. I inquired about her and she broke into a 10-minute monologue. I figured I could grab a couple of beers.

She talked about how she has been traveling Europe by herself and she has family in France that she made home base. She spoke a lot about her ex-boyfriend and her current one. She didn't need much prying for her to open up about her life. She knew I was leaving the next morning and we would never see each other again. We were single serving friends.[73] We were only there for that moment and then our lives would continue. The

---

[72] Nazi ass holes.
[73] Palahniuk, Chuck. Fight Club

world would continue to spin, as our lives moved on. But that night we were best friends.

She started asking questions about me and answering her own questions. She somehow knew everything about me. Or at least it seemed that way.

I began to get an uneasy feeling. My gut turned. It wasn't the beer. I am not sure what it was. It was that sixth sense. It was that feeling, which sends your "spidey senses" out into the night air feeling for evil. So it goes.

"Why are you holding back?" she said butting into our conversation about 90's nickelodeon TV shows.

"You are holding back...this isn't you...you are so much more than this."

"I don't think I am..."

"You are...you are scared..."

"I am not scared...what are you talking about?"

"Let me guess...a girl?"

"Sweetheart I am too old..."

"Wife?"

"There is no girl." I lied.

"You had a girl."

Jake, I tell you she reminded me so much of you. She was relentless. It is like I have a sign on my face that everyone knows my heart is 3 sizes too small.[74]

"All you want is the one you can't have and all you want to be happy are the simple things..."

"What are you talking about? Simple things? Why are you bringing up women in my life?" I shot back.

"You are so innocent..."

"I am too old to be innocent. The old are the guiltiest of them all. You can't live this long and be innocent."

"I don't mean that as in you haven't lived...but you just want to be loved... you look so scared to me, yet you truly are brave for doing this...

---

[74] Dr. Seuss. How the Grinch Stole Christmas.

yet you make exceptions for yourself...you can't let yourself be an exception...let me ask you something...are you truly happy?"

"I don't know how to take that... That girl is in the past. I am here...living my life...I am happy... I guess."

She was fucking spot on. It was uncanny. I ordered another Peroni. I tried to change the conversation. Maybe she got lucky. My story was not a rare story.

When you come across people like this in traveling it is like being the main protagonist in some Greek myth. I have found my soothsayer. As uncomfortable as it may seem, you sometimes have to play the cards dealt and hope for the best. I listened...I inquired. I joked...I drank...and what I found was that I was just stuck in the middle of a dancing lesson from god.[75]

"Listen...I am happy...look how blessed I am ... look where I am...what I am doing right now..."

"I was once suicidal..." She said with no hesitation.
Well that changed the landscape...

"Don't worry I am not anymore..." She said quickly... making me feel much better and breaking the silence in Firenze's night air.

"I know what it takes to be truly happy..." She continued again. "You are not happy...you say you have written two books but are afraid to put them out... that you hate everything you write...You don't let yourself get deep enough. No one is going to take away your cool card if they find out you actually care about something."

Sound familiar Jake?

I needed another beer. It was weird to hear the truth. It was odd to hear what I knew but never said.

I am terrified for anyone to read my writing because it was my journal. It would be me opening my world to the world. I felt a man could make a living in another way, but I saw no other option for me. But I was terrified. I was in love with a girl who became an idea. I passed up on other women, idolizing what I believed was a perfect match. I was happy but I felt lost in what my goal of life was. I couldn't find my passion. I couldn't

---

[75] Vonnegut Jr., Kurt

take control of my life. I had lost track of who I was by ignoring the little realities of life. I forgot the simple things about me that made me happy and created a man I thought everybody else wanted to see. It was an identity crisis. I was a forgotten soul and a man without a country but was a trip like this the answer, or was it another puzzle piece in the grand scheme of life as we go dancing by in a swirl of beautiful ignorance?

"I am sorry…my mom always tells me not to do this to strangers…but my thought is what can it hurt…it is a gift I have," Kelsey continued.

She spoke as if it was truly a gift. Something divine bestowed on her. It could have been good luck. I could have it written all over my face that I am not truly happy and was not fulfilling some life destiny I apparently had, but not yet discovered. Maybe, it was just my mind thinking too much about her words. Maybe, I was trying to think that I was special in some way? Would that have been such a problem? Would it truly have been so bad to think that at some point you were the center of the universe?

She didn't stop though. I sat there dumbfounded, just staring at her and drinking. I couldn't stop staring. She didn't always look back, but she knew I didn't look away. Something to be said about that.

"What do you want? Has anybody ever asked you that? Have you ever been able to answer? Can you answer now? It is not hard. What do you want?"

I have been asked this before. I have never been able to give a true and honest answer, until this moment. It may have been the liquid courage. It may have been the unconscious desire to scream from the barren landscapes of my soul. But, by god I had an answer and I have no idea where it came from.

"I read a short story by Kafka once called *The Hunger Artist*. I won't bother you with the details but at the end of the story all I could think about was one question. What do you hunger for? I don't know what I want but know what I am hungry for. I hunger to be loved. I hunger to never be forgotten. I hunger for immortality through my words. I hunger to be someone people talk about, for good or for ill. I hunger for recognition. I hunger to stay humble. I hunger to no longer worry about fiscal responsibilities. I hunger to be creative. I hunger to be inspirational. I hunger to matter. I hunger to leave this world a better place than how I found it. It is safe to say I am hungry…"

"Those are all things you believe you want. I have known you for ten minutes and I know I have done most of the talking but maybe this is good to hear from a stranger you will never see again…. but…you are screaming at me. Why are you scared to be you? You let the world overwhelm you so much you forget about yourself. You try to please the world and you end up pissing some people off and that is what kills you the most. You say you are on this trip and are blessed, but something is missing. I look at you and you are empty. You are so deeply saddened about something. The hole in your soul will never be filled by any adventure you believe you need."

What type of response did she expect? I didn't know how to respond. I am not sure why I responded the way I did. But all I could say was… "What is your biggest fear…?"

Without hesitating she said, "To die alone…" She quickly continued, "answer your own question."

I paused…I couldn't think of anything…I felt prepared to die alone, a sobering thought…but I said without truly thinking of the words, but feeling good about it, "I am terrified to be forgotten."

She hit back… "Everybody will eventually be forgotten. Life is no 'Tuck Everlasting' and we can only worry about what we do while we are still here, not how people are when we are long buried."

We walked back in silence. One should not think too deeply about themselves. It is not good for the soul.

When I woke up she was gone. Kelsey was one of those travel-dancing lessons. I danced. Sometimes it is best to just dance along with the music life composes.

Hope that made sense, my mind is flying…
LEVON

Old pal,

It is great to hear you are back pounding away at the pavement. I will take some credit for that. I know you will deny it because you are a spiteful ass hole. I must say I agree with good ole Kelsey from Texas. But that is neither here nor there. Keep running buddy. You will get where you need to go despite you forgetting where you came from. The two are not synonymous anymore in this too big world.

I am a managing editor on my school newspaper. However, I am struggling to stay out of trouble. I wrote an editorial the other week about how our school has been pushing the Flu shot, and how I believe the school has no place to force its students to take the vaccination. Well, apparently someone on the school board got pissed off and told the Journalism chair. Isn't an editorial supposed to be about a controversial topic? I refused to retract my statement. They are threatening to withhold pay. See how far journalism has fallen today! All I need to do is watch 5 minutes of Fox news to know the world is slowly crumbling and objective, yet creative reporting is now a fleeting memory in the golden age of the world. I guess I am like you in the fact that I constantly look to the past as the best year.

Cecilia has been trying to teach me not to keep looking into the past. I can't help but be preoccupied with all the different "what ifs." Have I told you about her yet? I can't remember anything anymore. I am smoking too much pot. She tries to get me to stop but it is my glass of wine at night. I also tried to be more social like you and Evie encouraged, but all I find myself doing is getting fucked up beyond control, just so I can stoop down to these peasant's level. I know, I know, you would tell me that true learning comes when you live with the majority and the reality is the majority of the world are the ones who aren't rich and intelligent, but average and poor.

I think I am at the point you mentioned in Yellow… Where you finally took the world for what it was instead of trying to change all the problems you saw. Maybe seeing and accepting the world for what it is, is the hardest part of growing up.

Stay thirsty for the world Levon,
J. Roberts.

Dear Son,

I am not sure why, but I enjoy calling you son from time to time. I am sorry it has been so long since my last reply. I am writing a lot, most of it useless. Maybe when I return home you can see some of it. Yes, I am offering to share. I am afraid that when I die my story will burn to ashes and I will have nothing left, no one to remember me. I keep thinking about the conversation I had with Kelsey when I openly admitted I was afraid of being forgotten. You won't forget me, will you?

Sounds like you have a good girl on your hands. Careful, for love is the crutch and the splinter in our lives. Us men are too hardened to admit our soft hearts can be penetrated but we are true romantics Jake. There is nothing wrong with that. Also fuck your editors and the department chair. Write what you feel, it isn't hard. I have been alone for 3 weeks now. I have passed into northern Africa and am headed down to South Africa, where my soul once ran wild with the wind at my back and the sun in front of my eyes. The longer you spend in solitude the quicker you realize true happiness is happiness shared.

The sun is different in Africa. They sky makes you feel smaller than it did before. So many memories are flooding back into me as I travel down the west coast. I am almost at the Indian Ocean. I can remember all the pain and anger from my youth that flooded me when I first saw how wretched us humans could be to each other. Remember Jake, just because someone is against evil, doesn't make him or her a good person.[76] This was a hard lesson for me to learn…Anyway I have no idea why I am telling you this. The sun reminded me of something I wrote when I was 19. I found it in one of my moleskins. For some reason I never included it in Yellow.

"The soft glowing abyss sizzled in orange and red hues. The water off the Indian Ocean swirled in ferocious torrents that echoed the lines emphasized in the clouds above us by the setting sun. Our eyes were open, and our mouths were closed. Our breathing was slight as if the sudden cough or hiccup would shatter the amber of the moment, we were caught in. We did not flinch for our youthful desire to feel all we could feel

---

[76] Hemingway, Ernest. Islands in the Stream

outweighed any other possible desire. Alone, but together we stood as frozen statues, our toes burying their way into the fine sand. We were terrified we would never be able to feel this way again, scared to look away from the sky for we knew in that moment we would see the world for what it truly was. At this very moment we would all cease to be children ever again. So, we fought as hard as we could. We resisted the urge to glance down and keep moving on with life. We held the second hand from moving by our eyes alone and what we realized was that even we had the power to stop time."

Have a beer for me. Pray I don't get lost, literally and figuratively, J. Levon.

Levon,

I am lost. Cecilia left me. She couldn't take my self-defeating attitude. She hated that I hated myself. I am not happy Levon. I need you to come home. I wait every day for another letter from you. I am stuck in this terrible cycle of monotonous bullshit. I am afraid I am losing my mind. What does losing your mind even feel like? The ocean keeps me grounded, but once the thundering sound of its waves disappear into the background, the pressures of friends, class, girls, social media, being connected all the fucking time drowns my senses. I need to learn how to disconnect.

I think too much Cecilia said. It is dangerous to think too deeply about life. It is even more dangerous to not think at all. I can't find the balance. It was only when I was with her, I could find that balance. She reminded me of the moron I was. I needed that in my life.

She will be my 'what-if girl.' My world has turned upside down like a river, which suddenly decided to flow the opposite direction. For though she was in my radius for such a small amount of time, she made a fierce impression. One strong enough to make a fossil imprint on my heart, only to be seen long after I am dead and the coldness inside of me flees like bats from a cave, as the sun finally sets. I will forever wander the underworld with my stone heart asking if anybody has seen the beautiful creature who is forever my what-if girl.

I need help Levon. I am not stable. I know you know what this feeling is like. I wish you could just call. I need my father. I even thought about going to church. Maybe there is a god? Maybe religion is real? Maybe my words are from some divine hand conducting my thoughts or maybe this is drunken stoned babble from a kid who thought he lived before he left his home? But maybe just maybe these are words of wisdom from a boy who loved to learn yet lived wildly enough to find himself where the wind blows warm and the beer is always cold. Maybe they come from a place where you can sleep late and love deeply with the only worry on your mind is who to love next. Maybe they come from a place where a smiling person is the norm. Maybe this is all a wish of a boy who never left home.

I am including something I wrote about a party the other day. I think you will enjoy it...

*** It was a complete weekend bender. All of us flying by the seat of our pants as if we were hanging off the back of a plane loving every stomach drop and tight turn, but just praying we wouldn't fall off. We had no guarantee on how the situation would come out but we knew it felt good at the time. And after three years at college I finally figured it out. Well, I figured it out for the next two weeks until another bender comes along and a new profound statement trickles from my drugged-up brain.

We were a volatile group. We numbed our brains together scared the few passing moments of sobriety wouldn't fulfill the moment enough. We were scared of what our brains may say to us. So, we sped them up, shut them down, slowed them to a turtle's pace. We yelled, screamed, laughed, fought, punched, threw shit in an attempt to find who we were. We wanted to feel, but we were counter-productive. Our whole lives we were told who we were. But we weren't what they told us. We were a blessed, over privileged generation that burned through time with no care to the present but what felt good. When you become retrospective on moments like this, it is easy to have regrets. At the same time, it is easy to have none. Moments in life are building blocks of personality. We are a compilation of who we meet and all we experience. If you do not experience anything how do you know you lived?

After pulling two Adderall induced all-nighters to get all of my work done. Not done well, but just complete. I decided I was too tired to go gallivanting around town with Brad.

Brad had the instincts of a 5-month-old puppy. First off... he only wanted to fuck. I mean I could think of worse addictions in the world but really it was all about getting his D into a V.

Sometimes his relentless pursuit was entertaining and sometimes it was frustrating. Though sometimes, I liked being dragged along on his adventures, as Brad always needed company the way women always went to the bathroom together.

He dragged you along to act as Tupperware… keeping the girls occupied until either he was done with the girl he was with or until he wanted the one you had been hanging out with.

See, this aspect of male friendships is extremely important because girls keep their friends around in a social setting to have an excuse to end relations with a guy if they were creeping. That's why girls always go to the bathroom together. It is simple societal cause and effect. Girls will never be alone, and if they are it is a red flag, but since they are never alone, a guy always needs a wingman. Some are good at it and some suck. I can hold my own depending on the girl, cause when wing-manning I don't try and prey on leftovers.

Not only did he want to fuck anything that walked but he also had the attention span of hamster on crack and the liver capacity of Fitzgerald. Needless to say the combination was terrifying… Beautifully terrifying because don't get me wrong, he was a crazy bastard, but he was our crazy bastard and none of us would change him. Because if anything Brad was like your puppy, he was a loyal bastard. He was always a loyal friend and he was true to himself, which is rare today. If you needed him, he was there. And he never pretended to be anything other than what he was. I always respected that. I gravitated towards realness.

So, I was playing DD. Or as we go, LDD aka "least drunk driver." I was driving everyone around with whiskey cup in hand putting to the back of my mind that drinking and driving was a crime or even frowned upon.

After dropping my roommates off at the bar, I headed back home to smoke two blunts and numb myself even more. With no care or thought of my surroundings or actions I filled every pleasurable sense in my weakened mind.

I was on my way to pick them up when I heard we were not going straight home but had to stop at the sorority house so Brad could try and round up a slut or two. Now, not to brag, but Vinny, Brad and I are no strangers to sorority houses, but what we walked into was an episode of the Real World. A house of blacked out, hormone ridden, anorexic, coked out girls (not women) with an attachment to drama like a fat kid had for cake. (Best cliché ever).

"She is a fucking klepto!" One girl shouted. (There is no need to differentiate their names or who they were. We caught up with a girl who had lived in our dorm

freshman year. She was the true definition of a smoke show, so she humored us by keeping us company while Brad coerced a girl to come back to our house. We eventually left around 3 a.m. and went home to a nice blunt and went to bed.

The next day when I finally came out of my coma around three in the afternoon it was the perfect time to hit happy hour at Chuckies's. Pitcher one...Pitcher two...Pitcher three. The afternoon went quickly as we all played pool and ate free chicken wings. No one was worrying about schoolwork. It was one of those moments that if you don't slow down and look around you will miss. It was one of those moments that you need to sit back and say, "if this isn't nice, I don't know what is?" (An ode to Kurt!)

After Chuckies's we were beginning to drag. We began drinking too early. So, what else were we supposed to do but buy as much cocaine we could afford...

The setting was not important as we drank anything in sight and snorted any white powder, we could get our hands on. Our friends were having a party and Chloe was there. Chloe was my former RA, that I used to hook up with. We had a good relationship, I think.

Regrets are scary fucking things to live with. They can simply pass by as bad memories. But every once in a while, one will stick. It will take your legs out from underneath you one day while waiting on the line at Dunkin Donuts waiting for your extra toasted everything bagel with cream cheese. By the time you get all the way back to your car and fumble with your keys for what seems like an eternity you feel a coldness trickle up your spine and all you can think about is that regret. You feel disappointment, shame and frustration. You quickly race through possibilities on how to redo this moment in your memory, but you realize you have done this already. By this point you have made it in the car, put your coffee in the awkwardly sized cup holder and got the key into the ignition. You either drive to work or turn around go home and indulge in whatever vice you so choose and life moves on. (This section was inspired by all your talks of regret).

I flew around the living room, playing drinking games as if I was betting my life savings. I went down the hall to take a well-deserved piss after best of 35 flip cup tournament. I saw Chloe as I wobbled to the loo.

Chloe was upset. I was not sure why. I never like to see anyone upset. I brought her downstairs in Robbie's house. They had an unoccupied living room with a couch. We talked for a while. I am not too sure what about. I remember trying to throw out big vocabulary, attempting to hide behind words. I blabbered relentlessly about my life's philosophy. It was all bullshit. I sat there throwing out Hank Moody, Hunter S. Thompson and Kurt Vonnegut quotes taking them as my own. I was ripping through whiskey and numb on cocaine. But she was smiling. I could feel her smile. The room was still dark because we were unable to find the light switch and also barely tried to find them. Something about the darkness, the night, that people drop their guard. In the night rules are allowed to be bent. It is a universal rule.

I made my move and knew it was on as I went from sitting beside her to thrusting my hips into position in front of her. She knew me well from the previous year. She knew my weaknesses. When someone pulls on the strings of my sweatshirt. When someone grabs my belt. I just love the touch, the feeling of someone there, of someone being close to you. I was longing for it. I needed it. So, I went looking for it.

We knew it was just going to be sex that night. As her back bent in ecstasy and we grappled at each other flesh, her perfect body wrapped around me, we knew it was a pure moment of modern-day hedonism. We were living for the pleasure. I was tired of being alone and she thought she had no sex appeal. She was sexy. We could solve both our problems with one night.

So, we went home.

Such fragile human beings we are...

After I finished, we finished... I sat back and realized I was doing what I swore I never would. I loved women, everything about them. Every curve, every shade, every flicker of their eyes made me fall in love even more. I couldn't help it. I fell in love three times a day. And when I saw Cecilia that upset, despite knowing she was just drunk and emotional, I wanted to make her feel better.

Pause...

As I read my work over, I realize a major mistake in my reporting. I wrote in the previous sentence, "And when I saw Cecilia that upset..." I said the wrong name. I fucked Chloe not Cecilia. If that isn't a sign of how fucked up this was, and a sign of my true feelings than I do not know what else could prove a better example. Sometimes I feel the best response in most situations is to say, "fuck it" and hope for the best.

It was simple; I was on the search for a woman, not women.[77]

Stoned and Lost,
Jacob

---

[77] The Game

Dear J,

I am alive and well. I know it has been months since you last heard from me... great job on the writing. You are doing what I knew you could do. I wish I gave you better words of wisdom. I wish I could tell you everything will be okay. I wish I could be there for you as you struggle. But Jake, this is your fight. The way we all must fight on our own. Just remember to laugh. The world is a funny place. I am rediscovering this. Do not worry about the world shitting on your doorstep. You are coming to your conclusions the way all-young men must. You are finding the world through your own illusions and mistakes. You need to live your own life and make your own mistakes, you need to go out into the wild and shake the world. I am only now discovering that I hid myself.

I wrote this the other night as I sat on a rooftop in Istanbul. It made me think of you.

It takes a coward to lie
It takes a coward to write
But both a brave man and
A coward are the same
For they both believe in doing the right things for
The wrong reasons
And the wrong things for
The right reasons
Both must live with the
Changing seasons

Sometimes I wonder... As these people fade in and out of my life, I wonder if they will remember me or if I will be just a single serving friend? I don't want to fade away Jake. I hate I have discovered all this too late in my life. Maybe that is the one piece of advice I can give you... that your stubborn ass can actually take and use. Don't wait to live. Though I may be alone at the moment, my heart is filled with you and Evie back home. How is that old hag anyway?

I don't know my next step, nor do I know yours, but remember I am with you. And know I keep you with me. I know you are afraid but use it Jake. Use that fear to drive you, don't let it bury you. And lay off the fucking cocaine you idiot.

Always move forward Sport,
J.H.

Levon,

I am realizing something. I don't even know your first name. Is that weird? What does the J and the H stand for? How have I known you almost six years now and I don't know your name. I am realizing there is so much about you I don't know. I don't know about the room. Tell me about the room. Remind me of home. Remind me of Lotus Lane. It is my happy place. Bring me back to my happy place.

Not a night or morning goes by when I don't think about where you are and what you are doing. Evie is good. She came to visit last week. Her last son was married but she didn't go to the wedding. He didn't invite her. I promise if I ever get married you two will be there. I want to see you grow old. Even older than you are now. I tried to fix things with Cecilia. She isn't having any of it. I graduate soon. I am scared, like usual. My anxiety is boiling over. I don't know what to do next. I think it is time you come home. I want to hear all about the adventures. When you come home can we go on adventures together?

I wrote a poem I thought you would like.

You aren't who you are supposed to be
Locked in craven silence
The raven cries
Scared of the chance
The child lies
Break out goddamnit
Scream goddamnit
Happy but jaded
Happy and you hate it
I don't have the secret

I just tell you what I see
And you are not who you are supposed to be
Don't sell yourself short
Remember the child within
Remember the feeling of your first summer swim
The feeling of grass between your toes
And dirt on your chin
Remember running in circles
Not caring who would win
You lost sight of you
Find your happy place
And possibly those bad thoughts will erase
So take off the mask
And take a deep breath

Come home Levon,
Jake.

Dear Jake,

    It was for her. In case she ever came home. I told her I would give her the home she always wanted. Ophelia always knew. She knew I wanted her back the minute I let her go, she knew I needed her so badly that I bought a home for her. I put myself in our dream, unfortunately I was dreaming alone. She decided to never come back, she decided she couldn't trust me. But I always kept faith. I always stayed hopeful she would realize there was no one else for us but each other.

    Everything in that room was for her. The painting station, the knitting area, the dog bowls for Madeline, the way the porch overlooked the ocean. It was all for her to come home to. She was incredibly artistic, although never openly admitted her ability. Her art was a release for the anxiety that strangled her every day. I always wanted to be a cure for her anxiety and did everything possible to curb its attack. The room became a time capsule of our relationship and my love for her. After I finished setting the room up, I locked it and didn't reenter for 10 years. When I did, an overwhelming uneasiness crept into my bones and a chill crawled up my spine. I shuttered and fear slapped me mercilessly in the face. The room, which once held my passion and love, now became a beacon of terror. I promised myself to lock the door and never reenter.

I still have a heart that beats, and I need to go after all I left her for in the first place. I have always had a vagabond soul, a "gypsy heart," Ophelia used to tell me. I will keep her with me everywhere I go. I will keep her in my heart as my feet pump the sidewalks of foreign nations. Remember, I am in your heart as well Jake. All those you love will forever stay with you. You can hear me in your words and in your mind. Walk fast Jake. Love with your heart. Burn with passion and the world will fall at your feet. You have a gift and you need to use it. Art is meant to be shared[78] and you have something I wish I possessed and that is the dream to actually be better than what you were brought into this earth as. Be better every day and there is nothing you can't do.

"I went out to the hazel wood,
Because a fire was in my head,
And cut and peeled a hazel wand,
And hooked a berry to a thread;
And when white moths were on the wing,
And moth-like stars were flickering out,
I dropped the berry in a stream
And caught a little silver trout.

When I had laid it on the floor
I went to blow the fire a-flame,
But something rustled on the floor,
And someone called me by my name:
It had become a glimmering girl
With apple blossom in her hair
Who called me by my name and ran
And faded through the brightening air.

Though I am old with wandering

---

[78] Passive voice was rare for Levon at this stage in his writing. It made me nervous.

Through hollow lands and hilly lands,
I will find out where she has gone,
And kiss her lips and take her hands;
And walk among long dappled grass,
And pluck till time and times are done,
The silver apples of the moon,
The golden apples of the sun."[79]

Jake, I know you want me to tell you I am coming home. But life has never been easy, and it won't get any easier. I have taught you all I know. I will return eventually but I will not lie to you and give you a time. You still have Evie. You will be okay Sport. Trust your heart. I am there.

Your Friend,
Levon.

---

[79] Yeats, W.B.

CHAPTER ELEVEN

"All the art of living lies in a fine mingling of letting go and holding on."

--Henry Ellis

Years passed and seasons changed. College flew by, the girls whipped past in a blur of indifferent faces. Levon and I continued our letters as he gallivanted around the world looking for something. His letters became shorter and more cryptic. It was obvious his mind was fleeing him faster than his body could quit on him.

No one controls destiny or fate. Creating your future is an illusion people like to tell you. We have no true control and it wasn't until the day Levon's letter showed up that I understood this fully. We have about as much control over our future as a convict has over his sentencing.

I was 26 and haven't seen Levon in almost seven years. Evie had become my surrogate mother. Most people in my life believed she was my mother. All my romantic relationships failed. They all said my heart and mind were somewhere else. I have no idea what that means. I just think I didn't give them the undivided attention they all so desperately yearned for.

It had been almost eight months since I last heard from Levon. All I knew is that he had boarded a boat somewhere around the Maldives and hoped to sail to Australia. Then I received a letter... It was a Tuesday.

Dear Jake,

If it weren't for second chances we would all be alone.[80] If only she knew. If only she knew how much I fell apart. If only she knew why I truly left. It was never a question of falling out of love. I did it because I loved her so dearly, I couldn't hurt her anymore. I had to lie about my reasons otherwise she would have never accepted my breakup and tried to fix herself.

Don't you get it?

No one knew how I fell apart. How I cried myself to sleep, woke up in night terrors and cold sweats. No one knew that I fucked anything that walked, hoping it would put a band aide on my wounded heart. It only opened the wound more. I didn't want to live. No one knew how I broke down and went to therapy. No one knew how my blood pressure went into stage-2 hypertension. No one knew about the suicide attempt. The multiple attempts. I never knew what to do with emotions.

If only she knew what I believed to have been a sacrifice and not what she saw as a selfish, immature and hasty decision. I never fell out of love. I fell so deeply in love I broke myself to help her. I lied to her, to help her. I shot the gun and stood in front of the bullet. I know it sounds fucked up. I just played the game, I didn't choose it.

Don't you get it now Sport? I destroyed myself for one. There can be no more noble, selfish, immature, idiotic, decision a man can make.

"Fleeing from a love that still pursued him, he had become a wanderer in strange countries."[81] And I continue to wander. Don't think I say his because I am unhappy. I am just doing all I know how to do. That is run. I am running. I have thought a lot about my death. It is inevitable, I guess.

I hope you don't hate me the way she hates me. I don't even know why or how I am still talking and thinking about her. I hope this letter finds you in good spirits. I have no more words for you Jake. Just know I am proud, and I love you.

Levon.

He was doing what all old people do when they say goodbye. I knew Levon well enough to know when he was saying goodbye. But for how long, and why now? I got a sinking feeling in my stomach. I wrote

---

[80] Isakov, Gregory, Allen. Second Chances.
[81] Wolfe, Thomas. You Can't Go Home Again.

back ten different letters. Levon told me he loved me. He couldn't have been in a good spot. I appreciated the story he told of Ophelia but at his point, without knowing more about the two, thinking about their relationship was a futile task.

I waited for a response. A year went by. Two years. I was a teacher in Boston, working with inner city children trying to save the world one crack baby at a time. Not only did I have to help educate, but I had to help teach people how to be parents. Sometimes, I think that all people should be born sterile and have to go through an application process to have children.

Still there was silence. Maybe he died? I had no idea. I wrote daily hoping he would show up at my apartment. Anytime something was out of place in my world, I thought it was Levon playing a trick on me. I hoped he was still out there with the sun shining down on his leathered skin as he sailed through waves and the salt water splashed over him. I pictured his smile as he took deep breaths of the crisp morning air in the jungles.

About a year and a half after the final letter, I came home to two men in grey suits standing at my door. It was a Tuesday. It rained for a week and a crow was following me everywhere I went. I was so preoccupied with the state tests that were coming up, I didn't pay attention to the fact I stopped writing Levon. When your words go unanswered for so long, you can only keep up so much hope. When you know you will not get an answer, then it is best to stop asking questions. The memories of Levon never left, but no longer was he part of my life. Lotus Lane was a distant past...a faraway memory of childhood. Before the formal suit-wearing clones uttered a word, I knew why they were at my apartment. Still, I let them speak, hoping I had committed a federal crime or something.

"Jake? Jake Roberts? Formally of 16 Lotus Lane in Branford, Connecticut?" The chubby one asked.

"Yes."

"Do you know a Jacob Helms Levon?"

"Sorry...who? I don't know a Jacob Helms...Jacob? What the..."

"Sir we are here to tell you about Mr. Levon. What is your relation to him?"

"Huh...why? What is this about?"

It was one of those situations in life when you knew the answers... you knew the outcome, but you played dumb in hopes it was different than what your heart told you. I played along until the reality set in firmly. I knew I lost my father. I knew Levon was gone. They kept talking but I heard nothing. The world crashed down around me. I don't remember anything that happened in the next couple days. PTSD I told myself. I don't remember how they told me Levon died.

I assumed it was inevitable. He was almost 70 years old and neither Evie nor I heard from Levon in almost two years. If he was alive, how could he not reach out by this point?

I was told I needed to head back to Lotus Lane to meet with lawyers.

When I arrived back to Lotus Lane, I wasn't sure what to expect. It was like walking into your girlfriend's family party. They could be friendly, or they could be hostile. We didn't know about any family, or who else would show up. It was just Evie and I. Evie was only there because she was evicted from her apartment and had nowhere else to go. I still didn't understand how they even had my information. It was truly the blind leading the blind, and I walked aimlessly amongst the shadows of unanswered questions trying not to accept the reality.

Maybe Ophelia would be there? When I drove past the house in my blue Jetta I borrowed from my roommate in order to make the impulse trip, the house still looked freshly painted, with its exterior spotless from the elements and the previous year's hurricane. Evelyn was obviously still hard at work in the gardens, which were immaculate.

Evie was there waiting for me when I pulled into the driveway. Her eyes puffy with tears and her hair in the usual messy bun.

She asked me if I was scared to go back into the house.

"Not one bit," I said. "There is no reason to be afraid of the dead. One should only be afraid of the living. When was the last time you heard about the dead attacking someone?"

Evie didn't respond... just gave a placid smile.

I climbed the long dark steps up to the ever-imposing front porch. The door creaked open just as the first time I ever opened it. The house was empty. No funeral, no one there to say goodbye. No Ophelia. The lawyers, still in grey suits, handed me a letter. I opened a sealed envelope. They said, "according to Mr. Levon, everything about his estate, is sealed in this. No one has heard from him in over two years and the bank is looking to collect." I have no idea what they were collecting on; I thought the house was paid in full but leave it to a greedy institution to declare someone dead in order to make financial ends meet. Corporate world makes me sick. Anyway, I didn't ask questions…too many emotions were involved in the situation. To my surprise it wasn't an official Will from the law office but a letter from Levon. I actually wasn't surprised at all.

Jake,

Find my Zanzibars chest. It will answer all your questions. I am sorry I couldn't answer them when I was around. I still had a lot of growing up to do Sport. The house is yours. Take care of Kurt and Ernest. Take care of Evie. Remember, whatever you do, be the best, and love with all you got because when you boil life down… work, money, homes, and everything else in between, we are remembered by the impression we leave on others. So, love them, even if they don't love you back. I have no more words for the world. It is your turn now son.

A thing of beauty is a joy forever:
It's loveliness increases; it will never
Pass into nothingness; but still will keep[82]

Your Friend and Father,
Jacob Helms Levon

---

[82] Keats, John. Endymion

CHAPTER TWELVE

Out of the blue, beyond any cause you can trace, you'll suddenly realize things are not how you perceived them to be at all. For some reason, you will no longer be the person you believed you once were. You'll detect slow and subtle shifts going on all around you, more importantly shifts in you. Worse, you'll realize it's always been shifting, like a shimmer of sorts, a vast shimmer, only dark like a room. But you won't understand why or how. You'll have forgotten what granted you this awareness in the first place.

You might try then, as I did, to find a sky so full of stars it will blind you again. Only no sky can blind you now. Even with all that iridescent magic up there, your eye will no longer linger on the light, it will no longer trace constellations. You'll care only about the darkness and you'll watch it for hours, for days, maybe even for years, trying in vain to believe you're some kind of indispensable, universe-appointed sentinel, as if just by looking you could actually keep it all at bay. It will get so bad you'll be afraid to look away, you'll be afraid to sleep.

Then no matter where you are, in a crowded restaurant or on some desolate street or even in the comforts of your own home, you'll watch yourself dismantle every assurance you ever lived by. You'll stand aside as a great complexity intrudes, tearing apart, piece by piece, all of your carefully conceived denials, whether deliberate or unconscious. And then for better or worse you'll turn, unable to resist, though try to resist you still will, fighting with everything you've got not to face the thing you most dread, what is now, what will be, what has always come before, the creature you truly are, the creature we all are, buried in the nameless black of a name.

-- *Mark Z. Danielewski, House of Leaves*

You get to a point in life when you are just plain angry. You don't know why, you just are. There is no real rationale, although, if you tried to understand the foundation and cause of this anger the answer doesn't come, so the world just seems grey. Some days the sun is a little brighter than the last, but overall this sullen feeling overwhelms your every being. Eventually, as Levon used to always tell me, the sun will rise and those days end.

At this point in my life I had only known disappointment. However, for two years I was happy. Despite the arguments, the frustrations and confusion during the time I lived at 28 Lotus Lane with Levon and Evie, I was happy. Those thoughts are what kept me going. I hold on to those happy thoughts and pray they will come again.

I don't do well with death. I know that. I knew that. So, when I found out Levon died, I knew I had to find my happy thoughts. I quit my job and moved into my new home on Lotus Lane. I saw Levon everywhere I went in that home. His presence was overwhelming. It took a while to get used to it. Kurt and Ernest barked incessantly at the fireplace, despite no fire. The house lacked a certain light when he left.

Two months after moving back into the old white colonial, Evie was out in the garden and I was on the front porch drinking my morning coffee when suddenly, warmth rushed over me. I had felt this warmth before. I wasn't sad anymore. People say happiness is a choice. Yes, this is true if you are someone who can control his or her feelings, but what Levon taught me is that no one can control feelings…they just are, and you live with them. Then, it hit me. I knew where I once felt this warmth. I shot up like a horse in the Derby and sprinted, dropping my mug to the ground smashing it into a thousand shards that skipped across the wood porch. I swung the front door open. It creaked louder than ever before, and I bounded forward like an Olympic triple jumper. I leapt the stairs, skipping a step with each jump until I got to the locked room. I paused in front of the looming white door. I had not been in the room since Evie and I broke into it. The room held too many questions, too many fears for me to ever revisit since my last journey into its presence, as if it were a living breathing entity in the home. I was always terrified of the unknown it kept. However, the fear dissipated as I stood on the threshold once again. I knew it was for

Ophelia but to me, it was not my burden to hold for Levon. We all have our burdens; I couldn't hold both his and Ophelia's. I didn't bother looking for the key and bull rushed the door. It didn't open with the first shoulder strike, but I wound up, stepped back again and rammed it, separating my shoulder in the process. The door swung open smashing against the wall. The curtains blew violently with the sudden burst of wind that rushed through the room. I saw it. I knew what Levon meant. His Zanzibar's chest was in the room.

Levon had a book called *Zanzibar's Chest* written by Aiden Hartley that he always referred to, but I never saw it in his collection. I knew the premise of the book. He mentioned it was the story of a young boy discovering who his father was through the writings he left in his Zanzibar's Chest. The old wooden chest in the back-left corner of the room slightly covered by the long white curtains, with ornate animals carved into it was still sitting there just like when I saw it many years ago. It was his Zanzibar's Chest.

No longer afraid, I walked confidently into the room directly over to the chest. My mind spun at what it could hold. How could it answer my questions? I had no idea what to expect. It could be anything from Levon's old baseball cards to precious gold from Blackbeard's treasure. Evie stood behind me with her apron still around her waist. She ran up after me when she heard the smashing of the glass and shattering of the door jam. She stayed silent. I bent down and gently rubbed the elephant by the brass clasp on the front of the chest. Its edges were splintered and the top scratched. This chest lived a life before it held a life. I flipped open the lid.

It was filled with pictures, receipts, napkins, and endless pages of writing. It was impossible at first to sort through it all. There was no reason to the disarray of writing. Some of it was dated. Some of his words were written on the back of receipts or bar coasters. Then Evie said in a soft voice, "It's her... It's their story..." Just as she finished her sentence, I lifted a piece of paper that said, "Stolen on 55th and 3rd" by J.H. Levon. Evie fell to her knees and sobbed. She grabbed me in pain, in happiness, in love... We found their story. Levon had the last word. What follows is the story of Ophelia and Levon. I hope you find as much hope, inspiration, happiness and love in it as I did. Evie and I spent the next year sorting through every piece of writing in the chest and put together the story. This is for Levon. This is for Ophelia. This is for anyone who loves love. This is for anyone who desires the unknown and hopes for brighter tomorrows. Yes, the world is filled with sadness and despair, but also so much beauty. Just as I found love unexpectedly in my pseudo family, so did Levon and Ophelia. It doesn't matter how long you love, but how deeply and passionately you love. I hope I made Levon proud because there isn't a day I don't wake up and try and live a life the old granite looking man wouldn't smile at, even just a little smirk.

     It's impossible to include all of Levon's writing, so we did our best to choose carefully the sections that show the entire relationship. It is impossible to encompass any relationship truly and fully in a couple of chapters. It is difficult to follow Levon's writing. He rotates between his story and an interior voice. For a man who wrote constantly, and read constantly, and knew so much about grammar and literature…by god, he had the worst fucking grammar I ever witnessed…Evie and I did our best to put together a coherent story encapsulating the sometimes-tumultuous love story of Ophelia and Levon. It is obvious Levon was under the influence of a substance while writing much of this story. It is unclear over how many years he wrote these scattered thoughts. Many times, it seems as if there were multiple authors due to the sporadic prose and change of voice throughout. However, it is still a beautiful story.

Levon…This is dedicated to you. You are finally a published author.

Stolen on 55th and 3rd

By. J.H. Levon

Foreword:

"This is not a love story. This is a true story."

How do I begin? How do I tell you every little detail through my eyes? How do I explain the feelings, the little intricacies, which made us beautiful?

At some point in someone's life they stop believing in miracles. Some people can tell you the exact moment they stopped. Some can tell you the exact moment they started. It could have been when they found out Santa doesn't exist, or it could have been when their first love broke their heart. Some people stopped believing in miracles after five months of praying for their father's pancreatic cancer to go away and he still passed. Some people discovered miracles do exist in their lives when they made it out of a war or survived a car accident. Miracles are talked about, but never fully defined. There are good miracles and bad miracles. Miracles could also just be coincidences, a series of fortunate or unfortunate events, or just an explanation with the benefit of captain hindsight.

I never thought about my stance on the whole miracle debate. Until one night, I was sitting in my 8 ft. by 9 ft. room in the midtown Manhattan putting off grad schoolwork and trying not to think about the lack of money in my bank account, when I received a text. It was from a girl, a girl whose story is about to be told. As I read the text I began to slightly tear because I knew what this text solidified. It told me I was in love and someone was in love with me. In that moment I believed in miracles. Not because it was love. That shit happens every day. It was because of the story behind the love. It was a story that, although I lived it, I remembered thinking, this shit doesn't happen in real life. I remember a feeling of no control as the world around me took over. I had no control as fate made situation after situation more and more beautiful.

To believe in the miracle I am about to write, you need to believe in true love as well. You need to believe in pure and honest love between two individuals. You need to believe that unconditional love is able to exist in this cold world.

She made me promise. She made me promise that I wouldn't stop writing. She made me promise that I would accomplish my dreams. I broke her heart. This is for her. This is for the girl who taught me what love was. This is for the girl who taught me what unconditional meant. This is to mend her heart. This is to mend my heart. This is for everyone who ever felt regret. This is for all those people who wish they could have a do-over. This is for Ophelia.

CHAPTER ONE: COLUMBIA

"Here we are, trapped in the amber of our moment, there is no why."

                                                                --Kurt Vonnegut Jr.

It was that clink, the clatter, the pitter patter, the heels on the floor, the toots, the hoots, the shouts, the cries, the laughter, the yearning, that deep burn, the scorning, the hatred, the soulless, the soulful, the hallows of the gallows, the empty streets, the darkened alleys, the bright billboards, the empty souls of the intoxication generation and the helplessly hopeful that kept me going. It was how these hopeless souls wanted to better the world. They seemed so angry but didn't know why. These are the things that made me fall in love with the city. These are the reasons I took my chances and made my cliché journey to the bright lights and plunge myself into the depths of the city whose only goal since its founding was to make money. But it wasn't the money I wanted, nor the fame, but the satisfaction that comes with feeling like you are the center of the universe. I wanted to feel important. I wanted to howl with the best of them. I wanted to love all there was to love and do it with no inhibitions or shame.

I didn't expect what was to happen next. I didn't expect to find myself acting this way. I moved to New York City for graduate school to get my masters in secondary education for English and History. I was attending Columbia University. I was an angry young man.[83] On the outside I was happy but so much bothered me deep down. And Lord knows I can't complain/ But even when I do it feels the same/ I'm getting high just to fight the lows/ Cause that's all I know.[84] It is the futility of man that we have such dualities. After I graduated the University of Rhode Island, I traveled through Europe, worked at the 9/11 Memorial and moved back home. Then the itch began. The itch you get whenever you have been in one place too long. I had this vision for what my life should look like at 23.

---

[83] Joel, Billy. Angry Young Man.
[84] Cole, Jermaine

You bet your ass living at home was not in that image. I eventually felt I needed to get out. Actually, my parents said I had to go. I needed to do something for myself. I decided to become a teacher. Why, I still do not really know to this day. Maybe it is because I felt the need to give? Maybe, it is because I wanted to leave this world a better place? Maybe, it is because I thought I would be good at it? Maybe, I just wanted to have weekends and summers off? We all say we want to make the world a better place but do we really?

The only way I could describe why I wanted to become a teacher goes back to when I was a child. I remember driving up to my Nana and Papa's house. My mother parked our red mini-van in the driveway, as the white house loomed over us. She slowly leaned to the back of the van from the driver's seat. My dad never drove. My mom always left her buckle on. I never knew why she didn't take it off when she tried to turn around. She would strain her body against the strap, stretching every bit of its fabric, just so she could make eye contact with the four of us jammed into the back of the van. It would have been much easier. I guess in hindsight it was more of a threat she would turn the bus around[85] unless we all listened to her every word. Knowing her I bet she never thought twice about the seatbelt. She placed her hand on the back of the passenger seat like she was driving in reverse and said, "Just remember, leave this place better than the way you found it." That is the way I feel about the life I live. No matter what I do, or who I meet, I want to leave this place or that person better than the way I found them.

I kept Timothy's journal with me at all times. It bothered me that I never read the ending. I don't like to finish books. Something weird I discovered about myself later in life. I kept rereading it. It was a drug. The brown leather notebook I found in pristine condition four years ago under that waiting room chair in Dulles Airport was now in tatters after having more liquor spilt on it than the floor at a rap album release party. When I found Timothy's Journal two years ago, I knew it would haunt me.[86] I think I like to be haunted.

---

[85] Billy Madison

[86] Confirmation the journal Levon, aka Drew, found in Yellow was real. I have searched the house looking for the journal but never found it.

Sometimes we stumble across things in life that
we know immediately, no matter how much we want
to let go, will linger and crawl up inside us for
the rest of our lives. This could be an object, a
moment or even a person. We are all haunted in
some way. But I can't stop looking at it, hoping it will drive me from this
spiral, like a fix after a long stint of sobriety. So, I have been keeping my
own journal, in hopes it can cure my neuroses. I hope it worked for him.

The semester started off like all the rest until I walked into the
classroom. There were the usual first glances at the cute girls in the class.
There was one…she struck me immediately. One of those women who you
take a second glance because there is no way god could create something so
beautiful. She immediately stunned me with her long blonde hair that curled
voraciously in front of her freshly tanned skin. Not a blemish in sight, her
chromatic blue eyes stood out like the first star in a cloudy night. She was
so damn hard to ignore it was almost sickening. The class was extremely
small, so I had to try and play it off like I wasn't staring at her. I don't
believe in that fairy tale love at first sight
crap Disney tries to shove down our throats. But
I do believe we are drawn to certain people. I
was drawn to her. It was an attraction when you
knew immediately your life was never going to be
the same after meeting this person. It was a
click. I believe in clicks.

Our professor was Jan. I would describe her as a real
whippersnapper of a lady. She stood 5 feet tall at best and had short brown
hair. She was a lesbian strung out on women's rights. I later found
out she was actually a research professor for
racial equality in public schools. She opened the class
with the usual corny icebreakers. I hate first days of anything, especially
when icebreakers are on the agenda, but I couldn't wait to begin so I could
learn her name. I was getting much better at my rapport with women. At
least I thought. It was easy for me to tell who was single, who was
complicated, who was in a serious relationship, or who was in the beginning
of first loves. However, after one full class, I couldn't figure this one out.
But I do know I will never forget the first time I saw her. Either way…I let
it go, first day jitters out the way and I moved on with my life. Life
consisted of either a burrito with guac, yes, I know it is
extra, or street meat, preferably lamb and chicken over rice with white

sauce and extra hot sauce, yes, I know it is spicy. This would be followed up with a joint, a fat lip, quick jerk off session and bed.

At the time I was moving into my first apartment in Manhattan with two of my best friends from high school Patrick and Rick. The fourth roommate was Rick's college roommate, Kevin. He was a nice kid, but he definitely felt like an outcast once Patrick and I moved in. Kevin had a serious case of only child syndrome. He always meant well, but never saw his rudeness. However, Rick, Patrick and I had been through everything together. The first time we were suspended, got drunk, got high, crashed a car, kissed a girl, fucked a girl, had a girlfriend, fell in love, threw up from drinking, snuck out the house, heartbreak. You name it; we were there for it. So, when we moved in with each other, we were already brothers. They were my family.

Life was moving as fast as life moves in Manhattan. The lights never turned off and the caffeine among other stimulants kept flowing. It was the pulse, as many artists have said before. I am not an artist. There was a feeling that you could never go to sleep because you would miss something.

Rick had a girlfriend named Stephanie. We all loved Steph, she was just a genuine sweet girl who grew up a couple towns away from us. Kevin had a 26-year-old girlfriend named Kayla. She was nice but never picked up on social cues. She pretty much lived with us. I had no time for her, but I was always nice because she was just socially retarded (I know not politically correct) and didn't mean to be as rude as she was. They were a match made in heaven. Patrick had just broken up with his psychotic girlfriend on their second go-around since high school. She came over the first week we moved in and she went absolutely ape-shit, breaking things in the apartment, even tossing a chair through his door. Now, newly single, Patrick was on the prowl. I was still caught up in past loves and truly didn't pay attention to girls when we went out. They all called me a pussy for this, I could care less. I guess I didn't have as much testosterone flowing through my bones as they did. I don't know what it is, but so many people today are fucking stupid. I won't say all, but so many that it is nauseating. Someone has to say it. My generation may have invented Facebook but we also invented molly, EDM music, and the quarter life crisis. Maybe I am just programmed differently?

School was flying by just as life was. I was student teaching in Chinatown at a school with 70% Asians and the rest a mix of Hispanic and

Black students. As far as public middle schools in NYC, this school was very good. It took a while to get comfortable in the school. My cooperating teacher was a real hard-ass and liked things done his way. It was tough to read him, but we got along all right.

The students in my classes at Columbia were all the same. We would all get drinks together after class to bitch about our students and our teachers. I hung out with the same crew. The most beautiful was Ophelia from Pelham; there was Beth a rich horseback riding Long Island Jew, Cynthia our token older prophet from Minnesota who lived in more homes than a Peruvian nomad, Jackie the 32-year-old Korean dry cleaner's son and Cross Fit enthusiast, and Justin the white, DMX loving, Bronx boy who only dated black chicks. After two minutes of talking to Beth I could tell she had a boyfriend, and during our second week of classes I found out Ophelia was engaged, and that was that. It is the way life goes, but I could not bring myself to wreck another home.[87] I have been really good since high school at not doing this. My heart couldn't take the guilt anymore.

Before classes Ophelia and I would go to Starbucks and get coffee. There was something about her. We clicked, we laughed. It was a constant battle of wits. We challenged each other. There was no filter, there was no mask, it was pure. It was honest. We both were extremely interested in what the other had to say, never backing down. The mask was gone with Ophelia. With her I was me, and that is rare in the world we live in. I was the witty, quick, smart kid that eluded me with other girls. However, she was engaged, and I respected that. She talked about her fiancé Bradley all the fucking time. Why wouldn't she? She was in love. There was something about us. I didn't think she felt it, why would she? Why would a beautiful woman, who was taller than me, engaged, and had her whole life planned out ever take a second look at the funny short kid in class?

Then one-day fate (Or miracle?) stepped in. While in Jan's class, we were all going over the facilitation's we had left. At least once during the semester, a pair of students had to facilitate a lesson for the class. I was working with a kid who I am sure had Asperger's named Daniel. He was the heaviest breather I have ever met and sounded like he was concussed every time he talked, smacking his lips and using an obnoxious amount of "umms." But then Jan said, "Levon you are going to work with Ophelia." I was fine with it. Rather work with a cute girl than Snorlax.[88]

---

[87] Confirmation of info about "Drew" in <u>Yellow</u> having sex with his high school QB's girlfriend.
[88] A Pokémon.

So, Ophelia and I discussed meeting up at my apartment and figuring out what we would teach. We were going to be teaching how to use a novel to teach history. It was an interesting topic.

November 17th

> "First you take a drink, then the drink takes a drink, then the drink takes you."[89]

I rolled over in bed to see two of my good girlfriends from high school passed out drunk next to me. The night before consisted of two bottles of fireball, drunk Jenga, seven whiskey gingers, three racks of Bud Light, two bumps of coke, a rock of molly, and a dance off with what I thought was a Mexican street gang but was really two street cart attendants yelling at me because I stole a Gatorade and a pretzel. My head was spinning. Then I got a text. It was Ophelia. I rolled over to my friends and said, "I am about to break up an engagement, I don't want to, but it is going to happen." They thought I was joking, so we all laughed. I was joking when I said it, but I sunk back into my bed and I stopped laughing. Chills ran up my back. I knew she was different. This was different.

After a couple hours of nursing a hangover with a bowl hit and some pizza...

She showed up to the apartment and everybody was hung-over watching football. You have to love Sunday Funday. My head was still spinning from the fireball shots at 4 am the night before. Yet, the first thing she said was, "Let's get a drink before we do any work." I thought, "well fuck it, it can't hurt." The only people I want to hang out with are the ones who know the best cure for a hangover is more booze. I still didn't know the area around my apartment that well, so we went to the original PJ Clarkes on 55th and 3rd. Dave Matthews wrote a song about it, when he stumbled into a past love at the bar. P.J. Clarkes had old-school 1950's vibe with checkered table clothes and waiters in white shirts and black bow ties. They sat us at table 53. Buddy Holly proposed to his wife at table 53. His picture hung behind our table. In the dim light you saw him twisting his beautiful wife around in a passionate embrace.

She ordered Pino Grigio, I ordered a Blue Moon. We each got clam chowder and an order of onion strings to share. Before we knew it the night took off, as the night so often does after the third drink. As her long

---

[89] Fitzgerald, F. Scott.

hair swooped around in endless waves, her blue eyes paralyzed the world around her. Only she moved, only she spoke. We shot into our usual battle of wits. We warred back and forth with quotes, book references and subtle backhanded comments. Our sarcasm was pushed to the limits. She would bite her bottom lip. I burnt my tongue on a potato in the chowder. She warned me they retain heat. After she saw me wincing in pain, she smirked out of the side of her face and politely said, "I told you so, you should learn I am always right." She was so cute as she politely insulted you. It was a dangerously beautiful skill to possess.

The world was bringing us closer together, but the reality of life kept us separated by a 3-foot table and a diamond ring on her left hand. Then I felt my stomach drop when the Paul Simon song came on. 'Me and Julio down by the School Yard' blasted through the ancient speakers. I reached up in joy, she grabbed my hand and in that moment, I felt empty as we stopped in silence. Did it feel so good because it was so wrong to be this way with her? Or did it feel so right because she had made a mistake and I was supposed to be sitting across from her. Was this another dancing lesson from God or were we both caught in a moment of adolescent weakness? It happened quickly. It happened without either of us knowing it.

She looked at me like no one ever has, before or since. She was screaming from her underbelly that she is damaged and needed help. She didn't want or need help... she just wanted what we all want. She needed someone to listen to her. She needed assurance she wasn't alone in this too big world. She needed to know that hope was not some cliché picturesque idea made up by people who had nothing else in their lives. She wanted love. She wanted to be understood. She needed someone to believe in her.

Ophelia stole my heart at 55th and 3rd. She stole it and refused to give it back. We clicked too well. She felt it too. When she was with me the world stopped its commotion and she became the center of my universe. She stole my heart that night and refused to give it back. She was taking all she wanted and gave all she could.

Under the dim lights she began a beautifully orchestrated blast of questions and statements, barely giving me time to respond.

"I deserved more," she told me.

"I am too nice," she said.

"Why don't you have a girlfriend," she asked?

"Why do I feel this way with you," she questioned?

"Where were you a year ago?

"I need you," she didn't say.

For what we felt in our hearts was impossible, for she was promised to another. She did not belong to me. She did not belong to us. Again, I found another girl who I was not allowed to have. Again, I was lost but this time I was not alone.

She questioned her fate. Was she making the right decisions? I tried to be supportive. I tried to be nice but something in my gut said she was making a mistake. Something was there. She was in my life for a reason.

We left the bar slightly intoxicated as she lit up a cigarette. It was misting out as the smoke cut through the tiny raindrops. The walk back to my apartment wasn't far. As we walked, we constantly swayed into each other. My oldest sister used to do this when we were children. I hated it then. I loved it now. The Madoff building lingered over the top of us. We continued to battle in dialogue as our words outpaced our strut.

We went straight to my room to work on our class project. She immediately jumped in my bed smiling from the slight buzz that comes after three glasses of Pino and a Marlboro light.

Something was different about the whole situation. Yes, an engaged girl was sitting on my bed blasting country music and laughing as if she hadn't laughed in the past decade. She flew from topic to topic like a skipping PowerPoint presentation. However, I just let her do her own thing and laughed it off. I needed to watch every single thing she did. I just let her be her and life went on in a beautifully orchestrated series of miracles.

"Behind every exquisite thing that existed, there was something tragic."[90]

I should have expected it. I am not sure what it was about me that girls tended to unload their deepest secrets. I know everybody has a dark side. I am well aware everybody has a story. No one can live to be 23 years old and not have a tragedy already in his or her life. If you ever come across someone who says they have never experienced uncontrollable sadness or anger over something by the time they are 23, you need to run. Run and

---

[90] Wilde, Oscar. The Picture of Dorian Grey

hide, for they may be from another planet. We are human and we all live on the same roller coaster.

I can't remember now, as I write this story what we were even talking about at that moment. I know it was not *Red Scarf Girl* or how to use a novel to teach history… Either way, it didn't matter because the world stopped briefly. It was warm in the room when she said it. She didn't really segway into it. She didn't really give me full warning.

"I had an abortion a month ago." She said waiting for a reaction…

The rest of that conversation will forever stay between Ophelia and I. No pen, pencil, keyboard, chalk or hammer and chisel will know that conversation. Some things in life are meant to be private.

She ended with, "I am 23 and about to get married, but this was a decision I had to make."

Ophelia spoke maturely about the situation. In her mind it was a necessary step. In her mind she was not ready. They weren't ready.

Then she acted out the abortion, leaning back, legs in the air, with sound and everything. That was a little strange, but for some reason comical as well, in a sick a twisted way. It didn't bother me. Two people shouldn't be this close, so soon. But we were just comfortable from the start. We had a flow between us that was rare in two people who have only known each other for 3 months.

When she left, she had a look in her eye as I closed the door. It was a look that said, "I am sorry I just put that on you." She stumbled over her words as she walked out the door. When Ophelia got back to her car, she immediately texted apologizing for "putting so much on me." She apologized for being "weird."

For some reason I couldn't judge her. This was just another layer. Stuck. She is stuck in my mind.

November 20th

From that day on there wasn't a moment I didn't think about her laugh, her smile the way her eyes glowed in the bar rooms. We spoke incessantly, never giving each other a break I told her to 'dream of the angels' before she fell asleep each night. She hid her phone from her fiancé and lied to him about her whereabouts. We never kissed; we never did anything inappropriate…we were able to love without any of the societal pressures of love. I didn't need to hold her hand, kiss her, and make love to her to know I loved this woman. She was my soul mate from the start. I knew because it was the feeling that sleeping separated us for too long.

You know that place between sleep and awake, that place where you still remember dreaming? That's where I'll always love you. That's where I'll be waiting. [91]

She drove in to the city. We went to a local dive bar near my apartment. She had wine. I had an IPA.

Ophelia asked, "I wonder why you have such an affinity for blue eyes."

"What do you mean?"

"Don't play dumb Jake, you have said it before and I can see it the way you look at me, at my eyes."

"Well, I do love blue eyes."

"But why?"

"That is easy Phia…because of the one that got away."

"Don't call me Phia…Who was she?"

"I don't talk about that stuff, Phia."

"I told you to stop…"

"I never agreed."

She heard in my tone that I could not yet talk about a love in my past. [92] The mystery kept her guessing. I don't actually think she wanted a true answer. She wanted to keep mystery in the relationship. But she still wanted more. If I gave her all I could, there would be no more to give and that would leave us both sad and empty, for she was using me to fill the voids in her life she could not fill on her own. People always use people. It is what we do. Sometimes we use people for the right reasons, and sometimes we use people for the wrong reasons, but in the end the outcome is the same. We all still use each other.

The questions continued as I brushed them off.

"What did you think of me?"

"How many people have you slept with?

---

[91] Barrie, J.M. Peter Pan.
[92] He must be referring to Sutton or Leah.

"Have you ever had a threesome?"

"What's your biggest fear?"

"Tell me what you are thinking."

It was never-ending. She pried and pried and pried. She stripped me down. She wouldn't let me off the hook. It was competitive banter. It was back and forth, it was engaging, it was refreshing, we bitched, we praised, we laughed, we did all we could without crossing the line. She looked through me and gave me those eyes. They were eyes I was not allowed to see. Neither of us knew what we were doing but we knew it was wrong and felt right.

"I have been here before," I said, "I have been in this situation. We shouldn't be here. We are playing with fire and I just know one of us is going to get burnt."

There was a pause between us both and at the same time it hit us. We knew each other. We have done this before, in another time, place... We have fallen in love before and destined to do it again.

`Serendipity: The effect by which someone stumbles upon something truly wonderful, especially while trying to look for something completely unrelated.`

`We walked by Serendipity on 60`th `Street...`

"What do you think of me?" She asked.

"Don't ask that," I said.

"Why not?"

"I can't answer that."

"Well what did you think when you first saw me?" she kept going.

"Please stop."

"Why won't you tell me! Why won't you say those sweet things to me?"

"I can't tell you those things, it is not fair. I think them but I can't tell you them."

"Why not Jake!?"

"You know I don't like when people call me Jake. It's Levon..."

"Okay...got it boss[93]...Jake it is... But why won't you tell me what you think of me?"

"First off we aren't in middle school... who cares...it will only make this situation harder. It will only confuse you even more. It is not fair to you. I won't do that."

---

[93] I wonder if Levon always said "got it boss" because of Ophelia?

"Stop being so amazing about this, it is only making me want you even more."

"Now you…stop saying those things Phia."

"You are a slow learner aren't you Jake. We can never work," she continued.

"I know we can't," I shot back. "We are opposite signs." She was an Aquarius and I was a Leo. Not that I believe in that sort of stuff…but for some reason I am an avid horoscope reader. The idea that everyone born in the same time period has the same personality doesn't make sense. However, sometimes when you make connections while reading your horoscope, it is comforting to think some of the shit in your life isn't your fault and is part of something bigger.

"Yup," she responded…

"You are engaged."

"Yup."

"You don't like to cuddle."

"Yup."

"You don't like to travel."

"Yup."

"We come from different backgrounds. You are a rich Westchester Jew… I am a middle-class kid from upstate."

"Yup."

"So why are we sitting here having this conversation?"

"Because despite all our differences and challenges Jake, I don't want to walk away from you. If you truly feel the same way about me then say something damn it! Tell me more!

"Look at your left hand. I have to go on with my life thinking you were a 'what-if girl.' You will just be that person that if we met in another place another time, the stars may have aligned, and we would have been okay. But there are too many conditionals in that statement."

"I think I knew you before," she said.

"Do you think part of this is the forbidden fruit theory?" I said shrugging off her previous comment, but not ignoring it either…

"Maybe"

"What if it is?

"Then it is."

"But hypothetically what if during a moment of weakness, you taste the fruit and realize the repercussions are not worth the flavor and now you are cast out of Eden?" I asked.

She responded in a way I did not expect…

"Well, how am I going to know it was a mistake, if I don't make it?"

November 24th

We looked at each other from across the classroom, locked in a gaze that no one else was invited to. We said a lot with our eyes, however for the first time in my life I had someone looking back at me.

I didn't feel the same anymore. It could have been the cough medicine or the subtle shifts in the ground underneath me finally added up to the point where I lost control.

An old love was in town recently. She said I don't look at her the same. I don't know why this is. I don't know what happened. But I couldn't put my heart through that situation anymore. I had put up with all I could. Life needed to be a balance of being sensitive and caring as well as a bro. I was struggling to find the balance in my life. I knew exactly why I didn't look at her the same or feel the same. It was because my heart now belonged to another. It belonged to Ophelia. But I couldn't have her. You don't control how you feel. The sooner you accept that, the easier life is.

But something was different in me. I felt something deep down inside my soul had changed. Was it Ophelia? Did she change me? What is haunting me?

After class...

"Jake, I don't get it," she said.

"Get what?"

"I have always been the good girl. I have always been the one who never cheated. I never left a good relationship for another guy. I have been in shitty relationships and met other guys and were like, yeah, I don't want to be in that relationship anymore... But Jake, you came around when I couldn't be happier and now you are all I think about and I am starting to feel guilty. I feel you could make me even happier than I am now."

What the fuck am I doing? "Either get busy living or get busy dying."[94]

---

[94] Shawshank Redemption

November 26th

Sitting in The Dead Poet in the Upper West Side, drinking with Cynthia, Beth and Ophelia I listened to them banter. They jumped from topic to topic as all women do when with more than two other estrogen producing beings. I was kind of buzzed after two beers on an empty stomach.

Some of the conversations were serious and some were fluff fillers. I jumped in with my usual smart-ass remarks. These remarks usually began with, "Wait really…, Don't you know that…, Can you say that again? Wait what did they look like?" Cynthia jumped into an intense story about how her aunt was murdered by her uncle. It came out of nowhere and was more like an episode of Americas Most Wanted than a tragic love story.

Ophelia powered through most of the night without ever taking a breath to pause between her Goose Island IPA, plate of waffle fries and stories of her childhood shenanigans. She talked about the entitled way she grew up. She was aware of her social status. She seemed openly ashamed of it. This was one of the interesting layers to Ophelia. She was extremely proud of her parents and all they were able to provide. She understood the sacrifices they made in order for her and her brother to have the life they lived. If you asked her she would tell you in a heartbeat she would trade every dime to have her parents around more often when she grew up. Ophelia understood the rest of the world didn't live the way she did but... Ophelia was lost in her past. Her friends were typical rich Westchester girls with too much money, too young, yet her old soul always trumped her upbringing. She loved her friends and understood how they were family when she grew up, but now she seemed lost between social circles feeling her way through the dark hoping at some point the search will end with love. She could live no other way than with money and knew she desired that type of upper-class lifestyle, yet she always put herself down for having that much money.

"I want to be two people at once. One runs away..."[95]

Ophelia jumped into her anxiety, problem, disorder, disease, burden. She believed it was due to a fear of change. She then listed her Barbiturate and Benzedrine history. She had been on just about every anti-anxiety/anti-depression medicine that was available to the public. She still didn't scare me away. Then as I listened some more, as Cynthia and Beth chimed in how they were on the same medicine and see a shrink as well. I was stuck drinking with three crazies. Maybe, I am the crazy one? But Ophelia didn't seem crazy to me. She was someone I wanted to love.

I waited for my feelings to change. I waited for me to finally realize that Ophelia is just unstable and that is why she thinks she had feelings for me. I tried to tell myself that it was her cold feet and that her recent abortion just shook her up a little. No matter what I tried to tell myself, my heart felt different. The wild stories of her youth she carried with her made her feel unable to let go of that badass lifestyle. Ophelia once stole her neighbors Porsche and crashed it because she didn't drive manual. She tried to play it off that she has changed, however I didn't believe it. The wild youth poisoned her everything. Nothing she said could turn me away. I was hooked. The claws were in. I accepted her. The things she saw as flaws are what made her beautiful. No human is perfect. We all have flaws, quirks and insecurities for a reason.

Maybe I was crazy and just fell for any girl who gave me the slightest bit of attention? I didn't understand it, but she was in my head now. I kept dreaming about her. I don't dream but she wouldn't leave my brain. What is it about her? We both know it is wrong for us to be talking the way we do. However, what is wrong sometimes feels so right.

Her demons played well with mine. Demons always live together. That is why angels find it hard to stand next to other angels. She was special. "She was a mean angel but a kind devil,"[96] and my savior.

---

[95] Heller, Peter.
[96] Unknown.

CHAPTER TWO: THANKSGIVING EVE

"Life starts all over again when it gets crisp in the fall"
-F. Scott Fitzgerald

November 28th

I was eating pizza with my parents on Thanksgiving Eve. She was at her home 45-minutes away. Her fiancé was in Connecticut. I answered her text like a good friend.

"I am so angry at Bradley" she sent.

"I need a friend." She continued. "What if I am making a mistake?"

I tried to tell her they needed to work it out. They needed to talk about it, and if she loved him this was just a little hiccup. People fight, couples fight, but if something is broken, you fix it.

"Ever since the abortion I view Bradley and our relationship differently. I don't know, it is just that I am nervous about money. He is 28 and doesn't have a degree. He may go back, but what if he is just going to be a construction worker his whole life? I want to get a doctorate. I feel like we have fundamental differences. Can he support me? Can he support a child? I can't do this all on a teacher's salary. Jake what do I do?"

"You try and work it out. For now, grab some wine and sit by a fire. You are more than welcome to come over and hang out. I will just be sitting here relaxing."

It was one of those invitations you throw out there not thinking they would accept. She accepted.

She came over. She met the family. She met the sisters and the commotion, which comes with the craziness of a family that drank, yelled and was merry.

She didn't miss a beat, and, in my house, it was easy to miss a beat.

When she left my dad looked at me. He spoke with earnestness and an airy tone his father use to speak with.

"I am going to tell you what my Father told me after he met your mother. Don't let that go. You need to go after it. Engaged or not, there is something about her. If you want it, go after it. You deserve that."

Then it hit me one day while microwaving a sponge so I don't need to buy a new one, (Life of a poor graduate student) I realized just exactly what Ophelia was contemplating. The only thing that would make a woman contemplate leaving a marriage is for another commitment. The feelings she shot in my direction were a lot stronger than I thought. I was young and naive. When she stared at me with those eyes that engulfed your soul like the sun slowly reaching out from behind a storm cloud, she was sizing me up. She was asking herself, is this a man I could be with the rest of my life? It was too heavy for me to think about.

It all seems too cliché to work out this way. Are we just two hearts full of battle scars trying to use each other's vulnerability as band aides? It seemed to be so wrong, but it fit so well. Was I falling in love with her? Or was I making excuses trying to fill a void in my heart?

December 14th

My feelings are hidden behind clouds. I do not know where these clouds are coming from. Sometimes I feel like she may just be using me. Like this is all one big practical joke. Sometimes I feel as if this is aligning too perfectly. It is just too ironic…too cliché. But maybe, that is why it is right. But maybe, those exact reasons are why it is wrong. My brain pangs for answers and my soul yearns for meaning in this too big world. My mind tells me, "So it goes."

Her eyes play tricks on me. Is she a siren? She clouds my judgment with her gaze. I feel I will be played for a fool, yet I am okay with it. Does that make me guilty of bad judgment? Does that make me a masochist? Does that make me a pushover? Does that make me a hopeless romantic? The answer is no. It just makes me an optimist. I just always like to think tomorrow is going to be better. I may talk a gloomy tale but, in my heart, I always hope for the best. A hopeful cynic. We are rare but we are special.

I do not pay attention to the things around me. I do not think about what I am doing; I just go with the flow, not taking life seriously. When my Dad tells me I am going to be okay and he is not worried anymore it just makes me more worried about my life. I have this overwhelming feeling I am going to fail, that I am not going to be successful somehow, I am going to fuck this whole thing up. But then again what if I don't? What if these words are just drunken, stoned babble again, and tomorrow I am going to wake up with a sober mind and my confidence intact? But something makes me worried. There is a part deep down inside that says something is wrong and that I am asking for trouble. But maybe, that isn't the case. Maybe, this was that good kind of trouble. The type of Trouble spelt with a capital T. Maybe, it was that special type of Trouble that reminded you why we are alive.

```
This is not a movie I said
This is not a soap opera
We are real people
With real feelings
There is a ring between us
You said yes to him for a reason
Yet, you scream infidelities at me
I whisper them back
This is a lose lose situation
However, we won't retract
In hollow souls and drunken talks
Xanax benders and wobbling walks
We confided in each other
We felt it from the start
We fell in love with no words
But had to stay apart
You wished for my sweet nothings
I gave you only kind words
You screamed for my answers
I gave you questions in return
Like binary stars
Two opposite signs
Mirrored reflection
Never can I call you mine
We have never even kissed
How do you know this is real?
It's the feeling I get she said
Don't you get it too?
There is something there she said
I think it is you.
```

CHAPTER THREE: THE KISS

"It's impossible," said pride. "It's risky," said experience. "It's pointless," said reason. "Give it a try," whispered the heart."
                                                                    -Unknown

December 15th

It was morning… around 10 am or so. I was still hungover when my phone vibrated.

"Hi…"

The silence after her greeting pierced through the phone. I could tell it happened. I knew she had done it.

"Hey…what's up?"

"Jake, do you want to meet up?" I heard her crying. I was just trying to take her pain away and put it on my shoulders. She didn't deserve to feel this way. Was she making the right decision? She was falling so deeply in love with me.

"Of course, we can. Do you want to come here?"

"Yes."

She hung up.

She didn't need words for me to know what she was thinking. I felt so comfortable with her, but did that mean we were supposed to be together? Did comfort equal passion and passion equal love? Passion comes from a Latin word which means to suffer. Were we meant to suffer together forever?

While writing this… I feel something is going on in the universe spinning this woman and I together.

Her white Range Rover slowly pulled into the snow-covered driveway. She stepped out into the cold December air, eyes fixated on me. Without a word we slowly closed the gap and hugged. More of an embrace.

"I want to take you somewhere," I said.

"Anywhere you want."

Her troubled eyes stared at the spaces between the slats of wood on my front porch.

I have mentioned Ophelia's eyes many times so far, but I want to take this time out to attempt, in a futile way, to describe just how special they were. She called them "Archer Blue" because of her Mother's side of the family. But they had the color of the Forget-me-not flower. They were a stunning blend of blue that paralyzed your thoughts. Icy cold, they warmed your heart with their soft gaze. They could inspire and destroy in between each blink. Every time she blinked it was as if the world fell into a black hole only to be illuminated when she reopened them.

"I am not going to tell you too much about it. I want it to be a surprise. But it is a special place I used to run to when I was a kid," I said.

I heard the crunching of the December ice under our feet. The snow had a one-inch layer of ice on top of it. When you stepped through your foot slipped forward and your ankle took the full brunt of the ice, making small slits up and down our shins knocking ice into our socks. She smiled at me in the cold air not saying much under her Russian bombardier hat, made from rabbit fur, as I blabbered on about different stories from my childhood.

Nothing felt different between us. I still felt the relentless draw to her. The addiction was getting worse. Or better, depending on the point of view. I knew she was hurting inside and just wanted to be with someone she knew would care for her. I still wasn't sure if she made the decision for her, or if I was the reason, she ended the engagement, but regardless, she was in pain and the cold was there to keep her warm. The bare trees whipped by our heads as our feet dug deeper into the snow. We trudged our way up and down the hillside and around the lake. We finally got to my spot. It overlooked the lake. I didn't really think about it being a romantic setting. When I was hurt as a child it was where I ran. I brought her there to let her in just a little bit. I couldn't let her all the way in. I wasn't even allowed to know myself that well, but I gave her just enough.

She sat down in the snow with no care she was in jeans or that snow was cold. Then on her next breath she flopped on her back and looked up through the twisted trees. The steam from her exhales engulfed her head turning the clear air into a mysterious fog hiding our hearts.

"Sit down next to me," She whispered. "This is what I used to do as a kid. I haven't laid in the snow in so long."

I ungracefully plopped down next to her, reminiscent of a child jumping into a freshly raked pile of leaves.

"What are you thinking?" she asked.

"Stop asking me that."

"Why don't you tell me what you are thinking? I can see it in your eyes. You are always thinking."

"Don't force the moment Ophelia."

"Tell me!"

"Stop Phia… I want to kiss you but I don't know if it is right. I don't know if you are ready for this. You broke the engagement for you right?"

"Yes."

"You have no regrets?"

"No."

"You made the right decision?"

"I couldn't marry him Jake."

"Okay…I want to make sure you made that decision for you and not me."

"I think I did. But I do want you. I want you so badly all the time and I don't know why. When I wake up, I want you. When I am working, I want you. I felt guilty that I could feel this way about another man when I was engaged to Bradley."

I kept looking at her and she kept staring at me. It was comfortably silent in the woods. The cold from the snow seeped through my peat coat.

"Stop looking at me like that," I whispered.

"No." she mumbled.

"What are we doing?"

"I don't know," she responded.

"Why did you come into my life? Why now?" I asked.

"Are you upset I did?"

"That doesn't answer the question."

"Tell me what you are thinking?"

She always asked me this. I knew why. I know what she was looking for in my answer. Every time she asked me, I dug deep into the hallows of my soul searching for some words I encountered during my life to describe the flurry of emotions and feelings that were snapping my senses in two. But I couldn't find them. I am not sure if such words exist in the English language. I wanted to tell her. I longed to tell her. Part of me thought the longer I staved off the barrage of questioning the better we would be in the long run. The other part of me silently screamed from every pore that I wanted her, that I needed this.

Instead of answering I stayed silent and continued the staring contest we started four months ago.

The mountain was quiet, and the snow was colder than usual. Our bodies curved together, holding each other for a brief moment of peace in our too crazy lives. We wanted the world to slow and words to become scarce as the trees creaked above us in our private winter wonderland. The shifts in our bodies let in brief cracks of brisk air that found its way to our exposed skin. We had only known each other for four months but it felt too right, too comfortable. I was longing for love and she was longing for someone to hold her. The normally emotionless femme fetal was breaking down slowly as the snow melted under our warm bodies making water stains on our clothes. There was no getting to know her. It just was right. We knew each other before this. We have done this before.

I leaned in and grabbed her chin, after another prolonged stare into her blue eyes, which were turning grey in the white landscape. "Kiss me and you will see how important I am,"[97] she said just before...

We didn't say anything as our lips touched. It was soft at first. It was a kiss that felt right. It was a kiss that every novel and movie try to replicate. It shook the underworld and knocked kings off their thrones. However, this kiss was real. I was kissing someone I was supposed to kiss. Neither of us wanted to move. Forever frozen together in the snow, our imprints will stay on the hillside till the end of time. In that moment pain ceased. She began to smile behind the kiss. There is no greater feeling than when a girl smiles behind your kisses and all you can think of in your head

---

[97] Plath, Sylvia

is "damn I love her." I continued to grasp her flushed face leaving ghost prints behind my fingertips. We were playing fate. We were playing love. We were young and reckless. We were young and vulnerable. She was the next chapter.

I could tell after our first embrace that we were in this for the long haul. However, darkness quickly flooded my brain. What if she was just rebounding? What if she broke the engagement for me and is lying? What if we don't work out and she is left alone? What if she wakes up one morning and changes her mind? What if I begin to show my heart and it is rejected? I keep putting up these walls unsure of when I am supposed to tear them down and let the world in. Love is a painful game.

We laid (Technically its 'lay' but that sounds like crap) in the snow until our bodies were completely numb. We trudged back through the ice-crusted field. It did not matter how cold and wet we were, nothing could spoil the moment. It was a moment you live a lifetime to experience. It was a moment you try to drink until you are drunk. It is a moment you inhale as deep as you can just hoping you could save a piece of it before you have to exhale.

We went back to my house, took off our shoes, sat in front of the fire and drank hot coco, with whiskey of course. We quietly smiled at each other, out of view of my parent's interested glare. Then we went upstairs.

She wanted to take me right there. She ripped off her shirt clutching me in the process. Her body perfect, and my mind now scrambled eggs. She just wanted to feel loved, cared for, and beautiful. I wanted her so badly, but it wasn't right. Not there. Not now. Not like this. But how insatiably we grabbed onto each other. How fiercely we fell in love...

She said later that night in a text.

"I knew when I kissed you. Nothing ever felt so perfect. It was like everything I was missing I found. A feeling I can't explain. But it was just all there. That feeling you are supposed to get that people talk about. I have it with you."

CHAPTER FOUR: CHRISTMAS PARTY

"No matter what I did as I looked through the sea of people, my eyes always found her."

-- *J.H. Levon*

December 21st – Winter Solstice

If you can survive my family's Christmas marathon, you are a special breed of human. This was going to put her to the test. When Ophelia entered a room, she doesn't simply walk in. She does not simply strut, prance, slide or anything like that. It is a soft walk that makes you take notice. It is as if she moved so silently you couldn't help but listen to the deafness.

When she softly made her way into house, the place was already a zoo. The old colonial house crammed in 80-100 people. There were state Senators, County Judges, Sheriffs, members of the rotary, teachers, principals, aunts, uncles, aunts who you called aunts despite not actually being related, childhood friends, neighbors, construction men, musicians, doctors, you name them, they were at my house.

She walked over to me, we hugged (embraced) and the night took off. She stayed right on my hip to make sure she didn't get stuck with a crazy uncle talking about how my cousin is in the midst of a divorce sending him to the looney bin. Ophelia even battled with the toughest critic of them all. My mother's token Jew friend, Sally Goldstein.

The liquor flowed. The moment buzzed. The music played. Our love grew. In the midst of a full moon under the Solstice sky we danced the night away... turning, spinning, flowing in a dreamlike ballet. It wasn't until later in the night when one of my sisters told me that when Ophelia and I were dancing everyone in the party stopped and just watched us. They were jealous of us.

"Remember we used to dance/ And Everyone wanted to be/ You and me."[98]

---

[98] Matthews, Dave. Stay or Leave.

As we made our rounds, politely having small talk with the plethora of empty faces, we ran into the Judge. Literally, he was the county Judge. He looked at me. He looked at Ophelia. He took another gulp of his homemade Kahlua. Two streams seeped out from the sides of his glass briefly before he whisked them away hoping to hide the fact his wife was definitely driving home.

The party was full of laughter, small talk, political debates and music trivia. All of the sounds together created a soundtrack that reminded us we weren't alone in this world.

He grabbed my hand, grabbed hers, put them in each other. Looked us both in the eyes and said, "You better marry her now. She is exquisite. You are now man and wife."

My face burned red. My family rosatia came out in full effect. Ophelia had never seen my face get that flushed. She laughed and grabbed my hand tighter. Ophelia stared at me the entire time with a grin like a child who just stole the big lollipop from the penny candy store. I was not used to this at all. But then I looked over my left shoulder at Ophelia and all of a sudden, the blood drained from my face, and I was home. It was all okay as long as she was there with me. Life was okay as long as I had her.

We stayed up all night talking. We talked about everything under the sun. We talked and we talked, and we talked as the lonely hours of the night clicked along. We knew that a night of comfort was far better than a day of loneliness.

Post marriage ceremony...

Ophelia said I smiled with my whole face, as she grabbed my flushed cheeks pushing them around the way a great aunt does at your grandmothers 80th birthday party. I didn't care, because I knew what she was doing. She saw through me. She stared at me enough to be able to intricately dissect every subtle shift in my face or body language. I could tell we were bad for each other from the start.

How do you know when something is too good to be true? When experience has taught you miracles don't happen, then why do we keep believing in them?

She kept telling me she was just drawn to me? She spoke to me as if she were writing her own romance novel. Does that stuff actually happen in real life? She was so content on running from emotion to emotion.

I found myself searching for a love story.
So, I can find inspiration again. So, I can find
the words I used to write. I want to punch the
keyboard as ferociously as I used to. I just feel
I have more to say to the world. I have more to
get out. I am dealing with the truest of all
emotions right now, I am dealing with love.

The night wound down. Our faces were sore from smiling. Our stomachs full of smoked eel, apricot kielbasa, cheese platters, pulled pork, smoked salmon, spinach and artichoke dip, and Stromboli. As we crawled into my childhood bed, I looked at her. I said, "I have something for you."

Her eyes lit up.

I couldn't waste a great moment to break the seal and fart. I had to see if she could hang. And I was holding it in all night. A girl who can't hang around a guy who farts is not a girl you date. She laughed an uncontrollable laugh. Something I had never seen or heard before. She laughed so hard that she stopped actually making noise and began shaking with her mouth open in ecstasy. Then promptly took her right foot and jammed it into my gut, karate-kid-style shooting me off the bed onto the floor. I sat up and brushed the extensive foliage in my room from my face (Since, I left, my mom replaced children with plants).

I looked at her laughing on the bed and I fell in love again...

Morning came and our hangovers set in, as the sun blasted through the third-floor windows. The sunrise was always her favorite part of the day. As the sun reflected through the attic windows, it casted rainbows on our tired bodies. She looked over her left shoulder.

Blinked once...

Kiss...

Good Kiss...

Really good kiss...

"I feel like we have met before..." she said.

"I need you."

"Can you tell me there is no one else?"

"Huh?"

"I just want to know that it is just me. I just feel...I need you and I would be crushed to know if there was someone else."

"It is just you," I said.

"It..."

"Phia... you are it. I am with you. It is us. You go left, I go left."

Tell me about your passions.
Tell me what makes you tick.
Tell me the things you have discovered about
yourself after all these years of searching.
Why do you do the things you do and how did you
get to be such a beautiful creature?
I want to get to know you so I can justify this
love I already feel for you.[99]

---

[99] Unknown

CHAPTER FIVE: NEW YEARS EVE

"Those who dance are considered insane by those who cannot hear the music."

-- *George Carlin*

January 1st

My bedroom window faced east, down 57th street. If the curtains were a little bit askew the morning sun blasted through the glass drawing lines of light over the room. Somehow, these slivers of sun always found their way directly into my eyes. I loved mornings when Ophelia slept over. She woke up with the sun every morning. I was more of a sunset kind of person. She loved the way the world looked in the morning dew. She loved the smell. Maybe not the New York City smell... I always thought she loved to watch the sunrise because it was her little moment to feel like she was the center of the world, when the rest of the world lay quiet, safe and relaxed.

The sunrise that day, was unlike any I have ever saw in NYC. I peered out through my squinting eyes at the light beams that were painted on my wall. I felt Ophelia moving next to me. Before I could even reach over, she was doing her morning yoga routine in bed. Her bareback faced me while she twisted and breathed in a symphony of movements. It was like having a close up view of flower petals slowly opening. So smooth and graceful, it was paralyzing to watch.

She noticed I was awake, slowly rolled my way, kissed me softly on my forehead and said, "Can we order Ess-a-Bagel!?"

God women are good at this...

We had different plans for New Years before we became official. So, we were obligated to our friends. Luckily for us our venues were right across the street from each other. Ophelia pregamed a little with us, met some of my crew and then off she went to her friends.

There was a group of about 45 of us who reserved a private room at some bougie (short for bourgeoisie, and I bet most people my age had no idea that's where the word `came from)` club in the Village. It was 3 floors, the interior mostly decorated with cum stained velvet couches, exposed rebar and purple lights. We had open bottle service. `That is just asking for trouble.` I began with vodka and cranberry. After drink one, I felt better as the liquor slowly numbed my senses and brain.

It is hard to recap nights where you are so intoxicated, there is no reasoning for your actions. We were a mix of high school, college and real-world friends trying to escape our worlds, yet stay together. I never understood why we had such a desire to get fucked up. But once the cocaine and molly started flowing, there was no turning back.

I began to feel funny. `Was it love?` No, this is a weird funny. I began to sweat even more than usual. I rubbed my thighs with my sweaty palms. `I have just been drinking, what the fuck.` I was rolling. I could feel my teeth bearing down. Drinks became easier and easier to consume.

I went to my High School friend Antonio.

"Yo, these drinks are going down way to easy."

"You like them huh?"

"Dude I am bugging…"

"Yeah that's because I have been slipping you molly all night."

"What!?"

"You looked like you needed it."

"How much did you give me?"

"I have no idea, I bought 8 grams and it's almost all gone, but a bunch of us have been doing it."

"You don't know?"

"Probably a little under a gram."

`No turning back now.`

So, I said, "Fuck it. Moderation is for pussies."

Spinning like a top from the excitement of the girl fight, the copious amounts of unmeasured vodka, and the unknowingly ingested molly, I saw the clock ticking down. `Or up, depending on your point of view.` Normally I would have been ramping up the drinks to pre-blackout status and combing the room for someone to kiss at midnight, but I wasn't. I was counting the seconds until I could run upstairs and kiss the most beautiful woman in the world. She was texting me like crazy. I could see my battery dying fast. This is a scary moment for any Millennial. When our phones disappear and we go off the grid, only bad things can happen.

11:45 "Baby, make sure you are up there at midnight! I can't wait to kiss you!" she texted.

11:49 "Just checked with the bouncers' honey...I will be there," I sent back.

11:52 "I miss you already and it has only been a couple of hours."

11:55 "MY PHONE IS DYING!! 9%...Please be there."

At 11:57 I went running up to the smoking section hoping to find the bouncer I had spoken to earlier. I had to dodge hordes of sloppy, emotionally charged, intoxicated, young adults pretending to be classy and sophisticated. Dodging the scourge of our youth is a skill I have developed over years of "Irish exiting" parties.

I finally got to the smoking section behind the main entrance. It wasn't the same bouncer.

"Dude! I have to get out there. I have to kiss my girlfriend at midnight," I said. However, it probably came out more like a dog with peanut butter stuck to the roof of his mouth[100] trying to speak.

"Yeah right...Look kid no one is allowed outside at midnight. Now, get out of here," said the massive black man with a built-in cowboy collar made of muscle.

I looked at my phone. Dead. Of course.

I reached around the massive torso of the bouncer and slid back the velvet purple curtains. Just outside, under the orange glow of the NYC street lights was Ophelia. Standing on her toes, stretching her neck out looking for me.

"LOOK! That's her! You have to let me out she is looking for me. I am just going to kiss her and come right back in... I swear."

Jerome looked at my face. Lord knows what he saw, but he turned around and pushed back the same curtain. His eyes suddenly opened wide. He looked back at me, then back out the window.

"Her? The blonde in the grey dress? She is with you?"

"Yes!"

"Shit kid why didn't you say you were dating so far out your league. You put that pussy on a pedestal buddy.[101] I would worship that girl. Damn she got that..."

"I get the point."

Jerome leaned back again and opened the door. He did so with one hell of a cherubic grin.

---

[100] Talladega Nights, The Legend of Ricky Bobby
[101] 40-Year-Old Virgin

I ran out into the sharp January air. I ran as if walking would be insulting. I looked at my watch 11:59. Ophelia didn't say anything. Sometimes you don't need words.

"Make a wish," I whispered as I wrapped my hands around her waist. (`Purposely standing on the high part of the sidewalk`). She closed her eyes, took a deep breath, slowly opened her eyes unleashing a serenading gaze. Then we heard the cheers from the surrounding bars. 12:00. We kissed. Our fates were sealed.

CHAPTER SIX: P.J. CLARKES

"It was one of those fine little love stories that can make you smile in your sleep at night."
— *Hunter S. Thompson*

January 3rd

Ophelia bought two tickets to the Islanders vs Blackhawks game. It was my Christmas gift. She loved hockey. She used to play as a kid. She was a self-proclaimed "Puck Slut." I didn't mind, there are worse types of sluts out there. There was supposed to be a massive blizzard that night. We contemplated not going. More than a foot was expected. Carpe that fucking diem.

We drank. The snow hadn't started yet. We held each other on the train. However, it wasn't suffocating. It was comforting. We drank on the train. When we got off the train the snow started to fall. We finally got to the Coliseum. Bought a couple beers took our seats in the first row right on the corner of the Islanders side. My roommates texted and said they saw us on TV.

I have no idea what happened during the game. When we were together, nothing else mattered. It was so hard to focus on anything other than her. Our conversations were infectious. I was in love with her mind. It was as if we have had a continuing conversation going that never ended. I was addicted to her presence. She looked at me differently. I could feel the affection seeping through her skin in every touch, pouring out her eyes with every stare. When we walked out of the Coliseum, we entered a whole new world. The vast array of grey that surrounded us when we entered the stadium turned into a scene from an Everest documentary. There was easily two feet of snow on the ground.

Ophelia flirted with a few people and after 30 minutes of becoming a human snowman standing on the side of the highway, we found a ride to the train station. She sat on my lap. When we arrived at the train station, we had to sprint to make the train.

```
    I know I was out of shape and intoxicated
but this was like an Olympic sport. Trying to run
in two feet of snow on a train platform was not
easy.
```

We laughed through our heavy breathing the entire time. She fell asleep on my arm during the ride back into the city. When we arrived, it was close to midnight and we hadn't eaten dinner.

We stood outside PJ. Clarkes. The city was empty. It was eerie how no one walked in the streets except for a few wasted businessmen trying to stumble home after the bushel of oysters and $20 scotches. We saw two cross-country skiers. Never again would we see the city in such a barren state. The city that never sleeps, lay hidden in the quiet winter night.

They sat us at Table 53. Behind us was a picture of Buddy Holly and his wife kissing on their wedding day at the restaurant. Ophelia looked at me and smiled. Brian was our waiter. He looked like Peter Griffin from Family Guy. We each got cheeseburgers. We ordered whiskey gingers.

A few finance guys lingered in the restaurant trying to remind themselves that the world wasn't as bad as it seemed. They spun their wedding rings like coins. They threw back scotch after scotch, dripping butter on their five thousand-dollar suits. Some were in hopeful high spirits, but that may have just been because they were high on spirits. The drinks got stronger and their actions more brazen. They hoped they were wrong about this too big world and their hopeless existence behind their cubicle, which kept them away from family, friends and fresh air wasn't a futile attempt at life. With every sip from their tumbler they all pushed themselves to the brink, slowly forgetting why they even entered the bar in the first place, soon to stumble back to their overpriced apartment, just to keep the routine going tomorrow. Anyway, I digress...

Before we knew it, Brian sat with us as we talked about love, life and everything in between. He got us a couple free drinks as the old restaurant began to breathe in the silence.

Soon it was just the three of us in the dining room. Brian went to procure two more drinks and bring the check, leaving us alone.

"What is your greatest fear?" I asked.

Without hesitation... "To lose my mind."

"What do you mean?"

"My biggest fear is to go crazy. It runs in my family. I always felt I have been on the edge my whole life. I am afraid one day I will lose my mind. I have seen how it can destroy a family. I can't do that to the people I love."

Before I asked anymore, she sent the question back my way.

"To be forgotten," I said.

"Is that why you write?"

"Maybe, I write for a lot of reasons. I write because I would go crazy if I didn't. Maybe our fears are actually the same. I do hope my words will one day make it out there. But really to be forgotten scares the shit out me. It may be an egotistical thing, but I want the world to know my name. However, it isn't fame I seek. I just want to be remembered."

Before I finished, Ella Fitzgerald, "Blue Skies" began playing. I grabbed Ophelia's hand and jumped up to the middle of the dining room. As the sun rose, and the world was catching its first glimpse at the new and beautiful day, we danced alone at the corner of 55th and 3rd.

As the music slowly hummed, I whispered, "Those who dance are considered insane by those who cannot hear the music.[102] Ophelia, you aren't crazy, you just hear the music."

We emptied out into the quiet snow filled streets…

"I want to do a snow angel," she said.

"Okay, then do it…you won't."

Without hesitation, cigarette in hand, Ophelia spun, leaned back and poof. She fell into the snow on 3rd Ave. In the middle of the road, in a full spread eagle, she stared at the sky and swung her arms and legs ferociously.

I fell in love again.

```
"She was never crazy
she just didn't let her
heart settle in a cage.
she was born wild and
sometimes we need people
like her. for its the horrors in her heart
which cause the flames
in ours. and she was
always willing to burn
for everything she has
ever loved.103
```

[102] Carlin, George
[103] Drake, Robert M.

When we got up to my apartment Ophelia had to use the bathroom. The bathroom was directly across from my bedroom door.

"Come with me."

"To the bathroom? I will pass."

"BABY!!"

"No, Phia I am good, I think you can handle it on your own."

"But I will miss you."

"How long does it take you to piss?"

"You are coming with me."

"No, I am not."

"No sex for you unless you come with me."

"That is not fair."

"I never said it was fair… No sex unless you come with me."

She would hold sex over my head. For some reason Ophelia saw me as just another man. Some guy who wanted to fuck any beautiful girl. I made love. She had too many poor experiences with boys who posed as men. I lied to her about my number. I was embarrassed for her to know. But I couldn't let the truth be bared.

"Fine I will go…"

I rolled my eyes. "Roll them back," she yelled from the bathroom.

I mean come on. I am still a guy. Seeing Ophelia naked was like staring at a sunrise for the first time. Her body was perfect in every way.

The lights were off. The only source of light came from the street lamps. I faced the shower, not her. She turned on the faucet to help her pee. Funny she invited me and got stage fright. She always turned the faucet on. It was cute. It is something I do to this day when I pee at night. I also brush my teeth with warm water because of Ophelia. It is in these little intricacies of people you fall in love.

"You have to kiss me now."

"No, no that's too far." I left the bathroom.

I turned around to see this beautifully intoxicated woman sitting on the toilet, pants around her ankles bopping up and down with a half pout, half smile on her face begging for a kiss. But the more I looked the more the butterflies flapped in my stomach.

"Get over here right now," she pleaded. I paused…

"I don't have a choice, do I?"

"Baaaabbbbyyyy! Please... just kiss me. Get your ass over here. How are you going to be intimate with me if you can't kiss me while I pee?"

Hasn't everyone thought of that?

Something about how she asked... the way she looked...the innocence of intimacy.

I fell in love again...

I walked into the bathroom and kissed her. She grabbed my head and began peeing. She didn't let go until the last drop fell into the toilet. She smiled behind her kiss, like our very first kiss and all I could think of was "Damn I love her." And a whole new level of intimacy began.

Just before I closed my eyes. I rolled over in bed so I could see Ophelia. She was already asleep next to me. When Ophelia slept, she always had a look of being safe. There was a soft smile with a calm demeanor. To watch her sleep made you feel at peace with the world. She was a true muse. Ophelia made you feel drunk with passion and high on life. My eyes were heavy from the day's events, but I had enough strength to utter one more sentence before I slipped off into a well-needed slumber.

"If saying I love you kills me tonight, then I was ready for death the day we met. I love you Ophelia."

I kissed her and fell asleep.

CHAPTER SEVEN: A WHISKEY LULLABY

...Unable to separate his angelic memories of the girl from the storms that were raging in his blood.

--Isabel Allende

January 24th

It was the day after our one-month anniversary. I planned a trip to the Museum of the Moving Image and watched Ophelia become squeamish over a quail dish at a Greek restaurant in Astoria, Queens. While we ate dinner, Bradley continued to text Ophelia. It was like Gollum in Lord of the Rings, having a conversation with himself.

"I love you Ophelia."

"I hate you Ophelia...how could you do this to me you bitch."

"I would have done anything for you."

"Are you fucking someone else?"

"I can't live without you."

"Do you not understand what this is doing?"

"I can't breathe air without you..."

The next day after Ophelia left to head back home to Westchester, I made a decision to reach out. Bradley was contacting all of Ophelia's friends and family telling them what a cold backstabbing bitch she was. I couldn't stand seeing this woman I cared for so deeply being put down over a decision she believed was right. I sent him a message online. Ophelia never knew I reached out. I couldn't tell her. I was only trying to do the right thing.

Bradley,

You do not know me. I am a friend of Ophelia's. I hope you understand I am only reaching out as someone who also cares about Ophelia. I understand how hurt you are. I understand how you feel betrayed. But life goes on and hurting her even more isn't fair to either of you. It sucks that she felt she couldn't marry you. I can only imagine that feeling. I can only imagine how your heart aches to have her back. She is a special woman and any man would be lucky to call her his own.

Please know the pain will go away. Know she didn't make this decision without thinking about you. Sometimes we need to shoot the bullet and stand in front of it at the same time. I hope you understand. She talks so highly of you. I know you will find someone special in your life but right now it isn't her. I am sorry if this is hard for you to hear, but I think it is necessary. Please stop contacting her. It is painful for everyone involved.

I wish you the best,
Levon.

I was getting dressed. It was like any other normal weekday getting ready for student teaching. Except it was a Tuesday.

Ophelia texted me, "They can't find Bradley, I am getting really nervous."

"It's okay," I said. "I am sure it will be alright. You used to say he always went off on his own sometimes. Maybe he is at his boat?"

We both knew it wasn't that. I lied when I said I am sure it would be alright. It was the only time I ever lied to Ophelia. It was a white lie. It was a lie you tell when you feel you have nothing else to say. My phone rang two minutes later. I knew. My knees went weak and I cringed as I saw Ophelia's name come up on my phone. Your body always knows when bad news is about to grace your presence.

"He did it!" she screamed, in a manner I never want to hear again. So piercing, so terrifying, so unnerving, I knew it could only be shared with someone she loved. Her world came crashing down on her in one instant. Bradley drove to Ophelia's summer home in Branford, Connecticut. He was a contractor and had keys to the house, because he helped maintain it. When Bradley's group of friends hadn't heard from him in over a day, they were worried and sent people to find his truck. They decided to check Ophelia's house at 16 Lotus Lane, and his truck was there, still running. So was he. Bradley died on January 24, 2014 due to strangulation from hanging and a broken heart.

"There is always some specific moment when we become aware that our youth is gone; but years after we know it was much later."[104] It was in this moment when she told me what happened

---

[104] McLaughlin, Mignon

through her cries and sobs; I realized all my
youth officially left me. I was faced with the
true darkness of this beautiful, yet tragic
existence.

   I guess this is the terrifying power of
love. It has the ability to make the world, with
its 7 billion people feel so small. It makes the
world feel as if there was only one other person
living in it. When you lose that person, your
personal heaven flees, and you are left with a
lonely hell.

   I didn't know what to say. I didn't know how to react. In some
situations, there are no words for comfort. Sometimes, silence is the best
Band-Aid. But I knew I needed to stand by her. It was his decision, not
hers, to do what he did. Death is never easy, and suicide leaves everyone
with questions. This is why we were in each other lives. I needed to be there
for her in this moment of pain.[105] I needed to take the burden from her.
Sometimes god sends you people you didn't know you needed at times you
didn't know you needed them.

   The guilt set in. I could only imagine what she felt as we both knew
this man would still be alive if it weren't for us. We did not tie that rope,
but in a sick twisted way, we killed a man. A man died for us to love.
Tragic? Romantic? It was nothing... It just was. I was angry. I was angry he
did this to her. I was angry he did this to us. I was angry he did this to his
friends and his family. I do not wish to curse the dead, but in my heart, I
screamed in pain for a life that would never be the same now that
someone's soul rested on her heart...

---

[105] When a friend first read his section, she stopped here and said, "Levon is
lying..." I asked her to elaborate. She said, "There is no way he was this
reflective and understanding. That is not how people react to death. Levon
shouldn't have these thoughts so soon after the suicide. Either he truly didn't
remember how he felt. He must have suppressed his feelings or blocked them
out. No wonder he snapped later."

January 28th

Four days later sitting in an auditorium listening to a lecture, I whispered in her ear, "I love you." I couldn't take it any longer, I had to fess up and say how I felt. Her eyes opened wide and her shoulders rolled back in relief. She reached into my backpack and pulled out my Moleskin. She grabbed my pen and responded.

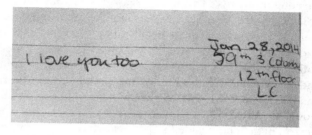

"I love you too."

I knew we needed each other.

And love it was.

January 29th

*(Written on 1/29 the day after I told you I loved you. Any words written in bold have been added a year later, after I broke your heart).

I have been through a dessert, I have sailed a sea, I have climbed mountains, hiked forests and trudged through jungles. I have shaken hands with the elite and drank beer with the locals who serve the elite. I have been so many places and seen so many faces and I cannot match a single one to yours and the way it makes me feel. **It lets me know, I have nowhere else to go. You are my destination and you are my dream.**

The city is dark, but it is still loud. My room is quiet and slightly too cool. I still feel you here. I still hear your laughter. I still smell your hair. **I can still feel your tears fall on my arm. I can still see your pile of clothes by the mirror.** I can remember you sitting on my floor doing your makeup or crying under the covers hoping the dark could keep you safe for five more minutes. **I still see your smile reflecting off the bathroom mirror as I tried to sneak a peek. I can still see you standing on your tiptoes holding your hair up looking at your outfit as you glance over**

your shoulder asking me with your eyes if you are beautiful. I look out my window and I still see you lying in the snow-covered streets glowing orange from the streetlights above. I still see your smoke coming up from your cigarette through the smog filled air of New York. **I still feel your presence everywhere I go.**

All of these moments pass by and they could be seen as just fleeting moments of youthful pleasure searching. But what I realize as the clicking of the keys begins to sound like thunderclaps over our relationship punching out the intricate details of our tale, is that we were two adults slowly teaching each other how to live. **We both added so much to each other's lives that when we departed a hole was created, which could never be filled by any means other than each other.** We were two people learning who we were during a scary time. **Someone above was looking down on us.** It was someone telling us we needed a dancing lesson in life and decided to pair us together. And once we started dancing…no one could stop us. **No one ever will stop us. Not when the music is still playing.**

Goodnight Ophelia.
Your love,
Jake

I asked Ophelia to bring a letter I wrote to Bradley's funeral. She didn't want me to go with her. Understandable. It was sealed. I told her it was between him and I.

Dear Bradley,

You only know me through over the shoulder text messages. This has been eating me alive lately. I am struggling to understand it all. When I found out you killed yourself, I didn't know how to react. I am the man who took your fiancé from you. I stole away your love and you have every right to want to kill me. Part of me believes I am the reason you are no longer with us today. I am sorry. Maybe, if I went to another school, Ophelia and you would have lived happily ever after? Maybe, I just should have said I had no feelings when Ophelia confronted me? Maybe, she was just a band aide to a bigger problem in your life? There are a lot of questions that are going to go unanswered.

Ophelia always spoke highly of you. She told stories about the bars you went to and you playing the drums and sailing along the ocean. She would tell stories of you cuddling with Madeline and your dog whispering abilities. She joked about your beard and all the other times you made her smile. She talked about your depth and how smart you were. She talked about how all you wanted to do was pass your music onto your children. I know you better than you think. I believe in another world we could have been great friends. I hope those happy thoughts are what you were thinking when you left this world. I hope you saw her smile as you closed your eyes one last time. I know it is what I want to see as I leave the world.

I want you to know that I love Ophelia. I am going to take care of her. I am going to be here for her. I am going to make sure I give her the life you wanted to give her. I will make sure she is always happy. Even though I never met you, I will carry you with me for the rest of my life. I know I will. I will honor you anyway I can. I hope you rest with the Angels now and are at peace with your son.

I had to remind myself that though he died young, Bradley had a fine time living. If he had lived it over a thousand times it wouldn't have made it any more enjoyable.

"Ce qu'on appelle une raison de vivre est en même temps une excellente raison de mourir."[106]

---

[106] Camus, Albert " What is called a reason for living is also an excellent reason to die. "

CHAPTER EIGHT: TWENTY-FOUR ACTS OF KINDNESS

So, you can leave with at least the consolation of having planted something in someone else's heart.

-- Isabel Allende

February 5th

Hello my old heart? Are you still there?[107] I feel alone. I don't know if this love can hold on anymore. The nights scare me. The night terrors were the worst. Ophelia would shoot up at night sweating, breathing heavy.

"He is here. I saw him. He is here, I swear Jake."

"Shhh, don't worry honey, it is just a dream…"

"No Jake! He is here… he is haunting me… I need him to go away."

I would hold her as tight as I could to try and help slow the shaking. It would help to put my heart close to hers, in hopes her heart would try and mimic my slower heart rate. What she never knew is I would go to the bathroom once she fell back asleep and have a panic attack. I curled up on the floor of the bathroom in solitude. I cried. I shook. Her anxiety, fear. Slowly beginning to diffuse into my body, into my mind. I still don't sleep…

"I don't know how to sleep anymore," she said.

"Sure, you do Phia, just close your eyes."

"I am afraid to."

"Don't worry I am here; it will be okay."

"My heart is haunted."

"Give me your heart babe. I will take care of it."

"I gave it to you a long time ago," she said before we fell asleep.

The morning of Phia's 24th birthday she woke up with a smile. I hadn't seen her smile in so long it scared me at first. I wondered if she finally cracked. She rolled over in bed and said, "I am so blessed Jake… I

---

[107] The Oh Hellos, Hello My Old Heart.

need to give back. We came up with 24 acts of kindness, from buying strangers lottery tickets, to buying books for the children's hospital, giving lollipops to kids, bringing cops donuts, giving flowers to a stranger and even helping the homeless with gloves. It was one of the happiest days of my life. For the first time ever, I wanted to give. Phia and I were so blessed, and we had so much to give the world around us. We gave smiles and we gave them together.

The final act of kindness was forgiving Bradley. She wrote a note to him. I still don't know to this day what it said. We went into the kitchen and she placed the note in a coffee cup. I gave her and lighter and lit it. It burned a bright green flame. As the last embers of her note burned away into a pile at the bottom of the mug she said, "All the art of living lies in a fine mingling of letting go and holding on."[108]

The next morning after she left, I looked at my desk and saw a black hair clip. I am still staring at the very same hair clip.

After that day we tried to live our lives the best we knew how. We tried to put the past behind and keep one step always moving forward. I tried to give her the life she deserved after so much tragedy. We did all we could to look forward. Grad school continued to buzz by us. The grey accusatory stares of our friends and family were never going to bring us down as long as we had each other. We spent every waking moment together. We watched every sunrise and sunset holding onto each moment in fear it would pass by. The city was no match for us. We lived a life people dreamed of, laughing at the moon. My poetry and writing flowed easier than ever before. The love we shared inspired my heart, my soul, my mind. It lit my way in life. I couldn't help but dwell on the fact no light lasts forever.

One night while dog sitting at my parent's home, we sat out by the fire on the patio. We drank whiskey on the rocks as we cuddled under the blanket my Nana made for me when I was born. The same blue blanket on the bed behind me as I write this story. She looked up at the sky and I watched her inhale the cold night air, as if with each exhale her past washed away. She was at peace.

"You calm my anxiety, my mind. No one has ever calmed me like you can," she said softly to not break the silence in the quiet night. Then she yelped, breaking the silence.

"Jake...I saw one!"

---

[108] Ellis, Henry

"Saw what?"

"My first shooting star!"

Her eyes glowed like blue beacons drawing me home.

"How have you never seen one before? Did you at least make a wish?"

"I didn't need to."

"Come on, everybody needs to make a wish, you have to."

"I don't need a wish because it already came true."

"Huh?"

"All I want is you."

Hold onto the small moments because when you are old and decrepit, they are always the biggest. She knew how special we were before I understood what we meant.

CHAPTER NINE: VIRGINIA LOVES YOU

"We loved with a love that was more than love."
--Edgar Allen Poe

She wanted to run. She wanted to run far and fast away from the world she once knew. She wanted to shed her clothes, her masks, and breathe like she did before the age of 14. Ophelia could handle the backhanded comments, the sheltered talk and crooked stares of the world who didn't understand. Her story was well known by our circles. People didn't know how to react. Do they say anything? Do they comment and maybe it backfires? Did she really drive him to kill himself? Why add to the guilt? She must feel horrible. Can she really love this other kid? Whose side am I on? Should I take a side?

During February break, we decided to get in the car and drive as far south as we could until we decided to stop with nothing but the wind at our backs and road in front of us. The night terrors were still frequent, and her eyes began to lose their blue luster. I knew we had to get out of town. We caught a driving high, blasting music with the windows down. Usually when you break the fourth or fifth state, driving isn't work anymore, the car becomes part of you and your mind erases all you are fleeing from.

Our first stop was in Old Town Alexandria along the Potomac, just outside Washington D.C. We found an old red brick Bed and Breakfast to lay our heads. Before we went to the hotel, we walked around the town, stopping in at bookstores, art studios and coffee shops.

After a long day of driving and walking around the old colonial town, my body needed some rest. When we entered the room, she grabbed me and threw me on the bed. Ophelia reached into her Louis Vuitton bag and pulled out an old ratty book. The binding was tattered and almost completely worn away. I looked at it questionably. I couldn't make out the title. She said, "I know you love his poetry, so I bought it when you weren't looking."

"What is it?"

"The Complete Tales and Poems of Edgar Allen Poe."

"Phia, how did you find this?"

"Just open it silly…"

Inside the cover were two red strings.[109]

"One for you and one for me," she said before she kissed me and smiled.

I noticed there was a page dog-eared. I asked Phia if she marked a page. She said no and that it must have been from whoever owned it before. I opened the book to page 89. It was the poem Annabel Lee,[110] and underlined was "We loved with a love that was more than love."

We both touched the page.

We made love for hours never wanting to leave the soft white sheets or each other's embrace. We grabbed at the lust and gave into the insatiable appetite we had for each other's flesh. We continued to make love. When we finished that, we made love again to the entire Road to Escondido album.

…She told me to keep writing. She told me to push myself and get down on paper what I am thinking. She told me I had a gift. She told me not to hide it from the world. I wanted to give her the world, I wanted to write about her with every second I had left on the planet, but when I sat in front of my computer my mind went blank.

"Jake, you just need to trust me. Keep speaking honestly in your words. It will come through, but always remember to not get attached. "In writing, you must kill all your darlings."[111] Ophelia loved Faulkner. No young person loves Faulkner. She was getting ready for dinner when I sat down on the large white bed. The bed was abnormally high off the ground. The height made it slightly awkward to climb into.

I began to type.

The room is warm, and my glass is cold. I can feel the condensation dripping over my fingers. The bed is warm. The comforter is soft. She hates the way she looks with no makeup. She says this often, but I do not pay attention to it. The days are whipping by so fast. The things, which used to occupy my mind don't hold their place anymore.

---

[109] The red string on Levon's left wrist now made sense. The note I found as a teenager made even more sense. The string was from her. It was how he stayed connected.

[110] "Annabel Lee" is the last complete poem composed by American author Edgar Allan Poe. Like many of Poe's poems, it explores the theme of the death of a beautiful woman." – Wikipedia.

[111] Faulkner, William

Ophelia turned away from the mirror, "What is your favorite state of mind? She said.

"What do you mean?"

"I love watching you write. I love watching you think. When you are so engrossed in something, I can actually see the wheels turning outside your head."

"I catch you looking at me when I am doing that. I still don't get what you mean?"

"What is your favorite place to be…in your mind?"

I can't answer that I thought. I couldn't come up with a single state of mind where I found myself comfortable. In all states there was something uneasy. There was something unsettling. She scurried over and leapt into bed with the excitement of a child on Christmas morning. The hair she just spent 45 minutes curling and primping now flew wildly as she bounced.

"Write me something. Now! Just let it go. Let it flow. I want to watch your brain move. You turn me on with your brain."

I looked at her. I looked through her forget-me-not eyes and looked down at the computer resting on my lap. The old hotel creaked…the town was silent outside the red brick walls.

So, I thought. I sipped and I thought. I could hear the wind ripping by the windows as it rushed up the Potomac. I could feel the brisk cold air sneak in the drafty windows of the old hotel. I could feel her eyes beating down on my fingers like hammers on nails. I was no longer typing but punching out her thoughts. She was giving me her words through her eyes. I could feel them sizzling my veins and crushing my brain into a twisted metal mess of confusion. But the confusion didn't scare me. The confusion made me feel comfortable. Then I realized, that no matter how much I loved simplicity, no matter how much I loved to shut my brain off and relax my true state of mind, what I enjoyed the most was the chaotic state of mind. I needed the world to spin out of control in order for me to feel comfortable. If there wasn't a problem, then it wasn't worth living. I needed the roadblocks I needed the challenges. I need her. I need you Ophelia. You make my days' worth living. No one said it would be easy…They just said it would be worth it.

~Author's Note~

Levon's writing stopped being dated from this point on. Evie and I tried our best to keep a flow of his thoughts, however it became difficult to piece any chapters or sections together after this. His brain was betraying him, and he thought too much about the situation.

After she fell asleep, I continued to write...

I am falling deeper and deeper into a spiral. The spiral grows deep into the ground. I feel like a drone with no original thought. I am trying to break free. I am trying to understand who I am. I am tired of telling people who I am.

She clouds my mind. She asks for a love story. The words used to flow so seamlessly from my twisted brain, but now they strain to move like honey being pushed through a straw. I push and pull for the creativity.

I can't lose it this close to the end. I am almost done with my degree. I have to be able to finish. But it is becoming so daunting. The threat of work makes me quiver. The looming threat of actually graduating and having to enter the "real world" pecked at my brain incessantly. I have always wanted to be older but now as I stood three-quarters of the way through graduating with a master's degree and a certification in teaching, but I don't know if I truly want to be a teacher.

When I close my eyes and picture myself ten years from now, I see a young writer in his prime. Living his life, the way he wants to live his life. I don't see a father mowing the lawn as a middle-class suburb family somewhere. That image isn't all that bad. If it happened, I wouldn't be upset. But I don't. I see a young successful writer traveling the world. I am not sure if there is a girl with me. I think there is. I think I see her. Is she there with me?

CHAPTER TEN: A KEY WEST SUNSET

*I feel like a part of my soul has loved you since the beginning of
everything. Maybe we are from the same star."*
                                                    --Emery Allen.

It was an interesting trip. It was a fun trip. It was a frustrating trip.
She kept asking me to write about her. She kept asking me to write about
our love. Why can't I? I give up. I want to write about our story about how
we are the way we are and how we got here, but I see nothing. I don't have
an original idea. She used to tell me there is no such thing as original
thought. I don't have the writing stamina I used to have. I don't have the
reading stamina. Typing now becomes painful for my hands as circulation
stops flowing. The buttons feel heavy. My brain is tired.[112]

We ran around Key West laughing along the way. My father's band
was playing at the Warf. They had a live webcam stream of the gig. Ophelia
and I danced away in our usual blissful ignorance as the world watched our
love from afar. A couple of Bradley's old friends were down there as well.
Ophelia posted a picture online and they reached out when they saw it.
Social media at work. I hid with my family. Phia went to speak with them. I
know she was terrified. How could she go from engaged to dating another
man in 1 month? Now she was vacationing with him a couple months later.
Katie and Edward were both Dartmouth grads. They came from money.
Edwards's dad owned a boating company who had a port in the Key's. Phia
finally got up the courage to invite me over and introduce me. We spent the
night drinking dark and stormy's and running around with reckless
abandon. I had his image I was Hemingway drinking with the locals and
smashing bottles on the ground. I think it eased a piece of Phia's heart
knowing not everyone in her former life hated her.

The next morning Phia and I had to take a boat to the Tortuga
Islands. She was terrified of the 90-mile boat ride. I was supposed to be
there and take care of her. Instead, I spent the morning throwing up in the
bushes outside of our hotel as she rubbed my back. Then a bird shit on me.

---

[112] Evidence Levon was breaking down.

The second to last night, while she slept, I slipped a gold locket onto the pillow next to her. I wanted her to know no matter where I was our love will be locked away right by her heart. Underneath the locket I wrote her a note, like I so often did in our relationship. I loved hiding notes around her home.[113]

[114]

---

[113] I found this note in the bottom of Levon's Zanzibar's chest. I am not sure why he still had them.

[114] "I do not tell you enough how much you truly mean to me. I do not tell you enough how much I love you. I know I am a pain. I know I am an ass. But never

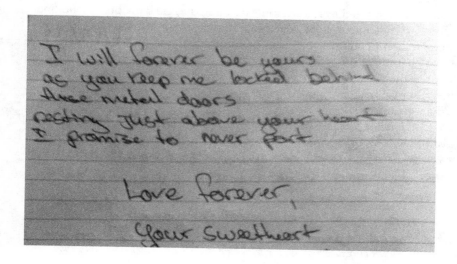

in my life have I met someone willing to put up with me and love me unconditionally.

I have been wondering for a long time what I would write in this. I wasn't sure how I would be able to properly convey why now I give you this gift and what it means to me...to you...to us.

I wish to forever be locked in your heart
A piece just for you
Alongside your pup
We make two
I forever wish to be remembered
For the love shared
Laughs had
With bodies bared
A mass of intertwining flesh
Under a mesh of emotions
That only when sifted
Only when the smog of life lifted
Is the one true thing revealed inside
And no words could be more true
Then I love you
I will forever be yours
As you keep me locked behind metal doors
Resting just above your heart
I promise to never part.

She wanted to reward me. She wanted to fuck my brains out. She wanted to ride me until we were both cum drunk on the moment. But for some reason I couldn't get it up. Sometimes I am too locked in my head. It wasn't her fault. She was still the most beautiful human I ever saw. She went to the shower. Whenever Phia felt sad, she sat in the shower. She said the water calmed her. I just thought it was easier for her to hide her tears. While she cried, I wrote…

I am searching for that inspiration. It comes in drunken bouts with reality. It comes with strong arguments of weak minds paired with strong souls. I should be with her. I know this. I am too prideful. I will stick with what I started. Hard words…True words…Words in hindsight…Words in guilt…

Did I do something wrong?

I miss the life of simplicity before. I have so much to live and love and do. She wants it all to herself. But she makes me happy. Love is blind. I am the blind and deaf. She asks for love stories but all I write about is heartache. All I write of is confusion, somber moments of realization, and reflection on times I was happiest. I can't show her my writing.

But I love her so madly, so deeply the passion is overwhelming. Like a pot boiling on the stove it can become too much and break the seal. Too much of anything is never good.

She wants so badly to be the love story that makes it. She shows me songs that are supposed to remind me of her. She doesn't understand that she cannot tell me what will remind me of her. She doesn't understand that when she tells me to give her attention, I will do the exact opposite.

I am my own worst enemy. That's all I have to say about that.

But I still love her. She still gives me butterflies.

And every time I touch you, you just tremble inside

And I know how much you want me that you can't hide

Why can't I figure this out?

When she came out of the bathroom, after I underperformed. I told her to not take personally, but knew she thought it was because I didn't think she was sexy or whatever it is that girls tell themselves when a guy's plumbing doesn't work. I gave her a note that explained how she was my dream.

"The night stars couldn't dull my feelings for you. We are from the same star my Ophelia."

The rest of the trip we blissfully played in the sun, with floppy hats, fresh fish tacos, melting gelato and bike rides with baskets. I thought after that trip nothing could hold us back.

I wish I knew why
sometimes I get a butterfly
I never choose when
sometimes it feels as if I get ten
sets of flapping wings
But everytime my soul sings

I wish I knew why
When I looked into your eyes
I get filled with more butterflies
No longer a child does hide
No longer do we just move with the tide

I think I know why
I get those butterflies
It happens in distant stares
grazing of our legs
or the smell of your hair

I wish I could tell you why
I always get these butterflies
even when we are tired or frustrated
part of me believes we made it

I wish I had the words more often
to brighten your day
to make you believe everything will be okay
But I can only tell you
that only with you
I get those butterflies

CHAPTER ELEVEN: IT WAS SUPPOSED TO BE A FESTIVAL OF FRIENDS

"Quis custodiet ipsos custodes?" (Who will guard the guardians themselves?)

--*Nelson Mandela*

It was the first fight we ever had. It came out of nowhere and left me on my knees begging forgiveness for something so tiny that I questioned my own actions. I didn't understand how she could make me feel so small. It happened during a family event. To get into the details and paint a beautiful picture of the weekend festivities is too exhausting. I am just trying to write about the fight. I have lost the poetry I use to write for her. It has become an obligation to love and be romantic. No longer is it allowed to flow. Anyway, I digress.

It happened on Memorial Weekend. We were at a family party that consisted of 150 friends and family on a camp. We drank, laughed, played games and enjoyed the fuck out of being American. The poetry is gone... where did it go?

She yelled at me. She yelled at me for abandoning her. I didn't abandon her I just didn't give her the undivided, uninterrupted attention she desired. She was so used to me never looking away but when I was with friends and family, I left her.

"Just because I can hold my own doesn't mean I need to. You haven't talked to me in two hours…"

"Phia come on."

"No, I want to go home and go to bed."

"Phia the night just started."

"Are you coming with me or not?"

"Phia don't make me choose that is not fair. I am doing all I can to make everyone happy."

"It's me or them."

"Why are you making this so dramatic?"

I saw in her eyes her anxiety was starting to boil. She was splitting at the seams. She needed to get out of the scene. But I was a spiteful ass hole and hated being told what to do. The beauty of our past and my love wasn't at the tip of my tongue. Instead, I was insensitively drunk on anger. I hate my anger.

The air was cold, and the sky was starless.

"You are a grown woman; you know the way home."

"You are a real dick."

"Not the first time I have been told that."

"Fuck off Jake."

As she walked away… "It's Levon you bitch."

How could she not understand the position she put me in? It wasn't fair. How could I not understand how she felt? Where did the empathy and sympathy go? Something so small, so simple, so stupid, but I will never forget it. Whatever, it was just a fight. All couples fight.

There were other people staying in my room that night. Phia got anxiety when sleeping in rooms with people she didn't know. I realized it would be a long night unless we found somewhere else to sleep. We lied back to back. I felt her shaking in the bed by the time I suggested we head downstairs. The tremors didn't stop when we were downstairs. I am not sure what caused me to begin singing, but I knew when I had trouble sleeping a soft voice was all I needed. I sang…

go to sleep you little baby
go to sleep you little baby
your momma's gone away and your daddy's gonna stay
don't leave nobody but the baby

go to sleep you little baby
go to sleep you little baby
everybody's gone in the cotton and the corn
didn't leave nobody but the baby

your sweet little baby
your sweet little baby
honey in the rock and the sugar don't stop
gonna bring a bottle to the baby

don't you weep pretty baby
don't you weep pretty baby

she's long gone with her red shoes on
gonna need another loving baby

go to sleep little baby
go to sleep little baby
you and me and the devil makes three
don't need no other loving baby

go to sleep you little baby
go to sleep you little baby
come and lay your bones on the alabaster stones
and be my ever loving baby[115]

The next day she told me she wanted to go back on anxiety medicine. I told her she didn't need it. We agreed to disagree, burying this underlying thorn only to let it fester months later.

---

[115] Harris, Emmylou. Didn't Leave Nobody but The Baby.

CHAPTER TWELVE: MY SISTERS WEDDING

"Anxiety compels a person to think, but it is the type of thinking that gives thinking a bad name: solipsistic, self-eviscerating, unremitting, vicious."

--Daniel Smith

Ophelia went back on medicine. It made her sick. Her stomach gnawed at her. When her stomach didn't feel well, she became anxious and her anxiety caused her stomach problems to get worse. Phia had a fear of throwing up so she stopped eating. She stayed in bed all day. I told her she was killing herself. The beautiful excited woman I fell in love with was fleeing faster than El Chapo from a jail cell. It killed me to see what she was doing to herself. I tried to ignore it, but you couldn't. Friends and family asked me if Ophelia was okay. It was obvious she was sick. Her eyes grew dark. They lost the Archer blue shimmer they once held. Her words became quick, her temper fast. Simple routine chores grew into dramatic bouts of fighting. Then suddenly she would be happy, and we would have a great day together, volunteering at dog shelters, going to pottery classes, making love until our bodies would cramp from fatigue, but something was off. Something didn't feel right. Unconsciously, I began to pull away. It could have been a fear she may actually lose her mind. Or it could have been that I was the one who couldn't handle my own anxiety and fear over the ebb and flow of our relationship.

Ophelia knew she was sick. She knew how she looked, but god bless her, because as my sister's wedding approached, she spoke with a confidence about Bradley and his suicide. She looked at me through the dark circles around her eyes and would smile as if she won. She blocked out the noise of the judgmental stares. I was not as strong. Women are better at dealing with pain. It is why they are the ones who give birth.

Before the rehearsal dinner Ophelia and I entered the old Philadelphia hotel...

Just before we got on the elevator we stopped and stared at the gold-framed mirror at the end of the hall. I was on her left and she slowly wiggled her fingers asking for my right hand. I was wearing blue jeans, brown shoes and a black peat coat with my blue hood sticking out the back.

She had on black spandex pants, tall brown cowboy boots, and an unbuttoned blue peat coat. Our faces were slightly flushed from the cool spring air we just escaped. Neither of us moved. We both scanned the portrait in front of us with tender, skeptical eyes. You could tell our minds fluttered with questions. In our eyes we saw two 4-year-old's holding hands scared about the next day. But we kept our emotionless, stoic compositions. Despite all the feelings of hope and how right the entire thing felt, our minds dwelled on the eventual end of this affair. Our minds seethed in negative thoughts and we could not escape. We smiled at each other looking at the physical atmosphere the two of us created when next to each other. But we knew we were doomed from the start. Neither of us knew if we were prepared for the roller coaster we were about to strap into, and we were both too prideful to admit we were scared to get on. Well, that's how I viewed it. She was beautiful and we were damned.

    ... Everything was blank... Moments I can't recall; laughs I am not sure I had...What was happening to me?

    Just before the ceremony I ran upstairs in the hotel to see Ophelia and pee. I drank 7 beers during the bridal party photo shoot and couldn't hold it anymore. I swung the bedroom door open. She wasn't there. I opened the bathroom door. She stood there with a tenuous smile. I brushed past her en route to the toilet. I never told her she looked beautiful.

    I don't remember the wedding...

    As we pulled away from the hotel, the day after the wedding I watched Ophelia. It was a moment when I couldn't look away. It was a moment when I fell in love again with her. These moments happened all the time with her. I fell in love with her twice-a-day, every day. This was one of those moments. So, I whipped out the Moleskin she got me for Valentine's Day and wrote...

"She was fierce, she was strong,
She wasn't simple. She was crazy
and sometimes she barely slept.
She always had something to say.
She had flaws and that was ok.
And when she was down she got right back up.
She was a beast in her own way, but one idea described her best.
She was unstoppable and took anything she wanted with a smile." [116]

---

[116] Unknown

It wasn't until months later I found out Phia left the wedding early and spent the night throwing up and shaking in the hotel room. I was so selfish and stuck in my own world I had no idea and didn't bother to find out. My immaturity in relationships was beginning to show as our relationship grew. I was too concerned about partying downstairs to realize what was going on.

She fought the good fight during the wedding. It is sad in hindsight because I can't even remember seeing her at the wedding. When I look back at pictures there are only two pictures of us the whole night. All the rest are of her watching me dance. Somewhere along the line I forgot how to dance with her. We began to fall apart and wouldn't admit it.

I no longer helped her anxiety...

"Never ignore a person who loves and cares for you because one day you may realize that you've lost the moon while counting stars."[117]

---

[117] Unknown

CHAPTER THIRTEEN: THE RETURN TO BRANFORD

"She was the love that made all the other loves irrelevant."
--Levon

Ophelia got a job at her old high school. I was so proud of her. She found a beautiful little cottage to move into. It reminded us of a hobbit hole in the Shire. One day she came over and was discussing the eventual move to the little cottage in Westchester. Then she asked if I would go back with her to Branford.

She wanted to go back to the house. Ophelia grew up in that house. It was her happy place. Like my rock overlooking the lake at camp it was where she found peace, but Bradley took it from her. She needed to go back for a wedding shower as well to get her bed and couch for the new cottage. But since the tragedy of almost a year prior she couldn't bring herself to return, for obvious reasons. I couldn't say no but I didn't expect to spend the entire day with all of Bradley's old friends and some of their parents. I did it for her. I can only imagine what Bradley's friends thought as we sat on a boat near the Thimble islands, drinking beer and whiskey. Ophelia held my hand the whole time. We both needed something to hold on to. We went to the bars they drank at and listened to the music they used to listen to. I have no idea how none of them threw me off the side of the boat and drowned me on the spot. It showed me good people still existed in this world. I was nauseous the whole time.

Phia left for a wedding shower and I was alone in the large home on the water. The house was modern in design but country on the inside.[118] I could still see Bradley's finger marks on the beam he hung himself from. It is not good to follow in the steps of the dead. Let the dead bury the dead. I couldn't stay in the house. I sat on the porch until she came home. I didn't sleep a wink that night. I never told her about the fingerprints. I was there for her.

---

[118] 16 Lotus Lane?

That night, before we left Branford for the last time, Phia leaned over to me, as we were just about to fall asleep. She whispered in my ear something I never forgot. "Jake, I feel like I can pour my soul into yours. I feel like we are connected in a way that I could never understand before I met you. But I am struggling. I finally found that someone, but it's so hard. Do you know what I mean?"

"No, I actually don't."

"I am struggling because words seem so feeble and simple and can never describe how I feel. I get scared to love you so much and I don't know what to do."

"Just love me and go to sleep babe."

We finished the move into the cottage the next day. We played house the best way mid-20-something-year-olds could. I installed a new fan, fixed the toilet, put up shelves, stacked wood, hooked up the TV and stayed with her every night the first week. I wanted that home to protect her and keep her safe when I wasn't there. It was the first time she ever lived away from home. Not because she didn't think she was able to live on her own, but because her parents were in their 70's. She always felt it was important to spend as much time she could with them.

I left the city every weekend to spend with her in that cottage. At first, I loved having a quiet retreat away from the commotion of the city. But my roommates didn't understand. They said she took me away from them. They were selfish, but were they wrong?

Each fall and winter morning, as the dew and crisp air crept over the large glass windows, I woke up and started a fire. She put on a pot of coffee and I began making breakfast. We played James Taylor Pandora station in the background. Our hearts were warm. Those were some of the happiest days of my life. We took Madeline for walks down by the lake and gardened together, laughing, talking and seizing every special moment. I read her books, while she knitted by the fire. Our favorite was *The Giver*. I, of course, planted orange lilies all over the yard. We had a Christmas together, put up a tree, and lights. We made ornaments with our thumbprints and even Madeline's paw print. It was the first time I had a family and I loved us. I loved the home we built together.

CHAPTER FOURTEEN: WINTER WAS COMING...

"Sometimes I am terrified of my heart; of its constant hunger for whatever it is it wants. The way it stops and starts."
--Edgar Allen Poe.

We planned to go out with my roommates. We spent so much time in the cabin that I never saw them anymore. I didn't resent that fact, it just was a fact. My roommates joked they only lived with two other people. Since I moved to the city, I spent very little time with them. I barely knew what it meant to go out I the city and this was a date I told Phia about a long time ago. She knew it meant a lot to me that we went out. I am social and social beings need to be with others.

Then just as we were getting ready her anxiety reared its ugly head. The panic attack ensued. I didn't know what to do this time. She told me she didn't need me and to go with my friends. I felt obligated, I felt I needed to be there for her, the way I always was. I stayed, but for the wrong reasons.

We left the city and returned to her cottage in the country. She stayed up all night reading anxiety help blogs. I always told her they would only make her feel crazier. She said they made her feel not alone. The next morning, she woke up laughing about the whole ordeal. I was angry... I was frustrated. I felt I had been pouring my everything into the relationship. How could she not see how troubled I was? How was she so happy and I was so miserable? What about me? Will I ever be able to do anything I wanted?

"What's wrong Jake?"

"Nothing..."

"Jake, I know when you are lying..."

"Just leave it alone."

"What, are you not happy?"

"I don't know."

"Do you not want to be with me?"

"I don't know..."

I didn't realize what I said. She paused and got out of bed. With the anger of a thousand childless women she screamed at me in words I didn't comprehend. She kicked me out. I walked to the train station like a scolded puppy. I spent the next five days trying to figure out if I wanted to be with her or not.

I came to the conclusion I wanted her so badly. The days without her hurt more than days with her, but for some reason I couldn't figure out how to convey such a simple message. When I returned to her home after the week was up. She told me. "This is your only chance. I don't give second chances Jake."

"But I didn't leave you."

"You questioned us, and that is enough. The next time I can't give you another chance."

She meant every word of it.

Happy but sad
Not knowing where to go
But happy where you are
Stuck in a life you can't escape
Stuck in a life you wish you could hate
Stuck where you have a love
But you need more
You desire the world
But have no drive to go after it
You desire to be loved
But you need more
Contradictions pile
You hate when she stays
But you love when she holds you for a while
Contradiction spills over
You know its three leafed
But you wished for a 4-leaf clover
So why do you love the sun,
But hate to get up in the morning?
Why do you believe it is good to be a role model,
But spend your nights stoned
Up all night
Chattering to yourself alone
Why do you know moderation is key,
But binge until the tile graces your knees

You want to stand up
But you prefer to sit
You wish to travel
But you have TV
You wish you could believe
But you have forgotten how to see
Look nowhere else
You mess of contradictions
As you create reality from fiction
Losing to a lack of self-knowledge
Losing because you decided to go to college
And get lost for some time
Howling at the moon
With fierce
Ballyhoo's
Toots
Growls
And stood tall with the menaces
Broke down the neighborhood fences
Created trenches
In mind, body,
And soul
Only to wake up
Cold
Shaking and alone
Pleased at life
As the sun sets
Over yet another wasted day
However, time enjoyed wasted[119]
Is never wasted time
And now as you look back at the uncertainty between the days
And they blend into a haze
And this straight life
Becomes another maze
Wonder is all you can do
Simply because you don't know you.

---

[119] Lennon, John

CHAPTER FIFTEEN: ONE-YEAR ANNIVERSARY

> *"It is a risk to love.*
> *What if it doesn't work out?*
> *Ah, but what if it does."*
> — *Peter McWilliams*

I planned an evening to see "It's A Wonderful Life" at an old movie theatre in the Village with a beautiful dinner at a wine and cheese bar. It was our favorite movie. To see it in a theatre was on our relationship bucket list. It was December 21st. It was supposed to be beautiful. We made it against all odds.

Just after the movie finished her stomach didn't feel well. She blamed the popcorn. Right after our food arrived at the cheese bar, she ran to the bathroom without saying a word. After about ten minutes I got worried. I texted and called. I texted and called again. For 45 minutes I sat alone. When she finally appeared, I drank all the wine and ate all the cheese by myself. I got the check and we left. We didn't speak.

She was still so beautiful that night.

```
I wrote this note that night as you slept
peacefully next me...I found my poetry again, for a
brief moment.
```

Love was just a word when I met her. I threw it around like we all do. Often, I found myself saying I fell in love 10 times a day with how many beautiful women pranced around the city in miniskirts, maxi dress and no bras. It was endless street porn tantalizing my every bit of immaturity to prepubescent stages. But then, she came along and changed everything. She changed the word love. Love had always had a definition in Webster's dictionary or any quick Google search, but she gave it a meaning. Because the word was finally meant for someone who believed in it the way I did.

It comes down to the details of things. It is in the little intricacies of life we fall in love with someone. These details are always the most important. I loved her for all of these reasons. I loved the way she rose from the bed and fell back into it smiling as the down comforter covered her face. I accepted all her quirks. The things she claimed made her weird or difficult, were what I loved. I loved her nighties, the way she needed to make a pot of coffee in the morning, I loved when she laughed so hard, she would stop laughing and shake with her mouth open. I loved the way she grabbed my leg under the table. All of her mannerisms began to form into me as I fell into an intimacy I would never recover from.[120] They all became truth. The way she held her favorite coffee mug, the way she laughed, the way she smelled, and the way her lips curled after certain words. It was the way simple things suddenly become gigantic things and lit up the world before you like a flame thrown into shadowy clouds. It was always a breathtaking display. No matter what they tell you, a person is a universe when truly loved. However, anything less of that is not love at all.

---

[120] Fitzgerald, F. Scott.

CHAPTER SIXTEEN: CHRISTMAS EVE

"You are not perfect sport and let me save you the suspense. This girl you met, she isn't perfect either. But the question is whether or not you are perfect for each other. That's the whole deal -- that's what intimacy is all about."
                                    --Robin Williams, Good Will Hunting

I stayed at the cottage the morning of Christmas Eve. My ex texted me because she knew I always spent Christmas Eve in Massachusetts with my uncle. Ophelia saw the text. I didn't hide it. I tried to explain how my ex lived nearby and use to love my family's Christmas Eve festivities. We drank, we sang, we danced, we laughed. It was a big Italian family. We were all close. It was the type of family I thought Ophelia wished she always had.

We were at my Uncle's house on the South Shore. Her anxiety began to grow. I felt it seething through every word she spoke to me. I don't even think she remembers the night as she pounded drinks hoping to outrun the idea my ex used to participate in the very festivities she was in at the moment. She was wasted.

When everyone fell asleep, we spent the entire night screaming at each other. It was one of those arguments that when you look back on you cannot even begin to repeat what was said due to embarrassment and the fact nothing was actually said. We spun in circles, no logical conclusion ever reached.

We ripped through cigarette after cigarette.

All I could say was I loved her. I don't even know why she was so angry. She was nervous I was going to leave again. I was frustrated my love wasn't enough proof. She reminded me love was a verb, not a noun. I don't think she even remembers the argument. I cried when she fell asleep knowing we were breaking apart. How could she not see my love was enough?

However, the rest of the time we were together it was beautiful. I couldn't see the good without dwelling on the bad. We humans are wretched things…

CHAPTER SEVENTEEN: ANNIVERSARY OF BRADLEY'S DEATH

"It may be the wrong decision, but fuck it, it's mine."
                                        -- Mark Z. Danielewski

There is no greater purpose in life other than to be happy. Whatever makes you happy, you should do. It is simple. If holding up in a shabby hotel and jerking off for the rest of your life makes you happy then do it. If mowing lawns makes you happy then do it. If making a lot of money makes you happy then do it. If having a close, loving family makes you happy then do it. If being a moral person makes you happy then do it. The problem is, what will eventually make you happy, always changes.

I thought happiness was my friends. For the longest time they were my family. I didn't realize how things changed.

She wanted me to stay with her in the cabin that weekend. She wanted me to be locked away with her again. The cabin I grew to adore, became a prison cell of anxiety and monotonous bullshit week in and week out. I resented her holding me there. I didn't have anxiety; why did I have to stay? Hiding from the world as she hid. It wasn't my battle I told myself. I can't keep fighting this with her. It was a selfish mindset, but it was my mindset.

I wanted to spend the weekend with my friends in New Hampshire. I wanted to party and be young and live my life. I forgot why we were together. I forgot how special we were.

I left her alone on the anniversary of Bradley's death. She was alone in that cottage and I selfishly ran away. I was a coward, but I couldn't stop it. When I made the choice to go and not stay, my decision to end our relationship must have been already cemented, I just couldn't accept it yet.

I was so in love with our memories, the laughs, the travels, the words I shed for her on coasters, napkins and journals. I was so in love with all the good we had it was painful to think of leaving… We always focus on the bad and I was too immature to put my rose-colored glasses on and see what a blessing she was in my life. I didn't see how much this simple decision hurt her when I was off getting wasted with my friends. Every sip of alcohol that weekend made me feel guilty. I hated that I felt guilty. But your gut always knows when you are wrong. Partly because I was guilty…but then I thought, who is she to make me feel this way?

I have no more to say about that. I was born an ass hole.

CHAPTER EIGHTEEN: IT ENDED

"Of all the words of mice and men, the saddest are, "It might have been."
— *Kurt Vonnegut*

I can't write any more. Some memories are too hard to relive. I gave up. My roommates told me to leave her. My friends said relationships shouldn't be this much work...

My immaturity, my anger, my resentment, my bitterness grew. It was a Tuesday.

I gave her a note at dinner. I said I was worried about our future. I lied. I knew she would never listen if I told the truth. The truth was every time she looked at me, she saw her past. She saw Bradley. She never forgave me for questioning our relationship that Fall, and it burned us alive from the inside. A small thorn that infected our relationship, we couldn't stop the disease from spreading. Our love made the drama, dramatic, and it fell apart. I was unhappy, she was unhappy. I felt I needed to save her from the pain our relationship was causing. I was now why she had anxiety and that very thing, pushed us away.

She was never going to beat this anxiety, beat this demon while I was still around. I needed to go. I didn't want to, but we were hurting each other. I loved her so much despite everything; I knew I needed to do this for her. It was sick and twisted the way my brain worked. But it was all I could come up with... They say relationships shouldn't be work but they require work. They say it shouldn't be this difficult. They say if it is broken you fix it. This was the only way I could see us fixing the problems we had. I had to end it. I had to do it for her. She had to take the last couple steps on her own.

Just like our first kiss, our final kiss came as flurries fell from the heavens, and a white blanket engulfed our hearts in the soft winter night.

...It was over...

I cried the entire train ride home. I knew I had finally fallen apart. I felt my mind losing control of reality and sanity. I felt myself going crazy.

Maybe she destroyed me…maybe I destroyed myself…either way the outcome was the same. I ended up alone.

When I got back to my apartment, I rolled a blunt, took four Xanax, finished a bottle of whiskey and sat in the fetal position.

She texted me, *"I never thought I could hate someone more than Bradley. I do now. I hate you for everything you ever did to me. I hate you more than the man who killed himself because of me. You gave up you piece of shit. I don't know what I did wrong. What did I do? When I had you, I had it all. Was I not enough? Is there someone else? I never thought you would do this, I never thought I could hate someone so deeply, all you ever said was a lie, and all you ever did was a lie. When you love someone you make it work, you fix it. And here on a fucking Tuesday you come up here and break up with me. I can never forgive you."*

I called out of work the next two days and what ensued was a bender that left New York City in a draught. I ingested everything I could to hide my broken heart. I smoked, I snorted, and I poured toxic liquors in monolithic proportions down my gullet. I couldn't teach. Everything reminded me of her. A piece of my heart was gone, and I was never going to get it back.

I thought about a passage from a book I read while we were together…

"Child, child, have patience and belief, for life is many days, and each present hour will pass away. Son, son, you have been mad and drunken, furious and wild, filled with hatred and despair, and all the dark confusions of the soul - but so have we. You found the earth too great for your one life, you found your brain and sinew smaller than the hunger and desire that fed on them - but it has been this way with all men. You have stumbled on in darkness, you have been pulled in opposite directions, you have faltered, you have missed the way, but, child, this is the chronicle of the earth. And now, because you have known madness and despair, and because you will grow desperate again before you come to evening, we who have stormed the ramparts of the furious earth and been hurled back, we who have been maddened by the unknowable and bitter mystery of love, we who have hungered after fame and savored all of life, the tumult, pain, and frenzy, and now sit quietly by our windows watching all that henceforth never more shall touch us - we call upon you to take heart, for we can swear to you that these things pass."[121]

---

[121] Wolfe, Thomas. You Can't Go Home Again

~Authors Note~

When Evie and I finally emptied Levon's Zanzibar's Chest we found a USB drive with the following letters. We do not know if he ever sent these to Ophelia. I truly believe the entire relationship is encompassed in these letters. It is clear to see the neurosis that brought them both down. It is clear the regret and pain Levon lived with in these letters. He mentions parts of their relationship seen nowhere else. The most honest version of Levon I ever read is in the following...

April 15th
My Dearest Phia,

(Please read this whole letter)

Ophelia, I felt I really needed to send you this letter. This is not to win you back. I know that is impossible. I wish it wasn't. This is not to try and sweep you off your feet. I know you well enough to know that when you make your mind up, it is made up. You have dealt with enough heartache in your life that when the one person who was supposed to protect your heart, me, broke it, you have every reason to turn around and never look back. However, I feel there are some things I need to say. This is not written in anger; this is not written is any bitterness. This letter is being written in remorse, but with more love you could ever imagine.

This is the culmination of your letter-a-day since I made you that promise 3 weeks ago when I showed up at your cabin. You said we shouldn't talk after that and you were right. You were always right. You have always been right, and I was too immature and prideful to realize. Oh, how pride was my epic downfall. During this time of no contact I did even more reflection than the previous month and I have the utmost clarity at this point. I am sorry for showing up because it just wasn't fair to you and your feelings/emotions. I am apologizing for many things in this letter, the first being the length of this, but you know how much I write, and this is a lot of letters mashed into one. I have been trying to respect your wishes of no communication, despite it being the most difficult thing I have ever done. I also want to say, I am so fucking proud of you. You deserved that promotion and you worked your ass off for it and no one else in this world deserves it more than you. I wish I could have been there to celebrate with you. I wish I could have cooked you dinner, kissed you and cuddled up with Madeline and you.

First, I want to apologize for coming up to the cabin unannounced and for begging, crying, looking needy and weak. That is not the man you loved, and it is not the man you deserve. You deserve a strong man, a decisive man, a man who can be your shoulder (like I used to be), and a man who knows what he wants. Unfortunately, I found that man too late. I hope you find him. I hope he treats you well. I hope he makes you happy, because the most beautiful gift in this world has always been your smile and it wasn't until I lost it that I realized how much sun it truly gave to my life. Coming up to your cabin, pouring my heart out to you was unfair. It was unfair to both of us.

It was September 9th and I walked into our class with Jan. I saw no one but you. I never knew why I couldn't give you the satisfaction that I saw no one but you. I know I wrote in my Moleskin that "I saw two attractive women," but that was not true. I saw one. I saw you. The next week you had a ring. I figured there was nothing I could do at that point and didn't want to be that guy. But the way we talked always struck me. It always caught me off guard. You would shoot back in these battles of wits always challenging me like no one else ever did before. However, you never talked down to me. It does not seem possible that I could have a connection with anyone the way I had with you. It was seamless from the beginning until my mind fucked it up for us. We were perfect from the start. The best relationships always start out as friendships.

But then we fell in love and we fell in love fast. It happens, it is life. You saw me for me. We spoke every day. You became my best friend. We began to crave each other's presence like I never knew I could. I don't regret a single minute of it. I hope you do not either. The reason I am writing this part is because you once said to me that if Bradley didn't kill himself, we wouldn't have lasted a month. This isn't true at all. We would have been together no matter what. Bradley just brought us closer. At that point I saw this beautiful, kind, loving young woman who got stuck in a situation she didn't want to be in. This woman tried to get herself out and I was able to be there for her. I fell in love with you during this time. I fell in love with how strong you were. I fell in love with how you were able to look at people who you knew were judging you and be confident in yourself. The whole time I thought it was me standing by you. However, it was you standing by me. You said to the world, this is the man I am supposed to be with and if you can't handle that then tough shit. I respect you for it and I love you for it.

After that day in the snow, we fell madly in love. We spent every waking moment together. We laughed, we cried, and we made beautiful love that can never be duplicated. No one could stop us. No one could get in our way. Your friends and family loved me, and my friends and family loved you. You became my best friend. I wanted to spend every waking moment with you. We would stay with each other at night knowing the next morning we had to wake up at 4 or 5 am, just to get to work. But a night of comfort was far better than a day of loneliness. I was talking to my Dad recently, about why I want to go back, and I had one simple answer. It was honest. I had never been involved in anything so honest. The times we spent together are some of the most beautiful times and ones I will miss as long as I live. I miss reading to you, watching you knit in front of the fire, playing with Madeline together, going on walks, listening to live music, I miss talking, cooking, making love, laughing, crying, road trips and being a part of your life. And having you a part of mine. You got me. And I got you.

As we fell madly, deeply and passionately in love my friends began saying, "Levon, you changed." I took this as a negative statement. They didn't like that I was growing up. They missed their friend the way I miss my best friend now, you. I realized that I needed to grow up and I enjoyed it. I didn't need to get fucked up every weekend. I loved our quiet nights. I loved our adventures. You were enough. You were so confident in our love that it made me love you even more. You were making me grow up, you were forcing me to be a man, to mature, to learn how to love so deeply I never thought possible. I cried with you, you saw every piece of vulnerability I owned. You broke down my walls like no one else. I let you in. I don't regret a single piece of it. I wish I wasn't so fixated on what I was missing, I never paid attention to what I had. And now, it hurts to let you go, because I know I have lost a diamond when I was busy collecting stones.

But I realized something when we broke up, I wasn't unhappy because I wasn't spending enough time with them, I was unhappy because I wasn't spending enough time with you. Time with them didn't matter when we spent all night staring at the stars. But when I was split, I grew bitter against both sides. This isn't your fault, it is mine. I only realized that I needed you so insatiably too late in the process. I realized it after I broke your heart to the point, I could not mend it. I am stronger now. I know what I need and want. I think you know it too. And now I have no problem saying to you that I would love to move into the cabin we built together and grow old with you. I am sorry I came to this conclusion too late.

Another thing I realized after the breakup was our disagreement about medicine. You wanted to take medicine. I just didn't understand why you still thought you needed it. The worst of everything with Bradley's death was over, I was with you; we were in love, why did you need to be medicated to stay with me? I was too foolish to see this was not something for me to argue against but to be there as a support. I was immature on how to be a support. I thought I knew how to be a boyfriend. I thought I knew how to help but I truly didn't. You began taking medicine and, in my eyes, completely changed. The happy go lucky woman I knew left. You were scared of everything. You were scared to eat, scared to drink, scared to go out. You began to hide yourself from the world and I didn't know what to do. I began to resent the fact that it was only us hanging out and I couldn't see my friends. It was me that changed, and I hate myself for it. But now, in hindsight, I know you were my best friend and I should have been there for you in this time more than I was. I should have not been so selfish. This just adds to the regret, which builds up inside of me like a balloon waiting to burst.

There is so much I am sorry for to list them all is impossible. But I will mention a few. I am sorry that I ran out of the car when we were going to the Patriots game in the city, I am sorry for the way I spoke to you when we were unloading the dishwasher in my apartment, I am sorry for not being able to be more aware during my sister's wedding to understand how much pain you were in and how much you were truly doing for my family, I am sorry for not supporting you when you were taking medicine, I am sorry for not communicating my frustrations better, I am sorry I wasn't there to support you on Bradley's anniversary. God, I am so sorry about that one. Phia I have fucked up time and time again and yet you still loved me unconditionally. I am sorry I couldn't realize any of this until it was too late.

When I came up to the cabin the most recent time, I should have just said I am fucking sorry and that I was an idiot. I felt I was causing your anxiety and it killed me that I was hurting you. It killed me that couldn't tell you that I believed I was part of the problem. You loved me so much I think it scared you. Your anxiety grew as you thought I was going to break up with you. I became frustrated trying to prove to you that I loved you all the time. How could I not be there for you during the anniversary of Bradley's death? How could I not have been there for someone who loved me so unconditionally? How could I have broken so much of your trust? This is not who I was raised to be. This is not who you fell in love with. That is not the man I am today, I promise.

I became unsure about us and if I was unsure, I was terrified of dragging you through the mud. I am sure now, and it is not going to change. If I was unsure it was an injustice to you. I wasn't treating you the right way and I couldn't hurt you anymore than you have already been hurt. In my sick twisted mind, I was doing the right thing when we broke up, I was doing something noble. I was protecting you. I was really just lying to myself. What would have been noble would have been to work through things and stand by your side through good and bad. The way you always stood by me.

Over the past month or so I have been thinking so much about what it means to be in love, what it means to be in a relationship, what it means to be happy in life. Clarence told George, "You see George, you've really had a wonderful life. Don't you see what a mistake it would be to just throw it all away?" I see my mistakes Phia and I can't believe I gave up. I can't believe I threw us away. Since the moment the words left my mouth, it has been baffling to me what happened. I am chasing after to try and get it back, to right my wrongs, to show you what we had was so wonderful it deserves another chance. George had these idealistic dreams that he needed more that he deserved more. He believed he needed to see the world. I used to always joke that I was going to be George, and the Camp my Baileys Savings and Loans. I had to come to the same realization George had, unfortunately I didn't have a Clarence. But Phia I had you. With you I had the World. George got another chance, but I guess that is why it is a movie. You have given me a great gift; one I am dedicated to return. You showed me love. You showed me unconditional love. I know you believe this is final. But nothing in life that is living is final. You have my heart. Every day I wake up and am reminded of our love, what I left, and my heart is dragged to the depths of my soul like a rock to the bottom of a vast ocean. Then I see a picture of you, I hear a song of ours, I walk by somewhere we used to hang out, or had a moment in and each and every one of those instances become my ZuZu's petals. It reminds me that all, which is good in this world, resides with you. It reminds me that I don't need more, that you are all I need in this too big world. You once told me after we broke up that as long as you had me you were safe, and you were okay.

Mary understood George better than anyone. She grounded him. I know what is important in life and it's one thing. It is a life with you. I know this is an uphill battle but just let me try. As George once screamed, "I want my life back! I want to live again!" You were what gets me up in the morning and what rocked me to sleep at night. Let me lasso the moon for you. Let's go on this journey together. Let us be each other's rock.

At first, I thought I had a different dream, I thought I was George Bailey meant to go travel and see the world, nothing holding me back. But that is not my dream, the clouds have shifted, and my vision is clear. It was you. It was always you. I knew I had to try and mend the heart I broke because I truly love you. Remember, you try and make things work with the people you love. But now you don't love me. You don't see me the same way. The grief, remorse, shame, disappointment I have in myself that I was unable to push through my own neurotic problems to the point where I pushed away the one woman who truly loved me unconditionally and wanted to have a life with me, with kids, and grow old, makes my stomach curl and a bubble rise in my throat. The days have become long and dreary even when the sun is up. You are my dream, but I am no longer yours, a tough pill to swallow and a tough reality to accept. My dream is now shattered, and it was shattered before I could hold it.

A little piece of me still has hope. Hope is a dangerous thing, but also a beautiful. False hope it may be, but hope nonetheless. I hope that somewhere deep inside your heart you still love me. I am only looking for a sliver of hope my love. A sliver is all I need, and I will prove to you I deserve you. I will prove taking one last chance on this wretched soul will be worth it. When I left and you talked to your new guy and your friends looking for advice, I know they all told you to not come back to me, that I ruined my chance and that I would do the same thing again. They are trying to protect you and I am happy you have those people in your life. But people change Phia. I know I have. I know I am a confident, strong mature man who truly knows what he wants in this life and will not drag you through the mud.

The best feeling in the world is knowing you actually mean something to someone, and you gave me this. You were comfortable with my silence, and you always knew when I needed a kiss. Remember why and how we fell in love. I am not playing Gatsby, I am not trying to recreate the past, I am trying to have you remember a feeling. I know you have that feeling deep down in you; it is impossible to escape (at least for me it is). When I was with you, the days passed like seconds on a clock, but when we were apart, they dragged on worse that a Lifetime movie. I hate being apart. It is a feeling I don't know if I will ever get used to. I know actions speak louder than words. I have had a double standard my whole life this relationship made me realize. I have always judged others by their behavior, but only judged myself by my intentions. It is unfair and I need you to see my intentions and behavior can match up. I know I pushed you away and now am expecting you to be there. It isn't fair. It isn't what you do to someone you love. Search your heart Phia, you know the man I am. I tell my students all the time their actions give a perception of who they are. My actions have given the perception of me being a flakey ass hole. My actions show a man unsure of what he wants. A man who is scared, with a gypsy soul, who doesn't care. My actions show a man who can say many loving sentiments but not back them up. Phia that was because I was a fucking moron. I was a child in a relationship, and you deserved a man. Losing you made me a man. Losing you, even though it was self-inflicted was a thousand slices through my heart. It was a blunder of epic proportions. Like I said before, my conversation with my father made me realize you are my dream. I am not giving up a dream, you are all I want and need. I am ready for my words and actions to meet up. I am ready to earn your love and prove to you my actions will match my words of unconditional love. I know now exactly what I need and exactly what I want, and I believe it is the same need and want as you. I know you wanted it once, I thought you could want it again. The thought that you now have someone else are thoughts that make me sick to my stomach. I know I don't deserve another chance and if you granted me a chance you believe it goes against your moral code and moral compass. You are a true woman of principle. I know at one point I was worth it to you. We had it once. I am trying to recreate a new future, a future where we grow together. Open your heart. I hope there is no way one month can erase your unconditional love. I hope there is no way these past events can take away me being your soul mate, me being your one. Phia it is me I know it is. I think you still know it too honey. Maybe one day you will let me come home to you. Maybe one day you will be my best friend again.

Regardless of how you feel towards me now, or what may have changed in your eyes please know I will always be here for you. If you ever decided to come home or let me come home, I will be here. I hope you are happy, I hope you find someone to make you happy and that treats you well and gives you every ounce of love that you deserve.

I know this all seems like too little too late. I am sorry about that as well. But you just needed to see this and know the best kind of people are the ones that come into your life and make you see the sun where you once saw the clouds, the people that believe in you so much you start to believe in yourself as well. The people that love you for simply being you. The once in a lifetime kind of people. I hate I had to lose you to get to this point to be so sure. But to finish this letter off, considering I have edited out over three pages and widened the margins because I felt bad you would have to read so much, I want to quote a movie we watched during our first Valentine together (yes I remember everything). I hope your heart hears it Phia, because although they may not be my words, they are my feelings. "I vow to fiercely love you in all your forms. Now and Forever. I promise to never forget that is a once in a lifetime love. I vow to love you and no matter what challenges might carry us apart, we will always find a way back to each other."[122] Maybe one day you will find a way back to me.

Goodbye my love, my best friend, my Ophelia, my Phia, my songbird. Until we meet or speak again,
> With love and flowers in your hair,
> Your Buppie, Your Peanut, Your Moron,
> Your Friend, Your Honey, Your Love Jake.

P.S. I understand if you do not respond to this letter. But if you do text, call or show up, I will answer, I will be there, I will still love you.

Another letter… Levon was breaking down…

My Dearest Phia,

Forgiveness is a difficult thing for anyone to do. There is no timeline on it and there are no rules for it, but so is the same with love. There is no rhyme or reason for who you love and when you love. Lord knows this is the case with us. However, we were meant to be. We fell in love during a time when we both needed each other. The only universal characteristic about love that I know is, when you lose the person you love there is no remedy to cure the hole it leaves, and time is only a band aid. (I doubt you will do this, but my sister did say if you ever wanted to reach out to her as a friend, and another girl, she would be glad to talk, and remain impartial. She said she just wants to make sure we are both happy and knows this is tough)
I don't know if the best thing to do is to continue to give you space or try and use my words and actions to prove this is meant to be. I know I can't, shouldn't and won't force anything, I promise. I also understand time is important in healing the hurt I caused and if time is what you need, I will wait as long as you need. But I know I can still hear it when we talk. I know

---

[122] The Vow

it is still there between us, it is not lost. I can try and be poetic and pray the hopeless romantic side can somehow strike a cord. I truly don't know. At this point I just want to make sure you are happy. I want to make sure you are doing and will do what makes you the happiest. I just believe I can make you happy. If you believe I can't anymore than it is something I will have to deal with not you. I just still believe I can. I did it before I can do it again. Like I said in my last letter I will always keep a sliver of hope for us. It may be false hope to you but to me it helps. It has only been 3 months. The longest three months of my life but only 3. We have gone through worse. We can get through this. Remember, people who are meant to be together find their way back. They may take a few detours, but they are never lost. We aren't lost yet (at least not in my eyes).

This past weekend up in Maine everything reminded me of you. From the Taco Bell we ate that night, to watching you ice skate, to the liquor store we stopped in, to Ricky's diner when we got super "Maine" on people. I couldn't even go to the loft where you had to drug me because I couldn't stop my hiccups. You held me that night. You calmed me down. You were there for me. I was talking to Tony about what happened. He said, "I am going to be straight with you Levon, two New Years ago, when we went out in the city, you looked me dead in the eyes and said, 'I have never been so happy in my life.'" Tony continued to say, "and then this New Year's I could see there was some tension with you two. But Levon, you both still made each other smile even when frustrated and angry. Not to be creepy but you two had the most romantic kiss that night, no one looks at each other that way anymore."

Phia, I will always love you, and the rain won't make a difference. You may think we are lost, but nothing you love is ever truly lost. The reality is that a bone is always stronger after it breaks.

I fell in love with your eyes. Your right one has always loved me and the left one always suspicious.[123] Both eyes can love me now. I promise I will never hurt you again. I have never broken a promise and I always tell you the truth. I fell in love with your heart. It was so courageous, generous, kind, fierce and burning with the desire to be held. I fell in love with your brain. You were quick, understood my sarcasm, and enjoyed intelligence. You didn't belittle it. Your wit always turned me on, and your personality lit up a room. I fell in love with the way you moved. You were always graceful in a clumsy sort of way. When you would do yoga in my bed as the soft spring air ripped through my blinds your body would move in a way that

---

[123] Good Old War, Amazing Eyes.

formed these lines always accentuating your beauty to a point where I could never look away. When you would sit cross-legged and stare at the fire not saying anything but just embracing its glow. I would stare at you and wonder how I could have been so blessed that someone like you could ever fall for a wretch like me. I have never seen anyone as beautiful as you and I never expect to either. I fell in love with you and that is the beginning and the end of everything. When we fell in love, we both knew we were slipping into an intimacy neither of us would ever recover from.

I know you want a man who will always be there for you. You want a man who knows what he has in you. You want a man who is going to put you first. You want a man who can spoil you. You want a man who will respect you. You want a man who can be weird with you, drink whiskey with you, play with Madeline with you. You want a man who is committed to you through and through and will stick with you no matter the challenges life throws at you. You want a man to go on adventures with but have quiet nights together. You want a man to support you and help you follow your dreams (like get a doctorate or open an art studio). You want a man to read to you while you knit in front of the fire. You want a man to eat corn chowder with you and drink IPA's. You want a man who can make you laugh, will play in the snow, dance in the rain and kiss passionately. You want a man who can sing to your soul with just a look. You want a man who will always know where your phone is. You want a man who can keep you calm when a panic attack hits. You want a man who can be empathetic, understanding, caring, loving, and appreciative. You want a man with a good family, one you get along with. You want a man who has good taste in music but always available for a good fashion tip. You want a man who you can marry one day and raise a family with. You want a man to be a kind caring father and a supportive husband. You want a man who is yours and yours only. You want a partner and a best friend. I was that man and I still am that man.

Maybe one day you will find a way back to me.

Love Always,
Your moron, your friend, your buppie, your peanut, your love, your Jake.

Evie and I believe the following is something he wrote in anticipation of meeting with Ophelia at some pint after they had separated. It was on the same thumb drive as the other letters.

Love changes people. Or maybe it is just people who try to change love instead of going with its everlasting flow. Our hands can be weapons and our lips become fists as tongues turn to knives when locked in an embrace. Forgive me for flinching because I wasn't used to the fight. Forgive me for my twitch when your lips were pressed against my neck. It all would have been much easier if we weren't so chemical. Our chemistry made me flinch when I should have just relied on physics. I want your love like I want gravity, the way two objects always fall at the same rate. So long as there is no more resistance we will fall together. No past can cling to us and no different upbringing could slow us down. We will protect our lungs and guard our hearts as we travel through this together. And when I tell you that I will fight for you, remind me that when moving forward anything that will threaten us will be beaten back by not one but two, together. I want "no matter what." We should feel the fear of falling but be so damned ready for each other that we lock arms and take the running start. Anything short of that isn't worth a drop. I only have a few falls left.

She reminded him (you remind me) of every good day he (I) ever had all wrapped up into one. Every sunny day with a cool breeze, every headfirst dive into the pool or night staring at the stars. Every sunrise, and every sunset. She reminded him of the feeling of wind in your hair and salt air tingling your nose. She tastes like the morning dew and smells like the soft spring light. When she speaks it is like someone slowly plucking the strings of a guitar. A sad beautiful song begins to play all on its own with every breath she takes. He loves her like he can never grab enough of her between his fingers. No matter how close he gets even when they make love it never feels close enough as if her flesh and bones keep something sacred hidden within her walls. Something he needs so insatiably he will grab leaving ghost prints until he can't grab anymore because she is no longer there.

All of this is meaningless unless I can share it with you. When people ask me about my future wife, I will always tell them her eyes are the only Christmas lights that deserve to be seen all year long. I will tell them her walk will make an atheist believe in god. If her voice sounded like my alarm clock my snooze button would collect dust. If she came in a bottle, I would drink her until my vision is blurry and my friends take my keys away. If she were a book, I would memorize her table of contents. I would read her over cover to cover hoping to find a typo, knowing I never would because though we all may be imperfect in her eyes, she could do no wrong. For she is the most beautiful piece of art I have ever seen. The hunger pangs I have dealt with waiting for her to come back have given new meaning to the term starving artist. She was art and I was starving for her.

I know they say some people are meant to come into your life for you to learn from, or to teach you a lesson. Some say there are people who you are meant to love but not be together. All of that is wrong when it comes to us. Yes, you have taught me a lesson, but there are so many more for you to teach me. Every day that continues to pass where I go without you in my arms makes me know I am not to exist without you by my side and me by yours. You should never be afraid to start over, it is a chance for us to build something special, something everybody else is jealous of, something they can't have. 1 universe, 9 planets, 195 countries, 809 islands, 7 seas and I met you.

One of my favorite memories of you is when you would smile in between our kisses. In that moment when I could feel your lips purse and smile, I would always forget about every argument, every disagreement, any anything negative in the world, because all I could think about was "damn I love her so much." Phia, you don't just cross my mind you live in it. The distance has only told me who is worth keeping and who is worth letting go. You are worth keeping every bit of.

Now, if we can. I would like to drink a little wine and just talk. Just catch up. Then I will leave. Phia you know how to find me. You know how to get in touch with me. If you find it in your heart after looking in my eyes that this is right, then I will be here. If you can say I ruined us. We can never be us again. Then that is that and I am forever sorry.

CHAPTER NINETEEN: END OF THE SCHOL YEAR

"The reason why we can't let go of someone is because deep inside we still have hope."

-- Unknown

And now she is just a stranger with my secrets.

It is tough because there are things, I can never tell her that could have possibly changed how this story ended. It doesn't do any good now. Lost and gone. Sometimes two people are meant to fall in love but aren't meant to be together in the end.

I just wish I could tell her that, the biggest reason I broke up with her, is a reason she would never believe and would probably scoff at. I did it for Ophelia. She needed this. Ophelia was perfect in every way, but she didn't love herself. She needed to go out on her own. Ophelia needed to heal, and I was getting in the way. I reminded her of so much pain in the past, we needed to separate in order for her to fully close the wounds. No doubt, the strongest woman I know, but also stubborn. If I told her that we needed to break up so she can learn to truly love herself and heal, in many ways, she would most likely slap me with her rings turned in and a 50/50 chance I get a swift kick to the balls.

In a slow steady voice my dad said, "Sometimes you need to just throw principles out the fucking door. Ophelia may believe she would be breaking her principles by coming back to you, but that's what love is Jake. You have to break your foundation. You have to compromise. If you love someone you make it work. Principles have nothing to do with it. Fuck her principles if that's the only reason she can't come back to you."

I gave up when I received the following text...

"Jake, you didn't take all of me. I am still me. I still have my values, my principles. I am still here fighting for what I want. Maybe I have changed, I don't know. There is something, which is still fighting, and it is telling me to protect my fucking heart. I can't trust you. I have to protect myself."

As Evie and I ransacked the USB drive trying make sense of the cryptic and sporadic notes we found a file titled "The Final Chapter." Evie knew most of the story between Levon and Ophelia because she kept in touch with Phia for a little while after they broke up. However, this part she never knew. I am not sure anyone knew what happened on Levon's birthday after they broke up. It was Levon's one last burst of creativity before he turned into the old man, I met on Lotus Lane. It truly was his Last Chapter.

THE FINAL CHAPTER

At that moment I wish I had died before loving anyone else.
                                        -- Ernest Hemingway

"The past is dead," my mother once loved to say. "Sink or swim,
kids. Fight or die."
                                        -- Alexander Maksik

Time is the most precious thing we have in this world. All we truly
have to give anyone is time. The struggle lies when time is not
only your biggest enemy but also your best friend.

My eyes were heavy when I woke up. It felt like my brain was pushing so far forward nothing else could fit in my head. I squinted as the sun showered through the venetian blinds. The white comforter glowed softly in the morning light. The world was blurry through my tired eyes but felt heavenly all the same. I could see balls of blonde curls twisting their way up from the soft white pillows. But I don't have venetian blinds or a white comforter or soft white pillows, or blonde curls. Then I saw her. This had to be another one of those dreams that has been haunting me for the last six months. One of those dreams that makes reality so hard, but falling asleep even more difficult because the pain of waking up without her was unbearable. It was like one of those dreams where I could feel her touch again... One of those dreams that made me want to sleep more than stay awake just so I could stay close to her for one more second. Even if waking up was the most painful moment of the day, at least at night I got to hold her. It had to be. But god had never been kind enough to bless me with such a miracle as sending this angel down to me for a second time. However, God has very little to do with this. Then as I rubbed the sleepies from my swollen hungover eyes, I realized I wasn't dreaming. Her light blue nightie peaked tenderly from the corner of the bed. She slept with a smile on, grasping my hand in a grip that cut off circulation to the tops of my fingers. Ophelia always seemed at peace when she slept. But how did this all happen? What the fuck am I doing here?

Fast-forward two days…

I am alone again in my bed, wondering what happened. It all seemed too good to be true. It all must have been too good to be true. At least we now have the ending to our story… One last dance. I drank too much last night and drunk called her. I have no idea what I said. What the fuck is wrong with you, how does that show maturity? I hope she can forgive me for my night of excess because I can't handle the thought of her going back to the other guy. I know she is a grown woman and can make any decision she wants, but it becomes frustrating when you know so unquestionably that she is the one and that you are meant to be with her that when she no longer sees it, you question how it's even possible. But what is healthy is for both of us to step back and not let the drama become dramatic. The timing may not seem right but there is no better time than now. We use time to heal our wounds. We use time as an excuse, and we wait for time to give us an opportunity for one more time. Fuck you time. You make me old when I want to be young and young when I want to be old.

Anyway, I digress. This needs to start from the beginning.

How it all started… again…

"Is it okay if I call Ophelia?" My mother asked me.

Without truly thinking that much I responded, "Of course, if you want to."

"You sure?"

I think I was. Ophelia and my mother had a relationship outside of me and I knew how much my parents meant to her. I could never stand in the way of that. However, I did not expect a phone call to turn into an adventure down memory lane, bringing about a whole flurry of feelings and emotions I am not sure anyone involved was prepared for.

They spent the whole day together. They rode horses, walked, talked, drank wine (Whiskey), played music, listened to music, laughed, remembered and found a common ground in knowing I was a moron forever ending something with someone as beautiful inside and out as Ophelia. They cried together because we all had missed this feeling of home.

That night she called me. I called her. Well, after she asked. Your heart starts racing. Everything begins to shake. You question whether you are ready for this... you question whether the world is ready. It is just a phone call... I heard it in her voice. I heard it in her tone. She wasn't angry. Ophelia desperately tried to hold onto the rage that burned so deep down inside her from the many tortured memories. Everything she ever tried to forget she held onto deeply while always trying to let go. But we felt it again. Funny how a simple phone conversation, just hearing the other person's voice can stir up emotions you haven't felt, nor knew you could feel anymore. It was a battle of words again, no topic off limits. She admitted to seeing someone. That's all I remember as I blacked out the conversation for 20 minutes after hearing this deadly news. However, what was I supposed to do? I want her to be happy.

That is what true love is. Being able to give someone up, knowing it is what's best for him or her. I just happened to think I was what was best for her. I couldn't be upset with her for trying to find someone. However, when she told me about him, I realized she was just searching for me in someone else. She found the older me, the richer me, the me her parents approved of with slightly more ease because he was more financially stable. She found the me her world wanted. She found the banker me. The me that fit her society slightly better than I ever could. (Actually he was nothing like me) One of the very things that attracted Phia to me was that I was a little different than the crowd she grew up in and now (but played a happy medium...just enough bad ass to get by and just enough conformity to keep everything together), just as she said she would never do, she went out and instead of looking for love, found comfort and ease in a man who would be a partner, but never a lover. She claimed how nice he was. Well, of course.

She knows me better than anyone. But she will get overwhelmed and push me away. Out of sight out of mind. She even said it to me that day. She may push me away because it is too complicated at this point and Alex is nice. He is simple. He will call her beautiful and pay for shit. And by being with him she will be doing the very thing her world wants. Marry rich and live an easy life of comfort. But this isn't the Ophelia I know/ knew. Ophelia has more talent and drive than anyone I know, but she needs someone to push her to go after these things. You want an art studio...okay how do we do it... you want to start a shelter for dogs (fuck cats), let's do it...you want to go back to law school or get a doctorate...how can I support you?

Once the luster and honeymoon period fades away he will become frustrated and try to change her or hurt her. I pray he doesn't change her. She needs to paint and ride horses, listen to music, knit, take care of Seeing Eye dogs. I know her. She has a wild heart and a special mind.

All of these thoughts rushed through my convoluted brain I became sick. I had to click back in. Don't show the hurt Levon. Be positive, show you are happy, show you are a strong confident man. Someone close to Ophelia told me that there was no spark, no excitement no luster, in her eyes when she talked about him. And her eyes were the truest things this world knows, so if it wasn't there, I am confident it truly isn't there.

When my mind came back to reality she was saying, "It just felt like home Jake. I missed your parents so much. It was nice to know I have a home somewhere."

"If it's okay with you... would you want to meet up tomorrow? Like nothing serious, just a coffee maybe a beer if we make it through the coffee." I asked.

You are such an idiot Jake. She hates you. Aquarius' hold onto their grudges the longest.

She will never say yes. She has someone new.
Don't start this again.

"I think that would be very nice."

"Wait, what?" I was shocked.

I could tell she was getting drunker and drunker. After her cigarette, I could tell she enjoyed talking to her long-lost best friend again. I missed my best friend. For the first time in sixth months I smiled uncontrollably. It is not because I didn't smile before or laugh, but it was always different with her. She understood me. She got me. I got her. Even if we weren't talking, I could hear her love in between each breath and on the end of every flicker of her eyes.

Like clockwork, she asked for more. She always wanted more. She always needed to justify her undying love and need of me and I wanted nothing more than to prove it every chance I had.

"I have been writing a lot. Keeps me busy."

"Show me something."

"I don't know Phia."

"Why? Is it about us…don't I have the right to read about my own life?"

"We are being honest here right?"

"Yes."

"I don't want this to sound insecure, because I am not insecure about my writing, but I don't want to push you away. It is kind of heavy and the last thing I want to do is overwhelm you."

"You won't."

"You don't know that."

"Send it."

"I don't have a choice, do I?"

"Nope."

"I guess nothing has changed."

I dug through my writing that I have been fanatically nitpicking over for sixth months. The first four months of our love story was eloquently outlined in 42 pages. My heart unfurled in 20,000 words. My vulnerabilities laid out, the truth for her to see.

With my heart at stake I poured myself a drink. What the fuck else was I supposed to do? I just opened up to the woman I love. I showed her it all. I don't want her to forget the feeling we gave each other. But I also wasn't scared because I knew she truly loved me. I know our relationship wasn't a sham. I know it was real. If she doesn't see it anymore, I need to help her see it but make her think it was her idea. (She is too spiteful for it to be my idea).

The time did not pass, waiting...waiting...

"How is it Phia?"

"I adore it, but I may be a little bit bias."

"You are definitely bias."

"But there is something missing Phia."

"What?"

"You."

"What do you mean?"

"It is missing your voice."

"You really respect my voice enough to want me in it?"

"I respect every bit of you."

"Let me try and write something."

"Please do."

"I am going to need your help, your guidance."

"No, you don't, just show me your heart. Give me your feelings. Try your best to not think and just type."

"Okay Hemingway."

"Write drunk..."

"Edit sober."

She is back. You truly know you miss someone when their very voice and thought of them makes you see the sun when there were only clouds. She made you believe in diamonds when all you saw were rocks. Then she sent it. I could tell she pulled from parts of our story I wrote that rung true to her soul. She knew I saw her. The true her. She wasn't just a pretty face, or a smart woman. She was caring, compassionate, confused, excited, artistic, funny, witty, scared and loving all wrapped into one. She tried to make sense of her world through wine-soaked glasses and smoke-filled lenses.

There are certain moments in life. When you find your fingers placed perfectly on your qwerty keyboard. Expected to come up with some rational, yet simultaneously idealist, thought. It was exhausting. I didn't want to be perfect anymore. I didn't want to live the life my family so carefully planned out for me. Did I love them? Unconditionally. Did I agree with them? Rarely. I guess that's the best way to define myself.

There were few things in life that didn't make me anxious. A kind word, plenty of trees, and the love of a dog. Maybe it's because they can't talk back to you, maybe because in my hopeless romanticism I felt the unconditional love was unable to be reciprocated. Regardless, a starry night, a bonfire, and impeccable drinks and people always eased my worried heart. I guess that's the best way to put it. My heart is constantly worried; of loving enough, thinking enough, and most importantly, to be enough. I don't believe I am half the woman I am without my façade. It has become such an intricate part of my character I started to wonder if it could ever actually unveil itself.

To rebel was a dream of mine. The dichotomy in my mind has been existent since I can remember. Do I follow the rules? Do I go against everything that was so carefully taught to me? The questions flowed. Many psychiatrists would tell me it was anxiety, I believe it is the figment of being a real person in an erred world.

The first paragraph. Who the fuck uses the word qwerty? Besides that,…She was honest. She didn't want to be the perfect little Westchester girl her family wanted her to be. She couldn't stand the thought of her Westchester Mansion, banker husband. She had too much of a free spirit. She had too much love for the world to spend it only pushing out babies and cooking meals for her overpaid narcissistic husband who pushed money around on a computer for a living. But she wanted security and comfort. She loved her family and all they provided, but her heart rested out in the wild. When the mind questions the heart, everyone will be split in two and become terrified as to which person we become. Her heart was with the strings of a guitar on a late summer night as a fire roared under musty stars and bright moons. Her heart beat for good whiskey and laughter with the people she loved. I knew this before she even typed it.

Then paragraph two. Her "worried heart" struggled to breathe free. When we were first together, I let her heart out of its shell. I released it to the world with my words. I always gave her kind words. But she always worried.

Would she love enough? Is she making the right choices? The world seemed to overwhelm her, and every decision seemed to be gigantic. She held the façade for the world masking her vulnerability. However, what she may not remember is that she showed me that vulnerability. She gave me everything she had at one point. I was there for the night terrors, the panic attacks, the shakes. I held her hair when she got sick and rubbed her back when she got panicky and loved her all the same. With me no mask need be worn. However, since I broke her heart, she felt a need to protect herself from me. I just hope I can prove to her fragile heart that I could never break it again. I don't want her heart to worry anymore, however I can make that happen.

Paragraph three. I was the happy medium. I wasn't exactly what the world wanted for her. She could rebel with me. Phia needed to know was that we all have a dichotomy of self. We all have an inner person we struggle to set free. I am not sure if she remembered was how we would set each other free when we were together. I do believe she is right about the world though. The longer I live the more I realize it is not me who am crazy but the world. Poor Ophelia has been stuck in a world that claims she is crazy however, in my eyes she is actually the only sane one left.

The next day everything would change. For good or for ill.[124]

"Do you still want to see me?" I asked.

"I would love to."

She didn't live in the cabin anymore. She moved to New Haven. It wasn't her. On my way to the train I picked out her favorite flowers. Our favorite flowers. We loved lilies, orange lilies. Her new man would buy her roses, because he just didn't know the woman he claimed to have fallen in love with in a single month. I bought her favorite bagels. Bialys and

---

[124] Vonnegut Jr., Kurt

everything bagels from Ess-a-Bagel. I wasn't sure if I should get her flowers. I figured fuck it. We couldn't have gotten anymore broken up.

The train ride was nerve wracking, yet I wasn't worried. I wore a shirt that would hide the sweat. It was the first time I saw her in six months. We had been broken up for seven months in a week. I unfortunately count the days. I could see her car from the platform. Fuck me I am committed. Sometimes in life you don't always know why you do certain things. I am not sure why Ophelia hung out with my parents the day before. I am not sure why she agreed to see me. I am not sure why I was standing on the train platform in New Haven Connecticut on my birthday about to go see my ex-girlfriend who I was madly in love with and she couldn't stand the sight of me. But I was there. I was smiling. Even in the face of certain rejection, for some reason I felt hopeful and that made me smile. We all have this sick struggle between our hearts and mind. With Ophelia this manifested as anxiety. We both were smart enough to know what was going to happen. We didn't count our chickens before they hatched but we weren't stupid. A love like ours will never die.

Her car was the same. Maybe a bit cleaner. The sunglasses I would always steal from her, still on the dashboard. Her Marlboro Lights still in the cup holder next to her half drank iced vanilla latte.

We drove to her new apartment. It was a high rise in a little white enclave. It was called the Postmark. It came with a field for the dogs to run and a public pool everyone with a balcony could stare down into. Everything was electronic and high tech. Everything was new and would be classified as modern architecture. She hates modern architecture. The building was designed with hard angles and white walls. There were granite countertops and stainless-steel appliances. Everything worked and didn't need to be fixed. If she ever had trouble a little Mexican could come and fix it free of charge. She could walk to the bars and be a part of society again. I loved that she was making moves to make sure she was happy. She needed to get out of the cabin once we broke up. It is for the same reasons why it hurts every night to fall asleep in my little cum cave of a room in Manhattan. She made all those steps to close the door on her past. She wanted to block out the memories of Bradley, of me, and move on with her life. Ophelia needed to move forward... So did I. It was important we kept trying to better our lives and ourselves. I didn't mean to show up and bring about a past she had been so desperately trying to escape.

This wasn't her. She was doing it to run. (Run from me? Our past? Our love?) Maybe it was to conform and find something comfortable? Maybe Phia was really feeling that pressure she wrote about? Now, she was in a beautiful modern nice building with a banker boyfriend. I am sure her mother was happy. But was Phia? She wasn't anxious and that is the important part, I guess...

I gave myself a tour of the sterile apartment.

The more I looked, the more I realized another schism between words and actions. She kept everything. For someone who moved out of a cabin to get rid of the memories of me she kept everything. I saw the box where every note I ever wrote, every poem, every letter stayed. She kept my pen. She kept my books. She kept my jewelry. Though it all laid hidden in crevices of her heart and apartment they were still there. When I would later ask her why, she said, "I could never get over you." I just wish she would listen to her heart more than her convoluted brain.

"Want to get a beer? There is an awesome brewery not too far."

"I would love that, what is it called?"

"Two Roads."

"Why is it called that?"

"Robert Frost."

"Perfect."

The drive took forever, but we continued to chat and catch up like we never missed a beat. We sang songs together that made us laugh. I smiled just looking at her. She was more beautiful than I remembered. Paralyzing beauty, her eyes glowed in the bright sun. I found myself slipping back into an intimacy I know I would never recover from.[125]

We drank slow at the brewery demanding each other to be as honest as possible. She said she had been with 3 guys since me. I said I had been with two girls. I had really been with eight. "I might have enjoyed the company of a woman or two... Or three but that had never stopped me from loving

---

[125] Levon was obsessed with this line from Fitzgerald. It appears in much of his writing.

you."[126] Of course she wanted to know more. I was nauseous at the thought of three other guys' penis' inside of her. I couldn't be upset for her trying to find happiness and sometimes by fucking people they can fill that void, but it hurt more than I thought it would. I used to say sometimes that knowing is better than not knowing. That is bullshit. Knowing fucking sucks.

She asked about the girls I had been with. But they were all just hedonistic fillers. I could never feel any emotion towards any of them. I tried to date. I tried to get over her. I would kiss them, and it would feel wrong. I would sleep with them and they didn't fit. It was just never right, and I felt I gave them all a fair chance. Nothing I did filled the void of her love in my life. I think she felt the same.

"None of them are you."

"Were they pretty?"

"They weren't you."

We talked about it all, but a feeling began to grab both of us just as the first beer disappeared into our bodies, loosening the seams on our hearts. It felt normal. It felt right. We would stare at each other and I began to tear slightly as I tried to explain something, I have held in for 6 months.

"Phia, this is going to sound fucked up, but I didn't break up with you just for me. A big part was I was scared I was going to hurt you because I was unsure about me and my future and my life, but I never fell out of love with you. But there is more to it."

"Then who did you do it for? I will never understand."

With tears welling up. `Because I am an emotional bitch.` "I did this for you."

"What?"

"You weren't happy. You weren't okay and as much as it pangs me to say this, I felt I was the cause. You felt me pulling away and you got anxiety and you stopped talking to me. I never want to cause your anxiety. You stopped answering my calls after work. You stopped answering me at night. You hid in the cabin scared, and I allowed it. I was so scared to hurt you anymore I allowed it. You needed to find your happiness and you needed to do it alone. And look at you now. I couldn't be prouder of you. You got out of the cabin. You are looking for the job that makes you happy. You are eating, gaining weight, traveling. You are smiling more than I have ever seen you smile. You are going out with the girls again and I love it."

---

[126] Fitzgerald, F. Scott

"So, what, now you see I am okay, and you want me back?"

"No... I just loved you so much that I knew if I told you this reason you would say fuck you and wouldn't have tried to help yourself just out of spite. You had to do that on your own, but now I am being selfish Phia. Because I don't want another day to go by without you by my side."

"I don't get it."

"I loved you so much I risked losing you, I can't take that risk anymore."

"I missed you so much Jake."

"You have no idea."

We finished our drinks and headed to a restaurant for some cheese fondue and wine. The small bar was open to a patio where a Jazz trio played for a crowd of a dozen or so. The evening air was losing the hot must of the declining day. Our masks we wore for the rest of the world faded as the walls crumbled and hearts became bare. I noticed the atmosphere was changing when she rested her head on my shoulder. She smelt the same. I could still make her laugh uncontrollably.

"Get out of my head." She said.

"You feel it too don't you."

"I am scared Jake."

"Am I crazy Phia? But please tell I am not. This is too good, too easy, too right."

"Stop Jake."

"Be honest."

"I feel it."

Then he called. She had a picture of the two of them as his caller ID. He even looked like me. She never had a picture of us two when I called. Fuck this kid. He was 35. He is going to die soon anyway. I told her to answer it.

She said no.

"Why are you here then?"

"I didn't ask you to hang out with my family, I didn't ask you to call after, I didn't invite myself for a beer, I thought this was a coffee and I will go home..." In mid-sentence, 'Fool in the Rain' came playing from the patio.

She grabbed me. We danced as we have so many times before. The crowd stared at us as they beamed with jealousy over young rekindled love. If only they knew the story. If only they knew the people, we left in our wakes in order for us to survive. If only they could feel how our hearts and minds played a tug of war with our lives crippling each other to a kerfuffle of emotions. We danced seamlessly, beautifully choreographed as god held us and spun us in a dancing lesson of life. Eyes locked, the embrace felt perfect as our bodies intertwined in the evening mist. The adults smiled at our innocence. But we were far from innocent. Then she kissed me. Without warning she shot in and her supple, soft and silk-like lips closed in quickly perfectly conjoining with mine. It could have been the wine. But she did it. Warring hearts gave way to true love, for neither of us believed in it until we met each other and this moment on our timeline only signified our incessant need of the other. And for that second as the inches of air slowly dissipated from between our mouths our hearts warmed, and our tension eased. As flesh met flesh, I was home again. She smiled behind the kiss. It is my favorite thing she does.

It wasn't the kiss that scared me. Despite the fact she just cheated on her new boyfriend who she seems very reluctant to call a boyfriend and more "someone she is seeing." She kissed me right after he called. Whatever the kid was 35 and had never been in a fight, which just doesn't seem possible to me.

Well I kissed her back and I couldn't stop after that. It was like I was a heroin addict who just got high after 10 years of sobriety. I needed it. I was drunk on the taste of her lips. She felt like home.

The song ended and we went back to our wine and cheese. I had to ask.

"Why did you kiss me?"

"I had to."

"No, you didn't Phia…I didn't just do that. You kissed me. Don't blame alcohol you had three drinks."

"I had to know."

"Know what? You need to talk to me…remember we have to be honest."

"I needed to see what it felt like."

"And…"

"It felt like home. It felt right."

"I know… it felt like I never left your lips."

"I am scared…"

"What's going on Ophelia? Why did you say okay to seeing me?"

"I have been feeling guilty lately."

"About?"

"Alex is so nice, and he thinks I am the one, but I feel bad because I still have feelings for you. I needed to see if they were true."

"And are they?"

"Jake... I still love you..."

"I never stopped loving you Ophelia."

"Do you want to stay over? No funny business, I just can't see you leave again."

I knew I shouldn't. I knew it was the wrong thing. I was going to awaken a feeling I have been trying to suppress for so long. Every part of me that tried to protect myself was saying nooo... goooo home... don't do this you fucking idiot.

So, I said, "I would like nothing more than to stay with you."

We were like two school children blissfully in love and ignorantly ignoring the realities of our now separate worlds. As the walls faded our lives began to seem that much more entwined. We kissed again as we got to the car and she put her head down in obvious frustration with the very emotions that were bringing us together. She wanted no more than to hate me. She prayed that kiss would feel like kissing a stranger or her brother. But what was done, was done.

"You had to come back Jake. Why now? Just when I found someone who made me happy."

"I didn't plan this Phia."

"You scare me."

"Why? Is it because we work and we both feel it?"

Her smile agreed but she did not speak. Words seemed futile as the war continued.

We drove back to New Haven in a hurry to find whiskey. Mission accomplished. We stumbled back to her place to take the dogs out. As we walked over to a local bar with both Madeline and Jett people came up to us. We talked to them about the dogs. She explained how we met in Graduate school. On the walk back I grabbed her in the dew filled lawn. I held her tight so our bodies would match up and she could feel my heart beat with hers. I kissed her passionately trying to unleash my soul through silent and frustrated lips. Although strangers we were for 6 months, we are strangers with memories.

We sat in front of the chest at the end of her bed. Underneath its cloth lid was our relationship. I read some of the notes. She took out my jar of love. A note for everyday of the year.

"It's always been you Ophelia."

"You would marry me?"

"In a heartbeat."

"But I am crazy."

"You are perfect."

"What if I get fat?"

"I will still love you."

"What if I lose my mind?"

"I will still love you. Remember you go left…"

"I go left," she finished my sentence.

Tears welled up in my eyes as I read my old love notes strewn about on napkins, coasters, receipts and matchbooks. It seemed our love so strong that anything I could get my hands on I would write her a love note. But along the way I stopped.

"I promise Phia, if we tried again, I won't stop. I want you to wake up every morning and smile at our love. Let it at least be the one constant in our lives. Let me keep writing you love notes."

What happened next, I didn't expect.

She reached over to the jewelry box sitting on her nightstand and took out our locket. The very thing that held our love. She asked me to put it back on her. She took out our ring and put it on her left ring finger.

"Are you sure I asked?"

"You want to try? To work hard at this? To me it is worth it but only if it is what you want."

"Jake, I want this. I missed you so much."

"I want this too…"

I read her Annabel Lee.

We went to bed. We didn't make love. I respected her wishes, even though the sight of her in that light blue nightie with her underwear sneaking out the bottom made my blood flow faster that a river at the bottom of a melting glacier. As she grabbed my hand and pulled it over her shoulder, we both took a deep breath and the moon glowed through the oversized window. Our breathing synced up and we became one. A few stars blinked and our hearts began beating together as if they never parted. We were home. But what is so easy by the moonlight is never as simple when the shades are pulled back and the realities of our worlds, we left behind began to creep back in with the morning light.

For the first time in six months, I slept...

I woke up before her and watched her sleep. We held each other the whole night. I snuck away to write her a note. I left it on the pillow for her to wake up to. But it wasn't the only message she woke up to unfortunately.

Alex knew something was wrong. He called and texted her. He called her beautiful. It made my stomach curl. I couldn't eat. She had to be honest with him. Phia told him she was confused and didn't know what she wanted. It was honest. Then she changed. She was closing off. I know her well enough to know when she starts closing off. She had to tell him because she kissed me and still felt something. And like she said, "he was sooooooo nice." Ophelia wasn't going to tell him.

"What if I am not being fair to him Jake?"

"I can't make these decisions for you Ophelia. But you see how we are, we are good. You feel this too between us. I know you feel bad for him, but this can't be ignored."

"What if I am missing out on him because I go with you and you just break my heart again?"

"What if you break my heart Phia?"

I could feel her anxiety brewing as she let her mind begin to question her heart.

She asked about my sister and how she forgave her boyfriend and how they are now engaged. She asked about my parents. She continued to kiss me throughout the day as we talked and tried to make sense of the Pandora's box we just opened. Every kiss just made us even more uncertain with how perfect it felt.

Then her stomach growled... I looked into her eyes and saw the anxiety. The moment again becoming too big, however there was someone else in my shoes now. I was no longer able to help her.

I pray it's not me but the situation. I love her too much to cause her pain and if my leaving her life is the only thing that gives her relief then so be it... So it goes...

Time was ticking away, and I had to do something. I grabbed a piece of string I cut from a dog toy. I put some tape on it to make it a ring. I placed this makeshift ring on her ring finger and made a promise.

I looked her in the eyes. She looked back. I grabbed her hand so tight I began sweating. Neither of us cared. I dug down deep. If there is

LEVON

anytime I thought to myself, it is now. Don't leave without her. Don't give up your dream. Sometimes you just need a friend to remind you where your heart is.

    "My dearest Ophelia. I know you are scared. I know I am scared. I know I didn't mean to come into your life like this and fuck everything up, but the reality is that I am here, and the past two days happened. Neither of us can ignore it. The passion is still here, the love has never left. But please know, I lost you once and I don't ever want to lose you again. I know deep down I am going to have to. You are the love of my life, like I have explained so many times. I have learned from my mistakes and I have grown to be a more mature happy man and one who knows exactly what you want. But not only that it is what we both want. I know you are scared I may hurt you again, but I am scared you may wake up one day and say you don't love me. But that is what faith and trust is and I want to build that trust back and I want you to take a leap of faith. If we both jump together at least we can fall together. I now have a plan for the future, I am happy with the man I am, and I know I can always be there to support you and give you everything in my heart. It won't be easy Phia…But it will be worth it. We will have to take it slow and build it back, but we have a start and that is unconditional love. We are going to fight, and we are going to become frustrated, but I will always stand by your side for good or for ill until they put me into the ground. I vow to love all your forms and never waver. I am sorry for ever letting you question our love, but I have only done what I thought was right for the both of us. I know you are what is right for me, but it doesn't matter what I want anymore. It matters what you want and if you are willing to try. Cause if you are, I am here. I will keep fighting. I will keep trying to show you that true love is something worth fighting for. When you know you know. I don't want to wait anymore but I will… I will wait until time lets me hold you again. I love you Ophelia and I always will. Love is the compass that points you home. Please let me come home again."

    She looked at the string with a glistening of tears. She looked at me as if she had longed to hear those words from me for so long. I just hope they weren't too late. However, nothing that is real, nothing that is alive is ever too late.

    "Ophelia, just promise me you won't wake up tomorrow and feel different?"

    "I promise…I just need a little time to figure things out…but I want to try, I really do."

    "So do I."

I had to leave because she was going out with her friends that night. As we pulled up to the train station, I looked at her and asked, "What is the etiquette here? Can I kiss you goodbye?" She looked at me and smiled, "Of course."

We kissed passionately like so many times over the past 24 hours.

"I love you so much Ophelia."

"I love you too Jake. Please text me later."

"Of course, and I can't wait to see you tomorrow. Have a good night with the girls."

While running up the stairs to the train corridor I stopped. I am not sure why I stopped but I stopped and looked back at the white Range Rover. She didn't look back. "A pain stabbed my heart, as it did every time, I saw this woman I loved go the opposite direction in the too big world."[127]

We texted until her girlfriends came over and then...Radio silence. The next morning instead of a good morning I get, "I can't see you today. I need to see my parents and clear my head."

Just like that it was over. I knew the minute I left she wouldn't feel the same. Our passion came from being together. I knew she needed time, but the more time went on the worse it was for me. Time dragged on and all I did was drown myself in booze and weed. The more I thought the crazier I became. There was a tone. She woke up and felt different. She promised me she wouldn't.

The insomnia returned. I can no longer sleep.

I just miss my best friend.

I thought about something my Uncle Don said to me at last year's Christmas Party. A large man, with a belly you could barely hug around and a laugh that shook the room... he spoke in a booming voice. He pulled me aside as Ophelia created a beautiful gingerbread house. That's just what I told her... She struggled with the icing. It was all over her. She was adorable. I digress...

"So, things are pretty serious with you and Ophelia," He said starting the conversation.

"Yes, we are."

"You don't seem so sure."

"No, No, I am...Just I love her so much I am actually scared."

"What the fuck are you scared about she is beautiful."

"How did you know if they are...you know...?"

---

[127] Kerouac, Jack

Don looked at me and without hesitation said, "If they are the one you are willing to make sacrifices for."

And this is my sacrifice. To let go…again…

The relationship was just too delicate at this stage and I understood that. She did what was right even though it is not what either of us wanted. We can kiss in the shadows and love in the depths of our hearts but again, the world did not approve of our love. I just pray our timelines will meet up again in the future, so I am no longer a statue in the past but a person in the present and future. Time still our enemy after two days of ecstasy we were thrust back into denying the truth. But love it still was and confident I still am now that we will survive this.

`You know you love her when you let her`
`go...again...`

Maybe, his lips won't feel the same after tasting mine. Maybe, his cuddling won't fit as well as we fit. Maybe, when she meets his family, she will begin to miss mine. Maybe, when she has her mansion in Westchester and her three spoiled little kids running around, as she no longer follows her artistic and professional passions. And she is going from book club to book club, drinking wine with the real housewives of Westchester, she looks back at this moment and sees me living in a farmhouse on the New England coast with my newf and English bulldog. Maybe then she will see true love is true love and no one person, moment, or conflict can ever separate two people. We will always have our past, but what I hope she realizes is that we also have a future and that makes all the difference.

I hope she never settles for someone who is just nice. I hope she never settles just for someone who calls her beautiful and gives her attention. I hope she doesn't just settle for what is easy because of comfort and money. I hope she knows it is about that feeling the other person gives you, the feeling we gave each other.

I lost my love once. I can lose her again. To do what is right is to let her go…again. Unconditional is Unconditional.

When I left, she took off the locket and our relationship with it. And so, it seems now we have an ending to our story, because I have to go right when she goes left.

So, I left to travel the world, but now alone.

"Benjamin, we're meant to lose the people we love. How else would we know how important they are to us?"
-- F. Scott Fitzgerald, The Curious Case of Benjamin Button

"His heart danced upon her movements like a cork upon a tide. He heard what her eyes said to him from beneath their cowl and knew that in some dim past, whether in life or reverie, he had heard their tale before."

-- *James Joyce, A Portait of the Artist as a Young Man*

CHAPTER THIRTEEN

"It's never too late to begin again."

--Levon

LEVON'S FINAL WISH...

By the time Evie and I finished sorting the scattered thoughts of Levon, we sat on the floor of the white room in a daze. We didn't eat. We emptied the Zanzibar's chest of everything it contained. I was surprised how much Evie never understood or knew about Levon.

"I get why he fell apart. We all used to tell him to stop being dramatic. We all made fun of him for being a little bitch...but I guess some hearts can't be mended."

At the same moment, Evie and I turned to each other and said, "we need to find her." According to our calculations it had been almost 40 years since Ophelia and Levon saw each other. The last time we had any sign of communication was 2014/2015. I spent the next year of my life trying to make sense Levon's writing, creating what you are now reading. I decided this novel would be the vessel for his story. This was the culmination of a year of late nights after work, trying to make sense of the old man's crazy mind. I heard Levon with every click of the keys. I knew he hated how I loved the heartbreak.

Finally, when it was complete, we knew the last step was to give it to Ophelia.

Levon definitely was yelling from above that we shouldn't find her, but we knew we had to. And he was dead and didn't have a say in the matter. He gave up fighting for her, and although he was gone and time passed, I knew the love was still there. If everything Levon wrote was true, there was no way Ophelia lost their love. We had to get this to Ophelia.

We needed to find her, wherever she was. Evie couldn't remember the name of the hot-shot banker, but she did say Ophelia stayed with him and married him not long after Levon and Ophelia's last communication.

"I hope she was happy, but the pictures she posted from the wedding never looked right. They made us all uncomfortable. You could see in her eyes, she was marrying to just marry," Evie said.

Levon always referred to her husband as "that guy" or "the hot-shot banker." He might as well have called him Voldemort. Evie said she would try old friends in New York to see if they could track her down. I went on the Internet and searched. Eventually, we found her living on a ranch in Colorado.

At first Evie wasn't sure if she wanted to come, she was much too old for a plane, but I insisted. There was no way I could make the trip without her. This was her story as well.

Ophelia's home was on the backside of Pikes Peak. The old farmhouse was the spitting image of 28 Lotus Lane. It shocked both Evie and me. The house sat on a sprawling horse farm with split beam fences lining its perimeter. We rang the doorbell and a young woman answered. She was in her early twenties with short blonde curls and the bright blue eyes. The girl walked on her toes, with her feet slightly turned in, making her look younger than she probably was.

Then we heard Ophelia from the back of the home, "Charlie! Who is here?"

As Ophelia came closer, her eyes came into view. I finally understood what Levon was so obsessed with. It all made sense, just by being in her presence. She had a red string tied around her left wrist with a tattoo that said, "Just Love." The J and the L bolded.

"Can I help you?" Just as she finished her question, Ophelia recognized Evie.

"Evelyn! Oh my god how are you, come in! Who is this? Is this your son?" she said motioning to me.

"No, no, this is Jake. He is an old friend of mine from back East."

"Jake, I like that name. Nice to meet you."

"The pleasure is truly all mine Phia."

"Sorry, its Ophelia, no one has called me Phia in decades."

Ophelia shot a stare at Evelyn and they had a silent conversation through their eyes. I was in a trance following the two old ladies into the house. Ophelia had three children but only Charlie still lived in the house. It was short for Charlotte.

The rest of the day was a blur as the two old women caught up, the way all old people catch up. They spoke of grad school, adventures in the city and people they once knew. Their conversation flowed the way Evie and Levon used to speak. Ophelia was intelligent and quick even in her advanced stage of life. I stayed in a trance and spoke very little. Ophelia glanced my way periodically during the conversation. We couldn't bring ourselves to mention Levon or the fact he passed away.

During the banter Ophelia admitted to being divorced for roughly 20 years. The hotshot banker husband had been cheating on her during all of his "business trips." She learned he never stopped seeing his ex-girlfriend and actually was living a double life. So, she did what all good women do who were scorned, lied to and abused. She took all of his money and left the poor bastard alone and broke. Ophelia now ran a horse farm in the mountains by herself.

Once the formalities of catching up slowed, she eventually asked, knowing we didn't find her in the mountains on a Tuesday afternoon in December for no reason.

Eventually, she asked, "I don't want to be rude, but why are you here?"

Evie looked at me. I knew it was my responsibility.

"Well, Levon passed away...sorry I mean Jake...It's hard to get used to that."

She didn't respond or look up... But she grabbed her neck. I saw a gold chain leading down into her orange blouse. Ophelia kept her hand near her heart gently touching whatever was attached to the gold chain.

"How did he die?" she eventually asked, breaking the silence.

"Well, we don't actually know. He was traveling. Last we heard, he was on a ship from the Maldives to Australia."

She smirked, "typical Levon… But how do you know he is dead?"

"No one has heard from him in a couple of years Ophelia. The bank finally declared him dead after he stopped paying them."

"No one that you know of actually confirmed he was dead?"

"Ophelia, it's been years, I have written endless letters. He would have come home by now…"

The silence stood suspended. It lingered like a night sky that stayed a bit too long while the sun forced its way over the mountains.

"Jake, you remind me a lot of Jake…I mean Levon. Sorry, it's hard to get used to that."

"What do you mean? I haven't said much… I mean…Well, he raised me."

"You are his son?"

"No, I was his neighbor in Branford, but he was the closest thing to a father I ever knew."

"He was living in Branford?"

"I think there is a lot you don't know about the man…" I said.

"I think there is a lot he didn't know about me."

When she finished, Ophelia reached into her blouse and pulled out a small gold locket. It was so small it looked like it belonged to a dollhouse. The gold was slightly faded.

"Follow me Jake I want to show you something. Evie if you don't mind, I think Jake should see this himself."

Evie motioned, and we walked through the country home to the back door. I looked back at Evie like a kid being dragged off to a summer camp he didn't want to attend. I went to the back of the house, where Ophelia walked me across a bountiful garden with purple, white and orange lilies, forget-me-nots and lavender. There was a large brown shed with a chimney. A small stream passed by the back windows of the old shed. When she opened the shed door, I knew exactly what it was. It was evident what it was for. It was a writing studio.

"I have never told anyone in my family why I always kept a writing studio. I designed it after Hemingway's loft above his garage in Key West," she said.

I slowly walked over the threshold and onto the hard wood floors. There was a fireplace, brown leather couch and an old wooden desk in the corner overlooking the stream. She sauntered over to the desk. Even in her old age I could see the magic oozing out of her. She screamed beauty from her chromatic eyes to her long legs. To the right of the desk was a large white cloth chest. She motioned for me to come over. As she opened the chest, paper spewed out onto the dusty wooden floors. I saw Levon's handwriting.

"This is everything he ever wrote me. I could never get rid of it. I don't know if I ever got over him. He was my one."

Then she pulled out an unopened letter. "I received this letter last week."

"Last week!? Is it from him? It can't be. But he hasn't sent anything in years…"

Ophelia turned the front of the envelope into my view… There was no return address. It just had a name. J.H. Levon.

"That son of a bitch! He is alive! I am going to kill him again! What does it say? Open it!"

"I don't know if I should open it." She said, not taking her eyes off the envelope.

Ophelia went to open the envelope and paused…She started to open the envelope again and paused. She sat down at the desk.

"Wait, you aren't just here to tell me Levon passed away…what is it?"

"You are as intelligent as Levon always made you out to be."

I opened my backpack and handed her the finished manuscript. Her eyes widened, sweat dripped off her gentle brow.

"It's done? He finished our story?" she asked.

"Well, technically I finished the story. It took the past year to compile everything and put in some sort of order. I just felt I needed to give it to you first. Levon would want you to have it."

She rubbed the top of the manuscript. "I love the title."

"Original I know."

I titled the book, Stolen on 55th and 3rd.

Ophelia then looked back at the envelope in her hand. She shook.
"I guess I need to open this…" She slowly opened the envelope tearing at
one side exposing a ripped sheet of Moleskin paper. There was only one
line, which is odd for Levon who rambled on, especially in his notes to
Ophelia. The line was written in the same blue ink Levon always used.

"We loved with a love that was more than love." -- Poe

She looked at me as if she knew me forever. A single tear trickled down her
face. Never looking away, her hands trembled as she mumbled, "Levon?"

It was dated December 21st. So it was…So it goes…